Jim Traft's first job [...] miles of barbed wire across a virgin, free range. Homesteaders, rustlers and small ranchers alike vowed to tear down the drift fence as fast as Jim and his mutinous crew could build it.

The running battle started with fists. It ended with bullets. And for all his guts, the tenderfoot would have lost—except for one person: beautiful Molly Dunn, sister of Arizona's toughest gunslinger, who had sworn to hang Jim Traft's body on the drift fence for the buzzards.

No quarter was asked or given!

THE DRIFT FENCE
was originally published by Harper & Row,
Publishers, Inc.

3/22

THE
DRIFT
FENCE

Zane Grey

PUBLISHED BY POCKET BOOKS · NEW YORK

THE DRIFT FENCE

Harper & Row edition published January, 1933

POCKET BOOK edition published November, 1957
10th printing........March, 1972

Standard Book Number: 671-75697-4.

THE
DRIFT
FENCE

◈

MOLLY DUNN sat waiting on the rickety old porch of Enoch Summers' store in the village of West Fork. For once she was oblivious to the approach of the lean-faced, long-legged young backwoodsmen who lounged there with their elders. Molly was sixteen and on the eve of a great adventure. She had been invited to ride to Flagerstown with the Sees. She had been there once some years before and the memory had haunted her. In her pocket she had money to buy new stockings and shoes, which compensated somewhat for the fact that she carefully kept her feet and ankles hidden under the bench. She wore her good dress and bonnet, and though not satisfied with them she was not ashamed.

Andy Stoneham, a tall youth with sallow face and fuzzy beard, edged over closer and closer.

"Reckon you're orful stuck up this mawnin'," he drawled.

Molly looked at the bullet holes in the wall of the old store. She had seen them before, and long ago when she was ten she had stuck her finger in them and wondered about the battle that had been fought there once.

"Goin' up to Flag, huh?"

"Do you think I'd dress up like this for West Fork?" inquired Molly, loftily.

"Wal, you used to, didn't you? You shore look purty.

But I can't see you've any call to get uppish. I've seen you in thet rig before, haven't I?"

"I don't remember, Andy."

"Then you've got a darn short memory," replied Andy, bluntly. "Didn't I take you to the last dance in thet dress?"

"Did you?"

"Wal, I shore did. An' didn't I hug you in it?"

"Did you?" queried Molly, flippantly.

"You bet I did."

"I've forgotten. But I've heard it said you're so big an' awkward you have to hold on to a girl when you dance. Else you'd fall down."

"Wal, how aboot kissin' you, too? On the way to the dance an' drivin' home?"

"Oh, did you!" retorted Molly, her face hot. Andy's voice carried rather far. "An' what did I do?"

"Wal, I figger thet you kissed me back an' then slapped my face."

"Andy Stoneham, you're a liar about that first."

"Haw! Haw! . . . Say, Molly, there's going to be a dance next week."

"Where at?"

"Hall's Mill. Come on an' go."

"Andy, I don't like that place," returned Molly, regretfully. "Besides, I wouldn't go with you, anyway."

"Wal, you shore air gettin' stuck up. An' why not?"

"Because of what you said—about huggin' an' kissin' me."

"What of thet? I did an' you liked it. Aw, you're funny. Haven't all the boys done the same?"

"They have not," declared Molly. "Who ever said such a thing?"

"I heerd Sam Wise say it. An' Bill Smith laughed, though he didn't say nothin'."

"So that's the kind of fellows you are!" exclaimed Molly. "Talk about a girl behind her back? . . . To kiss an' tell!"

"Wal, at thet we're not so gabby as your cowboy admirers from Pleasant Valley. Take thet red-headed

2

cowpuncher. Accordin' to his talk he's a tall fellar with gurls. He shore had you crazy aboot him."

"He did not," said Molly, hotly.

"Wal, you acted orful queer then. Danced all the time with him. An' three times walked out under the pines. Aw, I watched you. An' come Saturday night he was drinkin' heah, an' accordin' to his talk he could have had a lot more than huggin' an' kissin' from you, if he only got you alone."

"Andy Stoneham!—You let him talk that way aboot me?"

"Wal, why should I care? You've shore been mean to me."

"Why should you, indeed?" replied Molly, coldly, and turned away.

At that juncture a horseman rode up and his advent not only interrupted Molly's argument with her loquacious admirer, but had a decided quieting effect upon the other occupants of the porch. He was a lean range-rider, neither young nor old, and he fitted the hard country. His horse showed the dust and strain of long travel.

"Howdy, Seth," said old Enoch Summers, rubbing his bristled chin and stepping out. " 'Pears like you been humpin' it along. Whar you come from?"

"Me an' Arch Dunn just rode over from the Diamond," replied the other.

Molly's attention quickened to interest at the mention of her brother. Seth Haverly was his boon companion and they had been up to something.

"Wal, thar's news stickin' out all over you," drawled Summers.

"Reckon so."

"Git down an' come in. Mebbe a drink wouldn't go bad."

"Nope. I'm goin' home an' get a snack of grub."

One by one the men on the porch joined Summers. The fact that Seth Haverly did not want a drink, as much as his arrival, interested them.

Haverly had a still brown face and intent light eyes.

3

"Enoch, you know thet drift fence we been hearin' aboot for the last year?" he asked.

"Reckon I heerd the talk."

"Wal, it's more'n talk now."

"You don't say?"

"Yep. Me an' Arch rode along it, for ten miles, I figger. Straight as a bee-line. New three-wire fence, an' barbed at thet!"

"What you say? Barbed!"

"You bet."

Silence greeted Seth's nonchalant affirmative.

"Arch had a hunch aboot this fence goin' up," went on Haverly. "An' in Flag we found it was a fact."

"Wal, who's buildin' it?"

"Traft."

"Ahuh. He could afford it. Wal, what's his idee?"

"It ain't very flatterin' to West Fork," drawled Seth, with a grin. "We heerd some things thet'd be hard for you old cattle nesters to swaller, if they're true. But me an' Arch only had the word of some idle cowpunchers. We couldn't get any satisfaction from Traft's outfit. New foreman. Nephew from Missourie, we heerd. Tenderfoot, but I agree with Arch, who said he was no fool. Anyway, we asked him polite like: 'Say, mister, what's the idee of this drift fence?'—An' he looked me an' Arch over an' said, 'What do you suppose the idee is?' "

"Short an' sweet!" ejaculated a man standing beside Summers. "Wal, you two-bit free-range cattlemen can put thet in your pipes an' smoke it."

Whereupon he strode off the porch and down the road, erect and forceful, his departure expressive of much.

"Me an' Arch was sure curious aboot this fence," continued Seth. "We rode out of Flag an' started in where the fence begins. It strikes south into the timber at Traft's line, an' closes up every draw clear to the Diamond. At Limestone we hit into Traft's outfit. They've got the job half done an' by the time the snow flies that drift fence will run clear from Flag to Black Butte."

"Ha! A hundred miles of drift fence!" exclaimed some one.

4

"Ahuh," nodded Summers, sagely. "An' all the cattle will drift along to Black Butte an' then drift back again."

Haverly swung his spurred boot back to his stirrup and without another word rode away.

Molly watched the departing rider as thoughtfully as any of the others on Summers' porch. This drift fence must be going to have a profound significance for the few inhabitants along the West Fork of the Cibeque.

Then down the road from the other direction appeared the See buckboard, sight of which brought Molly bouncing to her feet. To her relief young John See was not in the vehicle with his parents. John had more prospects than any of the young men Molly knew, but he also had more than his share of their demerits. The buckboard rolled to a stop.

"Hop up, Molly," called See, gayly. "We're late an' it ain't no fault of yours."

"Good mawnin'," returned Molly, brightly, as she climbed to the seat beside Mrs. See.

"Mornin' lass," replied the rancher's wife. "You look like you could fly as well as hop."

"Oh, I'm on pins," cried Molly. "I'll never be able to thank you enough."

"Howdy, Caleb," spoke up Summers. "Reckon you've got time to come inside a minute."

"Mawnin', Enoch," replied See, which greeting included the others present. "I'm in a hurry."

"Wal, come in anyhow," returned Summers, bluntly, and went into the store.

See grumbled a little, as he wound the reins around the brake-handle, and laboriously got down. He was a heavy man, no longer young. All the loungers on the porch followed him into the store, but Andy Stoneham remained in the door, watching Molly.

"That lout's makin' sheep eyes at you, Molly," said Mrs. See.

Molly did not look. "He just said some nasty things to me," she confided. "Then the fool asked me to go to a dance at Hall's Mill."

5

"Molly, you're growin' up an' it's time you got some sensible notions," said Mrs. See, seriously.

"I'm goin' to Flag," trilled Molly, as if that momentous adventure was all that mattered.

"Lass, you're a bad combination. You're too pretty an' too crazy. I reckon it's time to get you a husband."

Molly laughed and blushed. "That's what ma says. But it's funny. I have to work hard enough now."

Caleb See came stamping out of the store, wiping his beard, sober of face where he had been merry. Without a word he stepped into the buckboard, making it lurch, and drove away. Molly was reminded of the news about the drift fence.

"Mrs. See, while I was waitin' for you Seth Haverly rode up," said Molly. "He'd just come in from the Diamond with my brother Arch. They'd been to Flag. An' he was tellin' old Enoch Summers about a fence that was bein' built, down across the country. A drift fence, he called it. What's a drift fence?"

While Mrs. See pondered over the query Caleb answered.

"Wal, lass, it's no wonder you ask, seein' we don't have no fences in this country. On a free range cattle travel all over, according' to water an' grass. Now a drift fence is somethin' that changes a free range. It ain't free no more. It's a rough country this side of the Diamond. All the draws head up on top an' run down into the West Fork, an' into the Cibeque. Water runs down these draws, an' feed is good. Wal, a drift fence built on top an' runnin' from Flag down country will keep the cattle on top. They'll drift along an' water down on the other side. Then they'll drift back."

"Why were they so serious about it?" asked Molly, curiously. "Isn't a drift fence a good thing?"

"Reckon it is, for Traft an' Blodgett, an' the big cattlemen up Flag way. But for us folks, who live off the Diamond, it ain't so good."

"Most of us couldn't live much worse," replied Molly, thoughtfully.

6

"You bet you could, lass. Haven't you always had milk an' beefsteak, an' shoes to wear?"

"Most always, but not always. Just now I'm walkin' in my bare toes," said Molly, with a giggle. "If I hadn't saved up money enough to buy stockings an' shoes I'd never come."

"Molly, you goin' to have a new dress, too," declared Mrs. See. "I didn't tell you we are goin' to a picnic. Goin' to be a big time in Flag on Saturday, most like the Fourth."

"Oh, heavenly!" exclaimed Molly, rapturously. "An' to think I almost didn't come! ... Mrs. See, you're awfully kind."

Mr. See went on with something in his mind. "No, Molly, we've been fair to middlin' prosperous down here in the valley. But this drift fence will make a difference."

"Caleb, isn't the land owned by the government? Couldn't any man homestead it?"

"Shore. An' there's the rub. Traft has no right to fence this free range. But he's a rich, powerful old duffer an' bull-headed as one of his steers. Who're we down here to go to law? An' where'd we go? Fairfield, the county seat, is farther away than Flag. It takes time an' money to travel."

"Oh, dear!" sighed the good woman. "Then it'll mean hard times."

"Wal, Susan, we can stand hard times, an' I reckon come out ahead. But this drift fence means trouble. It's a slap in the face to every free ranger in this section. They'll all take it Traft accuses them of stealin' un-branded stock that drifts down into the draws on the West Fork."

"What kind of trouble, Uncle Caleb?" queried Molly, soberly.

"Lass, do you remember the Pleasant Valley war over across the mountains in the Tonto? Let's see, you must have been about six years old. Ten years ago."

"Yes, I remember, mama wouldn't let me play out of the yard. We lived at Lunden then. But if I hadn't remem-

7

bered I'd sure know what that war was. Papa talks about it yet."

"Ahuh. Lass, some people say your dad was crippled for sympathy to one faction in that fight."

"Pa denies it. But he was on the side of the sheepmen. An' that riles my brother Arch somethin' funny. They never get along. Arch isn't much good, Uncle Caleb."

"Humph! I'd not say that, for Arch has good parts. But he's much bad, an' that's no joke. . . . Wal, if Traft's outfit ever finishes their fence—at least down in the Diamond, it'll be cut. An' as Traft runs a lot of hard-ridin' and shootin' cowpunchers, there's shore goin' to be blood spilled. It takes years sometimes to wear out these feuds. An' we've a lot of thick-headed hombres in our neck of the woods."

His ominous reasoning had a silencing effect upon his hearers. The women of that country were pioneers in suffering, and there were many windows and orphans. Molly thought of her brother Arch. He was only twenty-two, yet he had killed more than one man, and through many fights, but few of them bloodless, he had earned a reputation that was no source of pride to his family. Arch not so long ago had been a nice boy. Lack of work, and drinking, and roaming the woods with fellows like Seth Haverly, had ruined him. Now it would grow worse, and that would make it harder for Molly's crippled father, who had to sit at home and brood.

Molly conceived a resentment against the rich cattle-man who could impose such restrictions and embitter the lives of poor people. And as for Traft's tenderfoot relative, who had come out from Missouri to run a hard outfit and build barbed-wire fences, Molly certainly hated him. Funny if she should meet him! What would he be like? A change from long-legged, unshaven, ragged boys who smelled of horses would be a relief, even if he was an enemy. It was unlikely, however, that she should have the luck to encounter Mr. Traft's nephew from Missouri, which fact would be good luck for him, at least. Molly would certainly let him know what she thought of him.

It occurred to her presently that Arch had seen this

new foreman of Traft's and could tell her all about him. How was Arch going to take this newcomer? Seth Haverly was as easygoing a boy as Arch, but dangerous when crossed. Molly was prone to spells of depression and she felt the imminence of one here.

Wherefore, in order to shake off the insidious shadow, she devoted herself to the ride and to her companion, who needed a little cheering also.

It had been years since Molly had been so many miles from the village. She did not remember the road. From her own porch she always had a wonderful view down the valley and across to the grand upheaval of earth and rock locally called the Diamond, and at the rugged black hills to the south. But now she was riding at a fast trot of a spirited team through a winding timbered canyon, along the banks of the West Fork. As there was a gradual down grade, the gray cliff walls grew higher until they were far above. Only a lone horseman was encountered in all the fifteen miles down to where the West Fork poured its white torrent into the Cibeque. Here Mr. See took the main road, which climbed and wound and zigzagged up the long slope. Molly looked down and back at the wilderness which was her home. All green and gray, and so big! She could not hate it, somehow. All her life she had known that kind of country. She had played among the ferns and the rock, and in the amber water, and under the brown-barked pines and spruces, where deer and elk and wild turkeys were as common as the cows she drove from pasture in the dusk. She felt that it would take a terrible break to sever her from this home of forest and gorge.

FROM THE head of the Cibeque the road wound through
undulating forest land, heading the deep draws and glens,
and gradually ascending to the zone of cedar and piñon,
which marked the edge of the cattle-range.

There had been snow on the ground all winter, which
accounted for the abundance of gramma grass, now beginning to bleach in the early summer sun. Cattle dotted
all the glades and flats and wide silvery meadows; and
toward afternoon, from a ridge top the vast gray-green
range spread like a billowy ocean far as eye could see.

Several ranches were passed at any one of which See
would have been welcome to spend the night, but he kept
going all of daylight, and by night had covered more than
half the journey to Flagerstown.

"Wal, wife, we've made Keech's, an' that's good, considerin' our late start," remarked See, with satisfaction, as
he drove into a wide clearing, the hideousness of which
attested to the presence of an old sawmill. Rude clap-
board cabins and fences, not to note the barking dogs,
gave evidence of habitation.

The cabins, however, were more inviting inside, Molly
was to learn, and that the widow Keech was a most
kindly and loquacious hostess. She had two grown
daughters, and a son about fourteen years old, an enor-
mously tall boy who straightway became victim to Molly,
a conspicuous fact soon broadly hinted by his elders.

"So this hyar is John Dunn's girl growed up," said Mrs. Keech. "I knowed your father well, an' I seen you when you was a big-eyed kid. Now you're a woman ridin' to Flag."

Molly, however, was not to be led into conversation. This adventure seemed to her too grand to be joked about. She was keen to listen, and during the dinner hour heard much about Flagerstown and the fair to begin there on the morrow, and to end on Saturday with a *rodeo*. Mrs. See had not imparted all this marvelous news to Molly and she laughed at the girl's excitement.

"What you know aboot this drift fence?" finally asked See.

"Caleb, it's a downright fact," replied the widow, forcefully. "Harry has seen it. Traft's outfit are camped ten miles north of us. They'll pass here this summer an' be down on your Diamond by the time snow flies."

"Ahuh. So we heerd. But what's your idee aboot it?"

"Wal, Caleb, all things considered, it'll be good for the range. For no matter what folks say, cattle-rustlin' is not a thing of the past. Two-bit stealin' of calves is what it really is. But rustlin', for all that. An' up this way, anyhow, it'll help."

"Are you runnin' any stock?" asked See, thoughtfully.

"Cows, mostly. I send a good deal of butter in to town. Really am gettin' on better than when we tried to ranch it. I don't have to hire no-good punchers. People travel the road a lot these days. An' they all stop hyar. I've run up some little cabins."

"An' that's a good idee," said See.

Molly listened to hear everything, and particularly wanted to learn more about the young Missouri tenderfoot who had come out West to build fences for Traft. He would certainly have a miserable existence. And it was most liable to be short. To Molly's disappointment, no more was said about the drift fence.

"Wal, we'll rustle off to bed," concluded See. "Mrs. Keech, I'll want to leave early in the mornin'."

Molly shared one of the new cabins with Mrs. See. It was small, clean, and smelled fragrantly of dry pine. It had three windows, and that to Molly was an innovation. She vowed she would have one like it, where she could have light in the daytime and air at night. She was tired, but not sleepy. Perhaps the bed was too comfortable. Anyway, Molly lay wide awake in the dark, wondering what was going to happen to her. This trip to Flagerstown might be a calamity for her. But she must have it. She must enjoy every moment of it, no matter what discontent it might engender.

The hounds bayed the wolves and made her shudder. Wolves and coyotes seldom ranged down in the brakes of the Cibeque. Bears and lions were plentiful, but Molly had never feared them. Wolves had such a mournful, blood-curdling howl. And when the hounds answered it they imitated that note, or else imparted to it something of hunger for the free life their wild brothers enjoyed.

When at last Molly fell asleep it seemed only a moment until she was rudely awakened. Mrs. See was up, dressing by lamplight. A gray darkness showed outside the open window, and the air that blew in on Molly was cold enough for early fall, down on the West Fork.

But the great day was at hand. She found her voice, and even had a friendly word for the boy Harry, who certainly made the most of it. When she came out from breakfast, a clear cold morning, with rosy flush in the east, greeted her triumphantly, as if to impart that it had some magic in store.

Harry squeezed Molly's arm, as he helped her into the buckboard, and said, confidently, "I'll see you at the *rodeo*."

"Hope so," replied Molly.

Then they were off behind fresh horses and soon into the cedars. Jack rabbits bounded away, with their ridiculously long ears bobbing erect; lean gray coyotes watched them roll along; deer trotted out of sight into thick clumps of brush.

Soon they came to the open top of a ridge and Molly saw a gray, dim, speckled world of range, so immense as to dwarf her sight. The scent from that vast gulf was intoxicating.

12

"What's the sweet smell?" she asked.

"Sage, you Cibeque Valley backwoods girl," replied Mrs. See. "Anyone would think you'd never been out of the timber."

"I haven't, much," laughed Molly. "I've seen an' smelled sage, but it's so long ago I'd forgotten. Reckon I'd better be pretty careful up at Flag, Auntie See?"

"Shore you had. But what aboot?"

"Talkin'. I'm so ignorant," sighed Molly.

"You don't need to be dumb. You just think before you speak. You're such a pretty little mouse that it'll become you. I don't care for gabby girls, myself. An' I never seen a man who did, if he was in earnest."

Molly was silent enough for the next long stretch. She watched a sunrise that made her think how beautiful the world was and how little she had seen, hidden down there in the green brakes. But she reproved herself for that. From her porch she could see the sun set in the great valley when the Diamond sheered abruptly down into the Cibeque, and nothing could have excelled that. And what could be better than the wooded canyons, deep and gray and green, with their rushing streams? But this open range took her breath. Here was the cattle country—what Mr. See had called the free range, and which riders like her brother Arch and Seth Haverly regarded as their own. Yet was it not a shame to fence that magnificent rolling land of green? For a moment Molly understood what it meant to be a range-rider, to have been born on a horse. She sympathized with Arch and Seth. A barbed-wire fence, no matter how far away, spoiled the freedom of that cedared grassy land.

"Wal, lass, thar's the smoke of Flag," said Mrs. See. "Way down in the corner. Long ways yet. But we're shore gettin' there."

"Smoke," said Molly, dreamily. "Are they burnin' brush?"

"Haw! Haw! That smoke comes from the railroad an' the sawmill."

From there on the miles were long, yet interesting, almost every one of them, with herds of cattle wearing

13

different brands, with ranches along the road, with the country appearing to spread and grow less cedared. Ten miles out of Flagerstown Mr. See pointed to a distant ridgetop, across which a new fence strung, startlingly clear against the sky. It gave Molly a pang.

"Traft's drift fence, I reckon," said See. "An' I'd almost rather have this a sheep range!"

For all her poor memory, Molly remembered Flagerstown—the black timbered mountain above it, the sawmill with its pile of yellow lumber, the gray cottages on the outskirts, and at last the thrilling long main street, with buildings that looked wonderful to her. Mr. See remarked with satisfaction that the time was not much past four o'clock. He drove straight down this busy thoroughfare. Molly was all eyes.

"Hyar we are," said Mr. See, halting before a pretentious brick building. "This is the new hotel, Molly. Now, wife, make the best of our good trip in. Take Molly in the stores. I'll look after the horses, get our rooms, an' meet you hyar at six o'clock."

Molly leaped out of the buckboard with a grim yet happy realization that she would not need much longer to be ashamed of her shoes and stockings.

Three hours later, Molly, radiant and laden with bundles, tagged into the hotel behind Mrs. See, likewise laden, to be greeted vociferously by Mr. See.

"For the land's sake! Have you robbed a store or been to a fire?—An' hyar me waitin' for supper!"

"Caleb, it happens seldom in a lifetime," replied his beaming wife. "Help us pack this outfit to our rooms. Then we'll have supper."

Molly had a room of her own. She had never even seen one like it. Loath to leave her precious purchases, she lingered until they called her from the hall. It struck her again how warmly these old people looked at her. Molly guessed she was a circus and ruefully admitted reason for it.

The dining-room might have been only "fair to middlin'," as Mr. See put it, but it was the most sumptuous place Molly had ever entered. Sight of it added to the excitement of the few hours' shopping effectually robbed her of appetite.

"Wal, I reckon Molly wants a biscuit an' a hunk of venison," remarked Mr. See.

Molly did not know quite how to take that remark. She became aware, too, of being noticed by two young men at a near-by table. They were certainly not cowboys or timber-rangers. Molly was glad to get out and upstairs to the privacy of her room.

There she unpacked the numerous bundles and parcels, and laid out her newly acquired possessions upon the bed. How quickly her little hoard of money had vanished! Still, it had gone farther than she had anticipated. Mrs. See had been incredibly generous. A blue print dress, a white dress with slippers and stockings to match, the prettiest little hat Molly had ever seen in her life, ribbons and gloves and what not—these had been the expansion of the good woman's promise.

But not only the pleasure of looking and buying had Molly to think of. She had met more people than she had ever met before. She had been asked to serve in one of the booths at the fair. One of the storekeepers had offered her a position as clerk in his dry-goods department. And altogether the summing up of this day left Molly staggered with happiness.

"Oh, dear!" she said. "If it's true it'll spoil me." And she cried a little before she went to sleep.

Another morning probed deeper into Molly's faculties for enjoyment and wonder. Mrs. See had relatives and friends in Flagerstown, and they made much of Molly. Not the least of that morning's interest was a look at Jim Traft, cattle king of the range. It was in the bank, where Molly and Mrs. See had visited with Mr. See.

"Thar's the old reprobate," whispered See to Molly. "Jim Traft, who's fencin' off West Fork from the range!"

Molly stared. She saw a big man in his shirt sleeves and dusty top boots. He had a shrewd weather-beaten face, hard round the mouth and chin, but softened somewhat by bright blue eyes that certainly did not miss

Molly. If he had not been Jim Traft it would have been quite possible to like him.

As they turned to go out he hailed See.

"Hey, don't I know you?"

"Well, I reckon I know you, Traft," returned See, not over-civilly. "I'm Caleb See."

"Shore. I never forget faces. You live down in the Cibeque. Glad to meet you again. If you're not in a hurry I'd like to ask you some questions about your neck of the woods."

"Glad to accommodate you, Traft," returned See, and then he indicated his companions. "Meet my wife. . . . An' this is our little friend, Molly Dunn. Her first visit to Flag since she was a kid."

Traft shook hands with Mrs. See, and likewise Molly. He was quaint and genial, and his keen eyes approved of Molly.

"Wal, wal! I'm shore glad to meet you, young lady," he said. "Molly Dunn of the Cibeque. I think I used to know your father. An' this is your first visit to Flag in a long time?"

"Yes, sir. It seems a whole lifetime," replied Molly.

When Molly got outside again she exclaimed, breathlessly: "Oh, Mrs. See, he looked right through me! . . . I don't want his pity. . . . But I'm afraid the Dunns of the Cibeque have a bad name."

"Reckon they have, Molly dear," rejoined Mrs. See, practically. "But so far as you are concerned it can be lived down."

"But, Mrs. See—I'd have to stick to dad an' Arch," said Molly, suddenly confronted with a lamentable fact.

"Shore. In a way you've got to. I wouldn't think much of anyone who couldn't stand by her own kin."

Not until afternoon on the ride out to the fair-grounds did Molly quite forget Jim Traft's look and the ignominy of the Dunns. But once arrived there she quite lost her own identity. This girl in blue at whom everybody stared was some other person. Crowds of people, girls in gay apparel, cowboys in full regalia, Indians in picturesque attire, horses, horses, horses, and prize cattle, and every

16

kind of a vehicle Molly had ever heard of, appeared to move before her eyes.

Quite by magic, it seemed, she found herself separated from the smiling Mrs. See and conducted to a gayly decorated booth. There she was introduced to a girl about her own age, with whom she was to share the fascinating work of serving the public with sandwiches and coffee. Fortunately for Molly, her partner was nice and friendly, and certainly gave no indication that she had ever heard of the Dunns of West Fork.

Under her amiable instruction Molly, who was nothing if not expert at waiting at table, acquitted herself creditably. But she could not get used to the marvelous gown she had on, and was in a panic for fear she might get a stain upon it. She did not, however, have so much work that she could not see what was going on, and presently she was having a perfectly wonderful time.

Once she served three cowboys. They were hardly a new species to Molly. Nevertheless, she had not seen such brilliant scarves and fancy belts. She noticed, too, that these young men, like Arch and Seth, packed guns in their belts, a custom she had hardly expected to find at a fair. One of them made eyes at Molly.

After a while they came back, when Molly's partner had left, and if ever Molly had seen the devil in the eyes of a youth she saw it in one of these customers. Still, he was not bad-looking and Molly could not help liking him.

"Miss—Miss—What'd you say your name was?" he asked as he straddled the bench before the counter.

"I didn't say," replied Molly.

"Oh, ex—cuse me. My mistake," he returned, crestfallen at the subdued glee of his comrades. "Have you any pop?"

"No," replied Molly.

"Or ginger ale?"

Molly shook her head.

"Not any pink lemonade?"

"Only coffee an' sandwiches an' cake."

"Cake? Well, give us cake an' coffee," ordered the cowboy.

She served them swiftly and discreetly, deftly avoiding the bold hand that sought to include her fingers as she passed a cup.

"Do you live here?" he asked, presently.

"You know quite well I'm a stranger in Flag, else you wouldn't be so impertinent," returned Molly, severely.

"Aw!" He subsided with that exclamation. And his comrades proceeded to enjoy themselves at his expense. Molly's keen ears lost nothing of the banter. They were just brimful of fun. Evidently the bold one enjoyed something of a reputation as a lady-killer, and had at last met defeat. Presently, as he could not get Molly to notice him, and grew tired of listening to his friends, he threw some silver on the counter and said, loftily, "Keep the change, Little Snowflake." Then he strode away, and after a few moments the others followed.

From this time Molly was kept busy, and only gradually did it dawn upon her that a string of cowboys kept coming and going, for the very obvious reason of getting a look at her. More than once she heard the name Snowflake. Still, none of them were rude. Manifestly they had taken her for a guest of some prominent family in town, and a lady of quality. Molly enjoyed it hugely, though she had more than one melancholy reservation that it might have been different if they had guessed she was only one of the Dunns of the Cibeque.

Soon she was relieved by the young lady, Miss Price, who shared the booth with her.

"You've got the boys guessing," said this smiling worthy. "They've ragged me to death. I don't know them all, though. Just keep it up."

"I—I don't do anythin' but wait on them," gasped Molly.

"That's it. Guess they think you're cold when you're only shy," went on Miss Price. "But you can have a heap of fun. Keep on freezing them. Tomorrow night you'll have the time of your life."

"Tomorrow night?" faltered Molly.

"Sure. Big dance after the *rodeo*. Didn't my mother tell you? Anyway, you're going with us."

"I—I hadn't heard. It's terrible kind of you. But I really couldn't go. I'm such a stranger. An' if they—they think—"

"You dear kid! You are going. Mrs. See promised mother."

Molly thrillingly resigned herself to the unknown. The afternoon ended all too soon, and she rode back to town, babbling to the pleased Mrs. See about the adventure she was having. That night they were out to dine with relatives of Mrs. See. No other young person was present and Molly had the relief of being comparatively unnoticed. These serious older people talked about the affairs of the town and the range, all of which found lodgment in Molly's mind.

3

It was Saturday afternoon and the *rodeo* had just begun, which accounted for the deserted appearance of the grounds adjacent. Molly had remained longer than was really necessary. Mrs. See would be waiting for her at the stand. She was about to leave when she saw that she was to have a last customer.

A young man, in overalls and heavy boots, got off a dusty horse and approached the booth. He asked for something to eat and drink. Apparently he took no notice of Molly. His face wore a troubled look.

Of all the young men Molly had waited upon in two days, this was the first one who had not looked at her twice, and the only one who had not appeared gay or bold or pleasant. Molly felt a little pique and secondly more than a little curiosity.

He might have been twenty-two or -three years old and

evidently was not a cowboy. Molly judged that he would have been fair-skinned if he had not been so sunburnt. His nose had begun to peel, but these demerits did not exactly keep him from being handsome. Presently he laid his sombrero on the counter, which act disclosed light wavy hair, and a broad brow marred by deep furrows.

He struck Molly just about right, and considering her vast experience during these two days, she imagined she was a connoisseur in young men. He slowly drank the last of his coffee, and looking up, met Molly's glance. Then she knew he had not seen her before. He had gray eyes full of shadows.

"What'd you do if you were just about licked?" he queried, suddenly.

"Sir?" exclaimed Molly.

He repeated the question, this time more deliberately, as if now he weighed it.

"I—I'd get up an' fight some more," declared Molly, surprised into genuine sincerity.

He smiled. Then something beside surprise happened to Molly.

"You would? Suppose then you got licked sure?"

"It wouldn't make no difference," replied Molly, at last forgetting to watch her speech. And she smiled back at him.

He saw her really then as a girl, and not as an individual who might propound a personal point of view. Leaning his elbows on the counter, he regarded her with interest verging upon admiration.

"Very well. I'll take your hunch. I'll not quit. If they lick me—I should say *when* they lick me, I'll get up and fight some more."

His words were severe, his purpose almost grim, yet Molly realized the best compliment she ever had received was being paid her.

"I never saw you before," he went on.

"That isn't my fault," replied Molly, demurely, with level gaze on him. What a nice face he had!

"But you don't live in Flag," he protested.

"No indeed."

"Where then?"

"I'm from the Cibeque."

"Cibeque. Is that a town or a ranch or what?"

"It's a valley."

"Never heard of it. How far?"

"Two days' ride."

"Just here on a visit?" continued the young man, and it was manifest that every word carried him farther into interest.

"Yes. We leave in the mawnin'," said Molly, and sighed. Would she ever come back to Flagerstown? And if so, could it ever be so wonderful?

"That's a long while yet," he returned, and smiled again, with a meaning which made Molly's heart jump. "I haven't heard, but of course there'll be a dance tonight. And you'll be going?"

Molly nodded. She had begun to be conscious of confusing sensations.

"I'll bet every blame cowboy at this *rodeo* has a dance with you," he declared, jealously.

"Not quite."

He gave her a long gaze that began in doubt and ended with trust. Molly felt that he knew every last thing in the world about her and she wanted the earth to open and swallow her.

"I don't care for these town dances," he said. "But I'm going to this one—if it's true you're not engaged for every dance."

"To tell the truth I—I haven't one single dance yet," she replied.

"Well! Then your best fellow isn't here?"

"He doesn't happen to exist," said Molly, wistfully. Like all the others, he had taken her for somebody, and if he knew she was only Molly Dunn of West Fork he would not be so nice.

"Listen. This is a serious matter," he rejoined, gravely. "Young ladies aren't always to be believed."

"I wouldn't lie to anyone," retorted Molly.

"Honest! You haven't a best fellow?"

"I haven't *any* fellow," replied Molly, blushing rosily.

21

"I'm only sixteen. Did you think me as old as Methuselah?"

"Your age hadn't occurred to me. But I'd have taken you for eighteen, anyhow. It really doesn't matter. . . . Have you been in Flag lately?"

"Not for years. I was a little girl."

"Will you dance with me tonight?" he asked, without any pretense.

"Yes," replied Molly, equally sincerely.

"How many times?"

"I—I don't know about that. You see, I'm not used to city dances."

"Oh, it'd be quite proper, if that worries you. You see *I* might be taken for your best fellow. I'd sure like that. . . . Would you?"

"It'd not be terribly disagreeable to me," said Molly, archly, and after a roguish glance she looked away.

But he responded to that differently from what she might have expected. "Thank you," he rejoined, and stood up, with his gray eyes alight. "Save some dances for me. Good-by, Miss Cibeque."

He strode away and led his horse in the direction of the corrals. Molly stood there tingling, to be disturbed by the arrival of Mrs. See.

"I had one last customer," said Molly, as if apologizing for the delay.

"Child, everythin' closed at one. The *rodeo* is on," returned Mrs. See. "Hurry now, but don't forget the cash. We'll turn that over to Mrs. Price. . . . You've been a success, Molly. An' I'm tickled."

They hurried into the crowded stand, where some one had kept seats for them; and straightway Molly became absorbed in her first *rodeo*. After that, time meant nothing. The horse races left her weak and quite husky, for she yelled in unison with everybody else present. The staid Mrs. See hit a fat gentleman on the head with her umbrella, and that was only a minor indiscretion observed by Molly.

Then came exhibition trick riding by experts of the range. Molly could ride a horse herself and she knew what good horsemanship included, but this riding went far beyond anything she could have imagined. One rider, bareback, rode at full speed, and he slipped all over his horse, even underneath. But that appeared less wonderful than the splendid rider who rode two race-horses, standing with one foot on the bare back of each. Molly thrilled to her toes at that performance.

The roping of calves was not new to her, though she had never believed such swift time possible. The roping of two-year-olds was a sterner game. Next after that came the riding of bucking bronchos. In any horse country there are bound to be some mean horses, and Molly imagined she had seen a few. But she had not even known what a mean horse was like. There was a black devil of a mustang with rolling white eyes that simply made the cold chills run over Molly. Buck! He went six feet into the air, doubled up, and came down stiff-legged. And he threw three successive riders. Yet how these lean, supple, round-limbed, small-hipped cowboys could ride! Many were thrown. One red-headed fellow had a horse fall back on him. Another rolled clear over with his horse and still came up in the saddle. At this the crowd roared. Molly saw another boy carried off the field, but she had not observed what had happened to him. When that whirling, dusty, snorting, and yelling mêlée ended it was none too soon for Molly.

"Bulldoggin' steers next," said Mr. See, consulting his program.

"Goodness! Do they chase them with bulldogs?" ejaculated Molly, in amaze.

See laughed heartily. "Wal, thet's a good one."

"Caleb, this is Molly's first *rodeo*," reproved his wife, though it was plain the girl's remark had tickled her.

Molly was soon to learn more. A wicked wide-horned steer was let loose, and a cowboy, superbly mounted, came tearing down the field, to drive the steer furiously, catch up with it, and then to dive out of his saddle. He alighted on the neck of the steer, and swinging down by the horns he tumbled it head over heels, and rolled over with it. Molly screamed. But the cowboy came out of the

23

dust unhurt and victorious, for there he sat on the head of the steer, holding it down.

"There! What do you think of that for a cowboy?" exclaimed See, turning to Molly.

"He's wonderful. But he's crazy. Who ever heard of such a thing?" returned Molly, feelingly.

"Molly's right," agreed Mrs. See. "I think this bulldoggin' sport is brutal. Where's the sense in it?"

"Ain't none. But shore takes a slick rider to do it," said her husband.

"A cowboy once told me he didn't have an unbroken bone in his body. Now I can see why," commented Molly.

Nevertheless, though this style of riding, and downing a steer like a bulldog, made Molly cold and sick, she could not help watching it through. She would certainly have something to tell Arch Dunn. Fortunately, none of the riders were seriously hurt during this most perilous test of horsemanship and hardihood. And the rest of the program allowed Molly to recover.

"Wal, lass, an' how'd you like it?" asked Mr. See.

"I've had the most wonderful time in all my life," dreamily replied Molly.

"With the best yet to come," added Mrs. See. "This is all very well for the men, but it's the dance where a girl shines."

With that remark there came flashing back to Molly the strange thoughts and sensations roused by her last customer at the booth. Ought she not tell Mrs. See about this young man? Molly was inherently honest and she knew she should, but she was also in conflict with feelings new to her, and most confusing. She would wait. What would Mrs. See and Mrs. Price think of her if they knew she had promised dances to a stranger who had not even told her his name? That omission had not even occurred to Molly until now. All during the service at the booth she had been most careful of her tongue, and then the very last young man had made her forget herself and what was due her hostesses. Molly could not understand it. He had sort of carried her away. Still, he had not been bold like

24

some of the cowboys, or flirtatious like others. At least she did not think so. But then she might have been worng. The trouble was he had surprised her into liking him. No doubt of that! Who was he and what had troubled him and how had he been about licked, as he called it? Would it be possible for any young fellow to be so clever and so deceitful as to make up all that? Molly was startled. She had known boys to do queer tricks. But she loyally defended this one who had found her weak. He was as honest as he was nice.

Here Molly got down to the point where he had become so undisguisedly interested in the fact that she did not have a best fellow. There had been a soft, almost mischievous light in his gray eyes. Could he have meant that he would like to be her best fellow? Molly burned within and without. The tumultuous fact was that he could be her only fellow, if he wanted to be. And she was ashamed and shocked to confess it. What had good Mrs. See brought upon her?

This perturbing state of mind got side-tracked again at the hotel, from which there was a general exodus of ranchers who lived near town. Molly was thrown in contact with women whom the Sees knew. And at dinner they sat with friends, so that Molly was not able to think for herself, until she got to her room. There anticipation and delight assailed her again, into which crept a dread of what she knew not.

Then she spread the white gown and accessories out on the bed, to revel in them, and forget the proximity of catastrophe. The following hour was one of exultation and dismay combined. She fixed her hair this way and that, never satisfied. It was an apparition which stared wide-eyed at her from the mirror. Who was this girl? Her arms and shoulders were bare. She could not get over the feeling of being still undressed.

When Mrs. See came in, to exclaim in raptures over her, then Molly's last vestige of sense went into eclipse. She needed to be scolded and reminded that she was only Molly Dunn of the Cibeque, instead of being lauded to the skies, and told not one of the society girls at St Louis, where Mrs. See had once been, could hold a candle to her.

"Upon your haid be it!" murmured Molly, tragically.

And so they went out to the dance, which was held in the town-hall a few blocks from the hotel. They walked, and Molly trod on air. Never in her life had she felt anything like her sensations when she walked through the crowd before the hall, between lines of men and women, children, Indians, and then at the entrance, before a phalanx of polished-faced cowboys. Whatever happened, she would have that to remember.

Inside there was a goodly assembly, among whom were Mrs. Price, her daughter Ellen, and an awkward son about Molly's age. They at once appropriated Molly, and this perhaps was the time of greatest strain for her. It was scarcely necessary, however, for Molly to remember Mrs. See's injunctions. She scarcely had a voice at all. Fortunately, she was too little and dainty to be clumsy, and shyness only added to her charm.

There was a good deal of standing around, talking and waiting, with introductions in order, while slowly the hall filled comfortably. Then the music began and it was not a fiddle sawed by a backwoodsman, but real music, and Molly could have danced in leaden boots.

Waltzes and square dances, with the former in large proportion, were to be the program. Molly's first partner was the Price boy, who could not dance very well, but that did not spoil it for her. It developed that intermissions were frequent, but brief. The young people clamored to dance. They would let the old folk sit and look on and talk. Molly had the next dance with a friend of Ellen's, a young man of the town, very pleasant and attentive, and a good dancer. And the third with Mr. Price, himself, who declared he would allow nothing to prevent him having a dance with Molly. She enjoyed it, too, for he was light on his feet and full of fun.

All this while, which seemed interminable despite her enjoyment, Molly knew there was something amiss. The dance had really begun and she was there. Everywhere she turned she met smiles and admiring glances. They

26

bewildered her. Yet she was keen to note that this was no wild, continuous, stamping log-cabin dance. Hilarity prevailed, but not boisterousness. She wondered if there would be any drinking and fights. A dance without these would be new to Molly.

Then, after the fourth, when she was standing with a group near the entrance of the hall, she saw Him. She felt herself tremble. He wore black and looked tall and slim. His eager eyes, dark with excitement, swept the hall. Molly knew what they were searching for. She had never wanted anything so badly as for him to see her, yet she was afraid. He did see her. His smile and bow came before he had time to look her over. Then Molly's cup grew perilously full. But what would he do? She was standing with Ellen Price and her friends. Suppose this stranger would present himself! Molly thought she might pretend to have forgotten his name; then if he had any sense he could save the situation for her. To her relief, however, he did not approach.

The music burst forth again and another partner claimed Molly. But even in the whirling throng she did not lose sight of this young man whom she had promised dances. Now and then as she turned she saw him leaning against the wall. Met his dark glance! It followed her everywhere. He did not dance. He did not mingle with the crowd. During the next intermission she saw that he was noticed by girls, who whispered to one another, and by cowboys who gave him rather contemptuous looks. Both actions struck Molly singularly. In some sense he seemed an outsider or else he did not choose to make himself agreeable. The meaning of feminine glances sent his way was not lost upon Molly. And when she, too, dared to glance his way, to find him watching her, she would quickly avert her eyes. She realized that he hopefully and reasonably expected her to give him an opportunity.

At the end of the next number, which Molly had with young Price, she claimed to be a little tired and wanted to sit down. They found a vacant place, where they conversed for the brief interval.

27

"Shall I take you across to mother?" asked young Price.

"No, thanks. I'll wait here for my next partner," replied Molly, graciously.

"Excuse me then," he returned, and left her.

Molly hoped her stranger would be quick. But she had scarcely prepared herself for his sudden arrival.

"Is this mine?" he asked, bending over her eagerly.

"Yes," murmured Molly, rising.

Then he whirled her into the throng. His presence did not quite make her oblivious to his strong arm, his light step, his perfect time. But instantly Molly realized she did not need to help this young man learn his steps.

"I was afraid you'd forgotten me," he said, pressing her hand.

"Don't talk," returned Molly.

He laughed and obeyed her. Molly's head came about to his shoulder and she just escaped contact with it. Not that she wished to! She felt that her face must be burning and she would have liked to hide it there. She did not seem to be making any effort to dance. Yet she was whirling, swaying, gliding around among dancers who looked vague and dim. All the threatened feelings accumulated during the last two days took possession of her now.

The music ceased when they were at the farther end of the hall.

"Come. Let's get out before some of them grab you," he said. "I must talk to you."

4

HE LED her out through a corridor to a long porch, high up over a garden. It appeared deserted and shadowy. There was moonlight at the corner and just at the edge of it a bench. He found a seat for her there.

"You look perfectly lovely," he said, expelling a deep breath, as if in relief. "I just didn't know you."

"You—you don't know me, anyhow," returned Molly, not knowing what to say.

"Nor you me. But at first I thought you did. It sure was jolly. To think I almost didn't ride to town!"

"That would have been terrible, wouldn't it?" murmured Molly. She could not remain silent. He seemed to draw expression from her.

"It sure would. But I don't want to tell you about myself, now. I want to talk about you."

"An' I'd rather not."

"Aren't we mysterious?" He took her hand and held it.

Molly did not have the desire to withdraw it, nor the strength. But she managed to look up. How pale and eager he was! His eyes devoured her. And his face wore an ineffable smile.

"'All's fair in love and war,'" he said. "And I rustled you away from *them*," he indicated the distant dance-hall by an eloquent gesture, "to have a minute with you alone."

Molly's presagement that something was going to happen to her was near its fulfillment.

"There's a strange thing about you—a lack I can't understand," he went on.

"What—do you mean?" faltered Molly. Had he found her out already?

"Oh, it's the most wonderful thing for me. I mean about the—the lack of that best fellow you said you didn't have. How does it happen? Sure you're only sixteen. But that's quite grown up in this country. Have you a fierce father or brother?"

"You bet I have. Both!" replied Molly, with a little laugh. She was sure of her ground here.

"Then that accounts. I'm glad. I was afraid of something else. . . . Very well, I make application for the vacant place."

"Place?" echoed Molly, weakly.

"Yes. I most earnestly apply for the job of being your best fellow."

"Oh, you—you can't be serious!" exclaimed Molly, in confusion.

"Serious? I'm afraid it is," he said, running a hand through his hair. "You don't know me. And I haven't any recommendations. But I'd like you to take me on without these."

"It isn't customary," returned Molly, trying to be light when she feared he might hear the outrageous beating of her heart.

"I know that. But I've a weakness to be trusted with responsibility. If I hadn't I'd never gotten into the trouble I'm bucking now. . . . You'll have to take me on faith—or not at all."

"But doesn't it—it apply to me—that way?" asked Molly, tremulously.

"No. I'm a man. And you're a girl."

"Yes. I'm beginnin' to find that out."

He laughed as if her reply was encouragement and possessed himself of her other hand. Then undoubtedly he began to draw her a little toward him, but to do him justice Molly imagined he did not realize it. She did, however, to the imminent danger of rout of reserve and self-control.

"I would take you as my best girl—my *only* girl, I should say, without one single thing beside your Yes."

Molly felt irresistibly drawn to the edge of an abyss. Here was an opportunity quite beyond even her dreams.

"You're—you're—" Molly did not know just what he was, besides being very careless and foolish. He had her almost leaning on his shoulder now. She had not made the slightest resistance. She was as unstable as water. Still, she tried to think in spite of his nearness and her dawning emotions. "If I said—yes—an'—an' afterwards you went back on me!"

"Good Heavens! . . . Little girl, you had better say 'yes' pretty quick or I'll——"

He choked at the end of that passionate utterance. Molly knew what he meant. For the moment it paralyzed her. And then it was too late. He had her in his arms—tight against his breast. Molly closed her eyes. She did not realize her state beyond the exquisite contrast to what her backwoods admirers had roused in her. And suddenly that thought ended in a singular revulsion. She stiffened. She repulsed him with a stinging slap which, blindly delivered, struck him across the lips.

He uttered an inarticulate cry of surprise and regret. His hand went to his mouth, and then he applied a handkerchief there. The force of the blow had cut his lip.

"I apologize," he said, constrainedly. "Sure lost my head—but I didn't mean to insult you."

Molly, with as unaccountable an impulse as the other, placed a tender trembling hand on his lips. "I—I'm sorry," she whispered, wildly. "I didn't mean that—at all." And she followed the touch of her hand with a shy swift kiss. Then she gasped at her utter effrontery.

"Well!—You make sweet amends," he said, haltingly, as if she were beyond him. "By that did you mean 'Yes'?"

Molly dropped her head and covered her face with her hands. The tight, hot constriction in her breast eased its grip.

"I don't know what I meant, only it wasn't 'Yes.' "

31

"In that case you'd better explain."

Molly looked up, impelled by his tone. His eyes burned doubtfully down upon her. His face shone pale in the moonlight.

"I—I'm dishonest," she burst out. "I've slapped boys before when they—took liberties with me. I liked them, I suppose, but I didn't want them pawin' an' kissin' me. . . . I really gave in to you. . . . Only, I wasn't fair. I wasn't honest. I hit you because I—I wanted you to keep on believin' I was what all these people thought. . . . They've made me act a lie. Me—in these pretty clothes! But, oh, I couldn't help it. I was afraid all the time. I *knew* somethin' terrible would happen."

"You wanted me to believe you were what?" he asked, sharply, bending over her.

"Like Miss Price an' her friends."

"I think they might do well by being more like you," he returned. "I asked to be your best fellow. I sure never asked it of any of them."

"But you don't know me!" cried Molly, distracted.

"I can see and think, can't I? You're the sweetest, loveliest little girl I ever met."

Molly was brutally torn between the ecstasy of that and the mercilessness of her honesty.

"Fine feathers make fine birds," she replied, bitterly.

"You poor kid! . . . There's something queer here, but I swear it's not in you. I'm taking your kiss for 'Yes!'—Heavens! what else could a kiss mean?"

"No, no. It meant nothin'," said Molly.

"Are your kisses so common, then?"

"You're the first boy I *ever* kissed," she flashed at him.

"I'm very proud of that. Well, then, what else could it mean except 'Yes'?"

"I was beside myself. I told you. . . . I was ashamed—sick because I hit you. But I wasn't dishonest when I kissed you."

"You said you wanted me to think you like Miss Price and her friends. That puzzles me. I do think they can't compare with you."

"But you're only fooled," she said, despairingly.

32

"By what?"

"I don't know. This pretty dress, an' the place—an' everythin'."

"Why, it wouldn't make any difference to me what you wore or where you were," he protested, tenderly.

"Oh yes, it would!"

"But, you child, didn't I fall in love with you at the booth?"

This protestation was almost too beautiful and poignant for Molly to bear. It came in the nature of a revelation of her own beset state. In another instant she knew she would surrender and fall into his arms.

"But you don't know who I am!"

"You're my sweetheart!" he returned, triumphantly.

Molly suffered during one instant of glorious exaltation.

"I am Molly Dunn, of the Cibeque," she said.

"Molly Dunn. What a pretty name! . . . Cibeque? Oh that's the valley you told me about."

"Yes. They call it the brakes of the Cibeque."

"Dunn. I've heard that name, too. Oh yes, I got into an argument with a fellow named Dunn. Slinger Dunn, they called him. But sure you couldn't be any relation to him."

"Why couldn't I?" she queried, in a curious calm.

"Heavens! He's a desperado! Wonderful-looking chap. They call him 'Slinger' because of his habit of throwing a gun. He has killed several men. The sheriff here is scared to death of him. I happened to cross his trail, unfortunately, and gave him a piece of my mind. If I ever saw lightning in a man's eyes I saw it then. Whew! . . . Well, his companion, as tough-looking fellow as he was, dragged him away. Saved me a scare if not more."

"His right name is Arch," replied Molly, and rose to her feet.

"Of course, living around here you'd have heard of him. It must be disgusting to have a criminal like that roaming around with the name of Dunn. People might think he is related to you."

"He is."

33

The young man rose slowly, in consternation, and made an appealing gesture.

"Impossible, Miss Dunn. . . . Perhaps a very distant relation?"

"He is my brother."

"Good God! Your brother? You lovely, dainty, sweet little lady! . . . Why, I saw him again, drunk and dirty, hobnobbing with Mexicans and Indians. If he's a—one of your family, he surely must be an outcast."

"No. He was home the day I left to come here."

He appeared suddenly staggered, not only by the truth, but by the nature of his transgression.

"Oh, I'm sorry!" he began, hurriedly. "I've hurt you. I never dreamed—please forgive me. . . . After all, it was natural enough. Another of my damned tenderfoot blunders! But who would ever think that you——"

"Ah! Now you've said it," she interrupted, passionately.

"Miss Dunn, I was only going to say who would ever think a wonderful girl like you could have such a rotten brother.—Well, it makes no difference to me, I assure you of that," he said, bravely, essaying a fine effort to keep under restraint. He was regarding her fearfully and again he had turned pale.

The bitterness of reality had steeled Molly, yet she shook inwardly as he stood there, erect and earnest, doing her honor.

"Yet it does, or you couldn't have talked so," she replied, shaking her head gravely.

"I say it doesn't," he retorted. "And I certainly shall hold you to your word."

"Word? I didn't give any."

"You kissed me. Of your own sweet will! You can't get over that."

"No, I cain't. . . . But it wasn't a promise."

"It certainly was. More than a promise. Unless you lied to me."

"Lie? I wouldn't lie to you," she declared.

"Then I hold you to it. . . . Come, let's forget the—the

thing. You see, Molly, we fell in love before we got acquainted. Didn't we? Isn't that great?"

"I didn't say we—I fell in love," returned Molly, pondering over the significance of the words.

"Not in words—yet."

Again Molly felt the imminence of a precipice. She could not resist this young man, stranger though he was, and presently she would not care to try.

"I kissed you because I wanted to be square," she said. "With myself, same as with you. I sure wasn't when I hit you. That's all."

"How can you say that? Kissing me proved your honesty. And for such a girl as I hold you to be, a kiss means a good deal. It just about means everything."

Molly was mournfully becoming cognizant of that very fact. Desperately she cried out again that she was only Molly Dunn of the Cibeque.

At this he seized her in his arms, masterfully, yet guardedly.

"Stop harping on that," he demanded. "What do I care who you are? You might be Sally Jones of the Missouri. I don't care any more than you'd care if my name was Bud Applegate instead of Jim Traft."

"Instead—of—what?" faltered Molly, slipping out of his arms.

"Why, James Traft! Jim, for short."

"Traft? But that's the name of—of the cattle king."

"Sure. I'm his nephew. My Dad is his brother. I was named after Uncle Jim."

"You're the new foreman of the Traft outfit?"

"Yes, I am," he replied, nettled. "That's the very question your brother asked me. Only he was insulting and you're—well, I don't care to have *you* ridicule me. The idea of my being a foreman seems to stick in the craw of these Westerners. Why not? I'm no nincompoop."

"You're the fellow who's buildin' the drift fence?"

"Yes—I am," he replied unsteadily.

"Did you know that fence is a slap in the face to every person down in the Cibeque?"

"No, I didn't. Uncle Jim said it would rile a lot of no-good homesteaders."

"I'm the daughter of one of them. An' sister to another," rejoined Molly, in tragic finality, and with a flash of eyes she left him there.

5

UP TO eighteen years of age James Traft had often seen his uncle, the Arizona pioneer and cattleman, who made frequent trips East. There had grown up a bond of affection between them. James had from knee-high listened to stories of Indian fights and road-agents, gunmen and rustlers. The Westerner had never married; he was devoted to his brother, who was James's father.

Then had come an interval of four years during which Jim Traft did not visit Missouri. His vast interests had grown so complicated that he could not leave them. During this time James had been at loose ends, trying farming, clerking, and odd jobs without any indication that he might set the world on fire. At last a letter from the West at least changed the world for James.

Some passages in this blunt letter to his father were hard for James to swallow.—In the natural course of events all of Jim Traft's property would go to his nephew James. But that was something aside from James ever making good use of it. If he were a strong, resourceful boy with guts he might become a rancher. The cattle industry was growing. The days of the great rustler barons were gone, though cattle-stealing still represented altogether a big loss to the range. And so on.

The implication seemed to be that James would get all his uncle's money without having worked for it, and that there was a question whether or not he was big enough for the West. At first James had been humiliated and furious, and would hear nothing of going to Arizona. Nevertheless, his father prevailed in the end. Old Jim was caustic and crude; he had grown up in the stern school of the ranges, but he was the very salt of the earth and had genuine affection for James. He would be terribly hurt if James refused and he would never understand.

"It scares me a little, Jimmy," his father had said. "You've got to have the real stuff in you out there. I believe you have and I want you to go. Show Jim you're a Traft!"

Persuaded and made to realize his opportunity, for which he should sacrifice anything and strive with all his heart, James started West. His first acquaintance with the Great Plains had come from the window of a train, and long before he saw the vast gray slopes of Colorado and the white-peaked Rockies, the latent spirit of adventure stirred thrillingly in him. Then the wild timbered uplands of New Mexico and the red-walled canyons of Arizona won him to the West, long before he stepped off the train at Flagerstown.

He had telegraphed his uncle as to his arrival, but there was no one to meet him. What a funny, slow, sleepy, wide-streeted town! Every other building, all high-boarded and weathered, appeared to house a saloon. He knew his uncle lived out of town, though not far. James finally found a livery-stable, where he engaged a loquacious Negro to drive him, bag and baggage, out into the country. What he learned from this citizen of Flagerstown, in that short drive, was certainly not reassuring.

But James liked the pine forest and the gray levels along the road, and the black mountains rising in the distance. And he had a fine view of Jim Traft's ranch home. It was nothing at all like he had pictured. Uncle Jim had been long on cattle deals and short on description, so far as talk was concerned. Across one of the wide grassy flats the long, low white house stood on a pine-timbered knoll, and below it clustered a bewildering array of corrals, barns, and sheds. Cattle dotted the wide valley, and on the fenced meadows horses and colts grazed, too numerous to count.

The road wound along the edge of the timber, from which James had ample opportunity to see the ranch at different angles, and by the time he reached the house he was wild with enthusiasm about his future home.

A low-roofed comfortable porch fronted the house. Here James deposited his baggage, and paying the driver, he knocked. Nobody answered, however, so he went around to the back. A wide courtyard led out to the corrals. He espied men out there and directed his footsteps in that direction.

Soon he came upon three cowboys around a horse, and then his uncle, who stood with another man, watching them.

"Hello, Uncle Jim!" he yelled, and his rapid strides soon fetched him up.

"Howdy, Jim!" replied the rancher, as if he had seen his nephew only yesterday, and extended his hand. "Got your telegram, but forgot to meet you.... By gum! you've sprung up like a weed."

Traft had not changed. His garb, however, was new to Jim, and consisted of high boots, corduroys tucked in them, an old leather belt with an empty gun-sheath on it, gray soft shirt, and a vest that had been new years ago. He was a stalwart figure of a man, nearing seventy, but still erect and rugged, with a lined hard face expressive of his life on the frontier.

"Shake hands with Ring Locke," said Traft, indicating his companion, a tall, lean, sandy-complexioned Westerner whose narrow eyes were almost hidden under an old black sombrero.

Jim was cordial and prompt in his greeting.

"How do!" drawled Locke, whose accent proclaimed him a Texan. "I shore am glad to meet you, sah."

"This is the nephew I told you about, Ring," went on Traft. "He has come West to run the Diamond outfit."

Jim tried to bear well the scrutiny given him by this range boss of his uncle's, a right-hand man who had been with him twenty years.

"Uncle should have said I'll *try* to run that outfit, Mr. Locke," said Jim, frankly. "I'm not afraid. But I'm an awful tenderfoot."

Perhaps his earnestness favorably impressed Locke, for he smiled and replied, dryly, "Wal, it ain't bad to start when you're a tenderfoot, just so long as you know it."

"You bet I know it," continued Jim, hastening to follow that up. "When Uncle's letter came I was sure up a tree. It sounded wonderful. But I had listened to Uncle Jim's stories about gunmen and bad cowboys, wild steers and bucking bronchos, stampedes and rustling. It wasn't easy to decide. . . . But here I am. And I can take a licking."

"Wal, reckon you're likely to get it," rejoined Locke. "But in this heah country a lickin' ain't nothin', so long's it's not for keeps."

Jim took almost instantly to the lean Texan. But the three cowboys standing by, apparently like hitching-posts, yet with still eyes and faces, gave him an uncomfortable sensation. To be sure, they heard every word. What clean-cut, lithe-limbed young men! The one holding the horse had a gun hanging low from his belt. Jim faced this triangle of judges, for so they seemed, expecting to be introduced. But his uncle apparently neglected or avoided it.

"We'll go back to the house," he said, and led Jim away. "Have a good trip out?"

"You bet. I've got a stiff neck from looking out of the car window," replied Jim, enthusiastically. "No matter what you've read or heard, you can't get any true idea till you *see* it. I mean the plains, hills, valleys, ranges, and mountains. . . . Uncle, I liked all the whole long ride out. But Arizona best."

"An' how's that?"

"I don't know yet. Maybe the great red walls—the canyons."

"Ahuh. . . . Sorry I didn't meet you at the train. I reckoned I would. How's your mother?"

"Fine and well. Uncle, she was crazy to have me come, but scared stiff."

"Good! An' how's that storekeeper brother of mine, your dad?"

"He hasn't been so well lately, but I guess it's nothing much. He sent a letter and some things which I have for you."

"Did he kick about your comin' out?"

"No. All he kicked about was my making good. He gave me a stiff talk, you bet."

They reached the house, where Jim was conducted to a large light room, with walls and floor of clean yellow pine. A few deerskin rugs, a wood-burning stove, a table with lamp, an old bureau and mirror, and spare blanketed bed, constituted the contents, the simplicity of which pleased Jim.

"Come out on the porch and we'll talk," his uncle had said. And Jim, after securing the letter and parcels he had mentioned, hurried out to deliver them.

"Thanks. I'll look at them later. . . . Wal, Jim, you've growed. You're a pretty husky chap. Too heavy, mebbe, but ridin' the range will soon change that. By the way, have you been ridin' much since I saw you last? You used to take to hosses."

"Had two years of riding every day. You know I tried farming."

"Yes, your dad mentioned it. How'd you make out?"

"I fell down, Uncle," replied Jim, regretfully. "I just couldn't do it."

"An' why not?" asked Traft, as if he already knew.

"I don't know, unless it was too tame. Every day the same! I thought I'd die. But I stuck two years. Then dad sold the farm, which was lucky for me."

"What else you been doin' these four years since I seen you?"

"I was still in school for a year after you last visited us. Then the two years on dad's farm. And the last year I tried several jobs, only one of which I was any good at."

"An' what was that?" asked Traft, kindly. "Reckon it wasn't clerkin' in the store?"

"No. I'm almost ashamed to tell you, Uncle. It was on my own hook, though. I got an idea some shade trees would look fine round our place. So I drove out to the river and dug up cottonwoods and planted them. Dad laughed at me. Then our neighbor hired me to do the same for his place. Through that I got other jobs, and I was making good money when your letter came."

"Wal, I'll be dog-goned!" ejaculated the rancher. "Plantin' trees, an' cottonwoods at that. Son, it was a darn good idee."

Jim thanked his lucky stars he had confided something he had been afraid his uncle would think trivial.

"Wal, so much for Missouri," went on Traft. "You're here in Arizona now. Reckon I might have wrote you all about what I want and hope. But it wouldn't have been fair to you or me. Fact is I couldn't have said all I need to in a letter. Your dad would have throwed a fit. I reckoned it'd be better to get face to face an' have it out. Don't you figger that way, too?"

"I certainly do, Uncle, especially if it's as big and hard a job as I imagine. And if it's really true that you have made me your heir."

"Wal, naturally, all I have would go to your dad an' you. But that's not the question."

"It's a serious part of it for me," declared Jim, bravely. "I appreciate your kindness, Uncle Jim, but if I can't make good as a rancher—well, I don't want the property."

"Ahuh, I see. Wal, reckon your dad never guessed that." Jim felt the piercing intensity of eyes like a pale blue gleam, yet not lacking understanding. "However, what becomes of my property ain't the main issue with me. Blood is thicker than water. An' under any circumstances I'd want my only kin to have what I left."

"Then, Uncle, what is the main issue?" queried Jim, anxiously.

"Wal, I reckon it's I want you to be as near a son to me as possible."

"That's easy, Uncle, if it depends on sincerity and affection and obedience."

"They'll help, but it depends most on what I said in my letter. Guts!"

41

"I remember, and that worried me. But I hope I have some."

"Jim, the job I want you to take is the hardest in the West."

"I don't care. The harder the better," declared Jim, answering the stimulation of doubt. "I always told dad that I needed responsibility. He never gave me any. The fact that you will put responsibility on my shoulders is half of the battle right now."

"Son, that's straight talk," returned his uncle, nodding his head thoughtfully. "An' I liked the way you spoke up to Ring Locke. If he took a shine to you it'd help a lot. ... But, Jim, the hell of it is no rancher who knows the West ought ever to give a tenderfoot from the East such a job."

"Why not?"

"Wal, I reckon because of natural human feelin's. But I'm just bull-headed enough to want a Traft an' nobody else to take my place."

"If you were a young man, Uncle, could you take care of this job?" asked Jim, curiously.

"Yes. An' I reckon I could do it yet."

"All right, then," returned Jim, feeling his face blanch. "I'll commit myself here. I'll *do* it."

"Fine! I like your spirit, son," exclaimed Traft, warmly, and a smile transformed his hard lined face. "Now listen. I'm runnin' about eight thousand head of cattle, mebbe more. But we can never get a count. That's a lot of stock, Jim. Figger out the value at forty dollars a head, which is a low estimate. Wal, I lose from a thousand head up every year. Most of this loss can be laid to cattle thieves. It has gradually growed worse an' has begun to rile me. I used to laugh at this two-bit rustlin'. But it's no good deceivin' myself any longer. The thing is serious. I've reason to believe Ring Locke knows it's worse than he'll tell me. Anyway, he's the best-posted cowman on the range.—Blodgett runs a big lot of cattle. So does Hep Babbit. They're all losin' stock, too."

"Uncle Jim, this is bad," declared Jim, in surprise. "It's

almost like the rustler stories you told me when I was a kid."

"Son, if I don't miss my guess you'll shore live one of them stories," responded Traft, with a grim laugh.

"You're being robbed, but you don't know where the cattle go?" queried Jim, ignoring the start his uncle's statement gave him.

"Humph! We know darn well where they're goin'."

"Where?"

"South of here, in the brakes under the Diamond. An' the Diamond, I should explain, is high country south of here. On three sides it sheers straight down an' cattle can't get off. But on the west, for forty miles or so, it slopes off into the roughest canyon country in Arizona. Thicker than the Tonto. These canyons head up high in the timber an' run down deep an' rough. All of them have fine grass an' water. Lots of deer, bear an' turkey, too, if you like to hunt. Wal, a good deal of stock, especially cows with unbranded calves, drift into these draws an' work down into the brakes. There the cows are killed an' the calves stolen. It used to be these thieves would take the meat an' bury or burn head an' hide. But lately they kill too many. They just down the cows in a thicket or drag them into one, an' leave them there for the varmints. Locke's last report shore riled me."

"Then, Uncle, this tough job you're giving me has to do with the thieves," asserted Jim.

"Wal, I should sort of smile it does," drawled Traft.

"But why not intrust it to an experienced Westerner, like Locke?"

"Locke can't bother with it, an' wouldn't if he could, at least the way I want to stop it. An' as I told you I want a Traft to do this. Son, it'll be a big thing for the range, if we succeed. I don't want one of these gun-packin' cowboys to have the credit, when I can throw it to you."

"You're very kind, Uncle," said Jim, with a dry humor not lost upon Traft. "Are you sure anyone but a fool tenderfoot would tackle the job?"

Traft laughed. He was growing more at ease with Jim. "Some of my boys are achin' to get the job. Jim, my

Diamond outfit is the damnest bunch of cowpunchers in Arizona. An' it's this Diamond outfit you're to take charge of."

"Damnest bunch! Doesn't sound very good, Uncle. Just what do you mean?" returned Jim, dubiously.

"Huh! I'll leave that for you to find out. . . . Now to come out with my plan. I want a drift fence built from my ranch here clear down across the Diamond to where it jumps off. A hundred-mile fence!"

"What's a drift fence?"

"It's just a fence along which cattle will drift south as far as they can go, then drift back. It'd have several good uses, but the main one is to keep the cows an' calves from driftin' down into the brakes."

"Well, the building of a fence even a hundred miles long oughtn't be so difficult."

"Shore it won't. But keepin' it up after it's built is where the hell will come in."

Jim grasped subtly that here was the crux of the whole matter.

"There'll be opposition? Down on the Diamond," he rejoined.

"Shore will. An' for that matter all over the range. Even Blodgett is oncertain about fencin' the range. You see, a barbed-wire fence in this country is nothin' short of murder. An' these nesters an' homesteaders an' back-woodsmen will lose by it. An' as for cowboys, Lord! how they hate any kind of a fence! I reckon I used to. But I'm ahead of my day. I can see what is needed an' what is comin'. So, Jim, you can trust me so far as the benefit to ranchers is concerned."

"Uncle, have you an actual right to fence the range?"

"Shore, but it's open to question. If it ever went to law I'd have to prove my contention. An' whoever sued me would have to show why he was bein' hurt. No honest cattleman will ever take such action. An' I'm shore doubtful about any of the homesteaders goin' so far."

"Could you prove your contention, which of course is that you are being robbed?" queried Jim, earnestly.

"Wal, I could, if Ring Locke an' some of my cowboys

would testify. But they hate the idea like sixty. I'll expect you to find out what they know, an' then add evidence of your own."

"I see. So far so good. How about your moral right?"

"Jim, I'm glad you ask that. You're no fool, if you are a tenderfoot. The question of moral right is the most puzzlin' one—the most open to argument. My own conscience is clear on that. I *know* in the long run the range will benefit."

"How do you know? Prove it to me."

'Wal, you can see how us big cattlemen will profit by it."

"Yes, that's easy."

"Wal, the little cattlemen will have to stop stealin'."

"If there's no more to it, you're absolutely right. But won't you close the range or fence off part of it from them?"

"In some sense, yes. But only those draws an' canyons I told you about. There's shore water an' grass enough in them for ten times the stock they own. Any one of them will admit that. These honest ranchers will just stop appropriatin' calves they're not shore they own."

"The really honest fellows do that now?" queried Jim, in surprise.

"Shore they do, an' don't hardly think they're stealin'."

"An' the other kind?"

"Wal, we'll put them up a stump. Some of them will see the handwritin' on the wall an' quit. An' others will cut our fence an' go right ahead stealin'. That's where our trouble will come in. Mebbe we can stop it in a few years, mebbe not. Some of the ranchers here think it'll start a long hard fight. An' that's why they're leavin' it to me."

"Wal, Uncle, what do *you* think it will lead to?"

"Nothin' much compared to what I've been through. But I reckon some fence-cuttin' an' hard ridin' an shootin' will seem a whole lot to you. Ha! Ha!"

"It's not very funny," said Jim, soberly.

"Wal, son, your face was. Don't let my Diamond outfit see you look like that."

"I'm to hide my feelings from them?" queried Jim.

"Nope. You're not to have any, except gettin' mad, an' when you do that you want to let them see it damn pronto."

"Oh! ... Uncle, I can see this is going to be a lovely easy job."

"Wal, it'd shore please me if you'd find it that. .... Jim, I'm puttin' a lot on you. An' I reckon in a way it's selfish."

"No. Nothing of the kind," replied Jim, hastily. "I believe implicitly in you, Uncle Jim. I'll make your ideals and motives mine. ... Otherwise, I'm scared stiff, but I believe I like the tough job you've given me—if I can only make a go of it!"

"Wal, the best encouragement I can give you is that I like the way you face it," returned Traft. "Shore it's more than I expected, first off."

"Thanks, Uncle. That'll help a lot," declared Jim, feelingly. "I'd like some advice, too."

"Wal, I never was much on givin' advice. Nobody ever follows it."

"I'd try. But at least you can tell me what you'd do, if you had all your knowledge of the range, yet were only my age."

"Haw! Haw! That's a stumper. Jim, I reckon I'm goin' to like you, outside of blood relationship. What'd I do? Wal, let's see. .... First off I'd go to town an' buy the best cowboy outfit I could get, an' that means saddle, bridle, spurs, chaps, sombrero, gun, boots, an' so on. That would be for special occasions. Then I'd wear most the time just plain overalls. I'd pack the gun an' begin to learn to shoot it. I'd have a little straight talk with the boys who was to work under me an' I'd let them know I was to be boss. I'd always do my share of any an' all kinds of work. I'd show a disposition not to give any boy a job I wouldn't try to tackle myself. I wouldn't be too nice to take a drink, on occasions where it might be wise, but I'd leave drink alone. Also—an' I hardly need to tell you this—I'd leave the town slatterns alone. I'd lend my money free, but never my hoss or saddle or spurs. I'd always stand the brunt of any trouble directed against my outfit. That'll be hard, for you'll find each an' every one of your cowboys keen to do that same thing. Last, an' I reckon most particular an' hard, I'd stand up under the hell the Westerners will make for a tenderfoot. I'd run the gauntlet. I'd make all the decent fellows like me—an' most of them are decent—an' I'd make the others respect me."

Jim had the good humor and the nerve to laugh in his uncle's face.

"Ha! Ha! Ha! Is *that* all, Uncle? I thought you were going to give me something hard."

"Wal," declared Traft, gruffly, with a dubious look at this nephew, "I was a-goin' to add somethin' that I never could do, myself."

"And what is that?" asked Jim, suddenly.

"Get married pronto."

Jim whistled. "Heavens! I hope you haven't picked out a Western girl for me."

"Nope. But I'm hopin' you didn't leave no Eastern girl behind."

"Luckily I didn't, Uncle."

"Wal, that's somethin'. You won't find these Western girls special sweet on a tenderfoot. But you're not bad-lookin'. You shore have prospects, an' if you try you might win one of them."

"Whew!—Uncle, that's a sticker. I'm afraid I'll have to jump the traces on that one."

"Jim, I'm onreasonable," said Traft, wistfully. "But I'd shore like to hear the laughter of children round this ranchhouse before I die."

6

A WEEK elapsed before the Diamond outfit came in from the range.

Jim made the most of that reprieve. He was up at dawn and did not go to bed till late. He went at Ring Locke like a youngster who could not swim in a swift current and was going to hold on or die. But Locke seemed only kind and aloof. He answered some questions; he never vouchsafed any range lore. Jim was sharp enough to find out, however, that Locke had a keen eye for him, and this gave him some grain of comfort.

Apparently his uncle never saw him unless he bumped right into him. Jim refused to take all or any of the wonderful horses that were his to own and ride. He rode or tried to ride all the mustangs and bronchos about the ranch. At first he kept account of the times he got thrown, but he gave this up. He certainly did know, however, that he had many bruises and sprains and bumps. Moreover, he grew so saddle-sore that it was agony for him to struggle up on a horse.

During this wait he learned every nook and cranny of the ranch, and there were a thousand acres and more, including the timber. He could not avoid coming into occasional contact with other of his uncle's cowboy outfits. And these instances were painful to Jim.

He found also, on numerous trips into town, where it was impossible to keep from meeting people, that he was an object of very great interest to everybody, especially the girls and young women. Jim, remembering his uncle's wishes, and being far from a hater of the opposite sex, at the outset made himself most agreeable. Presently he confined himself merely to politeness. The interest he had observed did not extend as far as personal propinquity.

One morning he had returned from a disastrous determination to stick on the back of a mustang, and had again taken up a dirty job at the bar, when a farmhand approached him with a message: "Boss says the Diamond outfit is in waitin' fer you."

Jim let them wait awhile, until he got himself thoroughly dirty and tired and cross. Then he limped round to the bunkhouses. His uncle did not appear to be among the bunch of cowboys at the last house. No doubt he had beat a hasty retreat.

"I'll bet the old devil is snickering," muttered Jim.

He approached the young men, and before he got even close he saw they constituted a remarkable group. They had a singular similarity, and yet upon near scrutiny they were not at all alike.

"How do, boys!" he said, bluntly, as he halted before them. "So you're the Diamond outfit I'm to boss? ... Well, I'm not a damn bit gladder to meet you than you are to meet me."

Most of them greeted him with a word or nod. Jim found that he had not exactly spoken the truth, for he certainly sustained thrills when he looked these cowboys over. There did not appear to be one as old as he was, nor, for that matter, as big, though several were as tall. Lithe-bodied, long of limb and bow-legged, with small round hips and wide shoulders, lean and sharp of face, bronzed and sunburnt, with expressionless eyes like gimlets, they certainly belonged to a striking and unique class.

"Who was your last foreman?" asked Jim.

After quite a long silence one of them replied, "Jud Blue."

"Is he here with you now?"

"Reckon no one has noticed him."

49

"Where is he?"

"Wal, if he's where he ought to be he's in hell," came the laconic reply.

"How so?" flashed Jim.

"Jud was shot last month down on the Diamond."

"Shot! . . . Was it an accident?"

"Shore was, for him. But whoever did it was lookin' pretty straight."

Jim did not betray the shock this intelligence gave him, but he certainly made note of another circumstance his uncle had not imparted.

"Which one of you has been longest with my uncle?" he questioned.

"Hump Stevens, heah, was in the first Diamond outfit. Six years ago, wasn't it, Hump?"

"Round aboot thet," drawled a tall tawny cowboy who was stoop-shouldered.

"Stevens, then, ought to be foreman of this outfit," returned Jim. "And after him every one of you according to your service. Well, let's understand each other right here. I certainly am not stuck on the job and think I'm the last fellow on earth to tackle it. But my uncle has put it on me. He wants to leave his property to me. And I won't have it unless I can deserve it. And that means make good at ranching from the ground up."

Blank, still faces baffled Jim. It was impossible to tell whether or not these cowboys were in the least impressed. They certainly thought he was a liar.

"You can lay off till Monday morning," added Jim, curtly. And before he started to limp away he gathered that his first order to them had been received with a pleasant surprise.

Perhaps the ensuing hour was the most profoundly thoughtful of any since he had decided to embark upon this adventure. What an unknown quantity the Diamond outfit! He had needed only one look at these devil-may-care boys to realize it. Cowboys were not wholly strangers to him. These, however, were the dyed-in-the-wool range product. They were potential chain lightning and fire-brand. He was conscious of admiration, dread, and an

50

acute desire to make friends with them. After meeting them he realized he could not expect any material help from Ring Locke or his uncle. The matter was personal.

Wherefore he carefully kept out of their way for a day and a half. On Saturday afternoon he went to town, and he had not been there long before he heard that the Diamond outfit was painting some very vivid red. Jim laughed. After a while, however, it grew monotonous. And when he happened to encounter Miss Blodgett in one of the stores and have her subtly refer to his cowboys he became irritated. Must the whole town take up the situation which his uncle had precipitated? A second look into Miss Blodgett's hazel eyes confirmed the suspicion. She was the nicest of the girls he had met so far, a tall, rangy girl who looked like she could ride a horse. She had freckles and brown curls and was rather pretty.

"I met Curly Prentiss in the post-office," she announced, after he had greeted her.

"Who's he?" asked Jim, though he had an inkling.

"Don't you know Curly yet?" she rejoined, merrily. "Well, he's one of your Diamonds."

"Oh, I see! Fact is I don't know any of them. Was there anything particular about your meeting him today?"

"Not so very—for Curly. He used to ride for us. Finest cowboy in the world. But when he drinks—well, his tongue wags."

"Reckon it wagged about me on this occasion?"

"It sure did. . . . Mr. Jim, have you anyone to write home to your mother and sister?"

Jim eyed her with misgivings. These Western girls were as deep as the cowboys. Jim conceived an idea, however, that Miss Blodgett was friendly, or she would never have made that remark.

"You mean about the disposition of my remains?" rejoined Jim, dryly. "Thanks, but I'm going to see that will not be necessary. I've fallen in love with my new job. In fact, I like the West—and everybody out here. Good afternoon, Miss Blodgett."

And Jim went on, muttering to himself: "Dog-gone it!

51

They're all after my scalp, even the girls. I hope I'm not going to get sore."

Presently he went into a pool-room to buy a smoke. The place was fairly crowded, and at the very first table he saw a cowboy he recognized as one of his Diamond outfit. He was in the act of making a shot. But he straightened up. His fine tanned young face was flushed and there were other indications that he had been drinking.

"Boss, I ain't doin' nothin'," he said, slowly.

"Who said you were?" returned Jim, realizing that he must have looked sharply at the boy.

"You're lookin' for Curly?"

"Yes," answered Jim, suddenly inspired.

"Sheriff Bray just collared Curly. Honest, boss, Curly was behavin' himself strick proper. But Bray has got it in for us Diamond fellars. An' Curly"—here the cowboy came round the table to be closer to Jim—"Curly was pretty drunk an' noisy. It was a chance for Bray, who'd never had nerve enough any other time. This sheriff is a four-flusher, boss. He's never had one of us in jail yet."

"Which way did they go?" asked Jim.

"Down the street. The jail's across the tracks."

Jim hurried out and in the direction advised, not certain of his position in the matter. Still, he did not take kindly to the idea of one of his cowboys going to jail. Moreover, he had met Sheriff Bray and had not been greatly impressed in that individual's favor. Jim, while crossing the tracks, espied Bray dragging a reluctant and protesting cowboy along the station platform, followed by a small crowd. Running ahead, Jim intercepted them. This cowboy he also recognized, a tall handsome fellow with curly yellow hair, just now very red in the face, but not so drunk as Jim had been led to suppose.

"Hold on, Sheriff!" called Jim, as he confronted them. "You've got one of my boys. What's the charge?"

"Hullo!" gruffly returned Bray.

He was a burly man, thick-featured, with a bluish cast of countenance, and he wore his sheriff's badge and gun rather prominently. "Oh, it's young Mr. Traft. I didn't know you. . . . Wal, this boy was gettin' a little too obstreperous to suit me. So I'm runnin' him in."

"Obstreperous! What do you mean by that?" demanded Jim, arriving at his decision.

"Wal, thet's what I call it."

"Curly, what'd you do?" inquired Jim, of the red-faced, blue-eyed boy.

"Boss, I was singin'," asserted Curly. "This heah one-hoss occifeer sings in—choir an' he thinks he's—only singer."

"Wal, you can sing in jail," declared the sheriff, with a gleam in his eye.

"Bray, I reckon you'd better not run Curly in," said Jim, coolly. "Let's walk along across and get away from this crowd. I'll take Curly around the block."

"Say, for a tenderfoot you're startin' right in to play a high hand," sneered Bray. All the same he had his doubts, which Jim was quick to observe.

"Correct, Bray," rejoined Jim, as he took Curly's arm. Between them they walked him away from the curious onlookers, and round a corner to the entrance of the jail. Here Curly's face was a study. Manifestly before Jim's arrival he had surrendered to the majesty of the law, but this amazing champion in the shape of his boss had galvanized him.

"Bray, there ain't none of Diamond outfit ever been—in jail. It's disgrash," he asserted, belligerently.

"I'll vouch for him, Sheriff," added Jim.

"Prentiss, you come along," ordered Bray, roughly.

By this time Jim's blood had grown a little hot. He had recalled what his uncle had said about Bray and thought he might just as well face the issue. He jerked Curly free from the sheriff, and interposed himself between them.

"If you had any charge against Curly I wouldn't interfere. But you haven't. Why, he isn't half drunk."

"I'll arrest you both for resistin' an officer," threatened Bray, his hand going to his hip.

Jim saw the action, followed it with his eye.

"So you'd throw your gun on us," he said, with derision.

53

"Boss, let go an' stand aside. This heah ain't funny no more," spoke up Curly. The change in him, the ring in his voice, made Jim jump, but he did not release the cowboy.

"No, Curly, I'm responsible here," he replied.

Bray had subtly altered, which fact Jim grasped to have to do with Curly's sudden menace.

"Wal, Traft, I'll let him go in your care," he growled. "But I'm givin' you a hunch. Prentiss said somethin'. This Diamond outfit ain't funny no more."

"Thanks, Bray. I consider that a compliment to me. Come on, Curly."

Jim walked the cowboy down the block and up a side street until they got out of the center of the town. Neither he nor Curly broke silence during this walk. Finally Jim halted on a corner.

"Curly, will you go back to the ranch? I'd go with you, but I've errands to do."

"Boss, are you orderin' me?" queried the cowboy.

"No, I'm asking you."

"Then I ain't a-goin'."

"Very well, then. I'll have to make it an order. Will you go now?"

"I reckon. The Diamond ain't disobeyin' orders. But what'd you want to go do this heah trick for?"

"Trick? I've only kept you out of jail."

"Shore. An' the outfit will be sore at me."

"Curly, I don't understand you," protested Jim.

"They ain't a-goin' to stand for me bein' friends with a tenderfoot boss."

Jim began to get a glimmering. The tall cowboy seemed pained over this little service. He looked most disapprovingly at Jim.

"Curly, you needn't let that embarrass you."

Apparently Curly could not help being embarrassed. He wheeled and strode away. Half across the street he turned. "Boss, I forgot. I'm in an orful fix," he said, and strode back. "My gurl's in town. I haven't laid eyes on her for two months. Shore it won't be safe to let it go longer."

"Curly, are you asking me to explain to your girl or to allow you to come back to town?" queried Jim.

"Reckon I was just tellin' you."

"Well, I dare say you are in a fix. What do you want of me?" rejoined Jim, who divined that the cowboy did not like to ask a favor.

"It'd never do for you to see Nancy. I lost one gurl that way."

"Curly, I'll help you out. Promise you'll not take another drink today. Then walk out to the ranch and walk back tonight. That'll sober you. And you can see your girl."

Curly swore. He bent a strange blue gaze upon Jim.

"I reckon there ain't no help for it," he muttered, as if declaring an inevitable fact to himself. Then he strode away.

Jim scarcely knew how to take this last declaration and he went back uptown, pondering over it. These cowboys were certainly going to be problems. They were like children. But he had had a most pleasing reaction from his first encounter with one of the Diamond outfit.

Jim returned to his errands, which took him up and down the main thoroughfare of Flagerstown, and therefore past the saloons and pool-halls. It struck him that the town was growing rather lively as evening approached. All the hitching-rails were crowded with saddle-horses, many of which took Jim's appreciative eye.

Jim was entering the hotel, where he expected to meet his uncle and ride home with him, when he was detained by another member of the Diamond, who barred his way obviously if not rudely. Two other cowboys drew back.

"Excuse me, Mister Traft. I'm Hack Jocelyn, an' I'm wantin' a word with you."

He was cool, insolent, and something else Jim could not name.

"Aren't you one of my cowboys?" asked Jim.

"I've been ridin' with the Diamond, if thet's what you mean. But I ain't shore I'm stayin' with the outfit."

Jim had been told by no less an authority than Ring

Locke that horses and men could not separate the Diamond outfit.

"You're not, eh? Well, you want to be pretty sure, or you won't be riding for it. What do you want?"

Jocelyn appeared to be gauging Jim.

"I was in Babbitt's an' they told me they'd sent out a wagon-load of barbed wire to the ranch. Fer the Diamond outfit! An' I calls him a liar."

"Then you'll have to apologize. It was for the Diamond. And there's a carload more ordered."

"Hell you say!" ejaculated Jocelyn, in amaze and gathering anger. "An' what's it fer?"

"None of your business, Jocelyn," retorted Jim. "If you'd asked me civilly I'd have told you."

"But barbed wire is most used fer fences!" exclaimed the cowboy. His two comrades edged closer until they were beside him, watchful, hiding their feelings, if they had any. "An' nobody in Gawd's world would reckon the Diamond'd have anythin' to do with thet!"

"The Diamond is in for some new experience, Jocelyn. And you may as well know fence-building is one of them."

"Haw! Haw! It shore is. A tenderfoot dude foreman! Then barbed-wire fence! My Gawd! what's the range comin' to?"

Jocelyn had turned to his companions, to whom, in fact, his exclamation had been directed. Jim shot out a hand and spun him around like a top.

"Did you call me a tenderfoot dude foreman?" he queried, and despite his temper he was quick-witted enough to ascertain that Jocelyn was not armed. Otherwise he would wisely have restrained himself altogether.

"Wal, Mister Traft, I reckon I did," he drawled. He expressed the usual cowboy nonchalance, but there was also a vindictive quality in his words, if not their content.

Jim knocked him flat. He had not calculated consequences. In accepting his uncle's job he had burned his bridges behind him. But when Jim saw Jocelyn lying there, then slowly rising, his hand to his face, which was

56

black as a thundercloud, he awoke to another sensation. He would not, however, have recalled the blow.

"Jocelyn, you're fired," he said, as coolly as the cowboy had spoken. "But if you come out to the ranch and apologize to me I'll take you on again."

"You better be packin' a gun," declared Jocelyn, darkly.

"Aw, shut up, if you can't talk sense," returned Jim, in disgust. "You insulted me. And if you're not man enough to own up to it you can bet there's no place on the Diamond for you."

Jocelyn's two friends laid hold of him and drew him away.

Whereupon Jim turned to enter the hotel, where among several persons who had been spectators of the little byplay were his uncle and Ring Locke.

"Hello! Say, I'm sorry you happened to see that," said Jim, regretfully. "But, Uncle, he just made me boil."

"Come inside," rejoined Traft, and when the three of them were out of earshot of bystanders he turned to Locke. "Ring, he called Hack's bluff. An' mebbe he didn't poke that puncher's snoot! I damn near choked myself to keep from yellin'."

"Uncle!" exclaimed Jim, as surprised at this speech as at Traft's glee.

"Son, the only fault I can locate in you so far is you talk too quick an' too much. It'll get you in serious trouble."

"But I nearly burst at that," expostulated Jim.

Ring Locke shook his lean hawklike head forebodingly.

"Wal, it's six fer me an' half a dozen fer the other," he said. "It's bad an' good. More good, I'd say. If the new foreman of the Diamond had stood fer that—wal, he couldn't have had a chance. Mebbe the boys put Hack up to it. If so he'll be as nice as pie an' come back to square himself. If not—" Here Locke shook his head gravely.

"Ring, I'll bet you four bits he'll be out here tomorrow," said Traft.

"But suppose he doesn't come?"

"Can't we fill his place?" asked Jim, anxiously.

57

"Nope. We can't fill the place of any of thet outfit," rejoined Locke. "But I was thinkin' of what it'd mean. ... Young man, this same Hack Jocelyn has shot fellars fer less."

"It's true, son," corroborated Traft, somberly. "That's the worst of it. This gang of yours has made way with nine men since they rode for me. Six years! Shore some of them were damn good riddance."

"More'n nine, boss," corrected Locke. "Lonestar Holliday got drove out of Texas fer a shootin'."

"What!" gasped Jim. "Those fine clean boys murderers?"

"Jim, you're out West now," said his uncle, testily. "When two men get into an argument or quarrel an' draw —it ain't murder if one is killed. We couldn't run the range without cowboys an' they're shore a tough crowd of young roosters. ... Ring, fetch round the buckboard an' we'll go home."

On the way out Traft dilated on the serious and uncertain side of range life. Jim realized that his education on the West had but just begun. He had not been ignorant of facts, but they seemed vastly significant and perturbing at close hand. During the ride out and at supper he maintained silence. Later, when he had recovered from the effect of this first clash, he could not feel that he would have desired to have met it in any other way. But neither his uncle nor Ring Locke could understand his feelings. Jim himself found them rather complicated. He had been furious, then frightened, then cold. And now, instead of wanting to go home to Missouri, he surrendered still more to Arizona.

7

LATE ON Sunday afternoon, while Jim sat on the porch, his uncle called attention to a cowboy approaching from a direction in which he could not be seen from the bunk-houses.

"Bud Chalfack," announced Traft, with a chuckle.

"Who's Bud?"

"You'll see pronto. He's the peacemaker of the outfit. Bud's a diplomat, the slickest, coolest hand on the range. Whenever anyone is in wrong, Bud is elected to set him right."

"Ahuh," returned Jim, dubiously. He watched the cowboy stroll up the lane and down the path to the porch. Bud appeared to be a little fellow, but sturdy, bow-legged, and otherwise suggestive of long association with horses. He was smoking a cigarette, which he threw away as he reached the steps. He had an open, guileless countenance and he reminded Jim of a rosy-faced cherub.

"Good evenin', Mr. Traft, an' howdy, boss!" he said, cheerfully. "May I set down?"

"Shore, Bud," replied Traft, genially. "Reckon you look sort of weak. What ails you? Too much town?"

"Weak? I couldn't fork a bench at a feast, let alone a hoss. We been wrastlin' all day with Hack. But you ought to see the other fellars. They're laid out."

"Is Hack here?" asked Jim, quietly.

"He's down at the bunkhouse. I been sent fer him."

"Why didn't he come himself?"

"Wal, fust off he wouldn't come an' I reckon now he ain't able."

Bud's grave infantile face was averted for a moment, during which Jim shot a quick glance at his uncle, to be rewarded by a wink. Matters were progressing favorably. Jim drew a breath of relief and gave in to the fun of the situation.

"What ails him? Did he get drunk last night? Sick this morning?"

"Boss, I reckon both. But it ain't them. We was sorta put out with Hack. Shore we didn't mean to let him bust up the Diamond. An' he was daid set on thet. So after arguin' all day we got tired, an'—wal, Hack's in bed."

"I see. Then he can't come over to apologize and get his job back. Or did he want to do it?"

"Wal, Hack shore wanted the job back all right, but he hated the terms. He said, 'Jest tell the boss I'll apologize if he'll swear I won't have to dig no holes fer fence-posts.'"

Jim had difficulty in restraining a shout.

"Bud, I'm afraid Hack will have to dig holes along with the rest of us. I sure expect to," replied Jim, gravely.

The cowboy looked incredulously to Mr. Traft for corroboration of that statement.

"Bud, it's up to Jim. You'll have to fight it out together. You can tell the boys, though, that Jim will not give them anythin' he won't tackle himself."

"All right, sir. Thet's shore fairer'n any foreman I ever rode under. . . . But Hack won't never dig no fence-post holes. We had it out with him an' so I may as well tell you. He yells at us, 'Hell! if I gotta dig holes, let 'em be graves fer thet Cibeque bunch of calf thieves.'"

"Wal!" the old rancher exclaimed, and glanced from Bud to see how his nephew would take that. Jim did not feel like shouting with laughter over it. Nevertheless, he concealed his consternation.

"Bud, wasn't Hack just raving?" he asked.

"Shore he was ravin'. An' he'd reason, too. Boss, shore your uncle has told you what this drift fence will do?"

"He hasn't told me anything," replied Jim.

"Wal, some of us will have to, then," said Bud. "I ain't quite agreed with Hack an' the other boys of the Diamond. But I've only been ridin' hyar fer a couple of years. Hack swears we'll have to fight. He knows Seth Haverly an' his outfit of the Cibeque. Bad hombres, he called them. An' Slinger Dunn don't need no introduction 'round Flag. You can see his trade-mark in more'n one place. . . . Some of the boys agree with Hack. We'll have hell buildin' thet fence, an' wuss'n hell when we get it done."

"Bud, is the Diamond game to build that drift fence?" queried Jim, with sarcasm.

"You bet your life it is," flashed Bud.

"Are you going to stick together?"

"Wal, we reckon nothin' but death can bust the outfit."

"If I left it to a vote, how many of you would be for building the fence?"

"Boss, we've already voted. This mawnin'. An' Hack was the only fellar to drop a black mark in the hat. Leastways, we think it was Hack."

"I'm glad to hear that. Now how do you stand on the moral issue?"

"Boss, I don't just savvy."

"You're all cattlemen in the making. Is it right or wrong?"

"Wal, fact is, we're not all shore. But the most of us believe that Mr. Traft knows more an' sees farther, an' wouldn't never do no homesteader or little cattleman a low'down trick. We're goin' to believe he's right an' stand by him."

"But you all think he shouldn't have saddled this job on to a tenderfoot nephew?" queried Jim, penetratingly.

"Wal, I—I reckon we do," replied Bud, growing red in the face.

"There!" cried Jim, triumphantly, to his amused uncle. "See what you've done! . . . Come, Bud, I'll walk down to the bunkhouse with you."

He found half a dozen of the boys there, but missed Curly Prentiss. Hack Jocelyn lay on a bunk under a window, the light of which showed him rather badly bruised up. He had one black eye, which he endeavored to hide.

"Hack, you get your job back, but it was a half-hearted apology," said Jim.

"Boss, I'd never give in but fer this low-down lousy outfit," replied Jocelyn. "An' I'm tellin' you straight I won't dig no fence-post holes. I'll cut an' haul posts. I'll cook an' wash, an' I'll pack water an' run errands."

"Hack, you don't look like you were sorry you insulted me."

"Boss, I don't reckon it no insult. I was only bein' funny. But you shore do wear nice store clothes, don't you?"

"Can't I wear overalls all week and put on clean shirt and pants without being a dude?" inquired Jim.

"Wal, it depends on the pants an' the shirt."

"Matter of taste, eh? Well, I'll wear out my St. Louis clothes pronto."

Jocelyn peered hard out of his unclosed eye, at this new specimen of range foreman, and then gave up with a disgusted grunt.

Next morning before sunrise the Diamond rode out upon their momentous adventure. Thirty saddle and pack horses, one four-horse wagon hauling wire and tools, and the chuck-wagon, made quite a cavalcade. Ring Locke saw them off, but Traft did not show up. Locke's last word was one of commendation at Jim's wise move to pitch the first camp five miles out of town. Jim intended to drop bales of wire all along the way, then work back from camp.

By the time that camp was pitched Jim imagined he was at the head of the weirdest *rodeo* ever given in the West. But the only argument he had was with Curly, who took violent exception to the ragged, bony old mustang Jim chose to ride.

"But I'm tellin' you," protested Curly, at length. "He'll eat out of your hand till he gets a chance to kick your brains out. Thet ain't no hoss fer the boss of the Diamond. It's an orful disgrace."

"You'll have to put up with a lot, Curly," said Jim, patiently. "I can ride this nag."

"Ride him! There ain't no cowpuncher in this outfit who can do it."

"But, Curly, I have ridden him."

"He's only foolin'. Boss, he'll pile you up aboot tomorrow."

Jim started the work just after the noon hour and it beat any circus he ever attended. He dug the first hole himself, with his cowboys gaping around.

"There!" he exclaimed in satisfaction.

"Whoopee!" yelled Hack Jocelyn, in stentorian voice. "Boys, heah's the grave of the Diamond!"

His fellow cowboys whooped so wildly in reply that Jim felt constrained to believe Jocelyn's pessimistic augury. Then, under Jim's orders, they set to work, and they yelled and swore, and kept up a constant harangue with one another. Jim had three of them dragging in long poles, which were cut into seven-foot lengths, five feet of which were to stand above ground. Jim had thought out his plan and it bade fair to work. Bud Chalback, Lonestar Holliday, and Hump Stevens had volunteered to handle the wire, which, next to post-hole digging, seemed to be the most obnoxious to these aristocrats of the range.

Fortunately for Jim, it was not necessary to build the drift fence in a straight line. A general direction to the south, keeping to levels and the easiest way, was the rule. Jim marked the line and the holes for a certain distance, then went back to help in all details of the labor. It had happened that not so many months ago he had built a barbed-wire fence round his father's farm in Missouri. He had not forgotten that. His father had not only been an exacting employer, but he knew how to go about fence-building. So Jim had a distinct advantage over his cowboys, who certainly had never had any share in such work. All the same, they found fault with every single detail of Jim's plan and execution, sometimes so guilelessly and with such apparent sincerity that he knew they had

63

begun their mischief. He took especial care, however, every instance to explain and prove to them the fallacy of their criticisms. Here was too good a chance to miss.

The first day ended, and a dirty, sweaty, hungry string of cowboys walked back to camp.

"Who'd a thunk it? Hoofin' it to camp! As if barbed-wire-fence buildin' wasn't enough. Boys, we'd be better off in the pen at Yuma," declared Cherry Winters, throwing his sombrero.

"It's a helluva good thing none of us has to cook on this job," said Uphill Frost. "You've all got to thank the boss fer thet."

"Wal, Up," replied some one, "we'd liefer you was the cook, 'cause then we'd soon be daid."

"Look aheah, Jackson Way," retorted Frost. "You hungry-lookin' jack rabbit! I kin beat you makin' sour-dough biscuits any day."

"Shore you can. I ain't no cook."

And so the badinage went on. Jim shut his ears when he was a little way off, to avoid hearing their facetious remarks about him, but on occasions he caught some of it.

The amazing day ended with Jim's adding a lame back and blistered hands to his other ills. They had camped in the open field, where a few straggling pines had escaped the lumbermen, and the site was far from pretty. Jim unrolled his tarpaulin under one of them. He had never slept out in the open in his life. The cowboys would have laughed if they had seen him in his room at the ranch-house, struggling over the rolling and roping of that bed.

The cook had been highly recommended to Jim, by no less a person than himself, and that, too, in writing. He claimed to hear fairly well, but he was dumb. Shot in the throat once, by a vicious cowboy!

"Say, when is thet cadiverous galoot a-goin' to yell, 'Come an' get it'?" demanded Hack.

"Anybody know what his handle is?" asked another.

"Boys, our cook's name is Jeff Davis," announced Jim, importantly. "He hails from Alabama. He can't talk, but he wrote he could hear fairly well."

"Why cain't he talk?" asked Hack.

"A dumb cook! Holy Jupiter! We're Jonahed fer keeps!"

"Fine. He cain't cuss the daylights out of us."

"Wal, if he can cook—O-Kay!"

"Thar's enough rebels in this heah outfit now without havin' a rebel cook," growled another.

"Boys," added Jim, by way of answer to all these remarks, "Jeff claims to have been shot in the throat by a vicious cowboy. Made dumb forever. Think of it!"

"Wal, he might have been one of these fellars who talk too much," declared Hack, significantly.

The sudden and violent beating of a tin pan appeared to be Jeff's call to supper.

Uphill Frost, who had fallen into a doze, leaped up with a yell, "Injuns!"

He was the last to reach the chuck-wagon, perhaps by the fraction of a second. The things they said to the grave-faced cook, as he filled their plates and cups, were enough, Jim thought, to make a dumb man swear. Probably he alone caught a curious little gleam in Jeff's deep-set eyes. That gave Jim food for thought. Then the members of the Diamond stood around, or sat cross-legged like Indians on the ground. The ensuing silence fell like a mantle. It seemed so beneficent and wonderful that Jim imagined he had been suddenly transported to another world.

After supper they had a camp fire around which they sat and smoked. Jim enjoyed that hour. The infinite and various moods of the cowboys seemed to have flagged. Then one by one they, some without removing their boots, rolled in their tarpaulins. Jim took off some of his clothes, and when he stretched out in his bed with a groan he felt that he would never move again. How delicious that bed! He burned and ached all over, and tired as he was could not soon go to sleep. The canopy of white stars seemed so wonderful and strange. The air, which had turned cold with the night wind down off the mountain, blew over his face. Jim had heard his first coyote chorus at the ranch, so he was in a way prepared for another at close range. Evidently this visiting bunch sat round in a half-circle, just behind his bed, and barked, yelped, whined their wild concatenations. He enjoyed the music for a while, but he conceived that he might have a murderous instinct develop.

He endeavored to enumerate the especial happenings and remarks of the day. Impossible! It had been his intention to keep a diary. He did not think he could do the opportunity justice, though he would try. Besides, it would never do to record many of the speeches of these range-riders.

Suddenly he felt something tugging at the back of his bed, at the blankets under him. It made him start violently and instinctively frightened him. A coyote! Did the scavengering beggars steal that close? He yelled with much meaning but poor articulation.

"Giout!"

Then he popped up. He could see a few feet back of his bed. Nothing there! Perhaps it might have been a gopher or a rattlesnake about which the boys had remarked after supper. With a boot he beat around back of his coat which he had folded up for a pillow. Then with a still shaking hand he felt back there. And it came in contact with a rope. It had been tied to an end of the blanket over him, and this had been drawn half off. "Well, by gosh!" he muttered.

From all around strange sounds arose. He sat there amazed until he grasped the situation. The cowboys had played their first trick on him and were now trying to hold in a fiendish and bursting glee. Presently from way over near the chuck-wagon broke out a raucous: "Haw! Haw! Haw!"

Jim untied the rope and flung the end as far away as he could. Sons-of-guns, he called them to himself! But nevertheless, he was tickled. They would make life miserable for him. Nevertheless, he took this as an augury of good luck. His uncle had assured him that if they played tricks on him there was hope. If they suffered him in silence and let him severely alone the case was hopeless.

Jim lay back happy, despite his chagrin at being scared half out of his wits, and went to sleep.

Next morning he hobbled around cheerfully without mentioning the incident and went to work. That turned out to be a trying day, particularly in keeping at it. Upon returning to camp he washed his blistered hands, and then thinking to rest a little before supper, he sought his bed.

But it was gone. At first he imagined he had mistaken the place, but he soon reassured himself that he was right about the location. After a few moments he discovered his bed-roll high up in the pine tree, swinging by the rope. Jim swore under his breath. If he had to climb that tree, crippled as he was, it would afford these devilish cowboys a treat. He just would not attempt it. They stood and sat around, waiting for call to supper, and obviously they were aware of his predicament.

"Oh, were I a little bir-r-rd," sang one of them.

Jim decided he would make one gigantic bluff. He had been pretty lucky so far. Why not play that to the limit? Whereupon he went to his pack, and taking up his Colt, he aimed steadily at the rope above his head and shot. He cut the rope. As he gasped, the bed-roll fell with a heavy thump. Jim flipped the gun in a way he had learned through a week's practice, and carelessly tossed it over to his pack. Then approaching the cowboys he said, seriously, "I sure hope none of you hombres make me throw a gun on you."

They seemed to be a wide-eyed and stricken group.

"Boss, I shore ain't goin' to do thet little thing," spoke up Curly.

So they had to score another for the tenderfoot. That night around the camp fire they were thoughtful, and whispered behind Jim's back. He went to bed knowing the war was on, and that he was in for utter rout. Ring Locke had said cowboys when pressed would do anything under the sun. Jim had thought it all out, and he could only regulate his conduct according to theirs. The main issue for him was to earn their respect.

Nothing happened that night nor the next day, but on

67

the following night he was awakened by a terrible crash and jar. He lay there shaking. The stars above showed more numerously. The pine tree must have been struck by lightning, for its branches no longer sheltered him. It had fallen. But there could not have been a stroke of lightning, because the sky gave no sign at all of storm. The cowboys had provided the lightning. Probably they had sawed the tree nearly through during the day, when he was absent, and at night they had pulled it down. The tips of one of the branches lay across Jim's feet, which he moved after some effort. Nice gentle cowboys! Not for a long while did Jim go to sleep, after that.

By the end of the week they had finished the drift fence townward to where it joined Traft's ranch. They had also about finished Jim. Saturday night he spent alone in camp, except for the cook, who plainly showed a solicitude for Jim. Sunday he was to have gone in to see Uncle Jim, but he never left the camp. Late afternoon the cowboys began to straggle back in twos and threes, some of them still pretty drunk. Jim resented that. He watched them come, careful to see who were the sober ones. Bud returned, holding Hack Jocelyn in his saddle; and Curly performed a like office for Cherry Winters. Drink manifestly was Hack's besetting sin, for he presented a somber and ugly figure. On the other hand, Cherry was funny. Curly handled him roughly, even to tripping him up twice; still in spite of it Cherry succeeded in getting to Jim.

"Bosh, ish all ri'," he said, waving a deprecatory hand. "Be'n lookin' at redeyes, but I'm sober's jedge. An' I wanna tell you. Lash night—"

Curly dragged him away. At sunset Jim took a long walk, which in a way mitigated his mood. The supper gong recalled him. As he neared camp his keen ears caught Curly saying: "Wal, it's shore eatin' into my gizzard. I reckon he's pretty decent, considerin'.'"

"Curly, somethin' shore is eatin' you," returned Hack Jocelyn, sarcastically. "He's got no kick comin'. Ain't we buildin' this drift fence? What the hell!"

Jim wondered if this talk referred to him or his uncle,

and after a moment's consideration decided it was about himself. Curly, then, as Jim had grasped before, was leaning a little toward championing him. It was the one bright spot in a gloomy week-end.

On Monday at dawn they broke camp and drove south to the edge of the timber, perhaps another five miles. Here the camp site delighted Jim. It was on a grassy bench just where the pines began, and near a beautiful spring. The bare despoiled land they had traversed was no longer visible. This drive, of course, included the dropping of bales of wire along the way; and that, with the unpacking and making camp, constituted the day's work.

At this camp matters came to a pass where Jim grew beside himself with rage. And the incident that capped the climax was where Curly Prentiss, after gradually and perceptibly leaning toward friendship for Jim, suddenly became alienated. Jim laid this to influence of a clique of four in the Diamond outfit, the ringleader being Hack Jocelyn. And it happened that Jim had begun to need some little evidence of reward for his unswerving patience and endurance.

"Curly," he said, "you've got a saffron streak as wide as the road."

"Boss, is thet thar relatin' to my work on this heah drift fence?" queried Prentiss, with keen glance on two of the cowboys who certainly heard Jim.

"No. I'm bound to admit you do more than your share," rejoined Jim.

"Wal, then, I'm takin' your remark as personal, an' if *you* ain't just as yellow you'll step out with me."

"Good Heavens, Curly!" ejaculated Jim, wearily. "You wouldn't make it a matter of guns?"

"Wal, in this heah country a man has to protect himself."

"Ahuh. And how in the hell am I to protect myself from most of this devilish bunch without a friend?" queried Jim, bitterly. "I've been banking on you right along. You have helped me a good deal, though you may not know it. I like you. And I swear you were beginning to like me. Then all of a sudden you turn cold and mean."

"So that's why you called me saffron?" asked Prentiss, with curious little flecks of light in his eyes.

"Yes, it is."

"Wal, the outfit put it up to me this heah way. They accused me of bein' friends with you. An' they made me cut the deck. You or the Diamond."

"So that is it," replied Jim. "I never thought of that. Naturally you'd stick to them."

"Shore. An' I'm demandin' an apology before the outfit," said Curly, with the air of one who held a whip hand.

It was on Jim's lips, of course, to beg Curly's pardon, when something perverse prompted him.

"Suppose I won't?"

"Wal, then, as you cain't stand fer a little gun-play, I'll have to lick you," drawled Curly.

"You'll *have* to?"

"Shore will."

"Curly, you couldn't do that if you tried it every day we are building this fence."

This retort, as amazing to Jim as to Curly, came out of the past days of Jim's turmoil.

"Mister Traft, I'm shore differin' with you. An' I'll show you pronto."

"Well, let's get the apology over first," replied Jim, dryly.

It happened to be just before supper-time and all the boys were there. Jim did not require to be told that they had heard about what he had called Curly.

"Fellows, I've a word to say," he began, and the slow sly glances he drew made him want to swear at them. "I want to apologize to Curly before you all. I told him he had a streak of saffron. Well, I take it back. And instead of Curly I'll apply it to those of you who made Curly turn me down. I don't know who they are, but *you* know. It is pretty low down. This rotten job I've tackled for my uncle has got on my nerves. There's so much I don't know. Curly or any one of you could help me. I think he was leaning that way. But you made him quit."

Then Jim turned to Curly.

"There, Mister Prentiss. You politely invited me to a gun party, and then threatened to lick me. But neither of these made me apologize to you. It was because I had done you an injustice. Now I'll tell you some more before your grinning-ape pards. You can't lick me. And unless you make a blamed good stab at it right here and now I *will* say you're yellow."

Curly's face was more of a study than that of his allies, which certainly presented a good deal in puzzles. But presently at the prospect of a fight long deferred they began to beam.

"Boss, I reckon your uncle will—" began Bud, conscience-stricken.

"Shet-up, you durn little crow!" bawled somebody, presumably Hack.

Lonestar Holliday burst into the circle. "Fellars, heah comes thet Slinger Dunn," he whispered, warningly.

8

Two RIDERS had come out of the woods. They were not cowboys, yet Jim could not in a glance determine why he made that distinction. Had it not been for Lonestar Holliday's announcement and its instant and singular effect upon his comrades, Jim would not have made anything unusual about a visit from strange riders. That had already happened. Nevertheless, as the former horseman halted, Jim modified this opinion.

The rider looked like an Indian, yet his skin was dark bronze instead of red. His features were shadowed by the brim of an old black sombrero, yet piercing eyes shone out of that obscurity. He wore a buckskin shirt, much the worse for long usage. The rest of his apparel corresponded with any cowboy's.

The second stranger was a lean-faced, hard-lipped young man, with eyes that appeared to oscillate like a compass needle.

Both were mounted on long-haired, ragged, wild-looking horses. The saddles were superb, with long *tapa dores*. Rifles were slung in saddle sheaths.

The foremost of these two riders did not greet the Diamond, individually or collectively. And Jim, quick to note this and that none of his men spoke, waived any sort of greeting himself. But he stepped out in front with an air of authority. This placed him somewhat closer to the rider, in a better light, and he looked up into a handsome, still, strange face.

"You the new boss of this heah Diamond outfit, hey?" inquired the rider, in cool hostility.

"Yes. I'm supposed to be," replied Jim, just as coolly.

"Young Traft, from Mizzourie?"

"James Traft," corrected Jim.

"Howdy, Mister Traft! I shore am glad to meet you," drawled the rider, without any intimation that he intended to reveal his own name.

Presently Jim replied. "I can't return the compliment if you don't say who you are."

Holliday took a couple of slow steps, which placed him beside Jim, an action that somehow thrilled Jim though he might have misunderstood its significance.

"Boss, it's Slinger Dunn an' his pard, Seth Haverly, from the Cibeque," said Holliday, crisply.

"Howdy, Lonestar," returned Dunn.

It was noticeable that Holliday had no more to say. But Jim greeted the visitors and asked them to get down and stay for supper.

Dunn might not have heard, for all the sign he gave.

"Say, ain't you buildin' sort of a long fence?" he queried.

"Yes. It's getting pretty long," replied Jim with a laugh.

"How long's it goin' to be?"

"Hundred miles, the cowboys say."

"They don't say! . . . Thet's purty long. An' barb-wire, too. What kind of a fence is this heah goin' to be?"

"A drift fence to hold cattle, Mr. Dunn," returned Jim.

"What's the idee—a drift fence?"

"What do you suppose?" counter-queried Jim, just as curtly. Then he gazed up into burning eyes that positively gave him a shock.

The second rider came up. "Arch, let's be goin'," he said.

"Wal, I suppose a lot. But I'm askin' questions," went on Dunn. "This heah fence is old Jim Traft's idee?"

"Certainly it is."

"Does he own the land?"

"No."

"Is he aimin' to fence free range?"

"It will divide the range, that's sure."

"Wal, along heah it won't make no difference to no-body. But when it gets down in the Diamond it's goin' to be a bad deal for cattlemen in the brakes."

"So I've been told, Mr. Dunn," rejoined Jim. "I'm just beginning to learn the cattle business, and can't say one way or the other."

"Wal I reckon you won't go far," replied the other meaningly, and he rolled a cigarette without ever taking his gleaming eyes off Jim.

"Arch, I'm sayin' let's rustle out of this," interposed Haverly, reaching over to give Dunn a jerk.

"I'm going to the end of the Diamond with this drift fence," averred Jim. "And after it is finished my outfit will see that it stays up."

"Your outfit?"

"Yes, my outfit."

"Say, mister, you cain't have it in your haid thet *your* Diamond outfit will stick to you."

"I've got that notion."

"Wal, you're plumb off the trail. Even down in the

73

brakes we heah what Jocelyn thinks of you. An' Cherry Winters. An' Uphill Frost."

"I'm sorry to admit that some of my men ridicule me," said Jim, feelingly. "Perhaps it's deserved, for I sure am a tenderfoot. But all the same the drift fence goes up and *stays* up, if it takes half a dozen Diamond outfits."

Dunn poised his cigarette, arrested by a speech that evidently struck him.

"Traft, no drift fence will ever stay up in Cibeque County," he returned, presently, with grim passion.

"That remains to be seen. Thanks for giving me a hunch. And now, since you're neither polite nor agreeable, will you please mozey on out of my camp?"

Dunn's face showed the darker for a wave of blood. His companion roughly seized him, nearly unseating him from the saddle.

"Slinger, I shore ain't waitin' to be ordered out of no tenderfoot's camp," he said, gruffly, dragging at Dunn.

"You're a little late," put in Jim, with sarcasm. "My invitation included you. Now I say to both of you—*get out!*"

The instant Jim had delivered this contemptuous order he realized he had done something terrible. Not only Dunn's aspect, but Jim's men appeared to freeze. Jim had never seen such a blazing hell in human eyes as he encountered in Dunn's.

Haverly reached down, and grasping the bit of Dunn's horse wheeled it and the rider away. Dunn could be heard cursing his comrade and getting roundly cursed in return. They were watched out of sight into the woods.

Jim turned to his men. As he did so he observed Curly Prentiss move his right hand, containing a cocked gun, from behind his back. This revealed to Jim more of the nature of this encounter with the two riders from the Cibeque, but it in no wise mitigated his temper.

"I don't think much of you men," he said, with a ring in his voice. "If I told my uncle about this he'd fire every last one of you. You may be the great Diamond outfit, but to me you're a lot of four-flushers. What the hell do I know about Slinger Dunn and his kind? Some of you might have chipped in and stood by me."

"Boss, I reckon we stood by you without you knowin' it," declared Curly Prentiss. "You were doin' the talkin'. An' if we'd chipped in there would have been gun-play."

"Curly's right, boss," added Lonestar Holliday. "I don't know if Dunn seen Curly slip his gun out. But I reckon he did, as he was shore civil for him. This Slinger Dunn has a bad rep. He's killed several men an' shot up more'n you could count."

"Boss, I'll chip in a word," said Hack Jocelyn. "It shore was nervy of you to fire Dunn out of our camp. If you hadn't been a tenderfoot you'd never have done it. You want to look out for Slinger Dunn."

"Aw, I'm not afraid of him, even if he is a gunslinger," declared Jim, passionately. "How do I know it wasn't another trick, hatched by some of you? You may think you're having fun at my expense. Perhaps you are. But there ought to be a limit. You're such awful liars I can't believe one word you say."

"Boss, are you callin' us liars?" inquired Curly, in a queer tone.

"I reckon I am. Damn liars! You're more. You're a flock of swell-headed, cross-grained, cantankerous cowboys. Now put that in your cigarettes and smoke it!"

At least for once Jim silenced them. He had no idea of the magnitude of his offense and he did not care. He had been frightened, and if anger had not come to his rescue he would have betrayed it. That would be the finish. He had vowed he would never let any of this famed Diamond outfit see him scared. At that juncture Jeff called them to supper, but Jim stalked off into the woods and walked under the dark pines. He recovered from his fit of temper, but not from the sense of disaster that had slowly accumulated. This task he had undertaken seemed well nigh impossible. At length, gloomy and troubled, he stalked back to camp and to bed.

Next day the stretching of wire fence went on, and now with a remarkable celerity, compared with that done in the open country. The stands of wire were nailed upon trees, and seldom had a post-hole to be dug. Perhaps this had a cheering effect upon the members of the Diamond, but Jim regarded their attempts at approaching him, their sudden solicitude, their amazing amiability, with suspicion. He was right, too, for that night, when he opened his bed-roll he found the blankets soaked. Some one had poured a bucketful of cold spring water into one end of the roll. Jim pondered over this mean trick. Oh, he would get even, but what ought he do on the moment? He could strip a blanket off every one of his men and by so doing catch the guilty party. But he decided against that course of procedure. Instead he built a roaring fire, so hot that he almost roasted the boys alive before they could awake and move back in the woods. Such profanity! Jim had heard a little on the docks at St. Louis, but it could not hold a candle to this. He took half the night to dry his blankets, knowing, of course, that a huge fire would keep his men awake. Then he went to bed, and in the darkness before dawn he crawled out to yell words he had heard them often use:

"The Day's Busted! Roll Out!"

That day and another passed. The camp was moved ten miles down in the woods, into a wide pleasant draw where a creek ran, and wild turkeys gave Jim a thrill. The wagon had to go into Flagerstown for more wire, and the driver returned with a note from Traft, asking Jim why he had not been in to the ranch to report. Jim never answered it, nor did he ride in. Another week-end went by, including Sunday, when Jim was left in peace.

He was nearing the end of his rope now. As the days passed and the drift fence lengthened, these incomprehensible cowboys of the Diamond outfit were driving Jim to distraction. They meant to break him. They were going to. No tenderfoot out of Missouri could ever run the Diamond! So Jim had overheard.

They were bewildering in the infinite variety of their attacks, and he was almost helpless because he knew so little of the West, and horses, and of the nature of cowboys. To him they seemed inhuman—cool, still-faced or smiling devils, hiding their sincerity, if they had any,

76

possessed of a fiendish desire to nag him, worry him, inconvenience him, make him acknowledge defeat.

On Monday the wire-wagon went on ahead, along a line Jim had blazed on Sunday, and dropped its load, then went back to town for another, necessitating now a trip of three days.

Jim, driving the men hard that week, reached the end of the blazed line before the wagon returned. There was a wide deep ravine that had to be crossed. The country was growing rougher.

"Boss," said Bud, that morning, "there's a lot of bales of wire been rolled down in the draw."

The rest of the outfit whooped, but Jim could not tell whether it was from resentment or satisfaction.

"Who rolled them?" he roared.

"How'n'll do I know?" retorted Bud.

"Another funny trick!" ejaculated Jim. And he walked on along the line to the ravine. There far down at the bottom he espied a dozen or more bales lying scattered about.

"Go down and pack them up," ordered Jim to his men, who had followed him.

"Wha—at?"

"Up thet hill on foot?"

One and all they sat down in the shade, to begin rolling cigarettes. When Jim swore at them they smiled in the slow, cool way that always infuriated him.

"All right," he fumed, "I'll pack them up myself."

He strode down the slope, which he found steeper and longer than it had appeared at first glance. Like a toy he handled a bale of wire. Jim was powerful. He could throw a sack of grain or a barrel up into a wagon. However, by the time he had packed that bale up the hill he knew what a heavy load was. He had bitten off more than he could chew. But with those intent eyes on him so watchfully, he could not quit. He went down again, and this time was careful to zigzag up the steep slope. It took him two hours of the most trying toil to finish the job. Then, hot as fire, and wringing wet with sweat, he panted at the silent cowboys.

"Now—if you're rested—we'll go on—with the fence."

"Boss, we was just waitin' to see how soon you'd think of gettin' a pack-hoss fer thet job," observed Hump Stephens, amiably.

For Jim to realize how again, for the thousandth time, he had showed how utterly unfit he was to be foreman of the Diamond, did not improve his mood. He worked off the mood at length, as he invariably succeeded in doing, just as if he did not know another would soon be imposed upon him.

It was Curly Prentiss who discovered horse tracks along the line, and he showed them to Jim, no doubt in the interest of himself and companions.

"Fresh tracks, an' unshod horses at thet," he said. "Reckon we can lay it to some of the Cibeque outfit."

"I'm sorry I accused you fellows," he replied, regretfully. No matter what he did or said now, it was wrong.

Friday, at the lunch hour, Bud Chalfack approached Jim.

"Boss, I'm talkin' fer the outfit," he announced. "We figger thet we're aboot up on this week's work, an' we want this afternoon an' tomorrow off."

"What for?" queried Jim, in surprise.

"We want to ride in today. There's a fair on in Flag, an' tomorrow's *rodeo day*. Most of us are entered."

"But we can't stop our fence-building to go to *rodeos*," protested Jim.

"Shore we can. We-all cain't see any hurry aboot the fence. An' when the Fourth comes we'll be 'way down too far to ride in. So we want to have a chanct at this *rodeo*."

Jim actually could not decide whether this was insubordination or the legitimate claim of a cowboy. He felt helpless. If he refused they would go, anyhow. If he gave his consent it might well be that they had him "buffaloed," as Curly had been overheard to say.

"Very well, you go on your own hook," he said to Bud.

They rode off, a gay and superb group of young riders, who made his heart swell with pride and yet saddened it with the thought that he never could be received by them. He would have been delighted. He had never seen a *rodeo*. But they did not want him; they were ashamed of their tenderfoot foreman.

After they had gone, Jim strode off toward the woods. He was astounded to hear Jeff Davis call.

"Boss, you oughtn't go out alone. But if you must go, take a rifle."

Jim did not answer, though he was grateful to Jeff. The cook, then, had perpetrated a hoax on the Diamond. He was not dumb. And it was a sure bet that neither was he slightly deaf, as he had claimed. Here would be one on the cowboys, presently. Jim assured himself that he would not betray Jeff. He did not, however, take the latter's advice, but went on into the forest alone and unarmed.

He was beginning to feel a strange solace or help or something in the deep solitude of the woodland. It was early summer now. The ferns and wild flowers were springing up along the brown aisles. His step made not the slightest noise. He saw squirrels and birds, and once, gray vanishing forms that might have been deer. Huge cliffs festooned with moss and vines, from which dripped water, arrested him in his walk. There was a pleasant low sough of wind in the tree tops. If anything could have spurred his flagging spirits, the sweetness and loneliness of this forest would have done so. But he guessed he was about beaten. And that confession, gaining audible admission into his consciousness, could not be dislodged.

The afternoon passed, and he returned to camp, there to eat supper in silence, without appearing to remember that the cook had spoken to him. He slept well, but in the morning the old bitterness and hopelessness assailed him again. An impulse to ride to town seized him, and straightway he acted upon it. He did not quite acknowledge to himself that this was a signal of defeat, but it would probably come out when he faced his uncle.

He reached home about noon, to ascertain that his uncle was at the fair. Jim rode out there, and walked his horse. What a vacillating jackass he was! It would hurt Uncle Jim to find him a quitter. Ought he not to try again? Weary and distressed, he entered the fairground; and espying a gayly decorated booth advertising lunch, he dismounted and approached the counter. He gave an order to a girl behind. When he was about through he happened to look up, to see a pair of gold-brown eyes upon him.

And they wrenched out of him the query, "What would you do if you were about licked?"

It was when the girl had finally said, "I'd get up an' fight some more!" that Jim really looked at her with seeing eyes. If her spirited reply had stirred him, what more did the toss of her pretty dark head, with its glints of gold. She was a little girl, very young, and she wore a dainty blue dress. Still, there were contours under it that betrayed womanhood. She had a small, oval, almost dusky face. Her hands were small and brown, yet they struck him as strong and capable. She was Western, of course, but she was a little lady of quality. He kept talking, scarcely with any idea of what he was saying. And that suddenly betrayed to him a swift and remarkable interest in her. After that he knew what he was saying to her, and every word added to a realization of charm. By the time he had found out she did not have a best fellow he seemed far on a strange new adventure; and when he rode away toward the stands, with her shy half-promise of a dance that night, he changed his mind about his mission to Flagerstown. "I'd get up an' fight some more!" She had looked it, too. What a sweet and fiery little girl! Evidently she had taken it for granted that he had been knocked down. Well, he had been. But he had gotten up. And he would act precisely and indomitably upon her advice. Fight! He would whip each and every one of that Diamond outfit.

He gave his horse to a boy at the stalls, and went round to the stand, where he soon found his uncle, and was welcomed in a way that made him ashamed. It pleased his uncle that he had come to town in his work clothes.

The *rodeo* was on. And Jim sat enthralled. "The Diamond bunch will walk away with everythin'," his uncle had averred, but even that startling prophecy had not prepared Jim.

He sat there gripping his seat, yelling when the crowd yelled. And he saw Curly Prentiss ride wild bronchos that threw all the other riders; he saw Hack Jocelyn break the record for roping two-year-olds; he saw Bud Chalfack climb all over a horse, racing at breakneck speed; he saw Jackson Way ride two beautiful horses, standing with one foot on the back of each, and beat his opponents two full lengths; and lastly he saw Lonestar Holliday win the money for the perilous feat of bulldogging steers.

Out of sixteen events the Diamond outfit took nine first prizes. Jim scarcely could contain himself. That was his band of cowboys. He might have hated them before today, but now he loved them. He gathered vaguely that something tremendous had happened to him.

He rode out to the ranch-house in a trance, divided between pride for his cowboys and the momentous dance near at hand. He shaved and washed and changed his clothes, aware of an undue regard for his appearance. His uncle had guests, to whom Jim was presented as the boss of the Diamond. Jim acquitted himself creditably, and kept his miserable secret, strangely growing less miserable.

Then he was off to the dance, eager, with palpitating heart, amused at himself, amazed and glad. He now had opportunity to show some of these Flagerstown girls that if he was a tenderfoot he could interest and perhaps win a prettier girl than any of them. But he had not prepared himself for a vision in white—his girl of the booth— stunningly transformed by a gown, a brown-armed, brown-faced beauty with haunting dark eyes. She saw Jim at once. She bowed. And whatever had not already happened to his heart surely happened then.

Jim did not approach anyone; he saw only her. And he was in a torment waiting for her to give him the opportunity he longed for. If she did not he must go to her, and introducing himself ask for the dance. But she divined his predicament. How the dark eyes met his across the hall,

through the whirling throng! Soon she sought a seat with
her young partner, and obviously dismissed him. Jim
made haste to reach her, to bend over her.

"My dance!" he whispered.

She rose, her face like pearl, her eyes downcast, and
gave herself to his embrace.

9

IT WAS Sunday, and Jim had returned to the Diamond
camp, a bewildered and chastened young man. Except for
Jeff, who was asleep under a tree, the camp was deserted.
Jim went again into the deep shade and quiet of the
forest. There out of chaos his thoughts got some semblance of control over his emotions and order in themselves.

All the other egregious tenderfoot blunders he had
made could not in the aggregate sum up the magnitude of
alienating Molly Dunn. He writhed under that. And always he would protest—who could have imagined that
sweet dainty girl sister to a desperado, a gun-thrower, a
killer, a rustler of the very brakes it was Jim's task to
fence off from the range? Then, just as poignantly he
would add—but what difference did it really make who
was her brother and why had he been so asinine as to
distress and shame her with the connection?

He found excuse for himself for everything but that. It
had struck him almost dumb at first to realize that he had
lost his head and seized her, hugged her atrociously,
surely would have devoured her with kisses had she not
brought him to his senses with a cutting blow across his
mouth. That act, at once under the astounding dominance
of her voluntary kiss—a strange sweet little touch of cool

lips—had lost its heinousness. In the light of the present hour, when it came to him that there had been genuine sincerity, the wild impetus of first love, he realized he had not much to be sorry for there. But she had not known that. How would she ever know? Not that knowing would change her! Her eyes haunted him. What a magnificent blaze! In them had been repeated the fire of Slinger Dunn's.

Why had Molly Dunn kissed him? He recalled her pitiful confession, and that hurt Jim more than anything else. She was not what he had thought her and she yearned to be. Jim stoutly fought against the fading and receding of something beautiful. The dream, the glory of new vibrant emotion, had to pale before reality. Yet Jim could not renounce, nor could he resign himself to another bitter blow this West had given him. It was sudden, complicated, and disastrous. But was it irremediable? A grain of comfort lay in the fact that he had time to think, to go over it, to puzzle it out, to find what had actually happened to him, to conceive who and what Molly Dunn was, and understand her reaction to their meeting.

Most vivid of the things he recalled was the bitter reproach in her big eyes. Why had she reproached him? Not because he had unwittingly intimated of a wide class distinction between Jim Traft and Molly Dunn. She knew she was Molly Dunn of the Cibeque. The reproach had come from a deep and terrible hurt. Jim divined suddenly that maybe she, too, had fallen in love at first sight. The ecstasy of that was short-lived. It could not be true. His own state for weeks had been one of excitement, strain, growing to morbidness. Then a swift change to romance and sentiment had thrown him off his balance. He sank as deep into the depths as he had been lifted to the skies. All of which seemed only to add to the mystery and fascination and fatality of Molly Dunn. He discovered himself vainly trying to do battle against her own estimate of herself. Just a little backwoods girl to whom a white gown had added charm! But he soon scouted that. Molly Dunn had innate charm.

Through the pine trees he saw some of the cowboys

returning from Flagerstown, and the considerable distance between them did not drown sounds of their hilarity. Jim plumped down under a pine, overcome by an entirely new and unforeseen probability. Some of the members of the Diamond had been at that dance last night. Beyond the bounds of hope and reason was it that they might not have seen him there with Molly Dunn. Those hawk-eyed cowboys could see through walls. They had an uncanny genius for finding out everything. But they needed only to know a little to drive Jim to distraction.

He lingered there in the woods, not actually afraid yet, but certainly loath to confront them. Molly Dunn's terse statement that she would get up and fight some more, which he had appropriated as a slogan, in this vacillating hour lost its grip. What a pity if he could not be actuated by that spirit again! Perhaps it would revive, if he got sufficient cue for anger.

Long before the supper hour, which Jeff had early on Sunday, the cowboys rode into camp. So presently Jim felt the imperative necessity of showing himself, because longer absence would only aggravate any suspicions concerning him.

He dragged himself up and to the edge of the forest, only there bracing himself for the ordeal. Somebody saw him coming. Did they pursue their usual demeanor and pay no attention to him? They did not. To his horror they lined up on each side of the camp fire, and faced him like a lot of grim judges. Jim divined that whatever he had dreaded was about to be perpetrated. And some last shred of courage came to his aid as he ran the gauntlet of the merciless Diamond.

"Howdy, boys! Back early—I see," he said, cheerfully, if haltingly. "I changed my mind and went in to the *rodeo* yesterday. You sure gave me the treat of my life. I congratulate the outfit on so many prizes. You can bet I was proud of you."

Not a murmur! He bent over to move a couple of billets on the newly started camp fire, solely to hide his face. Then he sauntered on toward the tree where he kept his pack and bed.

84

"Wal, boss, we heahed ya' walked off with a prize yourself," called Bud Chalfack. "Some little blue-ribbon boy from Mizzourie!"

That sally of Bud's was greeted by uproarious mirth. Like a giant hand it pulled Jim round. His cowboys presented a group of nine young men in varying stages of convulsions. The devil himself emanated from them. Jim choked back a sharp retort. Then Cherry Winters, still quite drunk, staggered over to Jim, his red face a whole grin of impish delight, and he essayed to deliver what must have been intended for an important speech. But its manner of delivery and incoherence spurred Jim to a blunt, "Get out!" and a hard shove. Cherry kept on staggering, this time backward, and he kept on until he met with an obstacle in the shape of Jeff's woodpile. He fell on this, toppled it over upon him, and he did not arise. The gang whooped. They had all been drinking, and Bud looked pretty wabbly on his feet.

"Tenderfoot hell!" he bawled. "You got us—skinned to frazzle."

"Thanks, Bud, but I don't quite savvy," returned Jim.

"Boss, I shore—ben savin' somethin' up," raved Bud, beside himself with maudlin emotion. "Th' outfit's all heahed aboot you last night. But I *seen* you."

"Well, anybody not blind could have done that," snapped Jim, trying to pierce the secret intensity of Bud's rapture.

"But I ben—savin' it up," crowed Bud, slapping his knees with his hands.

"You better keep saving it," warned Jim.

"Aw, boss, I couldn't think of thet. It's too orful good. I gotta tell the Diamond aboot it."

If Jim had any dignity left it was that of the gathering might of fury. What did the little fool know? Jim resisted a fierce impulse to slap the gaping mouth. The cowboys clamored to hear. They sensed the long-hoped-for corralling of their tenderfoot foreman. Jim grimly gazed from face to face. Most of them were only in fun, and Bud was drunk. Curly, too, appeared a little under the influence of the bottle. But Hack Jocelyn was keen, cold, leering. Jim did not miss anything.

"Boss, I seen you on the porch," shouted Bud, triumphantly.

Jim gasped at that revelation. Oh, misery! How exceedingly worse than he had dreaded!

"Fellars, I seen our fastidinous boss from Mizzourie," went on Bud, swelling with his dénouement, "I seen him huggin' thet little hussy—Molly Dunn!"

Before Jim realized what he was doing he had leaped at Bud, to knock him over the pack-saddles. The blow had been solid, and at least for the moment another of the Diamond was down and out.

Curly Prentiss jumped out from the circle, slamming his sombrero down with a smack.

"You two-faced Mizzourie gent!" he yelled. "Bud's my pard. I'm shore gonna lick you for thet."

"Bah! You bow-legged cowpuncher!" blazed Jim. "If you can't fight any better than you dance—you'll never lick me."

That hurt Curly more than the blow to his friend. He threw his scarf one way, his vest another, his gunbelt at Jackson Way, and he almost sprawled on the ground ridding himself of chaps and spurs.

The delay gave Jim time to collect his wits. But even that and some semblance of coolness did not mitigate his welcome of a battle with any or all of this confounded Diamond outfit. The incentive he needed had been miraculously forthcoming.

Curly gave a capital imitation of a bull about to charge, when he was detained by Uphill Frost.

"Hold on a minnit," yelled that individual, impressively.

"Don't corral me. I'm gonna pulverize this gurl-huggin' foreman," replied Curly, swinging his arms.

"Shore, an' my money's on you, Curly, old buckaroo," said Frost, holding up a hand stuffed with greenbacks of small denominations.

There was a noisy scramble then among the cowboys to get money up on Curly. But it developed that not a single backer of Jim came forward. If Jim had not been so wretched about Molly and so furious at these pig-headed cowboys he would have howled with mirth.

"I'll take every bet," he declared.

"Whoopee!" yelled somebody, with an eye to fortune. "Give any odds, boss?"

"Two to one," answered Jim. "But hurry. I want to get this over and have my supper."

"Atta boy, Curly!"

"Larrup him unmerciful!"

"You're fightin' fer the Diamond!"

When Curly came lumbering in Jim stepped aside and hit him in the ribs. The blow gave forth a hollow sound. Curly whirled around and plunged, swinging. He delivered wide sweeping blows that, if any of them had connected with Jim, would have fulfilled the hopes of the yelling Diamond. But they expended their strength on the empty air. In a couple of moments Jim became aware that Curly could not hit him. The cowboy was a wonder in a saddle, but on the ground he was lost. He got his feet tangled up and he appeared the farthest remove from nimble. After hitting Curly a few times here and there Jim discovered a vulnerable spot in Curly's big handsome nose. Wherefore Jim began to concentrate on that. He whacked it with his left. Soon the blood began to flow and with it Curly's wild exuberance. But this did not improve his fighting. Then Jim landed his right and that upset Curly. He sat down quite suddenly. This also upset Curly's backers.

"Git up, you big cheese!" yelled Hack Jocelyn, and he did not mean to be funny. "Our money's on you."

Curly responded to that trenchant call. And now to his amazement was added fury. In the ensuing few moments he showed that his spirit was willing but his flesh weak. The blows he landed upon Jim were inconsequential. On the other hand Jim gave him a severe drubbing. After the third knock-down Curly merely sat up. It chanced that this time he was near Bud, who was also sitting up.

"My Gawd! pard, hev we come to this?" cried Bud, evidently sober enough to realize. "What'd he hit me with?"

"I reckon it was a hossshoe," said Curly, feeling his swollen and bloody nose.

Jim stepped closer and peered down at Curly.

"Well, Prentiss, have you got enough?" he asked fiercely.

Curly looked up without the least trace of resentment and nodded.

"Boss, I cain't say how it come aboot, but I'm shore licked," he said, and he grinned.

"Did I pick this fight?" went on Jim, quick to grasp the situation.

"You shore didn't."

"All right. Are you going to threaten me with that damn nonsense about gun-play or are you going to shake hands?"

Curly laboriously got to his feet. Something had pierced the armor of his stupidity.

"I reckon I'll shake," he rejoined, and he took Jim's proffered hand.

"Aw, you're drunk," growled Hack Jocelyn, in disgust, with a hard eye on Curly. "An' we had our money on you!" With that he strode surlily away.

Bud Chalfack essayed to rise, a task no means easy, owing to the billets of wood that surrounded his feet.

"Bud, you better stay there, because if you get up I'll only have to knock you down again," said Jim, menacingly.

"But I wasn't fightin' you. Thet was Curly," protested Bud.

"No matter. You're a little skunk, and I'll have to do it, unless you have another pard who'll take it for you."

"Ahuh." Bud looked around, and it was evident that at the moment not one of the cowboys seemed eager to take Jim's hint. "Boss, so you're one of them fellars thet's never satisfied once he gets a-goin'?"

"I'm afraid I am."

"But you're bigger'n me an' I didn't do nothin' except give you away. An' if you hadn't soaked me I'd hev told the fellars——"

"If you tell any more I'll beat you into jelly. And I'll do that anyhow unless you apologize."

"Aw! Fer callin' Molly Dunn a little hussy?"

Jim looked a grim affirmative.

"All right, boss. I crawl. But I didn't mean any insult."

"You didn't?—Say, you little dumb-head! Didn't you lie when you said you saw me hug her?"

"Boss, I think I was sober *then*," replied Bud, gravely. "I seen you hug her. You lifted her clean off the floor. She whacked you one—an' when you let her down, she went fer you sudden-like an' kissed you."

Jim faced the silent puzzled cowboys. He had extracted all the humor for them from the situation, and he believed for once he had the upper hand.

"Boys, Bud was drunk last night. He has heaped disgrace on me and insulted a fine little girl."

Bud took violent exception to this, as was manifest from his face and actions, without the speech that followed.

"Boss, it ain't no disgrace to hug a gurl in Arizonie. An' if it happened to be Molly Dunn you'd shore make this outfit proud. 'Cause Molly Dunn has handed the mitt to me an' Lonestar. An' she shore set Hack Jocelyn down cold an' hard. Hack is plumb crazy over her."

"But you called her hussy!" thundered Jim, trying to hide his rapture.

"But, boss, I didn't mean thet in no insultin' way," protested Bud. "Molly's a little wildcat. She's a devil. She has shore made this Diamond outfit sick. Why, me an' Lonestar was flirtin' with her down at West Fork, an' we never knowed she was Slinger Dunn's sister! ... Boss, I take thet hussy back."

"Very well, in that case I'm sorry I misunderstood you," said Jim, and offered his hand to Bud.

Jeff's noisy banging call to supper ended the incident. Jim imagined an almost imperceptible transformation in the air of the cowboys, except in Jocelyn and Winters, who were surly and uncommunicative.

Jim sought his bed early. There was no singing round the camp fire that night. Scarcely had darkness set in when the fire flickered and went out. The coyotes had uninterrupted possession of the silence. But Jim did not find slumber coming easily. He believed he had stumbled on a way to get the best of the Diamond outfit. He was not sure that his hope was not father to the conviction, but the more he pondered over his achievement the more elated he became. These simple elemental boys respected only achievement. They did not really in the least care who a man was. It was what he could do! And Jim believed he could whip every last one of them. Hack Jocelyn would be a mean customer. Jim had liked Hack less and less all the time, and Bud's allusion to Hack's interest in Molly Dunn aggravated the feeling. Jocelyn would be dangerous in a fight and not to be trusted in relation to a woman. Jim could have laughed aloud at this deduction. Already he seemed to be anticipating rivals! But so far as Molly Dunn was concerned he certainly could not trust himself.

Jim reflected. It had amazed him—the ease with which he had bested Curly, and he tried to reason out why. Curly was a big, lithe, strong fellow, who ought to have put up a very aggressive battle. But he had been born on a horse and had lived in a saddle. On the ground he did not know what to do with himself. Slow, awkward, uncertain, he had been at Jim's mercy. Whereupon Jim took stock of himself. He weighed around one hundred and seventy. He had a long reach, a fist like a mallet; he was quick as a cat and fast on his feet. Only a couple of years back he had been pretty clever with his hands. And this had come about naturally enough. When he was about fourteen years old he was friends with a boy who had a cousin come visiting from the East. And this cousin taught Jim and his friend something of the manly art of self-defense.

It began to look as if Jim had another asset which he had not counted on at all. The fence-building on a Missouri farm had been the first; now the second was this playful and friendly boxing habit. These cowboys had long since given him reason to resort to violence. But Jim knew he had been backward and perhaps afraid. From some source had come the courage of a lion. He chuckled to himself. No fear that these cowboys would haul in! By their very nature—their pugnacity and curiosity—they must grow worse. Each and every one of them would feel it his bounden duty to wipe up the camp-ground with the tenderfoot foreman of the Diamond. Jim reveled in a situation that a few days back had been well-nigh intolerable. No wonder they had been a pondering lot of young men! A gleam of light they refused to see had begun to penetrate their craniums.

But as for Molly Dunn! When Jim let clamoring thoughts of her dominate his consciousness his exultant glee died and his heart sank like lead in his breast. So some of these tough cowboys knew her! Had dared to approach her! The idea made Jim's blood run hot and cold. Still, Molly could not have helped that, if these cowboys had discovered where she lived or any place she frequented. West Fork! He had not heard of that place. But he would very soon see it for himself. Stone walls could not keep these riders of the Diamond out. How much less then could a girl do it? Molly had spunk, though, Jim thought. It was no use to let pride and distrust have sway over him. As he lay there, his face upward to the dark canopy of pines, through which starlight filtered, he realized he was infatuated. That was as far as he grasped truth. Molly was an enigma, but only that because of the allusions of Bud Chalfack. That confounded cowboy had been witness to the scene on the porch in Flagerstown. He had seen Molly's incredible response to Jim's embrace. Jim felt it as a sacrilege. How could he dream and ponder over something that had been profaned by the keen eyes of a vulgar cowboy? Jim writhed over this aspect of the situation. Then when Jim was abject a staggering thought struck him. Bud Chalfack had lied about the interpretation of the word hussy. Bud was a smooth-tongued, crafty cowboy. Jim had observed a hundred instances of his diplomacy with his comrades. He was the brainiest of the lot.

The thought of Bud's trenchant remark was sickening. If these cowboys actually knew Molly Dunn, if they had ever been in her willing presence—especially that hard-lipped, veiled-eyed Jocelyn—it would be for Jim no less than a calamity. Because he would have at once to turn his back on romance. Then suddenly he recalled Molly's shy swift kiss—timid if there had ever been a timid kiss—and later her sharp retort that he had been the first ever to have that from her, and loyalty and love leaped to her defense. There, then, the battle raged in Jim's mind—between uncertainty and gossip, between romance and realism, between faith and unfaith.

10

MOLLY DUNN filled the bucket at the spring and set it down.

She had been home from Flagerstown ten days—two weeks—exactly fifteen days, and they seemed years. All had changed. Her very identity was not the same. If she had ever had any capacity for happiness, it had fled.

She looked at the old wooden bucket. She had carried it as long as she could remember, and that was as far back as when she had been so little she could scarcely lift it. And the spring—all her life she remembered that. Once it had been an unfailing source of wonder and gladness. It was the biggest and finest spring of granite water of all the springs in the Cibeque Valley. It roared out from under a mossy cliff at the head of a shady glen, as large as a room and as deep as a well. Molly could see the pink-sided trout lying along the rocky sides; she could see the golden gleams deep down where the bubbles sparkled out of the shadow. Maple Spring was deep enough to drown her, and Molly wished she had the courage to fall in and sink. But she had accidentally fallen in there often, and she could swim like a fish. It would be of no use.

The glen, too, had been one of her perennial joys. The spring lent music and movement as it boiled and eddied round the great hole and then burst over a little fall to begin its melodious way down the winding gully. Many rocks and drooping ferns lined the banks; maples and sycamores leaned over the amber water, letting only gleams of sunshine through; huge pines and spruces rose from the bank above to tower high. Above the spring on a level bench were grass and flowers, and clean, flat, gray stones where Molly had played alone all her childhood and dreamed hours of her girlhood. It had been a hiding-place, too, for it was isolated and not close to the cabin or trail. The squirrels and jays shared this secret with Molly. Only in the fall when the wild turkeys came down, and the hunters followed, were the sanctity and sweetness of this glen disrupted.

But Molly gazed about with eyes hopelessly disillusioned or else blinded by the trouble that had come to her. All because of the wonderful ride to Flagerstown—a white gown, a dance—and Him! Molly felt she could never be again what she had been before that visit. She would be what he had mistaken her for or she would die.

Every day since her return home had seen a struggle. At first she had been hot and resentful in her humiliation. She had hated Jim Traft. She would be a worthy sister to Slinger Dunn. She would carry on so boldly with the riders that her name would become a byword on the range for—for—Molly did not know what, but she would find out. She would encourage that nice little cowboy of the Diamond—Bud Chalfack, whose name she had never known until the night of the dance. And she would flirt outrageously with Curly Prentiss. Indeed, she would no longer repel the advances of Hack Jocelyn, though she disliked and feared him. She would show Jim Traft that she could win his vain and stuck-up cowboys and cast them aside, for Seth Haverly and even for Andy Stoneham.

But opportunities for such conduct had multiplied and

she had not availed herself of them. Seth had been often at her home, and her brother Arch, but she knew why he came. And always Andy waylaid her when she went on errands down to the village. On Sunday she had espied Hack Jocelyn riding up the trail from West Fork, and she had dodged into the brush.

She resented her vacillation and was long in understanding. But as the days went by she had finally realized that she was terribly, miserably in love. Her amaze and scorn, her fury and contempt, her pride and her shame, her wretched attempts to sink under this malady and make of herself what Jim Traft must think her—all were of no avail and only added to her burden.

Lately Molly had begn to soften toward Jim, and that had been the forerunner of dreams and remembrances and longings. Once she had surrendered to this sweet fancy she was doomed. Before she knew it she could no longer fight herself or the thought of Jim. So that a few lonely afternoons in the glen, a few nights lying wide awake in the dark loft of the cabin, had been her undoing. The shame of it made her more furious than ever, but she was helpless. In the daylight she had some semblance of character. At least she could throw off yearnings and what she deemed idiotic enchantments, but at night she became a weak girl, with aching heart and mad tumultuous emotions.

Each morning for a week when she had come to the spring for water she had set the bucket down, to indulge in pondering, brooding thoughts. This morning they prevailed longer than usual. But at length she picked up the heavy bucket and took the trail home. She left the glen behind, and perhaps the most bearable of her thoughts.

The trail led to the clearing, to the forty acres of hideous slash in the forest that Dunn had homesteaded twenty years before. The rest of the hundred and sixty acres consisted of timber land. Dunn had never "proved up" on his claim, and therefore had no patent for it.

Arch Dunn plowed the red field and planted the beans and corn and sorghum and potatoes. He had spells when he stayed home and worked about the farm. But the last year or two he had left the harvesting of the crop to Molly and her mother.

As Molly passed along the trail, under the cedars and piñons and an occasional pine, she gazed out at the red furrows, now green-ridged with beans and corn; she saw that she would soon have to get in there with a hoe. It had never occurred to her before, but she certainly hated that beanfield. Here and there stood dead pines and cedars that had been "ringed" by an ax and left standing to become bleached and ghastly; and everywhere black stumps stuck up, surrounded by a patch of weeds. Farmers in the Cibeque let the stumps rot out.

The cabin, at the end of the clearing, fitted the scene. It consisted of two one-room log buildings, with a porch between, and one rough-shingled roof over all. The shingles were moss-green in places and the logs were bleached. In the chinks between, sections of clay had broken out. The fences were down, the sheds built of uneven clapboards.

Altogether Molly saw the homestead with gloomier eyes than ever. Yet it could boast of the finest view in all the Cibeque. To north and east the vast gray-cliffed and canyon-notched wall of the Diamond towered, a mountain face of a thousand features and never the same any two hours of the day.

She carried the bucket into the kitchen end of the cabin—a dark room, only in winter a place of comfort.

"You've been gone long enough to dig a well," remarked her mother, with sarcasm. Mrs. Dunn was still young and good-looking enough to be jealous of Molly. She had come from a station considerably above John Dunn's, and she was a bitter, unhappy woman. Since Molly had grown old enough to attract the attention of men, what accord that had existed between mother and daughter had gradually been broken.

"That bucket is heavy an' it's a long ways," replied Molly.

"You used to fetch it in a jiffy. You met some cowboy on the trail."

"No. It's funny, but I didn't this mawnin'."

"Well, you must have fallen in the spring, then."

"Wisht I had," returned Molly, flippantly. She went out and across the porch. Her father had gotten up and was slouching in his crippled way to the big blanketed chair where he passed his wakeful hours. Of late Molly had seemed to see him differently, with pity and tolerance. These feelings, too, applied to her mother. Dunn was not an old man in years, but he was in all else. His dark hair, shading gray, hung down over his knotted pale brow. He was a broken man, living in the past, ruined by some secret association with an infamous war between sheepmen and cattlemen, and devoured by passions that had outlived his enemies. Molly had affection for her father, despite the impatience and disgust which grew with the years. And of late, since her own trouble, she had begun to have some little understanding of her mother—of what it must have meant to be faithful to Dunn all these years. There flashed over Molly a consciousness that she could follow Jim Traft to the end of the world and slave her fingers to the bone for him. Then she laughed at her imbecility. For her to aspire to be the wife of Mr. James Traft, gentleman tenderfoot from Missouri, and the sole heir to old Jim Traft's land and stock—that was rather far-fetched and ridiculous. Besides, she did not do anything of the kind. But she could not control vagrant and perverse thoughts. Here flashed another. This same Jim Traft had importuned her to let him be her best fellow. How pale and earnest he had looked! It was impossible to repudiate his sincerity. To be his sweetheart! Molly had a stronger, sweeter, more suffocating rush of emotion. What would become of her if this thing grew? She must throw herself at Andy or Seth, or both of them, and kill this affliction. But could those louts kill it? Molly divined they could not kill anything except her self-respect. And that, strangely, had become a pronounced thing. She would now have it to contend with. Her pride—her vanity! All because she had been hugged by a handsome young fellow from Missouri! Molly let out a peal of ringing laughter that made even her father take notice.

"Lass, you've been queer since you come back from Flag," he remarked, in his quavering voice.

"I feel queer, dad," she replied. "I waked up from my backwoods sleep."

"Backwoods! You mean this heah homestead?"

"Never mind what I meant, dad."

He could not understand, and if she confessed the truth to her mother it would only add fuel to that strange animosity which had developed between them.

Molly plunged into one of her working spells. It could never have been said of her, at any time, that she was lazy, but she took streaks in which she was busy from dawn to sundown. Small as she was, Molly had strength and endurance. Her little tanned hands were pretty to look at, on the back; her palms, however, and the insides of her fingers were hard and cut and calloused. They occasioned Molly pangs of regret, though she had never felt ashamed of the labor that had coarsened them. It was just that the vanity inborn in her rebelled. She was vain of her little feet and trim ankles; and that was why she never went barefoot and barelegged any more. She would brush her hair until it crackled and shone gold glints in its dusky splendor. But she could work like a beaver, and she did this day, preoccupied and sad most of the time, yet cheerful during intervals.

Toward sunset, while Molly was at the wood-pile—one of her many accomplishments being skill with an ax—her brother Arch approached. This was an unprecedented action for him. Years before she and Arch had been like sister and brother, playmates, but that seemed long before he had taken to evil ways of the woods and had earned the sobriquet of Slinger Dunn.

"Molly, cain't you leave a little work around heah for me?" he complained.

She dropped the fagot she had picked up, and stared at him. What a handsome, shiftless, backwoods beggar! He had the build of an Indian. Horses had not warped his legs nor broken any bones. His soiled buckskin garments somehow suited him. For some amazing reason he had shaved the golden down from chin and lips, and his dark, tan face shone clean and smooth. Arch's eyes usually lost their piercing quality when they beheld Molly. Just now they were bearable.

"Arch, you shore ain't drunk," she said, thoughtfully regarding him.

"No. An' I ain't sick, nuther," he replied. "Never you mind aboot me. But cain't I be civil without you gettin' sassy?"

"Shore I hope so. An' now I know somethin' ails you, Arch."

"Set down. A feller cain't talk in there," he said, jerking a sinewy brown hand toward the cabin. "Dad is out of his hair. An' mother—wal, poor mother raves if you so much as open your mouth."

"Poor mother? Yes, an' poor dad, too. ... Arch, you said a lot."

"Molly, what chanct have we ever had to help make them different?" he queried, swallowing hard. "I never had no schoolin' atall. An' you—only a couple of years. What do we know? ... An' before I was sixteen I was Slinger Dunn!"

Molly was so amazed she could not keep track of flying thoughts. One held, however, and it was that if awakening consciousness of heretofore vague things could come to her it surely was possible for them to come to Arch.

"Arch, is it too late?" she whispered.

"Hell! yes, for me. But for you, Molly—wal, mebbe it's not. I hope to Gawd it ain't."

"Arch, if you want to know, I'm as down in the mouth as you," said Molly.

"You have been queer lately, since you come home. ... Mol, did anythin' happen at Flag?"

"A whole lot."

"Your feelin's get hurt?"

Molly gave a solemn little nod.

"Wal, tell me aboot it," he went on, with that wonderful flash of eyes.

Molly laughed. "So you can shoot somebody up?—No, Arch, you cain't ever help me that way."

"Is thet so? Wal, you never know. But all the same, tell me."

"Arch, it was awful for me," she replied, unable to resist sympathy. "Mrs. See took me, as you know. She was lovely. Bought me clothes—an' oh! such a beautiful dress. All white—what there was of it! Arch, I actually felt naked. She has fine friends in Flag. She introduced me. I was asked to help in a booth at the fair. ... Well, it's like a dream now. A dream you cain't believe. I—I was the belle at that dance, Arch. Can you believe it? I was crazy with joy—at bein' taken for a—a lady. I must have looked one, Arch. ... Then somethin' happened an' my heart broke."

"They found you out, Mol?" he queried, shrewdly. "Thet you lived down in the brakes? Thet your dad was John Dunn? An' your brother Slinger Dunn of the Cibeque?"

"Yes, Arch, I was found out," she replied. "But I didn't go back on you."

"Shore you'd never do thet," he said, somberly. "You oughtn't to have gone to Flag!"

"Must I stick here buried in the backwoods all my life?" she asked, passionately.

"Molly, thet stumps me. I reckon I'd have said yes a while back. But if you *was* made much of in Flag—if you *was* took for a lady, why, there's somethin' turrible wrong!"

"There is, Arch. That's the trouble."

"An' it's with dad an' me. An' with mother, too, cause she's stuck to him."

"Arch, I am a Dunn, too."

"Mol, I come out heah to ask you a fool question. I see thet now. But I promised Seth an' I'll keep it. He wants to know if you'll marry him."

"Seth Haverly? Heavens!—No!" she cried, aghast.

"I reckoned you liked Seth."

"Perhaps I did, once, a little."

"Wal, marryin' Seth wouldn't help none. Now you make me think, Molly, I'd be ag'in' thet. But you needn't never tell him. ... Andy Stoneham is a decent fellar, though. An', Mol, he's turrible sweet on you."

"That tobacco-chewin' lout!" exclaimed Molly.

"Who you gonna marry, then—to git you out of this heah hole?"

"No one, Arch. You see that marryin' one of these Cibeque boys would only nail me heah. ... An' the—the kind of a boy I—I—who could save me—wouldn't have me."

"He'd be a damn poor sort, then," flashed Arch, with passion. "If I was sich a fellar as you mean I could swaller a lot for you, Molly. Don't fool yourself. You're good enough for any fellar."

His earnestness, his sincerity, touched Molly. She went to the wood-pile and sat down beside him, meaning to thank him, to yield to this surprising sympathy in him, but all she did was to burst into tears.

"Wal, don't cry," he said, almost roughly. "Molly, I heah this Diamond cowboy, Hack Jocelyn, was seen in West Fork last Sunday."

"Yes. *I* saw him, myself, an' I shore ducked into the brush."

"Ahuh. Wal, thet lets you out, if you're not lyin'."

Molly dried her useless tears and presently faced him. "Arch, I used to lie to you, about the boys an' everythin'. But I wouldn't no more."

"Reckon Jocelyn hasn't rid down heah so often the last year for nothin'. Molly, is it you?"

"Yes, Arch, it's me."

"Don't you like him?"

"I did at first. But not now. He's older. He's daid in earnest."

"Humph! You mean aboot you? In love with you? Wants to marry you, same as Seth?"

"Arch, he's in love, all right, but he never said nothin' about marryin' me. An' of course I wouldn't have him if he had."

"Wal, I should smile not!" ejaculated Arch. "Marry one of thet Diamond outfit? My Gawd! . . . But at thet they're some pretty decent boys compared to Jocelyn. . . . Mol, he an' me are aboot ready to meet up."

"Arch, you can't help me by killin' any more fellars," cried Molly, shocked at the significance of his words. "That's one thing against me—your bloody record. An', Arch, if you keep on—if you should happen to kill one of thet Diamond outfit—well, I'll just go to the bad!"

He took that darkly, without a protest, as if consciousness was being driven home to a man inevitably lost.

"Wal, I reckon I want to tell you suthin'," he spoke up. "All this talk aboot marryin'. . . . I up an' asked Lil Haverly to marry me."

"Arch! You did? Lil Haverly—that—that——"

"Never mind what. Anyway, I did, an' I told her I'd turn over a new leaf an' go to ranchin' if she'd have me. An' she laughed in my face! . . . She'd let me be sweet on her, too, Molly, an' thet fooled me."

"She's no good!" retorted Molly, fiercely, suddenly and astoundingly conscious of her brother's pain.

"Wal, not much, mebbe. Anyway, it doesn't matter," he replied, sitting up. "Come. I'll help you pack in this wood."

Molly slaved and brooded the days away. She could make life bearable by getting so tired during the day that sleep made short shift of the long, dark, silent nights. On Sunday she accepted the calls of Andy Stoneham and other village boys. Her wild intention to flirt viciously, to play fast and loose with them, seemed an utter impossibility, once they were in her presence. One Sunday afternoon, while walking the trail with Andy from the cabin to the creek, he took her hand in his, as had been his wont in the past—a preliminary to his by no means timid love-making. Molly let her hand lie passively in his a moment, which encouraged Andy to squeeze it. She wondered about this. She had absolutely no interest whatever in the action, except as something further to study about herself. Coming to the shade of a piñon tree, Andy gave her a little pull, accompanying the move by one of his speeches. Molly freed herself.

101

"Andy, don't do that again," she said, quietly, with a glance, and walked on.

Presently he caught up with her, and falling into step with her went on beside her for a goodly distance, without speaking. It was some time after this incident that Molly realized he had never attempted another liberty with her.

The other boys, however, were hopeless in this regard, and the only way Molly could circumvent them was to entertain them on the porch. Two of these Sunday afternoons were rendered exciting by the fact of cowboys from the Diamond riding up and down the trail. Hack Jocelyn was one of them on both occasions. The other cowboys Molly did not know, though she had certainly seen the youngest one, frank-faced, and as rosy as a girl.

"Molly," said Andy, on the second of these visits, "you know thet cowboy Jocelyn belongs to the Diamond?"

"Shore I know," replied Molly. "Is that a crime?"

"Wal, reckon 'tis, leastways since thet outfit's been buildin' the drift fence. ... Jocelyn has an eye fer you, gurl."

"He's very handsome an' attractive. 'Most all the Diamond boys are."

"Ahuh. Why doesn't Jocelyn brace in hyar then?"

"He aims to catch me alone, Andy. An' it's just as well you're heah."

"Much obliged. Glad I'm good fer suthin'," replied Andy, with sour humor. "But jokin' out of it, this feller Jocelyn is up to tricks. Last night I seen him in Mace's saloon. He had money an' was spendin' it. Sort of stumped me to see Seth Haverly drinkin' with him."

"No, Andy!" exclaimed Molly, aroused.

"Wal, I jest did. Honest Injun. An' you ain't the only one surprised."

"Was Arch there?"

"Reckon not. Arch hasn't been around lately. Now what's he a-goin' to say to thet?"

"Say! He won't say anythin'. But he's liable to do somethin'. Seth an' Arch are like brothers."

"Molly, around hyar Arch is considered a dangerous

102

fellar, but one you can trust. Seth ain't so dangerous, they say, but he can't be trusted. Now we know thet Arch an' Seth, the other Haverlys, an' Hart Merriwell, an' Boyd Flick, an' some other make up the Cibeque outfit. One or more of them, on an' off, rode fer the Coffee Pot, the Hash Knife, the Bar O an' other outfits in the valley. But so far as I know not one of them is ridin' fer any outfit now—except their own."

Molly echoed his last words and she caught the significance of his lowered vocie and roving look around.

"It jest strikes my funny thet Jocelyn of the Diamond seems to be makin' up to Seth Haverly of the Cibeque. How does it strike you, Molly?"

"Not funny, you can bet," replied Molly, with a short laugh. "Andy, there's somethin' in the wind. I'm thankin' you for givin' me a hunch. Arch is strange an' sore lately. He's that touchy aboot the Diamond boys an' their work I cain't get a word out of him."

"Ahuh. Wal, Molly, you can shore get them out of me," rejoined Andy, solidly, as one who had hit upon a happy medium. "I heard folks talk aboot Jocelyn. An' I'll tell you what. If he keeps on ridin' down to West Fork it's gonna be plumb bad fer him."

"Oh—Andy!" faltered Molly.

"Slinger will *kill* him," whispered Andy. "My own idee is thet Slinger might stand for Jocelyn gettin' thick with Seth an' his outfit, fer after all this brother of yours is a lone timber wolf. But he'll never stand fer Jocelyn runnin' after you."

"Andy, I know he won't," whispered Molly. "But I've told Arch aboot it."

"Molly, air you shore you ain't interested in Jocelyn atall?"

"Yes, I'm shore. I was at first. Like a ground squirrel with a snake! But now—Jiminy, I'll run like a scared rabbit."

"Thet's good if it's true. Will Slinger believe you? Molly, excuse me, but thar's folks who say you're meetin' Jocelyn on the sly, along the trail somewheres."

Again Molly suffered a hint of her status in West Fork.

103

She passed by Andy's covert suspicion. What could he know of a girl's honesty? But she told him rather forcibly that at least her brother trusted and believed her.

"Ahuh. Wal, I'm glad. You know what a place West Fork is fer talk. Wuss'n a beehive. An' the drift fence has shore stirred up hell. Molly, do you know thet son-of-a-gun tenderfoot Traft is 'most clear to the brakes with his damned fence?"

"I—I—hadn't heahed," replied Molly, thrilling.

"Wal, he is. Most clear on the Diamond! Ole Enoch Summers says, 'Tenderfoot hell! Thet boy is Jim Traft over again, an' you two-bit calf-chaser hev gotta look out.'"

"Did Mr. Summers—say that?" gasped Molly.

"He shore did, an' to a whole storeful of fellars."

From that hour Molly was kinder to Andy. She relied upon him to fetch her news—the facts as well as gossip. And Andy, evidently sensing some change in her, accepted the part gratefully. Molly went to one of the Saturday-night dances with him. It was an ordeal. She was made much of, though some of the boys were rude, and some of the girls catty with their remarks. Where was the grand white dress with which Molly Dunn had killed off the Diamond outfit, including young Mr. James Traft?

Molly did not stay long, especially after she had espied Hack Jocelyn enter the hall. She was quick enough, and Andy helped her, to get out before Jocelyn saw her.

"Take me home, Andy," she said, nervously holding his arm.

"Wal, it's a huggin'-bee inside an' a fightin'-bee outside," replied Andy, sardonically. "West Fork as she is an' always will be, I reckon."

Saturday night at West Fork always had been exciting, and Molly could count on her fingers the times she had seen it. But no longer was it diverting. There were groups of men and boys outside, noisy and rough. Sounds of hilarity came from the saloons. Indians passed her with soft tread. She heard the jingle of spurs on all sides. Shadows passed in front of the dimly lighted windows.

The air was cool and sweet after the smoky hall. The dark bulk of the Diamond promontory stood up against the star-studded sky line. Molly was glad to turn off the street into the lane, and she held Andy's arm tighter.

"Molly, I ain't had a chanct like this in a coon's age," said Andy, as if stolidly realizing the opportunity.

"Andy, I'm afraid of Hack Jocelyn," replied Molly, simply. "I *cain't* be your sweetheart. I *cain't* let you handle me. . . . Do you want me to be afraid of you, too? Afraid to have you take me home in the dark?"

He did not reply at once. Evidently the facts were hard to assimilate by his slow mind.

"Wal, now you tax me aboot it, I reckon I don't."

Molly regarded that as more than an answer to her question. Andy, too, like Arch, had unplumbed depths in the darkness of which there must be good.

11

DRY, HOT midsummer lay upon the Cibeque. In the shade of the glen Molly spent hours idle on a rock, watching the big trout lying still in the clear water. The bees hummed by. The sumac on the stony slope had taken on touches of red and brown. Squirrels and jays were taking their high noon siesta. The lizards, however, were active. They loved the heat and the dry brush and the hot stones. Molly never wearied of watching them and she could sit so quietly that the tiny ones would crawl over her hand. Seen near, they were beautiful with their many colors and jewel eyes.

Things that concerned the life of West Fork revolved uppermost in her mind. The drift fence, so dominant a factor now, was well out on the Diamond. In the eyes of the Cibeque folk young Jim Traft was a perfect hurricane for work. Conflicting stories about how he worked and his fights with his cowboys were rife about the village. More cattle had drifted down into the brakes this summer than ever before. Vague hints that they all did not drift there of their own accord filtered to Molly's ears. Her father was perceptibly failing now, and her mother talked of going back to Illinois. Molly wondered what was to become of her, and she did not care much.

Arch had been home steadily for a month, more morose than she had ever seen him. But he had driven Molly out of the beanfield and had harvested the beans himself. She tried not to see that he and the Haverly gang had cattle deals frequently. They drove cattle in from the brakes and down the Cibeque, small bunches and short drives that had a sinister significance to Molly. Resolutely she refused to think the matter out clearly.

She went back home through the woods, watchful along the trail, sure that she was going to hear any rider or see anyone before he discovered her. A ten-acre pasture appeared to have more young cattle than it could very well graze. But they had not been there the day before.

Along the eastern side of the cabin a line of sunflowers blazed gold in the sun. Molly's mother had planted sunflowers every spring as long as Molly could remember. It had always seemed funny to Molly, but she guessed nothing was that any more. Her father drooped in his chair on the porch; her mother puttered around in the kitchen; some ragged saddled horses stood bridles down out at the edge of the timber. Molly knew that Arch would be out there. The still hot summer air seemed charged with a suspense.

Molly's mother sent her on an errand to the village. She was always glad when a trip of this kind could be made in the daytime. Her mother had a habit of forgetting until just before the evening meal. Molly did not start out toward the horses. She hurried out back of the barn and slipped into the woods to cut across to the trail, sure that none of the riders with Arch had observed her.

The dusty village street was asleep. So was old Enoch Summers in his store. Molly made the necessary purchase, and not tarrying to listen to his gossip, though his query about Arch made her curious, she made haste homeward.

When she reached the shady trail she went slower to regain her breath. At a thickly overgrown point, where the trail turned, a brown hand shot out from the green and grasped her arm. Molly was not the screaming kind. But she struggled with all her fierce young strength. It availed nothing, however, and she was dragged through the brush a step or two into a little clearing beside a huge fallen pine. Molly was frightened but not surprised to look up into the dark face of Hack Jocelyn.

"Howdy, sweetheart!" he drawled. "I bin layin' fer you."

"Let go," said Molly, and she jerked so hard that she freed her arm. "What do you want? . . . Did you have to drag me in heah?"

"Wal, there's some folks I'd rather not see me," replied Jocelyn.

"My brother Arch, for one, I reckon."

"No. I'm standin' tolerable with Slinger. I was thinkin' of thet sneak, Andy Stoneham. He's got eyes an' he thinks too much."

"Well, what you want? Mother sent me on an errand. She'll be waitin'."

"Let her wait. Reckon I've waited often an' long enough. I had to see you."

"If you *had* to, why didn't you come to my home, like any decent fellow would?"

"I've had reasons, Molly. But I'm glad to tell you one of them ain't pressin' no more. I've quit the Diamond."

This had decided interest and surprise for Molly, though she did not voice it. She peered, however, up under the big sombrero, at the cowboy's handsome, wicked face. It bore recent signs of battle.

"I couldn't stand Jim Traft no longer," went on Jocelyn. "I bin layin' fer a chance to quit a month an' more. We had some words. An' it ended in a fist fight."

107

"Did he lick you?" asked Molly, unable to resist her swift curiosity.

"I reckon he did," returned Jocelyn, ruefully. "He's a slugger with his fists, an' thet kind of fightin' ain't mine. I couldn't make him draw a gun while I was ridin' with the Diamond, so I jest quit."

"Ahuh. Quit so you *could* make him?"

"Shore. An' I reckon thet sounds good to you?"

"It means nothin' to me," replied Molly, lying with tight lips.

"What was this heah talk aboot Bud Chalfack seein' Traft insult you at the fair dance in Flag?"

"It's news to me. Was there such talk?" rejoined Molly, flippant to hide her start.

"There shore was, an' it's goin' the round like brush fire. Any reason fer it?"

"I cain't stop waggin' tongues."

"You danced with Jim Traft an' went out with him?"

"Mr. Jocelyn, if I did, that's my business an' none of yours."

"Molly Dunn, I'm makin' it mine," he said. "I reckon you'd lie even if there was anythin'. But you ought to have sense enough to know Jim Traft couldn't be serious aboot you."

Molly looked away into the forest, conscious of deep-seated pain.

"Good day, Mr. Jocelyn. I'll be goin'," she said, and moved away.

Like a panther he leaped at her, cursing under his breath. She was a leaf in his grasp and she realized it. He lifted her high, held her close, and it was only by contortions of her supple body that she escaped hot fierce kisses on her lips. These burned face and neck.

"You're stayin' heah—till I get through—with you," he panted.

"Let me—down. I—I'll stay," choked Molly.

He let her slide till her feet touched the ground, but did not at once release her. Molly burned with more than shame. She could have killed him if she had not been so scared. All cowboys were violent and rude at times, but this one was a man with a cruel hand as masterful and relentless as if she were a horse. She must use a woman's wit or she might have infinitely more to regret. The place was secluded, lonely, so far from any cabin that screams would be useless.

"I reckon you'd better," he said, giving her a shake. "Molly Dunn, you made up to me when I met you. An' now you're goin' to pay fer it. I'm through with the Diamond an' I'm throwin' in with the Cibeque. If you feel sweet fer Jim Traft, like them moon-eyed Flag girls, you can jest forget it. 'Cause I'm crazy in love with you an' I'm goin' to have you. An' you'll marry me as soon as I make the stake we—I'm figgerin' on."

"Marry you!—Mister Jocelyn, you're shore takin' a lot on your haid," said Molly, aghast and astounded at his effrontery. "I'm thankin' you because a man cain't do any more than ask that of a girl, but I must say no."

"An' why must you?" he queried.

"I don't love you."

"Wal, if I know gurls, you'll change your tune soon as I make my stake."

"Stake. What you mean?"

"Never you mind now. I want to talk to you aboot your brother. Accordin' to the Haverlys he ain't got any use fer me. No reason except I was on the Diamond an' thet I'm supposed to have been driftin' round heah on your trail. An' thet ain't no lie! Wal, you're goin' to set me straight with Slinger."

"Oh, I am!" quoth Molly. Her fear held her in abeyance, but she could not wholly suppress her leaping spirit. "If I know Arch Dunn that little job wouldn't be easy."

"We—I—I've figgered it out," declared Jocelyn. "It's been goin' the rounds thet Jim Traft made a show of you at the dance. An' we'll see it gets to Slinger's ears pronto. Wal, you're goin' to admit it's true, an' tell him I quit the Diamond because of it. Savvy, sweetheart?"

"I savvy that you are a deep an' cunnin' hombre, Mister Jocelyn," replied Molly, sarcastically. Not to have saved her another of his onslaughts could she have restrained from that retort. But Jocelyn's instant grin proved that he took it for a compliment.

"You can jest bet your sweet life I am. ... An' now soon as you swear you'll tell this to Slinger—an', wal, give me a kiss—you can run home to your mom."

Molly could not look back on any experience with men like Jocelyn. He lacked something most cowboys had. But she divined that with whatever sort of girls he had consorted he had won them to his will. It seemed rather a force of character than conceit. Where Molly had disliked him, had been vaguely repelled, now she thoroughly hated and feared him.

"I won't kiss you, but—I'll *think* aboot tellin' that to Arch," she replied, playing for time, to propitiate him enough to let her escape from a predicament she would never let herself in for again.

"I cain't let you go on thet, Molly," he said, cheerfully. The idiot actually felt sure of her. And he began to roll a cigarette, a shadow of a smile on his dark smooth face.

Molly averted her eyes, lest he read in hers the thought that was forming. Once out of reach of his long arm she could get away. The cowboy did not live who could catch her on foot. Molly calculated distance and moment, while concentrating all her energy. Suddenly like a flash she ducked and bounded at once, under the brush into the trail. Jocelyn shouted and crashed through. But Molly darted away. She could run like a deer. Her moccasined feet pattered on the hard trail. He thudded heavily after her, soon losing ground. Molly looked over her shoulder to see that he might as well have been roped, for all the hope he had of catching her.

She screeched a laugh back at him and sped on out of his sight, never slacking her swift pace until she reached the place she had cut across to avoid the riders. Once in the clearing, she went slowly so as to regain her breath.

The fool! The hard-lipped cowpuncher—to think he could bully her into knuckling to him! But otherwise she welcomed the encounter. Hack Jocelyn had quit the Diamond. It was a stunning fact against all precedent. He was making up to the Cibeque, and especially to Arch

Dunn. Some deviltry afoot! Molly divined that she was not the whole contention. She recalled Jocelyn's looks and words—his actions. How grimly satisfied with himself! He had built some big cowboy trick. What a clever ruse to win Slinger Dunn's friendship! If anything could have placated the lone timber wolf of the Cibeque, that crafty lie might.

Molly sat down on a log to rest. And the gist of this complex situation burst upon her in realization of menace to Jim Traft. That agitated Molly even more than Jocelyn's attack on her. Hackamore Jocelyn would kill Jim, and if he did not Slinger Dunn or the Haverlys would. Molly divined it, shocked that it had not dawned upon her before, and her warm pulsing blood turned to ice. Jocelyn had proved traitor to the Diamond. For that he would be welcomed by the Cibeque, though she doubted Arch's complaisance. An infernal scheme had been hatched and Hack Jocelyn was the prime mover in it. And what did he mean by a stake? Molly understood the word to imply what riders called food or money that they hoped to get by some lucky or clever break. Jocelyn had certainly meant the latter and no small amount. Molly racked her brains for a solution, which was not forthcoming. Then her mother, espying her on the log, called, loudly. Molly hurried to the cabin.

"I declare, but you take long to do anythin'," said Mrs. Dunn, harshly.

"Well, so would anyone if she got waylaid by a bully of a cowpuncher," retorted Molly.

"Who?" demanded the mother, with a keen look at Molly's heated face.

Instead of answering Molly ran like a squirrel up the ladder to the loft that opened over the porch. It had two compartments, one over each cabin. That over the kitchen was a storeroom, and the other, over the living-room, was Molly's. It had a window at the far end, a rude contraption that had been put in by Arch. The V-shaped roof was high enough only in the middle for Molly to stand erect. Since Molly had been a child this had been the only room she had ever had, but she preferred it to

111

the living-room, where her parents slept and quarreled. Arch Dunn used to sleep on the porch below, and then Molly had felt safe, but for years now, most of the night, only the pines and spruces had sheltered him. What furniture there was in Molly's boudoir was homemade, and some of it by her own hands. Yet until Mrs. See had taken her to Flagerstown she had been contented in this loft. But then she had been a good many things before that lamentable visit.

At any rate, Molly kept her cubbyhole, as she called it, clean and neat, and fragrant with the scent of pine and spruce boughs, upon which she spread her blankets. She lay down there now and tried to puzzle a way through the maze of circumstances which seemed to have involved her.

Following her mother's call to supper, Molly heard Arch's slow, clinking footfall. When he wore moccasins he could not be heard at all.

"Where's Molly?" he asked.

"I don't know. She got huffy because I asked her a question an' flounced out somewhere," replied the mother.

"Some of your questions are shore irritatin'," said Arch. "What was thet particular one?"

"She came home red in the face and panting, and when I told her it had taken her a long time to go to the store, she said she'd been waylaid by a bully of a cowpuncher. Then I asked her 'who?' "

"Ahuh. I reckon the gurl's gettin' too big an' pretty to be alone on the trails," returned the son, ponderingly.

"Big! She's only a mite, an' not so awful pretty."

"Molly is no kid any more. You can bet I'm findin' thet out. An' as fer bein' pretty—where's your eyes, ma? I heah she beat them Flag gurls all hollow at the fair dance. I heah a lot."

"I never hear anything," complained Mrs. Dunn. "I'm stuck in this cabin from sunup till dark. I want to get away before I die on my feet."

Molly had heard such ranting of her mother's for years,

but she was stunned to hear Arch reply that maybe soon they would be able to move away from the Cibeque.

"Arch! What've you done now?" queried the mother.

"Nothin' jest yet. But I reckon to make a stake soon."

"Humph!—Call the girl to supper."

Arch stepped to the end of the porch and called, "Hey, Mol."

Molly thought best to answer sleepily: "Yes, Arch. Heah I am. What you want?"

"Supper, you wood-mouse," he replied, and he waited by the ladder to give her a slap and then lift her down.

"No kid no more! Mol, you're as heavy as a sack of beans."

"Shore, an' worth aboot as much," retorted Molly. "You're plumb interested in me lately, Arch."

"Yep, I am, more'n you'd guess," he replied. "You an' me are goin' to have a little confab after supper."

Molly looked straight into his piercing eyes, though she felt her face burn and her nerves quiver. However she did not reply. She carried her father's meal to him and placed the board across the arms of his chair.

"Lass, what's Arch jawin' you aboot?" he asked.

"I haven't any idea, dad. He's got one of his spells."

"There's too much goin' on heah," declared Dunn. "They all think I'm blind, settin' on this porch. But my eyes are good yet for cattle-rustlers."

Molly saw Arch lift his lean head with the action of an eagle, and give his father a dark look. She felt perturbed herself at her father's pointed remark, though now and then he would make some caustic allusion to the movements of cattlemen.

He hated them, and made little distinction between ranchers and rustlers. His day had been one when sheep held the range. Molly ate her supper in silence, which, in fact, was what they all did.

"Wal, sister, you can have a walk with *me*," said Arch, dryly, as he got up from the table.

Molly did not need to look at him again. She knew there was something in the wind, but she felt only half frightened. Arch was a puzzle lately. She walked beside

113

him as he led her along the edge of the field toward the creek. The heat of the day was gone; the sun had sunk, yet the top of the Diamond blazed gold and red; there were deer in the pasture with the cows; somewhere a burro brayed shrilly. When Arch got to the head of the trail where it led down into the glen toward the spring he halted and said: "Reckon this is far enough. No one can heah you if you do squawk."

"Arch, you're not a bit funny," replied Molly. "An' you cain't make me squawk."

"Who was the bully of a cowboy thet waylaid you?"

"Hackamore Jocelyn."

"I reckoned so. On your way home from the store? I seen you go out the back trail."

"Yes. He must have seen me, too, for he waited along the trail."

"Wal, what'd he do, Mol?" went on Arch.

He was hard to penetrate, yet so far Molly had no great misgivings.

"Arch, I don't *have* to tell you everythin' or anythin'," she said, steadily.

"Reckon you don't, to be fair aboot it. But you ought to. Poor ole dad is done, an', wal, I reckon ma's no good. I'm no good, either, fer thet matter. But I'm your brother, Molly."

She had never heard him speak like that before.

"Arch, you—you don't trust me," she faltered.

"Hell! It's only the last few days thet I seen you was old enough to mistrust."

"Then—how can I confide in you?" she asked, simply.

"Molly, are you goin' to make me choke thin's out of you?"

"I'm not anxious aboot it."

"Wal, then, are you sweet on this Diamond cowboy?"

"Which one?" rejoined Molly, with a titter.

He laughed, too. "Thet's one on me. But fer the moment I mean this heah Jocelyn."

Molly told him bluntly just what she thought of Jocelyn.

"Wal, I'll be dog-goned. I been given to believe you was sweet on him."

"Who told you, Arch?"

"It come round aboot."

"Somebody lied. I haven't any use for Jocelyn. If you want to know, I'll give you the straight goods aboot him —so far as I am concerned—but, Arch, I'd a good deal rather not tell you."

"Why—if you're willin'?"

"Well, it'll make you mad, an' probably run you into another fight."

"Molly it's no shore bet thet Jocelyn an' I won't fight, anyhow. Seth has been talkin' too much for Jocelyn. He's too anxious. There's somethin' up. It looks to me like Jocelyn wants to double-cross the Diamond an' somehow throw in with the Cibeque. I'm not shore. But I don't take to the puncher. Mebbe I'm cross-grained. Mebbe it's because he's throwed a gun heah an' there. All the same, if he'd double-cross Traft he'd shore do the same by us."

Long before Arch had concluded that speech, Molly had made her decision to be honest—to hold back nothing, though at the suspicion he might presently ask pertinently about Jim Traft her heart came into her throat.

"Arch, you're on the track," she replied, swiftly. "Jocelyn has quit the Diamond. Had a fight with—Jim Traft, he said, an' jumped at a chance to quit. He had a black eye, a cut lip, an' some other fist marks. An'—an'—" Here Molly paused to relieve the oppression in her breast, and failed to do it. "Jocelyn tried to bully me into lyin' to you. Wanted me to tell you he'd quit the Diamond because —because Jim Traft had insulted me. Then he could throw a gun on Traft!"

Slinger Dunn whistled long and low, and afterward muttered a deep curse. His brown hand shot out like the strike of a snake and snapped a dead twig of cedar.

"Molly, you've shore cleared up part of this heah deal," he said, gratefully. "I'll bet a hundred Jocelyn aimed to throw in with the Cibeque."

"That's what he said, Arch," rejoined Molly, and impelled by released emotion, she began at the point when

115

Jocelyn waylaid her on the trail and recalled every word and action of that encounter.

"So much fer Hackamore Jocelyn," muttered Dunn. "I wonder now—I jest wonder what cairds Seth holds—or if it is his deal."

"I wouldn't trust Seth Haverly with his grandma's spectacles," said Molly.

"Wal, Molly, mebbe I'd better take your hunch. But I cain't believe Seth would double-cross me, leastways with a puncher from the Diamond. An' thet brings us to real talk."

Molly had only to look up to realize that herself. Dunn fastened a hand in her blouse, so close and tight as to pinch her neck, and with a slow pull he drew her up so that her eyes were scarcely a foot from his.

"What's this I heah aboot Jim Traft insultin' you?"

"I—I don't know what you heahed, Arch—but it's a lie."

"Did you meet him?"

"Yes, at the fair."

"An' went to thet dance with him?"

"Oh no. I went with Mrs. See. . . . But Jim Traft came —an' I—I danced with him once."

"An' thet's all? You wasn't out in the moonlight with him, on the porch?"

"Yes—we walked out a—a little."

"An' he grabbed you an' hugged you?" demanded Dunn, leaning down.

"Y-es, Arch—he did," whispered Molly.

"You let him?"

"He's big an' strong. . . . What could I—I do? But at that I slapped him."

"Which was proof you felt insulted. So how's it come you say you wasn't?"

"Listen—Arch—an' don't choke me," she gasped. "I —I wasn't honest with him. The truth is—I took to him —somethin' outrageous. An' he must have guessed it. . . . But when he—he had me in his arms—I hit him. I—I wanted him to believe I *was* insulted. He'd taken me for a girl far above one from Cibeque. . . . But I really wasn't

116

insulted—an' when I hit him I wasn't honest. An'—an'—"

Molly reached the subtlety of a woman in her instinct to protect Jim Traft. And she seemed to divine that her brother might not know more.

"Took to him somethin' outrageous!" ejaculated Arch, incredulously. "Molly Dunn!"

"Yes, Molly Dunn," retorted Molly, gaining courage with resentment. "Even if I do belong to the Dunns of the Cibeque I've got a heart."

"I ain't blamin' you, Mol," he returned, as if realizing the inevitableness of the fact, and he let go of her. "You're only a kid. An' he's shore a good-lookin' fellar. An' he can talk. But, Molly, the thing is he's old Jim Traft's kin. He's worth a million. An' he couldn't have no honest intent toward you."

"I'm no fool, Arch, if I am a kid," she rejoined. "I know when a man means bad by me. Lord knows I've had reason to. I shore knew today when Jocelyn grabbed me. . . . But Jim Traft didn't mean bad. I swear it."

"Molly, he must have talked you out of your haid," said Dunn, amazed.

"No. He didn't waste any time talkin'. I'd hardly got in the moonlight. It was that white dress, Arch."

"What white dress?"

"The one Mrs. See bought for me. It's lovely. He—they—everybody there said I looked—"

"You poor kid! Mebbe they was all to blame. Damn thet See woman, anyway."

"Arch, let me put on the dress for you."

"Molly, I don't need any white dress to know how pretty you are. . . . An' I reckon I hold ag'in' Traft your defendin' him."

"But that's not fair, Arch."

He shook his shaggy head doggedly.

"You cain't tell me honest thet Jim Traft didn't make you feel you was Molly Dunn of the Cibeque."

"No, Arch, I—I can't. He did. He was shore surprised. An' he let out what he thought. Afterward he tried to—to soften it. But—but then my heart was broke."

117

Dunn made a swifter and more expressive movement of his hand, passionate and vindictive.

"Hurtin' your feelin's thet way is a wuss insult than huggin' you," he declared, with a note of pathos in his anger.

"It hurt like sixty, Arch. But he didn't mean it. There *is* a difference between Molly Dunn of the Cibeque an' Jim Traft from the East—rich, educated, with family name."

"Ahuh. You said it, Molly. Family name. You're daughter of old John Dunn. An' sister to Slinger Dunn!"

"I told him that."

"Before or after?"

"It was after, of course."

"Shore it was. No, Mol, there ain't no overlookin' thet. He was only playin' with you. Shore, in some safer place he'd gone farther. Made a hussy of you!"

"*No!*" cried Molly, poignantly, as if at the thrust of a blade.

"An' you're givin' it away thet you'd let him go as far as he liked."

"Oh, Arch! How can you—talk so!" sobbed Molly. "That's a lie. *You're* insultin' me."

He shook his head gloomily, and averted his blazing eyes, to hide their thought from her. Then he strode away, leaving her there trembling and stricken.

12

FOR DAYS Molly lived in a perpetual state of nervous dread of events that had cast their shadows.

Arch remained in one of his brooding moods. He worked in the fields as if to make up for lost time. And he did not go to the village in the evenings. The Haverlys rode over every day or so and engaged him in long talks, which left Arch more taciturn than ever.

Then one morning when Molly came down she saw Arch's horse saddled and carrying a small pack.

"Where are you goin', Arch?" she asked, at breakfast.

"Up on the Diamond, an' I reckon you better stick around home," he replied, gruffly.

"What're you—goin' for?" she dared ask.

"Wal, fer one thing, to see if this outfit is lyin' to me. I didn't tell you thet Seth an' his new pard swear they posted a notice up north of the Diamond. They laid down the law fer thet drift fence. The Cibeque wouldn't stand fer the fence goin' farther than the haid of East Fork. Thet's in the saddle just under the Diamond. An' if it was built farther it'd be laid down pronto."

"What else you goin' for?" added Molly, anxiously.

"Wal, I reckon you ought to know," he replied, with a dark glance on her.

Molly in trepidation followed him out to his horse, where her mother would not hear. She laid a trembling hand on him, as he was about to mount. She did not know what to say. But terror of something possessed her. "Arch, if you really love me you—you won't—"

He stared down at her, arrested by her agitation if not her words.

"Who ever said anythin' aboot me lovin' you?" he asked.

"No one. But you *do,* don't you?" she implored. "Somebody must love me or—or I cain't live."

"You seem to've been tolerable healthy all along," he drawled. Nevertheless, he evaded the question.

"I've only you to help me, Arch," she went on, swiftly. "I'm tryin' hard not to run true to what they expect of Molly Dunn. An' I can be drove too far. I'll hate you if—if you—"

But he was flint. Molly gathered that her emotion somehow augmented his suspicions of her.

"You have run true to the Dunns, I reckon," he replied, bitterly, and rode away.

Molly hid up in the loft, tormented beyond endurance. When she could stand it up there no longer she climbed down and went out to look for her horse. She had not done her errands by horseback for a year or more, for the very good reason that she had no saddle and would not be seen in the village without one. The dignity of sixteen years had been embarrassing in many ways. Molly had ridden bareback since she was big enough to get on a horse.

She found the pony in the unfenced north end of the clearing. He was wild and she did not easily corner him. But finally, when she had him and was patting his neck she wondered what she had wanted him for. And she seemed struck with the fact that it was not beyond her to ride up on the Diamond to warn Jim Traft his life might be in danger. But worried as Molly was, she did not think that so dire a thing would threaten until the drift fence actually crossed the Diamond. Down in the valley the opinion was general that the barbed wire would never go so far. Moreover, Molly remembered more than once when Slinger Dunn had ridden off with intent to fight, and this morning he had not been like that.

Three days later, while Molly was in the village with her mother, she heard that her brother was there, drunk and quarrelsome. At the store she met Andy Stoneham, who was a clerk for Enoch Summers. While waiting upon Molly, he contrived to whisper: "Heaps goin' on, an' hadn't I better come out tonight?" Molly nodded, and joined her mother, conscious of a sinking sensation in her breast.

Old Enoch was full of talk. "High jinks goin' on around West Fork. Hain't been so busy since last fall round-up."

"What's goin' on?" queried Mrs. Dunn.

"Cattle movin'. Riders comin' through."

"This time of year! Well, that's strange."

"So it is, Mrs. Dunn. An' we can lay it to thet drift fence. Did you heah the latest aboot Jim Traft?"

"Where'd I ever hear any news?"

Molly felt the blood tingle in her cheeks.

"Wal, it's shore news," replied the storekeeper. "Young

Traft has had notices put up thet he'd make no claim to cattle already drifted down into Sycamore Canyon. His drift fence has crossed the head of Sycamore an' is now out on the Diamond."

"Well, is that all the news?" declared Mrs. Dunn, indifferently.

"Wal, most folks is agreed thet Jim Traft was shore more than square to the Cibeque when he done thet," went on Summers. "Mebbe there's more'n a thousand haid of steers, let alone cows an' calves, in the brakes of Sycamore. Seth Haverly an' his outfit sold near two hundred two-year-olds hyar yesterday. Forty-eight dollars a head! An' they've gone back fer another drive. Reckon they'll have most of thet stock, before the other boys get wind of it."

"Forty-eight a head!" ejaculated Mrs. Dunn, who appeared to be conjuring with figures. "Arch was in on that?"

"Wal, it seems not. He's had a fall-out with the Cibeque, or somethin'. Anyway, he was in town last night. It was Slinger who busted in here with news thet the drift fence had reached Tobe's Well. It shore upset all reckonin's around West Fork. Tobe's Well is way out on the Diamond."

While her mother completed her purchases, Molly waited in the grip of conflicting feelings. She could not help a thrill to hear Jim Traft kindly spoken of, nor a start at the information he had passed Sycamore Canyon with his fence. This was the dead line drawn by the riders of the brakes. Traft had disregarded their notice.

Molly calculated that he was then actually within ten miles of West Fork, and not more than forty, to the east end of the Diamond. She had ridden up and down the brakes of Beaver Canyon and knew the trail to Tobe's Well. She had also been over the Derrick Trail once, but had no confidence that she could remember how to find it.

After supper that evening she waited at the gate for Andy, something she had never before done, and she knew he would make stock of it.

121

"Shucks!" he ejaculated, when he arrived to beam upon her with his homely face. "It's different when you want suthin' of somebody, ain't it, Molly?"

"I reckon so, Andy. You see what bein' friendly does. I'm doin' a heap of worryin' an' I'm just low-down enough to want your help."

"Wal, you've cause to worry, Molly Dunn," he said. "Let's get out of sight somewhere. I'm plumb scared of thet Hackamore Jocelyn."

Molly led him back of the cabin along the edge of the clearing to the creek and halted beside a huge fallen pine. The amber creek babbled over the rocks below; the squirrels and jays were noisy; the woods was full of the golden glow of sunset.

"Molly, last night I happened on suthin' thet's got me scared stiff," he began. "After work hours I went up the crick to ketch a mess of trout. An' as I was comin' back along the crick trail I seen Seth Haverly an' some riders. I ducked into the brush an' squatted down. I reckoned they'd pass. But I'm a son-of-a-gun if they didn't stop in a little glade not forty steps from where I hid. With Seth was his brother Sam, an' Hack Jocelyn. The Haverlys stayed in their saddles. but Jocelyn got off. He acted oneasy. An' he walked up an' down the trail. They was waitin' fer some one."

"I'll bet it was Slinger," said Molly, who sometimes in excitement used her brother's sobriquet.

"It shore was. Wal, fust off, Jocelyn swore Slinger wouldn't come, an' Seth said he would. . . . Molly, they stayed there till dark an' I could repeat every blame word they said. But heah short an' sweet is what it all means. . . . Hack Jocelyn has got in with the Cibeque outfit, an' they're aimin' to double-cross Slinger. They're goin' to cut the drift fence an' lay the blame on to Slinger. They're goin' to kidnap Jim Traft an' squeeze a big ransom out of his uncle. Thet's the stake Jocelyn is playin' fer. But I seen, if Seth couldn't, thet Hack is playin' a deeper game than they savvy. Mebbe Slinger is on to him. 'Cause Slinger wouldn't heah of Jocelyn throwin' in with the Cibeque. He wouldn't go in the cattle drive they're plannin'. Thet all came out in their talk before Slinger got there."

"Oh—did he come?" cried Molly, breathlessly.

"Yep. Jest before dark. Hart Merriwell an' Boyd Flick was with him. 'Seth,' says Slinger, cool-like, 'I'm splittin' with the Cibeque. No hard feelin's. You've got mebbe a better man than me in Jocelyn. Anyway, I cain't take the share of this cattle money you sent me. Much obliged, Seth. An' heah it is.'

"An' then Seth says," went on Andy, after a pause, 'All right, Slinger. You're shore your own boss. An' if there's no hard feelin's on your side there's shore none on mine. But you ought to come in on thet kidnappin' deal. Why, it's a goldmine. Old Jim Traft won't blink an eye at a hundred thousand.'

"Slinger owned it was a pretty slick deal an' easy money, but he jest couldn't see it thet way.

"'An' why in hell not?' asked Seth, sore as a pup.

"'Wal,' says Slinger, 'I reckon there's more'n one reason. But particular with me is thet I happen to be goin' to shoot Jim Traft.'

"'So we figgered,' says Seth, 'but cain't you wait till we've got thet ransom money?'

"'Nope,' replies Slinger. 'I don't like the deal. An' if I happen to run into any of you Cibeque gents up on the Diamond, I'll take particular offense. Savvy thet?'

"'We ain't deaf, Slinger. But I, fer one, am shore plumb surprised,' answers Seth, slick-like.

"'Wal,' went on Slinger, 'I've been sort of surprised myself, lately.' . . . An' he shore said it full of meanin'. Slinger rode away then, an'—"

"You heahed all this last night?" interrupted Molly, poignantly.

"Yes, before sundown."

"But we heahed Slinger was drunk!"

"Nary drunk. Somebody lied to you. He was as cool an' hard as ice. Those fellars was scared of him, Molly. I haven't seen him since. Now to go on with what happened! You never heerd such cussin'. Some from Seth an' most from Jocelyn. Then they got their haids together

123

again. It was all right with them aboot Slinger goin' to kill young Traft. But they didn't want to spoil their stake. An' they reckoned they'd have to give up the ransom idee. Hack Jocelyn busts in then with another. An' it was that if Slinger did queer their kidnap deal by killin' Traft, they'd have a chanct to rustle a big bunch of stock an' lay thet on to Slinger also. This struck Seth an' his brother all right. An' they won over the other two fellars. Then they started off. One of the horses must have smelled me fer he shied an' didn't come far from jumpin' on me.

" 'Somethin' in thet brush,' said Jocelyn.

"By this time I was pretty scared an' I up an' tore through the brush. Mebbe Jocelyn didn't let out a roar. An' he shot three times after me. I don't want no bullets closer to me."

"Oh, Andy, they'll find you out," cried Molly, fearfully.

"Wal, mebbe, but I don't see how they can. I'd hate to have thet Hack Jocelyn meet up with me very soon, an' you bet I'll see him fust."

"But Jim Traft will never see Slinger first," wailed Molly.

"I reckon not. Molly, ain't you a little over-concerned aboot Traft?" asked Andy.

"No more than I am about Slinger," retorted Molly. "It's an awful mess. Oh, Andy, what can I do?"

"Do? Good Heavens! gurl, you cain't do nothin'," he declared. And his idea of the enormity of such a supposition made Molly conscious of her helplessness. Yet could she not ride up to Tobe's Well, find the Diamond camp, and save Jim Traft from both her brother and the Haverlys with their new and treacherous ally? Tobe's Well was only ten miles. She could ride there and back in less than half a day. If she once eluded Slinger! But she would have to wait until he left, for he might come home any time, and he would find her trail and run her down. It was not conceivable that he would ride directly into the Diamond camp bent on his deadly intent. Slinger was slow to act upon any project, secretive and wary. Like an Indian he would watch the trails.

Andy, roused to a sense of his importance, repeated parts of his story, and then guardedly leaned toward the possiblity of telling Slinger of the plot against him.

"Molly, you might let on you heerd all this yourself," continued Andy. "I reckon Slinger would believe you. Shore he would. An' thet'd let me out. I'm plumb afraid of Hackamore Jocelyn. He's got it in fer me because of you. Aw, I figgered thet. He only had to look at me onct."

"Andy, I'll not give you away," said Molly, earnestly. "An' I'm shore owin' you a good deal. . . . Yes, I ought to tell Slinger. Oh, I must think. . . . Andy, I'll go back now. I don't want to risk missin' him."

They walked through the woods in the gloaming, and Molly did not repulse Andy when he timidly took her hand. He deserved some recompense for his interest in her brother's fortunes and his loyalty to her.

She went as far as the gate with him. "Andy, you've been good to me lately," she said. "An' I like you for it. I haven't a friend in all this valley, unless it's you. I wish I could be more to you. But I—I cain't."

Bidding him good night, she ran back to the cabin. It was quite dark under the porch. No lamp had been lighted.

"You better come a-runnin'," came in a slow, cool voice from the gloom. "Who was thet with you? Looked like Andy."

"Oh—Arch—" panted Molly, feeling her way to the porch. "Yes, it was Andy."

"You like thet fellar?"

"Why, yes—more than I used to—which wasn't much."

"Wal, Andy ain't as no-good as some of them. He works. An' he doesn't guzzle drink all the time."

"Arch, are you goin' to be home a while now?" asked Molly, sitting down beside him. She bumped against his gun, which contact gave her an icy little shudder.

"Pa had one of his sinkin' spells tonight," said Arch, ignoring her query.

"He looked bad today," rejoined Molly, sighing. "Where's ma?"

"She got him to bed an' I reckon she's in there. . . . I been sittin' heah thinkin', Molly."

"What aboot?"

"Wal, fer once not aboot my own damn self. Pa's failin', an' ma's thet contrary. Course I'm home so little it don't matter. But it's tough on you, Molly. What're you goin' to do soon—when we bust up?"

"Oh—Arch!" faltered Molly, and she felt for his hand, slipping hers into it.

"Might as well face it," he went on. "I'm goin' to get killed or have to leave the Cibeque country. Pa won't last long. An' ma will go back to Illinois. Will you go with her?"

Molly pondered a long moment. "I wouldn't if she didn't make me. I'd hate to leave heah. . . . Arch, I can get work in Flag."

"Shore. An' it ain't a bad idee. But don't get any moonshine idees in your haid."

"What you mean, Arch?"

"Wal, aboot Jim Traft. Because you'll be in fer a heap more hurt than you've had."

Molly had fortified herself for the very thing hinted in his slow drawl, nevertheless it made her blood run cold.

"I'm shore in for more hurt any way you look at it," said Molly, sadly.

"Natural like. Life ain't no *fiesta* fer the Dunns. . . . If I'd only knowed when I was a kid what I know now!"

Molly thought the moment propitious.

"Arch, the Cibeque outfit is goin' to double-cross you. Hack Jocelyn is at the bottom of it. But Seth Haverly is as treacherous. They want you to throw in with them an' kidnap Jim Traft. Hold him for ransom. Course you know this, because you refused to be in it. But there's a lot you don't know.

"Wal, you darned little wood-mouse!" he ejaculated. "You was there last night?"

"Arch, I heahed more'n you," she replied, evasively.

"Ahuh. What was thet shootin' aboot, after I left?"

"Hack Jocelyn heahed a noise in the brush an' shot three times."

126

"Wal! I come darn near ridin' back. . . . Molly, what did you heah?"

Briefly then she told him what had happened along the trail, as related by Andy; and though the supposition was that she had been there she actually did not lie.

"—!" muttered Slinger Dunn, and he held her hand tight. "I had a hunch. I didn't trust Jocelyn. But thet Seth could be so low-down! My Gawd!"

"Arch, it couldn't be no worse," went on Molly, in agitation. "They mean to cut the drift fence an' lay it on to you. An' if the ransom deal falls through—owin' to you killin' Jim Traft—they'll rustle a big bunch of cattle. An' it'll all be laid on you!"

She felt him freeze, and he was silent so long that she could not restrain an appeal for him to abandon an idea of revenge and to go away somewhere.

"An' leave it easy fer them?" he queried, harshly. "I know their deal now. . . . I'll settle with them afterward."

He slipped off the porch. His moccasined feet made no sound and his dark form vanished in the gloom. Molly clapped a hand over her mouth. Of what avail to call out!

Shaken and wretched, she climbed to her loft and crawled to her bed. Through the hours of distress that followed, one growing resolve at last found permanence, and then she slept.

In the gray of dawn she was peering down from the loft, watching Slinger Dunn—when on the first time for long he rolled out of his bed on the porch and pulled on his boots and buckled on his spurs and gun-belt—when he slipped off in the gloom to return with his horse—when he packed blankets and biscuit and meat, and then rode away on his mission.

Molly sat there, thinking out her plan. She would let Slinger get some miles ahead, then she would follow, climb the Diamond, and when some distance from Tobe's Well she would make a detour and hit the trail beyond Traft's camp, and ride back to it. She could hardly get lost, going only a short way from the trail. The peril lay in being discovered by Slinger. He would probably half kill her. But if she accomplished her purpose and saved

Jim Traft from his enemies, she did not care what Slinger might do. In fact, that would be the end of Molly Dunn in the Cibeque. She would be hated from one end of the valley to the other. Traitress! A little fool who betrayed her brother and her kind for love of a man who had only played with her! An object of scorn she would be, and so far as Seth Haverly and Hack Jocelyn were concerned, she would be marked for life. Molly knew the Cibeque. Seth Haverly would choke the very life out of her, and Hack Jocelyn would do worse. These convictions added to Molly's terror, yet in no wise changed her mind.

Before her mother was up, Molly put on her buckskins and slipped down out of the loft with a blanket, which she carried out to the barn and strapped on her pony. She fed him grain. Then she coiled a lasso and tied it to the end of his halter.

The sun was rising like a rose in the cloudless sky. Dark and wild loomed the Diamond. It seemed to call to Molly, every moment added to her courage. She saw clearer the beauty and the good of her action, if it were successful. In time even her own people would see that.

"What you up early for?" demanded her mother.

"Didn't you heah Slinger?" asked Molly, who knew how to divert attention from herself.

"No, I didn't and you quit calling him that name," returned Mrs. Dunn, garrulously. "Haven't I told you enough?"

"Ma, if I guess right he's aimin' to add more to what gave him that name."

"Oh, Lord help us!" cried the mother, and she launched into a tirade against her son and ended against her husband and Molly and the low-down life in the brakes.

That likewise strengthened Molly. She made another resolve. If she got out of this adventure alive, she would ride to Keech's and hire the boy there to drive her to Flagerstown. There she would go to work. Molly roused to a glamour over this enterprise.

After breakfast, the first moment that offered, she ran

to the barn, and leading Jigger out she mounted him and rode into the woods.

Soon she came to the trail, in the dust of which she espied the tracks of Slinger's horse, and turning into it she rode north. Jigger was not shod and his hoofs padded softly. He could not be heard very far, and Molly vowed that she would see any rider before he saw her.

It was still and cool in the forest, and she soon reached the zone where the Diamond cut off the morning sunlight. Here the dark shade was almost like twilight. The trail followed the creek and often crossed it. The amber water foamed around the boulders. Great gray rocks lined the banks, and above stood the maples and oaks, and the lofty pines and spruces.

At every turn of the trail Molly would peep around before going on. Always, too, she had a keen eye for Slinger's tracks. This was easy riding and there were miles of the gradual ascent before the trail entered one of the brakes, which was merely a local name for canyon. Open forest, with scarcely any brush, afforded vistas on all sides. Molly saw deer, but no cattle. She was still down out of the cattle zone.

In a few miles the forest changed and thickened. The maples and oaks had been left behind. Clumps of young pine obstructed vision. The silver spruces began to lord it over the yellow pines. Manzanita appeared, and tufts of grass in open spots. Molly had difficulty in keeping the charm of the forest from breaking her vigilance. The wall of brown-streaked green rose on both sides. Through openings in the foliage she saw the lofty gray crags of the Diamond promontories. Soon she would be climbing in earnest, and then she must exercise extreme caution.

Presently she missed Slinger's tracks in the dust of the trail. Molly rode back, bending in anxious scrutiny. She had been careless. Soon she found where he had turned out of the trail. Molly slipped off her horse. What could this mean? She dared not go on for fear she might get ahead of him. Perhaps he was going to climb the Diamond by a trail known only to himself. Molly stood in dismay, pondering the problem.

Suddenly a rifle-shot clear and sharp up the trail gave her a violent start. A wild cry followed. Molly stood transfixed. Then came the clatter of rapid hoof beats. She drew her horse behind a thicket of pines.

13

JIM TRAFT, resting on the soft, fragrant matt behind a spruce tree, and waiting for the call to supper, inadvertently heard conversation most assuredly not intended for his ears.

"Nope. You cain't deal no more cairds to me," Curly Prentiss was saying to some one. "I won't take a hand in any more deals against the boss."

"But, Curly, we all reckon you wasn't at your best when he licked you," rejoined Uphill Frost.

"How so?"

"Wal, you'd been drunk. An' you know how weak likker makes you. An' you was sort of in fun. You didn't get mad."

A silence betrayed that no doubt this eloquence and persuasion were balm to Curly's wounded vanity.

"Mebbe so. Dog-gone! ... But he hit me on the nose an' seen how it hurt. Then he kept pokin' me again right there. An' thet's what he'll do to you, Up. He'll find out how anythin' ag'in' your belly hurts you. Aw, you know you cain't even stand a tight belt. You've et so many million sour-dough biscuits thet your insides is gone. An' you, Jack Way, if you pick a fight with our boss, Gawd help you! Because you're all weak spots. You've not got a well bone in your body. An' ev'ry time he cracks you with one of them big fists, you'll yell. I'll bet a month's pay."

"Take you up. Heah thet, Frost," grumbled Way. "Fact is, though, I'm afeard he will lick me. He shore put it all over Lonestar last Saturday. But we gotta fight him. *Somebody* has gotta do it or the Diamond is done fer on the range."

"Don't you believe sech talk!" declared Curly. "We're doin' a big stunt with this fence. Boys, the boss is a chip of the old block."

"Hack Jocelyn says so an' Hack's an old-timer heah."

"You'd be smart not to listen to him," replied Curly, in lower tone. "Hack's out fer trouble. Not fun! He's stuck on Molly Dunn an' he cain't stand fer the Flag talk aboot the boss winnin' Molly. There'll be a fight one of these days as will be a *real* one. An' I wanna see it."

"Natural you'd like to see Hack get licked proper," growled Frost.

"You can shore bet on thet," said Curly, emphatically.

"Wal, you an' Bud have double-crossed us," complained Jackson. "Bud is clean out with it. He says: 'You can all go to hell. I'm sidin' with the boss.'"

"Boys, you cain't blame Bud much. The boss kept me out of jail, but thet ain't a marker to what he done fer Bud. An' if you look back hasn't this heah Jim Traft done somethin' fer each of us, 'ceptin' mebbe, Hack? Now I ask you?"

Both cowboys were significantly silent.

"I'm gonna pick a fight with him, anyway," concluded Up Frost. "He's sore at me an' it'll be easy."

"When you aim to pick it?"

"I had my mind made up more'n onct. But when I get near the son-of-a-gun, I don't stick to it."

"Ahuh. You jest cain't help likin' Jim Traft. If Hack Jocelyn wasn't in the outfit we'd all be fer the boss pronto."

"Up, if you tackle him, I'll do it, too, soon's he licks you," put in Jackson Way. "An' mebbe we can get Cherry to try ag'in, if he licks me."

"If? Haw! Haw! Say, you couldn't hire Cherry to stand up ag'in under them sledge-hammer fists. Fer fact is he was sittin' down all the time."

131

"Wal, we can get Hump to tackle it."

"I don't know. He an' Hump's been tolerable civil lately. It's workin' on Hump."

"Curly, air you helpin' to keep this outfit from bustin'?" queried Frost, scornfully.

"I reckon I am," replied Prentiss, in colder knife-edged tone. "An' you can expect trouble between me an' Jocelyn any day."

"Hell you say!"

"Wal, Jack, I told you. . . . Let's go an' try to talk Hump into suthin'."

The cowboys strolled away into camp, arguing and complaining, while Jim Traft lay there amused and touched and singularly pleased. This incident occurred at a camp on Pine Creek in the forest on what was called the Saddle. It lay half way between Black Butte and the Diamond. Not for weeks had Jim seen or heard anything so encouraging to him. He could not contain his delight. The drift fence was going on. He had not been in Flagerstown for weeks, but letters from his uncle kept him informed of the news at that end of the fence. He had long since worked and ridden out the soreness of muscle and bone, that had made him suffer so excruciatingly. He was now strong and hard. He could stick in a saddle. He could dig fence-post holes all day. In truth he seemed vastly changed and improved, and almost happy, despite periodic spells of depression. The months did not pale Molly Dunn's charm.

The call to supper disturbed Jim's reverie. He got up, and keeping the thick, low-spreading spruce tree between him and camp he walked off into the woods, and circling, came back to camp on the other side. Meantime he had evolved a plan to help Uphill Frost and Jackson Way to realize their ambitions in regard to a physical clash with him. The prospect simply filled him with glee.

He found the boys at supper, and a sudden cessation of voices proved he had interrupted something unusual, for cowboys seldom talked during their brief meal-time.

"Sorry to spoil your talk, boys," he said, with sarcasm

and putting on a severe face. "But I can't go without my meals to let you gab about me."

"Boss, you might flatter yourself," replied Bud Chalfack.

"Sure. But not this time," said Jim, as he surveyed the mask-like faces. "Hack looks mighty innocent and indifferent. The rest of you, though, strike me bad."

"We was only talkin' aboot the fence," put in Frost. "Me an' Jack stand by our argyment of this mawnin'. You're runnin' thet line wrong lately, keepin' to this thick woods hyar."

"Well, tomorrow we'll run off a way, then, into the open draws. And I'll give you and Jack the job of digging post-holes for a few days."

A long howl of mirth made the welkin ring. After that had subsided Uphill and Jackson rendered the air blue around camp.

Jim stood it a while and then, though it was not out of the ordinary, he pretended to take exception to such profanity.

"Shut your dirty mouths," he ordered. "If you want to rave you can do it without such cuss words."

"Wha-at!" bawled Uphill. "Ain't this hyar a free range? Cain't I open my mouth?"

"Why don't you eat with it? This is supper time. And the rest of us are hungry."

"You heerd thet, Jack," roared Up, in real or assumed wrath.

"I shore did," yelled Jack.

Whereupon the two of them burst out into another long string of profanity. Jim got up and deliberately punched Uphill in the mouth and then Jack. That certainly and effactually stilled the profanity, as well as all other vociferations.

"After supper I'll oblige you boys with all the satisfaction you want," said Jim, sitting down again.

Uphill's face was brick red and he appeared about to explode.

"You bet—you will—boss," he choked.

Jackson Way bent thoughtfully over his supper, with

the somber air of a boy who had been let into something unawares.

Another silence fell. This time Hackamore Jocelyn broke it.

"So the Diamond's come to this!" he exclaimed, in derision. "My Gawd! no wonder we're the talk of the range."

Jim bent a clear straight gaze upon his one real enemy.

"Jocelyn, the Diamond is doing fine, according to reports from Flag," he said, deliberately. "And I can see how it could do better."

"Ahuh. So can I," replied Jocelyn, with far less subtlety than Jim's.

"Aw, hell," interposed Bud Chalfack, "there ain't no outfit on the range thet could run this drift fence."

"Wal, cowboy, you mean would run it, an' thet's no lie," returned Jocelyn, sneeringly.

"All stale talk, Hack," spoke up Jim. "Can't you think of something new? I sure get tired of it. You've got a reputation for hatching up tricks and deals. Why can't you be original in your gab? It'd amuse us, anyhow."

Jim had spoken cheerfully, yet with scintillating pointedness. And this remark fell like a blanket upon the company. Most of the cowboys took a bold look at Jocelyn, to see what effect this strong talk from the boss might have. Jocelyn's lean face paled and he bent over his plate. The tension relaxed, but Jim felt that he had inserted a wedge into the breach.

Uphill Frost finished his meal in remarkably quick time for him. And he arose to make most elaborate preparations for the fray.

"Boss, tell me where you want your carcass planted," spoke up Bud, quizzically. "An' give me word to send home."

That resurrected the humor of the cowboys, except in several instances.

"Any money to bet, Up?" inquired Curly.

"This ain't goin' to be fun," quoth Frost.

"I should smile not. Lay you ten to one you cain't lick Jim."

"Jim!" ejaculated Uphill, with a fierce snort. "Who's Jim?"

"Why, our boss, you damn fule," replied Curly, innocently.

Jim got up with alacrity, and threw off his vest.

"Bud, you be my second," he said, cheerily. "Fetch those soft gloves of mine."

Bud complied and Jim pulled them on. These were heavy, soft, woolen gloves that Jim wore occasionally.

"Let me see? What's the idee of gloves?" asked Uphill, suspiciously.

"I don't want to hurt you badly, Up. These gloves are like pads."

"You don't say. Wal, you might have a hoss-shoe or nail hid in them. Lemme see. . . . Ahuh, I'll take my chanct with your bare fists."

"Come on. Let's get it over," said Jim, business like. "We've fence to build, you know."

After a few passes at each other Uphill swung in like a snorting bull, and Jim making a feint with his right came up hard with his left. It connected. Bam!

Up got rid of breath he could not retain.

"Wow!" yelled Curly.

"Got Up's bread-basket fust off," added Bud, merrily.

"Fellars, we'd better move back," suggested Cherry. "Fer if the boss soaks him thar ag'in we'll be dodgin' biscuits."

Up had begun valiantly, evidently adhering to a preconceived plan of battle. Jackson Way behind him kept calling encouragements. They danced around, and presently Jim ran in to take a couple of blows in order to plant another, at the pit of Up's stomach. *Biff!* It had a solid sound. Up let out a groan. His face changed remarkably, and from that instant he became a changed man. He left his face and head wholly unguarded, endeavoring to stem the attack on his lower anatomy. Jim could have landed at will on nose or eye or chin. But he wanted to hit Up's weak spot and he fought accordingly. He got in two or three blows, glancing ones, and not quite on the mark. Yet they spread consternation and terror to poor

135

Up's heart. He had nothing left to get enraged upon. He grew mortally afraid that he would sustain another blow in his vital spot. And he made a ludicrous spectacle.

Hack Jocelyn stood in the background, smoking a cigarette, disdainful and aloof. The other cowboys, including Jackson Way, gave vent to their riotous feelings.

Jim took the fight in hand then.

"You cussin' cowpuncher," he said, imitating the vernacular of his men. "You lazy hole-diggin' gopher! Take this one in the gizzard.". . . . *Wham!* . . . "You bow-legged, biscuit-eatin' rhinoosceross!" . . . Pop!—"Right on the kisser! Forgot you had a face, hey, Up? Look out now." . . . Crack! Smack! . . . *Zugg!*

That last one, a solid blow over Up's rather stout middle, elicited an awful groan from him. He sagged, and bent forward like a jack-knife.

"Fer Gawd's sake!" gasped Up, his face convulsed. "Boss, don't hit me—there—no more."

Jim lowered his fists and ceased prancing around the bewildered cowboy.

"Very well. Have you got enough?"

"A plenty," groaned Up.

"All right, then, provided you call it square for keeps and shake hands. Otherwise—"

"Boss," interrupted Frost, hostilely, "I've been ag'in you, jest natural an' cussed. But there was no sense in it. An' hyar you are!"

Uphill showed the true manliness back of his contrary, cowboy, cantankerous spirit.

"Now, Jack, come on. It's the only way for us to settle the difficulty."

"I reckon so, boss," returned Jack, ruefully. "But it ain't fair."

"Why not? Sure, I didn't start this. If you want to apologize—"

"Nope. I ain't takin' nothin' back. But my pore body has too many sprains an' dislocations an' cracks to stand your hammerin'. All the same, I'll take my medicine."

And he did take it, putting up a better fight than Frost's, though of obvious pain to himself and less fun for

136

the cowboys. He brought the blood from Jim's nose, an inconsequential blow, yet one loudly applauded by his companions. Shortly after that Jim caught him in the ribs. Jack went down in a heap, rolled over, and laboriously sat up, his face ashen.

"Jim—it was—bad enough—hittin' all my other—places," he panted. "But them busted—ribs! I knowed you'd find them. . . . Would you mind—callin' if off fer keeps?"

"If you want," replied Jim. "But you've bloodied my nose! And I reckon I'd like to soak you some more."

"Aw no! Take it out on Hackamore," replied Jack, beseechingly, and he got up to offer his hand to Jim.

His suggestion instantly charged the atmosphere with something more compelling.

"Strikes me," said Jim, quickly. "How about it, Jocelyn? You've a sore head. You've been mean and full of poison talk. And I haven't been as decent as I might have been. Let's have a whack at each other. It can't do any harm and it might do good."

"I wouldn't soil my gloves on you, Mister Traft," drawled Jocelyn, with undisguised malignity.

"Oh, wouldn't you? I reckon you're thinking more of your handsome face."

"Yep, I ben told it's handsome lately, an' I'm shore keepin' it so," returned Jocelyn, with caustic significance. No one there could have misinterpreted him.

Jim bit his tongue. It was no time for him to say more or make a move. Jocelyn packed his gun and had the look of a man who would strain any chance to use it.

That incident marked the definite break between Jim and Jocelyn. There was no hope of a better state of feeling. Jim hoped this disgruntled cowboy would keep to his threat to quit the Diamond. But Bud and Curly had warned Jim to let Hack alone to take his own time. They assured Jim that Hack would go presently, but they could not quite figure just what he was up to. Jim was glad of their advice and this late evidence of friendship. It seemed, indeed, that Jocelyn was now the only thorn in the flesh of the Diamond. Day by day he became more alienated from Cherry Winters and Hump Stevens, who had been the last of his stand-bys.

Another Saturday came. Some of the boys went to Flagerstown. Hack had disappeared before daylight, and according to Bud and Curly his horse tracks led south.

"Boss, he's gone to West Fork," claimed Bud, with a wise look.

"Shore as you're born," agreed Curly, wagging his bright head.

"Curly, let's ride down there, too," suggested Bud.

The idea found favor with Curly, who looked at Jim for approval.

"It ain't a bad idee, boss. We'll hit the Sycamore trail at Tobe's Well an' go off the mountain there. Thet's aboot at the haid of the brakes. We'll get a line on driftin' cattle, an' mebbe other thin's, too."

"Go, by all means," replied Jim, and he found himself fighting an almost irresistible longing to go with them.

That was the longest week-end Jim had put in since his advent in Arizona. He was on pins and needles until Bud and Curly returned, late Sunday night. To his disappointment, they seemed uncommunicative and brought no news of any moment. They had not seen Hackamore Jocelyn. They did not mention either Slinger or Molly Dunn. They reported considerably more cattle than they had expected to run across. Numerous dead cows, and old carcasses, neither of which had been killed by wolves or lions, lying in the open along the trails, attested to a changed and startling condition of affairs since the drift fence had been started.

Jim was too sick at heart to go into the subject of stolen stock any deeper that night. What had he expected of the boys? When he lay alone in the dark, his eyes peering through the canopy of foliage at the stars, he confessed to himself that he had yearned for even a word of Molly Dunn. Next morning at an opportune moment he asked Bud.

"Shore I seen Molly," replied the cowboy, frankly. "At the village. But she didn't see me. Looked sweeter'n a

138

peach to me. Changed a little, though, somehow. Curly says so."

"Did you hear anything about Hack?"

"Yep. An' it ain't good news," replied Bud, soberly. "Curly reckoned we'd better not tell you."

"Why not?"

"Wal, you might ride off down there."

"Bud, tell me if there's anything to worry you."

"It ain't worryin' us exzactly," rejoined Bud, scratching his head. "I wanted to tell you, an' Curly talked ag'in' it."

"Jocelyn went to see Molly Dunn," asserted Jim, quietly.

"He shore did, which ain't none of our bizness, since thet little devil has no use for us. But, boss, this is damn queer. Hack is makin' up to the Haverlys. An' thet means the Cibeque outfit!"

"Well, what of it? I wish he'd quit us, as he's hinted."

"What of it? Gosh! I don't know. But if Hack quits us I'll shore tell you what Curly an' I think."

Hackamore Jocelyn did not ride into camp until late Monday night. This was a break against rules, and Jim saw that the cowboys were keen to get his reaction to it.

"Where've you been, Jocelyn?" he asked.

"Down in the brakes to see my gurl," replied the cowboy, almost gayly. He had not been drinking. There seemed to be a singular elation or buoyancy about him.

"Why didn't you get back Sunday night, same as Curly and Bud? They went down to West Fork."

"Hell you say!" In a twinkling Jocelyn was his old self. "Wal, if you want to know I was havin' too sweet a time with Molly."

"I'm not inquiring into your private affairs," said Jim coldly. "But if you take another day off without permission, I'll fire you. . . . Do you understand?"

"Wal, I ain't hard of hearin', Mister Traft," replied Jocelyn, softly.

No more was said. Jocelyn ate his supper alone. The cowboys sat silent. Jim sought his bed presently, and tried to find ease from his pain in slumber.

The drift fence went on mile after mile, and one camp followed another. Three week-ends in succsssion Jocelyn rode down to West Fork, but on each occasion he returned some time late on Sunday night. The other cowboys ceased riding to Flagerstown. Curly and Bud rode off alone the second week-end, evidently bent on a mission of their own, which Jim guessed to be the movement of cattle, as well as of Hackamore Jocelyn.

Early in August, Jim Traft, acting solely upon his own judgment and responsibility, celebrated his fencing off the many heads of Sycamore Canyon from the brakes of the Cibeque, by posting notices that the Diamond would lay no further claim to stock in and north of Sycamore, and west of the drift fence.

It was a strategic move on Jim's part. It caught the fancy of every cowboy in his outfit, excepting Jocelyn, who, nevertheless, was staggered by it. Jim had just wanted to be generous to the riders down in the brakes. He had authority to do what he thought best. What did a few herds of cattle, more or less, matter to his uncle? But a singular reaction to this proclamation was the effect upon his cowboys and the several homesteaders living in the proscribed limits. Jim won his cowboys by that act, and further alienated Jocelyn. The homesteaders called at his camp, unmistakably friendly and grateful. They all profited by it. One of them told Bud that he could now make a good start at ranching.

"He was stealin' a few cattle right along," vowed Bud. "An' he admitted it. Any honest cattleman will admit he's run a few haid not strictly his. . . . Dog-gone it, boys, Jim Traft has hit one plumb center."

But so far as Jim was concerned this splendid news, which he knew would travel like wild-fire all over the range, was more than offset by Jocelyn's talk. The shrewd cowboy had divined how his talk about West Fork and Molly Dunn hurt Jim, and after that he kept everlastingly at it at meal hours or round the camp fire. At first it was just conceited comments upon his girl and her attachment to him. Gradually, however, it developed into a vulgar parade of conquest, at which times Jim would make himself scarce. It threatened worse, and Jim vowed if he heard any more derogatory to Molly Dunn that he would force the issue with Jocelyn, come what might, and dismiss him from the Diamond.

In mid-August the drift fence, now up on the great triangular promontory, received its first backset from enemies. Half a dozen stretches, where it crossed the heads of Rocky Canyon, had been laid low, with wire cut and hopelessly tangled, and posts broken down. Two days of hard labor were required to repair the damage. Jim had his consolation in the slow anger of the cowboys. It frightened him, too, for he now saw indications of his uncle's prophecy coming true.

"Boss, let me trail them hoss tracks," begged Curly Prentiss. "I can find out in two days who cut our wire."

"Suppose you do, Curly. What good will that do?"

"Wal, we can stop it from happenin' ag'in. An', Jim, shore as Gawd made little apples it will happen, onless we hit thet trail."

"How do you propose to stop it?" queried Jim, aghast at the flashing-eyed cowboy.

"Thet's fer you to say, after we ketch these hombres."

"Well, let's wait a little. A few miles of wire, a few days' extra work—what's that to us? I'll admit, though, if they keep on we'll be up a stump."

"Shore. We cain't help matters by waitin'. Bud an' I agree it's thet Cibeque outfit, though we cain't prove it."

"Prentiss," spoke up Jocelyn bitingly, "I reckon you know it's onhealthy to speak names when you cain't prove nothin'."

"Hack, I can shore prove one thing damn pronto," snapped Curly.

"An' what's thet?"

"I take offense at your speakin' up fer the Cibeque."

"Ahuh. But what does thet prove?"

"It proves you can git my game any minnit."

"Wal, if thet's so there ain't any helluva rush. I've a date with my gurl, Molly, on Sunday, an' I shore wouldn't want to miss thet."

"Aw, you're a liar, Hack!" retorted Curly, passionately.

141

Jim got between the two, and by backing Curly away from the camp fire he prevented more trouble for the present.

"Boss, he makes me see red," raved Curly, when they were alone. "I could uv stood his crack aboot the Cibeque, 'cause Bud an' I don't know shore who cut the fence. But he's all the time throwin' pore little Molly Dunn up to me. I liked her orful well, Jim. An' I cain't believe she's thick with him. I cain't. Mebbe she is. But I jest cain't believe it. He's a — liar!"

"Thick!" echoed Jim.

"Shore. He claims he's thick with Molly. Haven't you heahed him?"

"No. What do you mean by thick?"

"Wal, it's pretty low-down fer a gurl as sweet an' young as Molly."

"But you— It might be true?"

"Hell yes. Thet's what hurts so. Shore he'll marry her sooner or later, if it's true. Gurls like Molly don't grow on all the bushes. An' I reckon most uv the cowboys would take her if she *was* a d— little hussy. Bud swore he would."

"How about you, Curly?" asked Jim, in strangely level voice.

"I would, too. In a minnit," replied Curly, with his fair head lifting in a way to thrill Jim. "What chance has thet pore kid had? Her father's no good. An' they say her mother will cock her eye at a cowboy. An' Slinger Dunn! He'd be enough to ruin any gurl."

Jim made no immediate reply. He sat on his bed and pulled the petals off a tiny aster, which he had absent-mindedly plucked. Twilight was stealing down through the forest, melancholy and tranquil. The heat of the day was dissipating. A bell on one of the hobbled horses tinkled musically. The vast forest sighed with a breath of breeze, moving down from the heights.

"Curly, I wish I were as much of a man as you are," said Jim presently.

"Aw, boss, thet's nonsense! You shore are an' more," burst out Curly, nonplussed yet pleased. "It's bin a drill

142

fer you—this Diamond job. But the outfit's with you. Honest, Jim, an' heah's my hand on it. We caint' count Jocelyn. But to hell with him! He's bin a disturber always, an' he's growed wuss. I reckon you'd better fire him pronto."

"Curly, I couldn't answer for my temper—if I faced him again tonight," replied Jim, unsteadily. "Perhaps tomorrow or soon."

"Jim, ain't you takin' this hombre too serious? After all, you're boss of the Diamond. An' who's Hack Jocelyn?"

"It's not who he is, but what he claims, that's dug into me," replied Jim, frankly, lifting his head.

"Claims! You mean aboot Molly?" asked Curly, incredulously.

"Yes. Only I take it harder than you, Curly."

"Fust Bud, an' then me, an' now you! Aw! . . . Who'd ever thunk it? Thet black-eyed little devil."

"Curly, I'd bet my life she's decent," declared Jim, with emotion.

"So would I. But it's a long shot, an' we're takin' odds!"

14

THE DAY came when Jim Traft had his first look at the country from the rim of the Diamond.

It was from the western promontory under which the Cibeque curled like a winding snake. The rest was endless green, relieved by bare spots and gray specks, which were the homesteads of the inhabitants. West Fork lay almost under the rim, a few cabins and fields, a gray line of road between some houses. Far to the south the dense forest began to lose its grip and showed bare grass flats and ridges. Westward the slopes ran up in long slants, like the ribs of a washboard, ending in a craggy mountain range.

Standing above the forest to look back through the wilderness he had built the drift fence, Jim gazed down over a gradual descent to the open cattle country, rolling and vast and dotted, ending in deep purple distance.

The splendid panorama transported Jim. He gazed long, and ever his eyes traveled back to the picturesque little homestead in the bend ot the Cibeque, where he imagined Molly Dunn lived. He could see a log cabin, a ragged clearing in the woods, and tiny specks that must have been cattle or horses.

He lingered there a long while. This, his first sight of Arizona land from a lofty prospect, had staggered him with its vastness, its magnificence, its tremendous note of solitude and the wild. For weeks a subtle happiness in his surroundings had been almost imperceptibly stealing over Jim. He had grown to love the forest and life in the open. He could not hate this beautiful wilderness, because through it he had received the cruelest hurt he had ever suffered. And when at length he clambered over the rocks, up to a level and to his horse, he realized that Arizona had claimed him.

On the way back to camp, while riding across one of the grassy draws which headed on the western side of the Diamond, Jim found another placard nailed to a tree. It was identical with one Hackamore Jocelyn had brought in from the head of Sycamore, and its crude misspelled message read the same. This one, however, had a round black spot in the center. Upon tearing the placard loose Jim saw that the spot was a bullet hole. It stirred a curious heat in his veins. And he was reminded of Curly's admonition, not to ride around alone through the forest. "To be honest aboot it, boss, I'm more afeared Hack Jocelyn will take a shot at you than one of these Cibeque hombres," said Curly.

"Curly! I can't believe that of Jocelyn," expostulated Jim. "It's not hard to believe it of Slinger Dunn. But one of my own men. No!"

"Wal, heah you are—the same old tenderfoot! You're daid wrong, Jim. Jocelyn would do thet little thin' if he had a chance. Mebbe it's on his mind an' thet's why he hangs on heah. But Slinger Dunn would never shoot you or no other man in the back."

"You rate Slinger Dunn above Jocelyn as a man?" queried Jim, in surprise.

"Lord! yes. An' it's hard to explain, boss. But you'll get it some day. . . . Please take another hunch from me. An' from this next camp we're makin' I'm advisin' you to have one man whose job is to keep back off the fence line an' watch."

"That's not a bad idea, Curly," replied Jim. "You can take turns, one man a day. But it'll slow us up."

"Listen, Jim. This heah drift fence won't be done this fall, an' what with patchin' it up an' savin' our hides, we'll shore be next year on the job, an' then some more."

"Gosh! Curly, but you're a pessimistic cuss."

"Wal, I don't know jest what thet is, but I reckon it's a compliment."

Next day Jim moved camp to Quaking Asp and inaugurated the scout duty for one man. It was hailed with satisfaction, except in the case of Jocelyn, who ridiculed it as another "new-fangled idee from Missourie."

"That lets you out, Jocelyn," retorted Jim, like a flash. "I don't know as I would have trusted you, anyhow, with a job so important as that."

This was throwing down the gauntlet with a vengeance, and certainly against the advice of Curly and Bud.

"Mister Traft, you're gettin' mighty pert these days," returned Jocelyn, the ugly expression changing his handsome face.

"Yes. I'm finding out what little good it does to be civil to some people."

"Ahuh. Wal, your wise joke was more'n oncivil, I take it."

"Jocelyn, you can take that crack of mine any way you like."

"Shucks! We're shore bustin' out brave now."

"Keeping my mouth shut in the past wasn't proof I was

afraid of you, Hack Jocelyn. I've politely invited you to fight—twice. Beware of the third time."

Bud slouched in between the belligerents, sloe-eyed, and hard of face for him, but he did not speak.

"Shore," drawled Jocelyn, with that peculiarly mean note. "I know you invited me to a fist fight. An' I couldn't take you on. My sweetheart won't have me all bunged up."

Jim felt the cold tightening of his skin, which heralded the receding of blood from his face. Either this crafty cowboy had guessed his secret or he had learned something from Molly Dunn. And in the passion of the moment Jim inclined to the latter suspicion. If he replied to Jocelyn, or even glanced at him, there would be no more possiblity of restraint. Yet Jim quivered in his eagerness to get his hands on Jocelyn. Curly saved the situation for him.

"Hack, you ain't showin' much respect for our boss," he said, and interposed his long frame before Jocelyn.

That worthy let out a guffaw. "It ain't so long thet you did the same. Now you're eatin' out of his hand. Wal, Curly Prentiss, you lay to this. Heah's one who'll never do it."

"Reckon none of us figgered you would. Hack, you may have the edge on me an' Hump, an' mebbe Lonestar, when it comes to years on the range. But we ain't quite looney."

This droll speech, delivered in apparent good humor, effectually silenced Jocelyn, who without more ado left the group.

"Boss, I'd reckon he'll last heah till one more pay day," ended Curly. But several of the boys, outspoken and less humorous, took issue with him on that score.

Another Saturday arrived, and at noonday, when the cowboys knocked off for the week, Jocelyn, with more than usual of his donning his best and gaudiest, made a parade of his start for West Fork.

Jeff Davis, the dumb cook, electrified Jim and prostrated the cowboys.

"I'm a quiet man an' I like peace," he began, in a

perfectly clear and resonant voice. "Thet's why I never talk. But that — — — a Jocelyn has got me riled. An' if some of you — — cowpunchers don't shet him up, I'll slip some coyote poison in the — meat!"

Such profanity had never before been heard in the Diamond camp, at least since Jim had taken charge. The boys gave the cook wide-eyed and gaping stares, then after their usual manner when enraptured, they whooped like Indians and rolled on the ground. Upon partial recovery they delivered themselves with characteristic remarks.

"Our tongue-tied cook!"

"Deaf an' *dumb!* Haw! Haw!

"An' mebbe he cain't cuss!"

No other of the Diamond outfit left camp that weekend. They had a lazy, jolly time of it, interspersed with some thoughtful conferences about the obstacles ahead. Jim could not feel that they had accepted him as one of them yet, but they had changed so materially that their humor had lost its sting.

At Quaking Asp a stream of cold water ran down into the canyon, and half a mile below the rim there were pools full of fine trout. Bud took Jim fishing. Now it chanced that fishing had always been Jim's favorite pastime, but he had never seen a rainbow trout. The tackle was not much, Bud averred; merely hooks and lines which he dug out of his kit. They cut poles and caught grasshoppers for bait. Jim had the most thrilling few hours of his Western experience, always putting aside those fatal hours with Molly Dunn. He caught a number of nice trout, and Bud caught a string as heavy as he wanted to pack uphill. When they arrived at camp with fresh fish for supper they were received with vociferous acclaim.

On Sunday they assayed to go again, and Curly begged to be taken. He was put to catching grasshoppers, and the spectacle of that long-legged, awkward-running cowboy, whooping wildly and batting grasshoppers with his huge sombrero, was something to see.

They had a great day on the brook, the climax of which was when Curly slipped off a rock and fell in to his neck.

It wanted an hour to sunset when they arrived in camp. To Jim's amaze Hack Jocelyn had just ridden in and had kicked his chaps off. Jim's quick eyes noted the cowboy's gun belt hanging on the pommel of his saddle. The sight seemed to make every fiber in Jim leap. Jocelyn presented a marked contrast to the debonair braggart of a courtier who had left for West Fork only the day before. His garb looked as if he had slept in a hay-loft. His face was haggard, dark, and sullen. Not many hours past he had been under the influence of liquor.

If Jocelyn saw the approach of Jim and his companions, he gave no evidence of it, but went on in forceful harangue to Cherry Winters and Lonestar.

Jim caught the tail end of a speech that drew him up, strong and sharp. He dropped his string of trout. In a few strides he was upon Jocelyn, and with hard hand jerked him round.

"Were you speaking of Molly Dunn?" he demanded.

"Wal, if it's any of your — mix, yes, I was," returned Jocelyn, deliberately, and the way he squared himself and dropped his right hand to his side was not to be overlooked. Only he had forgotten that his gun hung in his belt over the pommel of his saddle.

"Jocelyn, you're fired," rang out Jim.

"Nope. Beat you to it, Traft. I quit," replied Jocelyn.

"When?"

"Wal, if I recollect, it was yestiddy."

"All right. Get out of my camp. You can't even eat here."

"Traft, thet ain't Western—to send a man out hungry," said Jocelyn, darkly.

"Is it Western to speak vilely of a girl?" flashed Jim, hotly.

"Depends on thet gurl, Mister Traft."

"Jocelyn, what you said *may* be true, though, by God! I think you're a liar! One way or another you're a dirty skunk!"

Then Jim lunged out with all the fury of might and grief. His big fist covered one of Jocelyn's malignant eyes. The cowboy fell over the bench, knocking Winters down. Jim leaped after them, and plunged upon Jocelyn, to kick him fiercely, and then fall on him like a battering-ram.

Curly was the first to leap and grasp Jim. But he could do nothing.

"Help, somebody!" he yelled. "Bulldog him, Bud! . . . There! . . . Why, boss, shore you'd killed the fellar. Come now. . . . You shore lost your temper."

Between them they dragged Jim off the bloody-faced Jocelyn, who sat up groggily.

"Some of you—lead him out of—camp," panted Jim, struggling for breath. "Then come back for his horse and pack. . . . And his wages, too."

Jim turned away unsteadily, with Bud still holding his arm. "Let go!" growled Jim, roughly. "Or I'll biff you one."

"Boss, I ain't fit to face my Maker jest yet," drawled Bud, complying with this command.

They crossed to where Jim had his bed and pack. "Fetch my bag, the one I keep my money in," said Jim, as he sat down. He was visibly shaking and the sweat dropped from his face. Bud brought out the little bag and opened it.

"Wal, I don't see how we could hev avoided thet, boss," he said, resignedly, shaking his head.

"Avoid hell!—Ought to have jumped him long ago." Jim looked at his big, dirty, red-stained hands. "Get out the money, Bud. . . . Let's see. I'll pay him the month out."

"Pay him nuthin' you don't owe," declared Bud, carefully calculating and counting out the amount due. "I'll give it to Cherry an' let him hand it over."

Jim did not look up from the ground until he had recovered his balance. Jocelyn had evidently been led off into the woods, for Cherry appeared to be following with his horse and Hump Stevens with his pack. They disappeared. Whereupon Curly and Bud returned to Jim.

"Best job fer the Diamond in six years," said Bud.

"Ahuh. But bad fer the boss, Bud," added Curly, gravely.

"Boys, I couldn't stand him any longer, I couldn't," broke out Jim, spreading wide his hands.

"Shore you couldn't. But Jocelyn will never get over thet. I don't mean the lickin', though you near busted him. It's what you called him an' orderin' him out of camp. Thet'll go over the range. It'll aboot make Hack Jocelyn an outlaw."

"I'm not sorry. I suppose he'll kill me, but I couldn't have done otherwise."

"Wal, Jim, it's *done*," rejoined Curly. "He's shore slated fer wuss company. I'll bet my spurs Slinger Dunn will kill him. But the thing fer you to make up your mind aboot is—if you ever meet Jocelyn ag'in, no matter where, grab your gun an' begin to shoot. Savvy?"

"Boss, will you promise to do thet little trick?" asked Bud, just as earnestly as Curly had spoken.

"Yes, boys, I promise," replied Jim.

"Fine an' dandy," declared Curly. "You're no slouch with a gun an' Hack ain't so much. It'd been plumb murder fer me to draw on him. But the chances are slim you'll ever meet up with Jocelyn alone. If he gets in the Cibeque an' Slinger Dunn stands fer it—which I'll gamble he won't—he'll be jumpin' out of the fryin'-pan into the fire. Jocelyn is only another cowpuncher thet's gone to the bad. I've seen a lot of them. The Cibeque will be the wuss off with Jocelyn. They'll cut our fence an' rustle our stock. An', boss, if you don't hold the Diamond back, every damn one of thet two-bit outfit will be daid or in jail before the snow flies."

"Boss," added Bud, impressively, "Curly an' I know right now thet the Haverlys are cuttin' our fence an' rustlin' our cattle. We didn't ride down to West Fork fer nothin'."

"Why didn't you tell me?"

"Wal, you had trouble enough. An' we reckoned we'd keep it as long as we could."

"If you give me proofs I—I'll not hold the Diamond

150

back," declared Jim, and probably that decision marked the West claiming him for its own.

"Wal, we cain't lay a hand on proof jest this minnit, but it'll shore come," replied Bud.

The Diamond operated out of that camp until wagon loads of fresh supplies and more wire arrived from Flagerstown. Then they pushed on to Tobe's Well, which was the end of the road. Thereafter all transports had to be packed on horseback.

Each succeeding camp site had added something to Jim's appreciation of Arizona; and Tobe's Well outdid them all.

Tobe, an obscure bear-hunter, had long ago built a log shack there, after which the canyon and the bubbling well of crystal spring water had taken his name. The situation was wholly different from the other camp settings. The canyon headed on the west slope of the Diamond, in a deep bottlenecked, gray-cliffed gorge. The floor consisted of several acres of cleared land and as much more in pine and spruce. The well was a huge spring at the upper end of the clearing and the wonderful flow of water boiled and bubbled up in the center. Under a magnificent spruce, the dead top of which tipped the rimwall above, stood the old log shack in ruins. There were several outlets to this miniature lake, little rivulets that wound away under grass and fern-bordered banks to merge into one stream in the center of the gorge. Soon it gathered velocity and plunged with low roar through the canyon neck, thereafter to fall precipitously down to the Cibeque. Giant pines and spruces stood far apart around the well, too lordly and self-contained to mingle branches or shade. White and purple asters, gold daisies, and blue flags waved in the summer wind. Birds and squirrels appeared tame and friendly. A herd of deer, does and fawns, stood with ears erect to watch the wagons roll clatteringly in at the rocky gateway.

"Boss, this heah is one waterhole you cain't fence off the Diamond,'" declared Curly, with a chuckle.

And indeed it seemed imperative to run the drift fence considerably below the gateway. Tobe's Canyon was one of the brakes of the Cibeque, not so large and open as the Sycamore, or Deer or Long Horn Canyons. It was however, a big country in itself, extremely wild and rugged up on the slope of the Diamond, and a noted place for bear and lion. The cattle that drifted down Tobe's Canyon had never been recovered by their owners.

"I'm going to have my fall hunt right here," declared Jim.

"Wal, heah's a gent who'd like to chop wood an' pack water fer you." said Curly.

"An', boss, if I do say it myself, I can cook rings around Jeff," added Bud, eagerly.

"You're both on," replied Jim, gladly.

"But, Lord! we're forgettin'," went on Curly. "We won't hev the fence up by October, an' if we do get it up it'll only go down ag'in. . . . An' then we'll be huntin' wire-cutters an' cattle thieves."

On the second day at Tobe's Well the drift fence was run below and around this famous waterhole and back up on the Diamond.

Jim had a rather uneasy conscience. Tobe's Well lay below the rim, and there was no other water close either to the north or south. Of course all the water from the well ran on down the mountain and cattle west of the fence could find it. But somehow the thing did look as if he was fencing off a waterhole. And he ventured to ask Curly what he thought the West Forkers would say about it.

"Aw, hell, let 'em drink whisky," declared Curly. "Boss, you're too turrible conscientious. Our side will say we're savin' the drift of cattle. Their side will say we're fencin' off grass an' water. It's nip an' tuck. But wait till you heah some bullets hissin' past your ear!"

The sixth day from that fell to Jim as his turn for the scout duty he had initiated. He had saddled and mounted while yet the others were at breakfast.

"Boss, how fur do you aim to ride back along the line?" asked Bud.

"I'll make for Sycamore, strike the fence, and work this way," replied Jim.

"Wal, keep your eye peeled," said Curly, gruffly.

Jim rode out of the canyon and up to the rim above, from which he gazed down with a stinging sensation of pleasure at the wild camp site, the does and fawns grazing with the horses, the blue column of smoke curling upward, and at the circle of cowboys round the fire.

Lonestar's mellow voice floated up: "Oh, I am a Texas cowboy, jest off the Texas plains. My trade is cinchin' saddles—"

Jim wheeled his horse off into the pines, conscious that his full heart could not quite attain the joy of realization. He loved the West; he was proving his mettle to his uncle and his father; he had begun to fit in with these elemental, dare-devil cowboys; he liked life in the open and the wild. But he could not rid himself of the pang and oppression in his breast, of the persistence of a bitter sickening doubt and regret. Long weeks, even months, had not killed his love for Molly Dunn. Time and thought, long hours in the lonely nights and bitter reflection, had proved to Jim that the one constant, ever-growing thing had been love. Some day before long he would ride down to West Fork and see Molly Dunn. See for himself what she was and if there was not reason for his blind faith!

So his thoughts came and went, repeated themselves and augmented, while he rode through the forest. There was no trail, but he had his direction and knew he could not miss Sycamore. Cattle were numerous and many of them wild. He saw not only unbranded calves and heifers, but two-year-old steers. And he remarked this as something against the large cattleman. It could do no less than tempt the little stockmen and the homesteaders of something morally dishonest, if not so according to range law. And once a man had stolen unbranded cattle, he was on the down grade. This was Jim's personal conviction. Curly Prentiss would argue, "Wal, how do I *know* this heah unbranded calf ain't mine?" Jim had to concede the point, but he thought it could become far-fetched. The free range and mixed cattle were mistakes. Jim, however, admitted he could not see any remedy at present. The drift fence was a start.

Arriving at Sycamore, he rode west a short distance until he came to the fence, when he turned south to follow it. He walked his horse, keeping back a few rods, and he peered ahead with keen eyes. He covered several miles in this cautious manner and came out on the bank of a swampy swale, from which water drained down into Rocky Canyon. Aspen thickets, clumps of new spruce and pine, filled the head of this canyon. Cattle were drifting down.

Jim found the fence down in a section clear across this gateway to the brakes. He really had not expected to find a cut, and hard on his surprise and dismay roused his slumbering wrath.

He proceeded, though less cautiously, with his rifle across the pommel. And along toward noon he rode down the wooded slope under Tobe's Well. Cattle were working down here, too. Not drifting! Jim prepared himself for another surprise. The bottle-neck width of Tobe's Canyon had been sheared of its wire fence. A clean-cut job it was, every wire strand having been cut on each side of trees and posts.

Jim descried fresh hoof tracks in the dim, seldom-used trail. Such was his wrath now that he followed them, keeping on the grass and under the pines where his horse walked quietly. Once the animal neighed, much to Jim's annoyance. That worried Jim, but did not deter him. And as he worked down, keeping intense vigilance on all sides, he could scarcely fail of impressions as to the wildness of Tobe's Canyon.

His intent was to trail this fence-cutter clear to his hole, wherever that was; and Jim's excitement kept him from realizing the miles he descended, until he got down on comparative level, in the midst of a most beautiful forest of spruce and pine. Few indeed were the open glades and aisles. He heard cattle or elk breaking sticks back of the trail; the black squirrels and blue jays noisily resented his presence; he saw a squirrel-hawk flash down through an opening and crash into a tree, to flop violently and fly off, clutching a furry victim in his claws. That was a near bit of cruel nature to Jim.

Suddenly his horse elevated his ears and stopped. The trail ran straight for twenty paces, and turned at a huge brown pine. A man stepped out, silent as a shadow. Jim recognized the lithe buckskin-clad form, the dark face, the eyes like holes that exposed fire behind. He leveled a gun, took deliberate aim, while Jim froze in his saddle.

He saw red belch from the gun. A sharp impact as from a violent gust of wind struck him. Then a terrific shock, a tearing rent of flesh, a thundering crash! Jim's horse plunged to throw him.

15

VIOLENT COLLISION with ground or tree ended Jim's acute consciousness. His first sensations afterward were the chill of water on his face and a burning pain in his breast. Then he felt hands on his forehead.

He forced his weighted eylids open, to see bright sunshine and spread of foliage over him. He lay half sitting up against a log. Beside him knelt a girl. She uttered a broken cry.

"Oh—Mister Traft—you've come to!" she exclaimed, huskily.

"Molly Dunn!" Jim's voice was not very strong. She straightened up a little so the light struck her face. It appeared pale and convulsed, with big dark eyes dilated in horror. Both her little hands were red with blood. This fully clarified Jim's stunned faculties. "Am I bad hurt?"

"Oh—I don't know! I—I'm afraid!" she cried.

"Show me where I'm shot."

"Your breast . . . heah!"

Jim's shirt was open. Even with the girl's help it took nerve to feel for the wound. His whole breast burned. A wet scarf lay pressed tight over his heart. Warm slippery blood! It had saturated his clothes. It was flowing freely. Then his fingers located a hole in his flesh that seemed on fire. Despite the shock to his wits Jim knew he had not been shot through or near the heart. The bullet hole ranged upwards. Had it missed his lungs? The moment was fraught with terror. And as he felt of it he was gazing up into the strained eyes of the girl. He localized the sharpest pain higher up. The bullet had come out on top of his left shoulder. From here the blood poured. Something cold and ghastly released its clutch upon Jim.

"Bullet—glanced," he muttered. Then he asked if there was any other wound.

"Molly, I'll not die," he said.

"You hit on your haid," replied the girl.

"Thank God!—I was so terribly frightened. What can I do?

"You had water here?"

"I filled your hat in the brook."

"Tear this scarf in strips," directed Jim. "You'll find a clean one in my pocket. . . . Inside. . . . Now tear that— and fold into pads. You've only to wash off the blood— and bind the pads on tight."

She complied with his instructions, without hesitation, though her hands shook.

"But this top hole! You're bleedin' so! Fast as I wipe the blood off—"

"Put one of the pads over it. Press tight. Now I'll hold it there. . . . Knot the strips. . . . Slip under my arm— over my shoulder. Now the other pad . . . and tie tight."

The difficult task was at length accomplished. Molly sat back on her heels, plainly weak. Tiny drops like dew stood out upon her forehead. Her hair was wet. She made a move to brush it back from her face, then, aware of her bloody hands, she essayed to do it with her elbow, holding them out so as to avoid contact.

"'Molly Dunn, you've got my blood on your hands—all right," said Jim, with significance.

But it escaped her. "I shore have—and it sickens me," she whispered. Then pouring water from his sombrero she washed them, and wiped them upon the grass.

Jim felt faint, and he was suffering severe pain, both of which in the thrilling agitation of the moment seemed nothing to be concerned about.

"I must get you back off the trail heah," she spoke up, suddenly.

"Yes. If you help me I can manage," he replied. With her assistance he labored to his feet and walked, leaning on her. For a little girl she certainly was strong. They seemed to go far. Jim grew dizzy. He heard running water, but could not see it. Blurred spruce trees stood up all around. His head swam, and when the girl stopped to let him down it was none too soon for Jim. He spoke, but apparently she did not hear. Then his sight cleared. She was coming with water in his sombrero.

"You aboot fainted that time, Mister Jim," she said, lifting his head so he could drink.

"I—should—smile," whispered Jim, as he lay back. Presently he had recovered again, not only to the mounting pains, but to a thrilling sense of this extraordinary situation.

"What—happened?" he asked.

"Shore a lot," she replied, mournfully.

"Do you know who shot me?" he went on.

She hung her head.

You needn't tell me. I know it was your brother, Slinger Dunn. . . . He stepped out from behind a tree . . . didn't seem in any hurry. But I was paralyzed. I forgot I had a gun."

"It's beyond me—that you're alive. Oh, I'm thankful."

"But what'll we do?"

Jim felt the lump over his breast where the lower pad had been bound. It was right under his shirt pocket over his heart. His finger located the bullet hole in his shirt and at the same instant his watch.

"See here, Molly," he said, curiously. "Take my watch out."

She complied. The watch was of heavy silver and had

been long in the Traft family. Evidence was not wanting that it had served its day. The bullet had struck the case, making a heavy dent and then had glanced upward.

"That accounts," whispered Molly. "I wondered aboot it. Slinger doesn't often miss what he shoots at."

"Saved my life!—Well, I'll be jiggered!" exclaimed Jim, fondling the watch. "And I came awful close not fetching it!"

"Oh, such luck! Thank Heaven! . . . But, Mister Traft, what'll we *do*?"

"Do? I haven't the slightest idea. I couldn't get on a horse. . . . I'll probably be laid out. My, but it throbs and burns!"

"You'll have fever. An' maybe blood-poisonin'. We got to have medicine," she rejoined, tragically.

"It won't do to send you up to my camp."

"Why not? My horse is heah, tied over there."

"The boys would know your brother shot me. I don't want that."

"Shore they'll find it out, anyhow."

"Well, I suppose, But if I'm on my feet I could keep them from—"

"Mister Jim, you needn't let Slinger off on my account," she interrupted.

"I'll have something to say to him when I'm all right again," declared Jim, grimly. "What'd the— Why did he shoot me? On account of this drift fence?"

"No. Reckon it was aboot me."

"You!"

"Shore. It's gone all over the country—what you did— what *we* did—that night of the dance . . . out on the porch."

"Bud Chalfack—the devil!" ejaculated Jim, stirringly aware of Molly's scarlet blush. "He told it! . . . Oh, I'm sorry, Molly! That was such a—a crazy thing for me to do."

"Reckon I was just aboot as crazy," she replied, generously, and smiled just a little wistfully. "But Slinger didn't heah what *I* did . . . an' he shore wouldn't believe me. I was scared he'd choke it out of me."

"What does he think, Molly?"

"It couldn't be no worse, Mister Jim."

"The damn blockhead! Some of these Arizona fellows make me see red. . . . I'll make it my business to hunt Mister Slinger up."

"Oh, don't do that! I beg you!" she implored.

"Suppose I busted in on him somewhere. At your home or in the saloon at West Fork—before other people. He wouldn't murder me outright, would he?"

"No. But he'd make you draw. Arch is the most awfulest man when he's mad."

"I didn't know whether he was mad or not, but he sure looked awful," replied Jim, forcing a laugh. "Molly Dunn, how'd you happen to come along here and find me?"

"Slinger just the same as told me he'd kill you," she replied, grave, dark eyes on him. "I waited this mawnin' till he was gone. Then I trailed him. My plan was to keep behind him till we were up on top, then I'd ride off the trail an' go round to your camp."

"Well! What for?"

"I wanted to warn you aboot Slinger. An' that you was in 'most as much danger from the Cibeque outfit."

"Molly Dunn!" he cried, incredulously. "Then it wasn't an accident? You actually came to save me?"

The distance to the little brown hand on her knee was not far, and his quickly bridged it. She seemed neither shy nor cold.

"It shore wasn't no accident, Mister Jim," she said.

"You must have risked a good deal, Molly."

"I didn't think aboot it. But if they find it out down in the brakes—well, the Cibeque wouldn't be no place for me. An' Slinger will aboot kill me."

"Oh, I'm sorry! And grateful! Molly Dunn, I've got to think up some way to prove it. . . . But you must not let Slinger or any one see you. How far is it to your home?"

"Reckon aboot five miles, down through the woods. I can keep off the trail."

"How'd you happen to find me?"

"I trailed Slinger to where his tracks went off into the

woods. Then I stopped. Pretty soon I heahed a shot—then a cry- then a horse comin' my way fast. I hid behind a spruce. An' I seen Slinger ride by. I didn't know what had happened. But I tied my horse an' slipped up the trail. First I saw your horse. He was makin' off, draggin' his bridle. Then I found you lyin' by a tree. you'd fallen off an' hit your haid."

She released her hand from his and gently touched Jim's head above his temple where even a slight pressure caused him pain.

"I'd better fetch your horse," she added, rising.

"Don't go far or stay long," said Jim.

The slight buckskin-clad form vanished in the green. And only then did Jim take note of his surroundings. He lay in sort of a lean-to made of spruce boughs, dead and brown. He could see one small bit of blue sky; all the rest was green. He heard a low murmur of running water. The place was secluded, and redolent of dry sweet pine needles.

But the effort to sit up caused him so much pain that he was glad indeed to lie back. He must not forget that he had been shot What an adventure! His thoughts simply whirled, and he had to force them to a logical plan. He absolutely must send the girl home soon. Could he dare let her risk coming back the next day? The idea overcame him. Sooner or later the cowboys would find him, though the last place they would look would be down the trail from Tobe's Well.

Soft thuds on the ground made Jim aware that Molly was returning with his horse. They ceased. Then he heard a rustling sound. and then the soft flop of leather. Next she appeared with his saddle blankets and his coat.

"Mister Jim, didn't you have a gun?" she asked.

"So I did. A rifle. . . . I had it across the front of my saddle when Slinger stepped out from behind that tree."

She disappeared again. And he lay there, subject to renewed emotion. Presently she returned with the rifle, to deposit it by his side. How pretty, slim, and graceful she looked in buckskin! He told her so. She just gazed at him with great, reproachful, melancholy eyes.

"Have you worn the lovely white dress since?" he added.

"No. . . . I'm savin' that to be buried in."

"Molly! . . . You should have said married. How sweet —"

"Mister Jim, you're shore talkin' too much—not to say too wild. Your face is hot. An' time is flyin'. What'll we do? I've hobbled your horse."

"You must go home at once. Don't let anybody see you. . . . Will you come back tomorrow?"

"Yes," she replied, with gravity, as if only she knew what that promise implied.

"Thank you. Better fetch some medicine. I'm going to be pretty sick. . . . And some clean linen to bandage my bullet holes."

"There's a canteen on your saddle," she said, and stepped outside the shack to procure it. Upon returning she placed it beside his rifle. Then on her knees she scraped up a soft pile of pine needles, and spread his saddle blankets upon them, and folded his coat for a pillow.

"There's a bed for you. I reckon you won't get cold. If you do, use one of the blankets. . . . An' now I'll go."

Jim gazed up at her as she knelt there.

"Molly . . . kiss me," he importuned, quite beside himself.

"Mister Jim!"

"I'll be here alone, unable to move. . . . Slinger might come back and kill me. . . . Kiss me, Molly."

"No. He won't come back."

"I might bleed to death or die of fever," he went on, wildly.

"You're out of your haid."

"Of course I am. But I know what I'm asking. Please kiss me."

"You ask that of *me*—Molly Dunn?"

"I don't care who or what you are."

Twice he reached for her, but she was just a little too far away.

"You mustn't move," she said, in alarm, edging close

161

on her knees. Then he could reach her. How large and dark her eyes appeared in her pale face!

"Kiss me, and go."

She bent over his forehead as if impelled, yet earnestly.

"No!" he cried, seeing her intent, and moving impatiently.

Then blushing duskily scarlet she bent lower, closing her eyes, and laid cool sweet lips on his. Before Jim could catch his breath to speak again she had fled.

"Low down of me to take advantage of her that way," he muttered. "But, after all, was it? . . . Curly would say, 'Thet shore aboot spills me.'"

Whereupon Jim called Molly every adorable name that he had ever heard or could make up, and in some measure satisfied himself of sincerity. After which he lay for long in a dream, the pleasure of which made him almost unconscious of pain. From that he fell into a fitful slumber.

When he awoke the light low down had shaded and rays of gold slanted through the forest. He was uncomfortably hot and thirsty, but the pain had somewhat dulled. It hurt him, however, to move over on to the bed of boughs, and he was glad to stretch out. Common sense told him that his situation was pretty serious, if his condition was not, but he could hardly dwell on anything else save Molly Dunn's return the next day. What endless hours to wait! Suppose she did not come? But that girl would come. Jim knew it positively. Nevertheless, he tried to consider his predicament.

The boys would scarcely be apt to search for him until next day. He had often been absent from camp until late. Then they would ride north to Sycamore, and the chances were favorable that they would not find him until the following day. Jim hoped they would not. Slinger Dunn, though, might come back to see his victim. After pondering this, however, Jim inclined to Molly's conviction that Slinger would not come. There was nothing else to speculate upon then but the girl. Jim suddenly felt glad for the solitude of the forest and the long night hours that he must pass wakefully.

He watched the gold fade from the tips of the spruces. The sky turned gray. Twilight enveloped the green surroundings in obscurity. Soon all was black except a small space of sky overhead where pale stars blinked, and grew clear and white. The stillness was something that Jim soon felt he could not endure. But it did not last. A sigh breathed through the tree tops. The night wind had begun its dominance of the forest. Soon from all around came rustlings and stealthy sounds.

From time to time Jim had to take a swallow of water from the canteen. These movements caused him acute pain, but when it subsided he suffered only the dull throbbing ache in head and breast. He could stand it. He did not mind only when it interfered with the pondering of his problem. Some late hour in the night relief from his mental struggle came, if not for the physical distress under which he labored. He had made up his mind about Molly Dunn, and a sweetness, a gladness, pervaded his soul. Then he fell asleep.

Jim awoke at what he imagined must be the dark hour before dawn. He lay flat on his back, and it took a moment or more for him to realize he was not in camp, but alone in the deep forest, wounded, and parched by thirst. This he satisfied, and had begun to mill over his predicament again when his heavy eyelids closed as if weighted with sleep.

When again they unclosed not only had dawn come, but the sun had arisen; and squirrels and jays were holding forth noisily.

Jim's throbbing headache had departed, and aside from the painful itching and contracting of his wounds he seemed to be doing pretty well indeed. At any rate, he told himself so. He sat up, finding that only the use of his left arm and shoulder hurt him severely. About this hour, he reflected, and with considerable gratification, there would be consternation in the Diamond camp. Curly and Bud, on the rampage, would scatter those cowboys like a bunch of quail; and lonesome riders encountered in the woods were going to have to give strict account of their presence.

Sooner or later some one would find him, and if no one did he might be able in a couple of days to reach camp. Perhaps he was not very practical this morning, for he almost felt grateful to Slinger Dunn. Young Jim Traft, head of the Diamond outfit, shot by a fence-cutter in the Cibeque—how that would fly over the range! And how would his uncle take it? And Ring Locke? Jim realized that he would have risen in their estimation. All the same, he did not intend to betray Molly Dunn's brother. Jim had the nucleus of a plan hazily forming in his mind.

Waiting for Molly Dunn was not in the least wearisome, though the moments multiplied into hours. Jim had too much to thrill over—to conjecture about. How would she take him? He tried to imagine the expression of her face—of her wonderful eyes at the critical moment.

Thus dreamily engaged, he was not prepared for low clatter of hoofs down the trail. He sat up with such a start that he wrenched his shoulder and had to pay a severe penalty. The forest was very still, except for birds and squirrels. The rhythmic beat of hoofs subsided, and likewise Jim's mounting heart. Then the sound came clear again. The hoofbeats were soft, and the horse that made them was neither heavy nor shod. They swelled clearer for a little, slowed down, and then ceased.

"It's Molly," said Jim, softly, and yet he endeavored to fortify himself against mistake. The moments dragged, and he was becoming nervous and discouraged, when a rustle of brush and soft footfalls just behind the lean-to brought him up transfixed and thrilling.

Suddenly the slight gray form he had in his mind's eye appeared before him. She was bareheaded and the sunlight glinted from her disheveled hair She carried a bundle.

"Oh, there you—are! I was—shore scared!" she panted. Her eyes appeared unnaturally large and black in her small pale face.

"Morning, Molly! I reckoned you'd never come," he said, gladly.

"Are you—all right?"

"I had an awful night. And I was bad until just now," he replied.

She sat down, and depositing her bundle, she put a hand to her bosom as if to still its heaving. She averted her eyes. It was plain she could not look at him. She appeared worn and troubled, as if she had passed a harassed, sleepless night. She seemed such a wistful, pathetic little figure. Jim's heart filled with tenderness and he could scarce contain his tremendous secret.

"Molly, did you get home safe?" he asked, anxiously.

"Yes. Slinger didn't come, an' ma never heahed me."

"That's fine. I'm sure glad. I've worried a lot." Then, noticing that she wore a blood-stained bandage around her left hand, he asked solicitously if she had not injured herself.

"No. I just put this on to fool ma, so I could go to the store," she explained in a matter-of-fact tone. "An' I told Mr. Summers I'd cut myself an' was scared of blood poison. I bought this medicine, an' I've fetched some clean linen, a towel an' soap, an' somethin' for you to eat."

"You're just wonderful, Molly!" said Jim, and meant it in a multiplicity of ways.

She gave him a fleeting flash of eyes. "I'll fetch some water," she returned.

Jim noted, as she glided away with the canteen, how cautiously she peeped around the spruce tree before venturing farther. She was gone some moments, that dragged for the eager Jim. Then presently she reappeared as noiseless as a shadow, to set the dripping canteen down beside him, and knelt to undo a buckskin thong around the bundle.

"It's goin' to hurt right smart," she said, practically.

"Molly, I could stand to be carved into mincemeat by you."

Whereupon she laid a cool hand on his forehead and temples, and then slipped it inside his open shirt to feel of the bandages.

"Wal, you don't 'pear to have fever, but you shore look an' talk flighty," she said. "Will you hold still an' keep

165

quiet? This's goin' to hurt like sixty. I've done it more'n once for Arch."

Jim nodded his acquiescence, and thought it would be safer and facilitate the operation if he closed his eyes. She cut the strips of scarf that had served as a bandage and then she essayed to remove the pads. They had evidently crusted with blood and they stuck tight. She saturated them with water and pulled gently at them until it appeared that more force must be used. Jim made the mental reservation that it hurt twice times sixty. But once the pads had been removed, how soothing to his hot skin and the irritated wounds were the touch of her cool hand and the feel of water!

"Mister Jim, from what little I know aboot gun-shot wounds, I'd say you're not so bad off this mawnin'," she said.

"I dare say my—favorable condition can be laid to my beautiful and splendid nurse," he replied, without opening his eyes. He thought he caught a suppressed titter, but could not be sure. Then he attended to her applying a stinging solution to his wounds and a deft and thorough bandaging of them.

"There. I can't do no more for you," she said. "I reckon these bullet holes are healin' clean, but it'd be sense to have your men get you to Flag, pronto. . . . An' then stay there, Mister Jim."

"Thanks, Molly. I'm very grateful to you," he rejoined, opening his eyes to smile up at her. "I'll go to Flag, of course, if it's necessary. But I'll come back. . . . Molly, is it safe for you to stay with me awhile?"

"Safe? I reckon so, now I'm heah," she replied, thoughtfully. "Ma won't miss me. . . . But all the same I ought to *run*."

"Run? From what?"

"From you, Mister Jim."

"Please leave off the Mister. We've known each other a long time, now. It'd be perfectly proper."

She laughed, and her mirth had just a touch of bitter mockery.

"Why should you run from *me*?"

166

"I've been with you only twice an' you made a fool of me both times," she replied, resentfully.

"I never did," he protested. If he could stir her, even to anger, he might overcome the aloofness he sensed in her this morning. But failing in this, he thought he knew a way.

"You shore did. That night on the porch at Flag! You grabbed me just like Hack Jocelyn an' other cowpunchers I know. An' yesterday—that was worse. Your persuadin' me!"

"Molly, consider. There was no excuse for me at the dance. But yesterday there was."

"Maybe for you. But not for me. I shore wonder what you think of me."

Jim saw the delight of playing upon her simplicity must be forsworn. She seemed to be smarting under shame. The moment had come, far swifter than he had anticipated, but he welcomed it, hastened to end forever her doubts of him.

"Molly, if you'll look around I'll tell you what I think of you," he said, in the coolest, easiest tone he could muster.

The dark head whirled. Her spirited action, the fire of her eyes, the receding of hot color, implied a doubt of him and her resentment at it. Yet there seemed something else in her expression, not conscious hope, but a pathos due to the dream she only half divined.

"Will you marry me?" he asked, simply, but with deep emotion.

Perhaps nothing else could have so altered her. At length she burst out:

"Mister Jim!"

"Let's dispense with the Mister. Call me plain Jim, and say 'yes'."

"Boy, now I know what ails you," she said, in self-reproach.

"No, you don't. I haven't come to that."

"If you're not out of your haid, what on earth are you?" she cried, wildly.

"In love, Molly."

"In love! . . . With *me?*" she whispered.

He got hold of her hand, to find it trembling. "Listen, child," he began, determined to convince her. "You remember our meeting. Well, I think I fell in love with you then. If not then, at the dance surely. And last night I made up my mind to ask you to marry me. I've been shot, I know, Molly. And I'm excited. But I am absolutely in possession of all my wits. I love you very dearly. And I want to make you my wife."

"Me? Molly Dunn?"

"Yes, you, Molly Dunn."

Then Jim Traft devoutly thanked the god of love or faith, or both, whatever it had been that had prompted him to broach this most impelling and sacred of all propositions to a woman. For though Molly Dunn was wholly unconscious of it, the instant he had convinced her was one of a singular transformation. He had convinced her of so marvelous a thing that it worked a like change in her.

"Oh! . . . I cain't believe it," she exclaimed, incredulous with the amazing truth. "My God! What would Slinger say to that? An' ma an' pa an' Andy—an' that grinnin' Jocelyn?"

"Molly, it doesnt matter in the least what they'd say. But a great deal what *you* say."

"Wal, Mister Jim—"

"Stop calling me that," interrupted Jim, imperiously, and he shook her. He divined not only that she really cared for him, but that she could never hold out against him. It shone in her startled eyes. She betrayed it in other unconscious ways. "Call me Jim. . . . Do you hear? *Jim!*"

"Shore I heah you . . . Jim," she replied, sweetly.

"It sounds very nice. Now what do you say, Molly?"

"I'm shore upset. An' I'll be so—so proud all my life —an' happy that you love me an' want me. . . . But, Jim, I cain't marry you."

"Molly! Do you love some one else?" he queried, sharply.

"No."

"Don't you—couldn't you care for me?" he implored.

She gave him an enigmatical little smile, as much mournful as derisive—something dedicated to the stupidity of man.

"Jim, heah you have lost your haid," she went on. "I'm Molly Dunn of the Cibeque. They always called me that. My brother is Slinger Dunn. An' this last shootin' will make him an outlaw."

"It needn't, Molly. No one need ever know. I'll not tell. And I'll find a way to change Slinger."

"But that's only one reason," she protested. "My father has lived for years under a cloud. No one can prove he belonged to that murderous outfit. But it's behind. . . . My mother isn't much good, either. There's talk aboot her an' this an' that cowboy."

"Molly, I wouldn't be marrying your family," replied Jim, sagely.

"Jim, I may be pretty, like a wood-mouse, as Arch calls me, but I'm nobody," said Molly, mercilessly. "I'm no—no fit girl for you."

"Why not?" he demanded, stabbed again by that fierce, jealous doubt. "You've sure got good looks. You've the face, the hands—the instincts of a lady. There must be good blood in your family somewhere."

"Yes. My mother came from a Southern family. She brags aboot it to this day. It's a lot to do with her fittin' so poor in a log cabin."

"Molly, if—if"—he tortured himself to get this out—"if you've had affairs with any boys—that damned Jocelyn—or anyone—affairs you're ashamed of—just forget them. I *know* you're the kind of a girl who'd tell me. But I really don't want to know. I think you've had a rotten deal down here in the Cibeque. What chance have you had—among these louts? Curly Prentiss said that. . . . So, Molly, turn your back on the whole mess and come to me."

"Jim Traft, do you think I'd ever disgrace you *now*?" she flashed, with tears welling down over her cheeks. "Just that you said would make me love you, if nothin' else could. But it also makes me see clear. . . . I—I cain't marry you."

169

Jim did not press this point any further, for her demeanor, the way she clung to his hand, the tremendous agitation that shook her, the traitorous eyes which she did not realize, were facts that moved him with tumultuous joy.

"But, Jim, I reckon you've heahed talk aboot me," she went on. "An' you're shore the one man I'd tell everthin'. Don't you let any lies aboot me stick in your haid."

"I didn't, Molly," said Jim, which he feared was not wholly truth. But on the other hand, under circumstances of extreme exasperation, had he not clung to some strange championship of her? Then he told her of Hack Jocelyn's vain boastings, of his innuendoes, and at last his open, vile claim.

"Slinger will kill him for that," she replied, furiously.

"I'd have done it myself," declared Jim. "The boys had to pull me off him."

"I saw his face an' taunted him with it," she said. "Hack admitted you licked him. . . . Jim, he scared me bad that time. He lay in wait for me along the trail home. An' he jerked me into the brush. That's when I learned he was quittin' the Diamond an' makin' up to the Cibeque. He was playin' for a big stake. My brother had no use for Hack. An' Hack aimed to win him over by makin' me tell him he'd quit the Diamond because you insulted me. When I didn't take kind to this deal, he grabbed me up in his arms an' near broke every rib I own. An' he kissed me, Jim—all over except my mouth. . . . You bet I was scared an' I changed my tune. He let me down then, an' pretty quick I broke an' ran."

"And that's all the claim Hack Jocelyn had on you! . . . Molly, all the time I *knew* he was a liar. But, oh, it nearly broke my heart."

"Jim, he never had no claim on me," she replied, earnestly. "Some of the other boys have tried to make up to me by grabbin' me. *You* did, Jim Traft!—It must be a failin'. But, I cross my heart, Jim, no boy ever got anythin' like you got from me."

"Darling!" cried Jim.

That and the stealing of Jim's arm round her waist, drawing her down, would have been Molly's undoing. But he heard a soft step. He felt Molly freeze under his arm. A shadow crossed the light above him.

16

Jim had only a glimpse of Slinger Dunn looming over him, gun in hand. Then Molly, with a scream, threw herself upon Jim protectingly.

"So heah you are, you wood-louse," grated Slinger.

"Arch, I found him—on the trail—bleedin' to death," cried Molly.

"When—an' what you doin' up heah?"

"I—I went ridin', Arch. Yesterday. I heahed a shot. Then you came by like mad. An' I found him."

"You was meetin' him heah."

"No. No. Honest to God—I wasn't."

"Molly Dunn, I've had my doubts aboot you lately. An' now I'm shore."

Jim managed to move enough to get his eyes from under Molly's disheveled hair. He needed only one look up at Slinger Dunn's face to understand Molly's terror.

"Dunn, she's not a liar," he said, hurriedly. "She couldn't have known I was on the trail. I was trailing the man who cut the drift fence."

"Aw, she'd lie an' you'd swear to it." His piercing gaze rested curiously on Jim. "How'n hell do you happen to be alive?"

"Your bullet hit my watch."

"Wah, heah's another," said Slinger, with strange intensity, and he brought the gun up to align it with Jim's head. But quick as a flash Molly covered Jim.

171

"For God's sake, Slinger, don't kill him," she begged.

"I shore will. An' I jest aboot as lief bore you, too. . . . Git up."

He kicked Molly, and his boot came partly in contact with Jim's thigh. The brutality of it, after the deadly speech, seemed to liberate Jim from a cold paralysis.

"Let go of me, Molly," ordered Jim. "If he's such a skunk as that, he might kill you. And if he means to murder me you can't stop him."

"Now you're talkin', Mister Traft," returned Dunn, harshly.

Molly not only refused to move, but she got her arms around Jim, and clung to him, shielding his vital parts with her quivering body.

"Arch, you cain't shoot him—when he's down—crippled—defenseless," she burst out, passionately. "It wouldn't be human. It wouldn't be like Slinger Dunn. . . . If it's on my account, you're wrong—terribly wrong. He never meant—bad by me."

"Molly, I reckon he's *done* bad by you. An' you're not only lyin' for him, but givin' yourself away."

"You cold-hearted devil!" she exclaimed. "How could you have a decent thought? . . . Kill me, too!"

"Ahuh. You damn little hussy! . .But being' daid wouldn't hide your shame, Molly Dunn."

"Oh, Arch, there's no shame. . . . There's been nothin' but thoughts an' feelin's that have changed me. . . . I love him. Cain't you see it? I love him!"

"Wal, I ain't blind," replied Slinger, and reaching down he laid hold of Molly and tried to pull her off. But she clung like a leech. Then with a curse he shifted his hold to her hair. Even then he could only budge her by savage force, and he had to step on Jim's shoulder to keep her from lifting him with her. Suddenly Molly, fierce as a wildcat, flung herself upon Slinger, and fought him for the gun, which he held out in his right hand.

The girl's courage, following her declaration of love, roused the lion in Jim. With all his might he kicked Dunn's hand, knocking the gun out of it.

172

"Hold still!—Somebody comin'!" whispered Dunn, hoarsely, stiffening.

Molly slipped out of his grasp, down to the ground. Jim listened. but could hear nothing save the pounding of his heart. Dunn stood strung like a listening deer, gradually relaxing his intensity. He might have been mistaken. But during this short interval he had removed his eyes from Molly, who suddenly snatched up the gun. She held it low, with both hands tight, pointing up at Dunn's body.

Jim could not bear the terrible intent expressed in her face and eyes. He grasped the gun, turned it aside.

"Molly, you mustn't shed your brother's blood—even to save my life," he said, very low. And at his words she relinquished the gun.

Slinger Dunn seemed to be calculating desperate chances. That Jim would not instantly turn the gun on him never flashed into his consciousness. Jim grasped this and thought he might turn it to good account. The last thing he could be forced to do would be to kill Molly's brother.

Then the brush crashed.

"Hands up!" came in cool, sharp tones that made Jim's blood leap.

Dunn's back was turned. Swiftly he elevated his arms high above his head. Jim moved to see that Curly Prentiss had appeared round the corner of the lean-to. He held a cocked gun.

"Come round heah, Bud," he called. And with more crashing in the brush Bud Chalfack followed his extended rifle into view. Both cowboys stepped closer, eyes quick and hard.

Jim slipped Dunn's gun out of sight—an act as impulsively swift as the thought that prompted it.

"Face around heah," ordered Curly, and as Dunn pivoted he showed no surprise, but an alert, cold suspicion.

"By Gawd!" shouted Bud. "Look, Curly! If there ain't the boss . . . an' Molly Dunn!"

Jim seized avidly upon his opportunity, though his wit and spirit far exceeded his physical strength.

"Hello—boys!" he began, huskily. "So you found me —at last. . . . Put up your guns."

"What's wrong heah?" demanded Curly, and Jim's heart felt a rush of warm gladness and thrill at the significance of the cowboy's mien.

"Nothing wrong, Curly—now—you've found me," replied Jim, cheerfully, though he realized his appearance must have given the lie to his words.

"Boss, you're pretty white—an' there's blood on your shirt," returned Curly, sharply.

"You bet. Put down your gun—and you, too, Bud. I'm nervous."

"Wal, you look it," growled Curly, complying with Jim's order. Bud likewise lowered his weapon. "I reckon you'd better talk fast."

"Curly," burst out Jim, in relief, "yesterday I found a cut in the drift fence. And horse tracks on the trail. I followed them down here. . . . Somebody shot me, knocked me galleywest off my horse. . . . When I came to, Molly Dunn was bathing my face. Pretty lucky for me she happened to ride along. She was on her way up to camp —to warn me that Jocelyn and the Cibeque outfit had planned to kidnap me—for ransom. She heard the shot and found me. . . . Well, it turned out the bullet had glanced off my watch and cut up through my shoulder. We tied it up. I wasn't able to get on my horse. Molly wanted to ride up to camp and fetch you, but I thought it'd be best for her to go home. You fellows would probably trail me, and if you didn't she could ride up today. . . . Well, Molly came today, and it seems that her brother trailed her. Found us here. And, well—the truth is, he thinks I'm a bad egg—and had evil intentions toward Molly. That upset me—and made Molly sore. We were having hell when you came up. . . . And, I reckon— that's all."

"Slinger Dunn, you're shore a hell of a bright fellar," quoth Curly, with all the sarcasm of a disgusted cowboy. "Let your hands down. An' mebbe you'd do well to make yourself scarce around heah. But before you go you put this in your pipe an' smoke it, you — — hard nut of a Cibeque gun-slinger!—My boss, Jim Traft, wouldn't never have evil intentions toward *no* gurl, much less so sweet an' luvly a little lady as your sister."

"Slinger, sumbody ought to beat the daylights out of you," added Bud, with even more scorn. "An' I'll bet you a hat the boss will do it sometime. . . . Me an' Curly both made up to Molly. Was we good enough fer her? No, we was not. Mebbe Jim *was* good enough. But you can gamble both he an' Molly are above your low-down suspicions. . . . Now you mozey along, and hereafter stay on your side of the fence."

Slinger eyed them while they delivered their separate speeches, and then looked strangely down upon Molly, who had rallied somewhat from the ravages of emotion, and lastly at Jim. There was little to be made of his impassive face, strong and hard as brown stone. Then he strode out to disappear in the brush.

The situation lost its suspense.

"You dog-gone old tenderfoot!" said Curly, sitting down beside Jim, to place a hand on him. "Gone an' got yourself shot fer the Diamond! I shore hope it ain't bad."

Bud crowded in beside Molly. "Boss, I wuz orful scared fust off. 'Course we didn't see who it wuz. . . . Gosh! I never wuz so glad aboot nothin'. . . . Did thet bullet go deep?"

"Not very. I bled a good deal. And I'm sore. But I should think you could hold me on my horse and get me up to camp."

"An' so little Molly found you!" ejaculated Curly, tossing his sombrero and shaking his curly head, while he bent bright knowing eyes upon the confused girl. "My Gawd! the luck uv some fellars! . . . How air you, Miss Molly?"

"Not so well, this minute, Mr. Prentiss," replied Molly, with a wan smile. "But I'm shore glad—the way it's turned out."

"Howdy, Molly!" drawled Bud. "You look orful purty this minnit. So you saved our boss? Wal, I reckon now the Diamond will belong to you."

"Boys," interposed Jim, with a happy ring in his voice,

"I know *a* diamond that will be Molly's, if she'll take it—along with the boss of the Diamond."

The cowboys looked bewildered volumes and were speechless, which loss of function absolutely testified to a state so rare in them. And Molly was hopelessly stricken, and confused. She had no strength left, even if rebellion was in her.

"You boys take yourselves off in the woods for ten minutes," ordered Jim, audaciously.

Curly got up awkwardly, after the manner of cowboys, and Bud followed suit. It was just as well, thought Jim, that he had flabbergasted them and then had not allowed them time to recover. Signs were forthcoming of potential and scintillating cowboy wit.

"But say good-by to Molly," added Jim, relenting.

Curly had dignity and selflessness. "Miss Molly, you shore hev my thanks. Jim has won over the Diamond, an' if, as he hints, he's won you—wal, I don't wonder, an' I reckon him the luckiest fellar on the range. Good-by an' good luck."

Bud, however, availed himself of an opportunity to make sheep's eyes. "Molly, good-by, an' so long's it can't be *me*, I reckon you've made the best deal by ropin' the boss."

They slumped away into the spruce, leaving a pleasant jingle of spurs.

"Oh, they're terrible—an' lovable, too," burst out Molly, lifting a flushed face.

"You bet they are. But that tickled me, Molly," declared Jim. "I've had a time with them. And of all the tables turned on them, this with you is the best!"

"But, Jim, it cain't ever be true," she murmured, sorrowfully.

"Forget your trouble now, Molly dear," replied Jim. "You must hurry home. I'll find some way to let you hear from me. A letter—or I'll come to West Fork."

"Oh, you mustn't! It wouldn't be safe!" she cried.

"Molly, I think we turned the table on Slinger, too. That fellow is no clod. . . . Darling, do you know you told him—*you loved me?*"

"What else could I do?" wailed Molly.

"But, Heavens, tell me you didn't lie!"

She turned away her face. "No, Jim."

"You do love me?" he implored, drawing her close.

"I cain't help it. . . . But don't ask me—never no more —what you did."

"I shan't, if you're going to be distressed. But, Molly Dunn, that offer stands!"

"Don't!—What do you think I'm made of, anyhow? . . . But, Jim, the wonderfulest thing I ever lived was when you hatched that lie to save Slinger. . . . That Prentiss boy is a real hombre. He'd have shot Slinger in the wink of an eye. An' my brother knew it. . . . Jim, if I hadn't loved you before that I'd have done it after. . . . Perhaps it's all for some good. You shore have changed me. Who knows? Maybe even Slinger Dunn might be made to see."

"I had the same thought, Molly," said Jim, earnestly. "And some day I'll follow it up. . . . Now you must go, Molly."

He released her, won to solicitude by the gray hue and strain of face she betrayed. But suddenly she surprised him by flinging her arms around his neck and pressing lips and cheeks to his. "Oh—Jim! *Jim! . . .*" Then she rose and ran into the spruce.

Jim lay back spent, elated, conscious of recurring pangs in his wounds, overcome by his feelings. So that sooner or later, when the cowboys returned of their own accord, it was no wonder they were concerned.

"Lemme see where he got plugged?" growled Curly, and with Bud assisting, he untied the bandages. "Wal, Bud," he continued, presently, "it's only a groove, an' we could do no better by it. . . . Reckon it's the gurl thet took the sap out of him."

"Ahuh. Anyone could see he was light-haided," replied Bud, plaintively. "Ain't it funny what a lovely female can do to a fellar? But, my Gawd! if I'd been Jim—"

"Idiots!" burst out Jim, opening his eyes and sitting up. "Shut up and get me to camp."

"Ex-coose us, boss," said Curly, hastily. "You see, we

177

was comin' back—reckonin' your—the little lady had gone—but jest then she pounced on you, an'—"

"Curly, you needn't explain," interrupted Jim. "You are a couple of two-faced demons from Hades. Find my horse. He's hobbled here somewhere."

"Wal, boss, I understand you," drawled Curly, as he got up. "My conscience has stung me more'n onct fer mistrustin' my friends on account uv a gurl."

They ambled away into the woods, snickering and talking low, and presently Curly's mellow laugh rolled out. Jim had to love them, realizing they were secretly delighted with his conquest of Molly Dunn. But what would his uncle Jim say? Jim wisely decided to withhold the matter until sometime when he could contrive to have the old bachelor cattleman see Molly in that white dress. Then the rest would be easy. Just here, however, he happened to remember Molly had refused him and importuned him not to ask her "never no more." The poor harassed, conscientious, adorable child!

Presently Jim's reverie was disrupted by the advent of the cowboys with his horse and their own. Bud found his saddle, and then came into the lean-to for the blankets.

"Come on, you boss of the Diamond," he said, making no effort to help Jim up.

Jim slowly crawled to a post of the lean-to and using that as a support he labored to a standing position. For a moment he felt dizzy. Then it passed.

"Fetch this medicine and towel," he said, as he walked out.

Bud was singing one of his Texas ditties: "When a boy falls in love with a pretty turtle dove, He will linger all around her under jaw—"

They made no move to help Jim on his horse, and he certainly gave no hint that their aid would have been most helpful. This cowboy school was a hard one. Jim remembered something about the Spartans, and concluded that Curly's and Bud's mothers had been Spartans. He swung up into the saddle to fierce shooting pangs through his shoulder.

They rode off, with Bud leading the way, and Curly beside Jim.

"Boss," he said, abruptly, "are you shore Slinger Dunn didn't shoot you?"

"Say! Whatever gave you that idea?" queried Jim, who did not need to feign surprise.

"Wal, when he turned round he shore expected to be bored. An' fact is, I come damn near borin' him."

"You'd have made a terrible mistake, Curly," rejoined Jim, seriously.

Jim managed fairly well in the saddle on the level ground, and even up the first gradual ascent of the trail, but when they reached the steep and rough part he had to hold on to the pommel. And he had never before suffered such sickening weakness and pain. But he stuck it out. He realized that he could do it, else these cowboys would never have let him tackle it alone. Nevertheless, he ground his teeth to keep from calling out. If anything in the world could have kept Jim Traft from falling out of his saddle, upon arriving in camp, it would have been the warwhoop the cowboys let out when they saw him. But even that could not do it.

17

A WHOLE week had to pass by before Molly Dunn came out of her trance. "I shore been walkin' in my sleep," she said.

Good luck facilitated an otherwise insupportable situation. Her parents never learned she had been away from home nearly the whole of two days. Slinger had arrived at the cabin before Molly, and Molly had a suspicion it had been through him, somehow, that their mother had not become aware of her absence. She felt Slinger's eyes upon her, at times when she was not looking at him, but he never spoke to her, never gave any indication that he heard her. More significant of his mental chaos were the hours he spent sitting idle. Sometimes he would go into the field and work, careful to take a rifle along. Molly would catch a glimpse of him, leaning motionless on a spade, looking off into the forest.

"Whatever ails your brother?" inquired Mrs. Dunn. "I hear him walkin' the porch at nights."

"Ma, I reckon he's in love," replied Molly, mischievously. "Folks get queer when they're that way."

"*You* know, don't you?" said her mother.

Molly nursed a calamitous conviction that she did. And she became grief-stricken.

She fell into a state in which there were no moments of relaxation, or dream, or relief from misery. Her heart was broken and she wanted to die. She thought of drowning herself in the great Maple Spring, and pictured herself lying at the edge, down in the clear water, her face white and her hair waving, and her eyes wide open, staring up at the cruel world which she had chosen to relinquish. There was some consolation in this picture. Arch would find her and suffer sorrow that he had been partly the cause of her demise. The thought of a conscience-stricken mother was not unpleasant. And then Jim might be the first to discover her lying cold and dead in the spring. Where he had driven her! The aching ecstasy of this thought vanished in sudden pain and self-reproach. Why should she make Jim suffer? He had done nothing but fall in love with her—nearly lose his life through her. He had lifted her out of obscurity. He had exalted her. No! She could not make him any unhappier than he was already. She had to forswear thought of suicide.

She could not do her work, which involved her in trouble with her mother. She moped all day, most of it in some corner; and she chose the dark and bare and squalid places, that seemed to be in harmony with her moods. At dusk she sat out in the clearing, on a stump, and watched the bats and the night-hawks. She did not sleep well.

Many hours she crouched at her little window in the loft, and during those when the gloom and silence of dawn seemed like her life, she suffered most.

A second Sunday came. Would she date all the rest of her life from that last day in the woods with Jim Traft? What would become of her? When Andy called she begged him to excuse her. "Why, gurl, you're sick! You look turrible!" he said, anxiously.

Then in the afternoon young Keech came on horseback. He was very mysterious, and Molly felt she would presently be rude, but he whispered to her that he had brought something for her which he had left outside by the fence. He gave no explanation and departed even more mysteriously than he had come, even winking at her.

"Darn fool!" muttered Molly, who had no patience these days. "Whatever is he up to?"

Nevertheless, curiosity consumed her and she went out by the gate and searched in the bushes. There she stumbled upon a large package, neatly tied in paper, the like of which she had seen in the big Flagerstown store. Molly was puzzled. Had young Keech begun to "spark" her in this romantic manner? It was highly improbable, because if he had fetched her presents he would most assuredly want to see her reaction to them.

No! That package was Jim Traft's first message. Molly divined it, and passionately she reproached herself for her doubt of him. Still, he might have forgotten her. This might be a joke, or anything.

Molly watched her chance to carry the parcel in unobserved, and up to the sanctity of her attic. Then, with trembling hands and beating heart, she opened it. Inside were three smaller parcels, and some books, one old and several new. One parcel was a box of candy tied with ribbons. Another contained the most beautiful silk scarf Molly had ever seen. The third was a little sewing-kit, containing everything imaginable.

"Shore it's from Jim—bless his heart!" she murmured, and searched frantically for a note. There appeared to be none, and her wild hopes subsided. She examined the books and thrilled at their titles. The old book was a school grammar and had the look of long thumbing. Then on the fly-leaf she discovered handwriting: "James Traft. Wellsville High School. Sept. 1, 1878."

"Wal, I'll be dog-goned! He's sent me his school-book, of ten years ago! . . . Now what in the dickens does he mean by that?"

Molly was thrilled, puzzled, and then suddenly dismayed. "It's a hint for me to study how to talk correct," she muttered, resentfully. But anger would not abide with her. One single query drove it away. Why should Jim Traft want her to make up for her lack of education? There could be only one answer. And straightway Molly was lifted to the skies and plunged into the depths. She had imagined—most absurdly—that he had repented of his rash offer, and had let her go at her own valuation. But he had not. He wished her to study. He believed in her. He meant—But Molly dared not follow on that thought.

Molly hugged the grammar, miserably sure of her mingled pain and joy. She put it under her pillow. She kissed the silken scarf and tied it round her neck. And all the rest of that afternoon she sat by her window, devouring both the candy and the story-books. A hundred times she looked dreamily out, to whisper: "Why didn't he write me a letter?" And after a while it dawned upon her wondrously that Jim Traft, despite his demands, was trying to make it easy for her.

All during the next week, Molly studied, day after day until her eyes ached. She taunted herself, but she could not help it. The brooding thoughts of making away with herself recurred, but they could not gain any hold in this new and strange consciousness. There seemed to be a joy even in her torment. Why could not her life be like that of the girls in the story-books? When she had punished herself greatly with their power over her, then she went back to the grammar.

The next Sunday Molly waited all day for another possible visit from young Keech. But he did not come and she had to fight bitter disappointment. Reason came back to her, however, after she had become thoroughly wretched. Keech would have to ride to Flagerstown—a whole day, and another back home. Then it would take the same time to make the trip down the Cibeque and back. Four days out of one week! That was too much. But he might come again the following Sunday, and she lived on hope of that.

Meanwhile September was far on its way. The golden flowers of autumn had begun to line the trails and fields. In the glen the ferns were turning brown. High up in the notches under the Diamond the scarlet and purple, and gold, had begun to burn in the sunlight. Fall had come— the season Molly loved best.

Slinger still stayed at home, though now he went to the village; and Molly detected that he drank. Once or twice he had spoken gruffy to her. And he had cut the corn and packed it in to the crib; he had repaired the fence to keep the hogs out; he had begun to haul and chop the winter supply of firewood.

Molly marveled and sadly divined the torment in him. No doubt he had expected a visit from the Flagerstown sheriff, or the cowboys of the Diamond. But they did not appear. And no word of Jim Traft having been shot by fence-cutters had yet reached West Fork. Molly believed now that it never would, and so she told her brother.

Other news and rumors were rife, however, some of which might be true. Work on the drift fence had not progressed beyond Tobe's Well. All the labor that the Diamond put in was in repairing sections that had been laid low. Small herds of stock had been reported on the trails, driven by riders whose names were not even whispered in West Fork. Money appeared plentiful in the village. There had been several shooting frays, of small consequence, one of which had been an attack on Andy Stoneham while walking the trail to Molly's home.

Another Sunday arrived, and with it, after Molly had waited long agonizing hours, young Keech with more of a mysterious air, more assurance that he shared a great secret, more winks and grins. He nearly drove Molly mad. He stayed for a whole insupportable hour, during which, before her drooping father and her inquisitive mother, and once or twice her sharp-eyed brother, Molly had to maintain her equilibrium as well as the demeanor of a village maiden entertaining a visitor. At last Keech said he wanted to run down to West Fork, and Molly accompanied him as far as the lane that led out from the barn, where he had left his horse.

"Thar's a pack fer you inside, hid in the corner," he informed her with a meaning grin. "I'll drop in on my way back, in case you want to send a letter."

"Letter!" faltered Molly. "How—how soon'll you be back?"

"Reckon aboot sundown. I'll whistle," he returned, and rode off down the lane.

Molly watched him guiltily. He seemed to take it for granted that she was a party to this courtship of Jim Traft's. The affair certainly could not be kept secret very long, even if young Keech justified the trust Jim had in him. Molly knew these youngsters. Soon everybody would learn that she was accepting gifts from the nephew of rich old Traft, and that would only be another black mark for Molly Dunn of the Cibeque. Not that Molly cared on her own account—she was thinking of Jim, and how her people and neighbors of West Fork would only have more against him. It would never enter their heads that he might have honorable intentions. Oh, if she could only let them know his honesty—his goodness!

She went in the barn and found the pack. Three times as large and heavy as the first one! Molly's fingers burned to open it, but she resolutely hid it and ran back to the house. She would return it. But no, she had not the strength to do that, let alone hurt Jim's feelings. She would write and tell him not to send any more.

Up by her loft window, Molly labored over that letter and her tears fell upon it. She was aware that she was placing in Jim's hands documental proof of her lack of education. It hurt her, but she was not ashamed, and she wrote as she would have talked. She had meant to make it short, which intention turned out to be impossible. For she had to explain to Jim why he must not send more

184

presents, why he must forget her. And then she seemed driven to add more, the content of which she scarcely realized and that she dared not read over.

She was sad while she waited in the lane for Keech, yet conscious of something she had not felt before. She was proving to herself and to Jim that she did not wholly lack decency and consideration. A melancholy consolation came to her. This was the end of her brief little romance.

Keech trotted down the lane, and received the letter as a matter of course. "I'll rustle along, Molly. I'm stoppin' at the head of the Cibeque. Have a little sparkin' to do on my own hook. Haw! Haw! . . . Good-by till next time."

Molly watched him ride away into the gloom of the forest. And when he had gone she stood there, looking up at the grand bulk of the Diamond, from the rugged rim of which the afterglow of sunset was fading, and felt vaguely that somehow she was a forlorn little soul, cheated of love and happiness. Yet she was glad she had arisen to the heights, even if forever afterward she must be plunged into the depths.

Under cover of the thickening dusk she secured the pack and carried it to the cabin and up to her secluded abode. There was at least one exceedingly good feature about her room, and it was that nobody ever got up there. Molly could not remember when anyone, except Arch, who had patched the roof, had invaded her retreat.

Panting, Molly sat down by her window, with her hand on the precious pack. She would revel in opening it, and in its contents, which must do for all time. Little chance of her ever having another suitor and less of her ever wanting one!

Dusk had settled down now. Her window was open, and a cool air began to move down from the mountain. The pines stood up like a black fringe. She could see the hideous dead trees in the clearing, and the pale blot of the bare fields. A cowbell tinkled, and somewhere a hound bayed. It seemed very sweet and peaceful there. Molly felt that strife and anguish were matters of the heart.

At last she lighted her lamp, and in its uncertain light

she opened the pack, ashamed of her rapture, yet utterly victim to it. Carefully she assorted the parcels, little and big, searching for a letter. But again there was none. And Molly was glad. If she read written words of love and hope and demand from him she would be as unstable as water. Suppose he should take exception to her letter of renunciation and boldly come to see her? Her heart gave a wild leap, then subsided proportionately. He would not come. He had pride and he would never stand more than a second refusal from Molly Dunn.

More books, and these from St. Louis! To her amaze all the parcels were marked with the name of that distant Eastern city. He had sent for things. The Flagerstown stores were not good enough for her. How could she ever resist his way of making somebody of her? Then for the ensuing hour she marveled at and gloated over a multiplicity of pretty and useful little presents. He did not submerge her with an overwhelming sense of great expenditure. He had tact and taste. "Oh, the darlin'," she murmured, "if he ever sees me again—it's shore all day with me!" Then she crawled into bed and cried herself to sleep.

During the next few days Molly went through a hundred variations of mood, ranging from lofty pride to self-pity, from resignation to furious revolt. And then she seemed to fix upon a settled wretchedness. Yet the days passed and life had to be lived and neglected work done.

On Saturday afternoon she went to the village with her mother, the first visit there for a month. It was the one day in the week when there was any activity at West Fork. Molly felt a reluctance to being seen, yet a tingling curiosity in regard to possible rumors. She knew she could tell instantly, when she met any of the girls or young men, if they had heard of the marvelous romance that had enmeshed her.

But she was to discover that, so far as her acquaintances were concerned, Molly Dunn was the same old Molly Dunn as ever. Strange to realize, Molly was chagrined. If they could know how far she had been removed from the ordinary life of West Fork!

Old Enoch Summers' establishment, that combined several stores in a row, all connected, stood on the main Saloon, a place of doubtful character, and one which Summers openly frowned upon, but in which rumor gave him a large interest. Board porches high off the ground, with wide steps in the middle and at each end, were a feature of West Fork's few business houses. Saddle-horses and buckboards, along the hitching-rails, attested to visitors in town. And in the next block all the available room along the plank sidewalk was taken up by wagons and buggies.

Molly for once was glad she had come with her mother, of whom it had been said that she had scant civility for Molly's admirers. They came at length to Summers' store, where Molly had to run the gauntlet of numerous men, old and young, strangers and acquaintances. It was a busy hour for the village merchant and his clerks. Mrs. Dunn and Molly had to await their turn, and when Mrs. Dunn met the worst gossip in West Fork, to become avidly absorbed at once, Molly, as a matter of self-preservation as well as taste, strolled on through this store into the next. Presently she found herself quite near the door, and curiously took a peep out. A young man had just ridden up to the porch. And when Molly recognized Jim Traft she nearly dropped to the floor. Fate had led her aimlessly to that door—for this. Then as the usual hum of talk of the loungers outside abruptly ceased, Molly realized that she was indeed not the only interested one. Jim surveyed the group on the porch, then dismounted and threw his bridle, to step up half the steps.

"Good afternoon, gentlemen," he said, coolly, and his resonant voice carried. "My name's Jim Traft and I'm looking for Slinger Dunn."

Molly bit her tongue to keep from crying out. Her next impulse was to rush to Jim. But that would be a crazy thing to do. He certainly would resent it. Her quick glance flashed over his lithe figure. He wore corduroys, high top-boots, and a brown shirt. Manifestly he could not have had a weapon upon him. Relief mitigated Molly's terror. He did not mean to fight, and certainly

187

Slinger, no matter how provoked, could not shoot an unarmed man before all these people. Jim did not look exactly pleasant, but how fine, Molly thought, and manly and clean-eyed.

"Wal, Mister Traft, you'll find Slinger in Mace's saloon," drawled some one.

"Thanks," replied Traft, and flipping a silver dollar to an urchin there, he said, "Johnny, go in and tell Slinger Dunn that if he isn't afraid to come out Jim Traft would like to see him."

The boy snatched up the coin and bounded off the porch. Jim stepped up another step. He appeared composed, but pale. He had some deep motive in bearding Slinger Dunn right in his own den. Molly fell prey to a tumult of thrill and shudder. She could not have rushed out now, for she was riveted to the spot. Traft's message had caused a low exclamation to run through the occupants of the porch, a dozen or more of whom Molly could see through door and window. Jim surely would have espied her had he looked in. But he faced down the porch, toward Mace's saloon.

"By gum! Slinger's a-comin'!" said some one.

"Reckoned thet'd fetch him," replied another. These two stood near the door and partly shielded Molly. She wrenched at her fettered feet, to move a little forward, the better to see. However, she could not see Slinger yet. People in the store behind her approached.

Then the slow step of a spurred boot sent a combined fire and ice over Molly. Slinger came into view, crossed the porch to confront Traft.

"Did you send thet kid in heah?" and Slinger jerked his left hand backward. His right hung significantly free and low, "askin' me out if I wasn't afeard?"

"Howdy, Slinger. Yes, I did," replied Jim, and he stepped up the last step. After a keen fearless glance straight into Slinger's eyes, he extinguished the cigarette he carried and dropped it off the porch. It was noticeable that he wore gloves.

"Wal, you want to be careful aboot sendin' fer me thet way."

"No offense. I just wanted you outside."

"An' what fer, Mister Traft?"

"Several things, Slinger, and for that reason I'm glad some of your friends and town folks are present," replied Traft. A small group of men had followed Dunn out of the saloon, but did not come up on the porch. In fact, they edged out toward the hitching-rail.

"What you want?" demanded Dunn, in mingled anger and amaze.

"First I want to tell you I'm sorry my outfit suspected you of cutting our drift fence. We found out who did it, and though we never said it was you, we think we owe you an apology. So I'm apologizing for myself and the Diamond—to you, publicly."

"Wal, it wasn't necessary fer nobody to apologize to *me*," returned Dunn, with a grim laugh. "All the same, I hadn't nuthin' to do with cuttin' your drift fence."

"Well, that settles that. Now you settle *this*. There's talk going around about your sister and me. Some of it is credited to you. Did you tell Hack Jocelyn and Seth Haverly that you not only heard I had insulted Molly—mistreated her, but you *believed* it?"

"I reckon I did, Mister Traft," replied Slinger, not shorn of his personality, because nothing could have done that, but plainly staggered.

"Thanks," said Traft, raising his voice. "Now listen. You are dead wrong. I fell in love with Molly—pretty pronto, I admit. And I asked her to marry me. *Twice!* ... Was that an insult? I shall ask her again. Will that be an insult?"

"I cain't see it thet way."

"I did—well, embrace her *before* I asked her. But I meant no insult. I was just excited—out of my head. Could that be held against me by any fair-minded person —knowing I followed it up with an offer of marriage?"

"No, it couldn't be," declared Dunn.

"Thanks again. . . . Well, Molly refused me. And one of the reasons she gave me was that she was Slinger Dunn's sister."

Molly saw Arch flinch, and tremendously agitated as

she was she felt a pang for him. This Jim Traft had a tongue as deadly as a bullet.

"Now, Slinger Dunn, listen," added Traft, his voice rising to a ring. "You're going to hear something. If you were half the man you think you are you'd quit this lazy, drinking, gunslinging life for your sister's sake. She's a fine little girl—good as gold, damn your stupid heart! And she deserves a better fate than to be disgraced and degraded by a rotten two-bit of a desperado brother. . . . But you've not got sense enough to see what she's worth. And as for your talk about her, well, you are a dirty, low-down skunk. You're a yellow dog. You're a liar, and suspicious, miserable Cibeque blood-spiller. Now, I'm not much on guns, but if you're not a coward—a *coward* —you'll lay off that gun-belt. And I'll swear, if I don't beat you as you deserve, I'll borrow a gun from somebody here, and fight you your own way."

Without the slightest hesitation Slinger unbuckled his belt, containing the heavy gun, and handed it shakily over to some one. He sailed his sombrero off the porch, exposing a livid face. He made a gesture, eloquent of supreme fury, and added to it with incoherent speech. Then like a panther he leaped at Traft.

Molly saw Jim move as quickly, just as Slinger reached him, and appeared to strike at the same instant. The blow cracked. Its force, added to Slinger's momentum, sent him off the porch, where only a remarkable agility kept him on his feet. But he thumped solidly against the hitching-rail, which broke. Horses snorted and jumped. The crowd let out a whoop. Fights were mostly as common as meals in the Cibeque and infinitely more amusing. People inside the store crowded out, and joining the men cut off Molly's view. She edged out, back to the wall, fearful, yet tremendously impelled. She had gloried in Jim's brave front, but she felt he would be helpless in a fight with Slinger. Bumping against a bench, Molly stepped up on it.

She saw Jim go down off the steps to meet Slinger. Then began a fierce exchange of blows, with Slinger slowly forced backward in front of Mace's saloon. Something was wrong, or unusual, Molly vaguely gathered from the exclamations and whispers of the villagers. Slinger Dunn had the reputation of being able to whip his weight in wildcats. But evidently he was slow in getting started here. Suddenly a blow upset him, and he plumped down ridiculously. The crowd warming to the fight greeted that with yells.

Slinger bounced up, only to be knocked down again. Then pandemonium broke loose. The young man from the Diamond might not be going to get mauled into a pulp. He might be cordially hated, but that had nothing to do with the surprise and glee of the West Forkers. Molly could no longer distinguish the shouts, the jeers, the egging on of the contestants, the riotous advice.

Bounding up with the agility he was noted for, Slinger took a couple of nasty digs in order to get hold of Traft. He clinched and plainly sought to trip his antagonist or wrestle him down. But Jim was the heavier and stronger, for with a whirl and a fling he sent Slinger sprawling. This occasioned a sudden silence. Was it possible for Slinger Dunn to be worsted?

"Stand up and fight—you Indian!" yelled Traft. And indeed Dunn had the look and the suppleness of an Indian.

Dunn, now bloody and dirty, responded as if he had no control over himself, as if this taunting voice could drive him to anything. He crouched and bored in, fighting low, until Traft swung up under his guard. Dunn's head jerked up. Another blow sent it back, and a third, square on the nose, making the blood fly, landed him on his back.

This time Slinger did not bounce up. Something was being battered into his consciousness—something that had already dawned upon the crowd. He slowly and cautiously rose, a stream of red running from his nose, down across his tight lips and protruding chin. Again he changed his tactics, proving that a fury of confidence had succeeded to grim realization, and that where an ordinary fighter would have been whipped he still had resource to spirit and energy. He tried a square stand up, give and

191

take. It grew evident that had he adopted this style in the beginning he would at least have done better, for he hit Traft now and then. But the latter could take punishment. If it hurt he gave no sign. His method grew clear to the bystanders, and wagers were shouted out, backing him to win. Molly, in a fit of wild joy at Jim's unexpected and wonderful ability, jumped up and down on the bench, and it was not certain that she did not cry out.

Soon down went Slinger again. The blow that prostrated him was from Traft's right, and was a swing, delivered fast and closely, no doubt to beat his antagonist back and out of balance. Anyway, Molly saw her brother go piling into the dust.

"Reckon now Slinger will rooster him, an' it's shore aboot time," declared a young fellow in front of Molly.

"Yep. An' I'm damn curious," replied his companion.

Other remarks were not wanting. Evidently Slinger Dunn was not yet beaten. Molly had heard of the "rooster" trick in fighting, but had never seen it. And her lot had been to see many an encounter between boys of the Cibeque. She had seen more than one dance interrupted, with the dancers fleeing to the walls, while a fierce battle ensued in the middle of the floor.

But fear for Jim had fled from Molly. He could meet any of Slinger's backwoods tricks.

Slinger slowly circled Traft, keeping well away. Undoubtedly Traft was ready for a new attack. When he got rather close to the wall he divined that Dunn was trying to back him into such a position, whereupon he stood stock-still and waited. Suddenly Slinger dove down with incredible swiftness, on the back of his head and neck and elevated his feet even higher than his arms had been.

His boots were armed with long spurs. He began to kick at Jim. He actually appeared to stand on the back of his neck and his elbows.

"Rooster him, Slinger!" bawled a lusty-lunged lout. And the crowd of West Forkers roared.

Molly saw Jim back from this amazing onslaught, and that was what he should not have done. For Slinger, hunching himself on his elbows, quick as a cat, forced

Jim to the wall. He dodged one vicious kick that raked the wall. Another caught him on his extended arm, tearing his sleeve from wrist to shoulder. Molly saw a glimpse of red. Then a cruel spur cut open Jim's chin. At this Molly screamed at her brother, but her voice was lost in the din. If Slinger did not kill Jim he would surely disfigure him for life. She leaped off the bench and darted here and there to get through the circle of men. Suddenly a louder yell, hoarse and thrilling, made Molly desperate. She squeezed into the front.

Jim, in bent position, had both arms round Slinger's legs. The terrible spurs stuck up, but they scarcely moved. Jim threw Slinger from him with such force that he turned clear over, his head and shoulders acting as a pivot. He fell with a flop. Jim made one jump and landed square on him with both heavy boots. This overbalanced Jim, who went down, but he went down kicking. Rolling over, he was up and at Slinger just as that hideous blood-and-dirt begrimed individual tried to rise.

Jim fastened both hands in his neck and lifted him and flung him sheer against the wall, where his head rang like bone on wood. But Jim did not stop. As Slinger, eyes rolling, tongue hanging out, was sinking down, Jim banged him against the wall again, and finished with a terrific sodden blow. Slinger sank down limp and senseless.

The crowd grew silent. Molly had sense enough to hide behind some one. Jim gazed down a long moment at his beaten antagonist, and then with a scarf he wiped the blood and sweat and dirt from his face. He turned sidewise, so that Molly saw a pale tense cheek.

"See here—you fellows," panted Jim, "I come down— here—to lick him—and to offer him—a job. . . . Reckon he's not worth it. . . . But I'll go through with my part. . . . Tell him—when he comes to—that if he can play square—there's a place on the Diamond for him."

Then Jim parted the crowd and disappeared. Molly slipped back up on the porch in to the store, and never even thinking of her mother, she hurried through to the other corner store and went out the side entrance. Sobbing, and in a terrible condition of mind, she ran home.

18

IT DID not help much for Molly to be home, safely hidden in her loft, except that presently she could breathe freely and would not be seen. Her world of the Cibeque had come to an end. She had been publicly championed, in a royal way that left no peg for the poison-mongers of West Fork to hang calumny upon. Jim Traft had beaten her brother half to death. He had proclaimed his love in the street, for those who ran to hear. He had blazoned abroad the incredible fact that twice Molly Dunn had refused to marry him and that he meant to ask her again. He had called Slinger Dunn all the dastardly names he could lay his tongue to, had banged and pounded and kicked him to insensibility, and then he had told the crowd Slinger could have a place on the Diamond, if he were man enough to take it.

Not one of the romances Jim had sent her in book form could reach up to the heights of this true happening in West Fork. How impossible to believe! Yet Molly knew her eyes and ears were to be trusted, if not her heart. Jim Traft had done a marvelous thing. It was breath-taking. He had a noble spirit that might not be wholly realized in the valley, but his ability to whip the wildcat of the Cibeque and then offer him a job on the greatest outfit of the range, would be appreciated. That kind of language was understood down in the brakes.

Molly began to divine that Jim was invincible. He had brought brains and brawn with him, and the West had taken stock of it. He had given his enemies a hard row to hoe. Molly had spent so many hours dreaming and thinking about Jim that now in the light of his decisive and open stand she could understand him. And she summed up her reaction to it all in a tragic whisper: "My land! If he comes heah I—I'll fall at his feet!"

Her mother's return warned Molly that she was liable to have a bad half hour, and she tried to fortify herself.

"Molly, you up there?" came a trenchant call.

"Yes, ma."

"Come down pronto."

Molly started promptly, but lagged slower and slower, and she thought she would drop off the last steps of the ladder. Her mother stood there, arms akimbo, gazing at her with an entirely new and astounding expression.

"Why'd you run home?" she demanded.

"There was a fight—an'—an' it scared me."

"It needn't have—since it was in your honor. . . . Molly Dunn, did you hear what that young Traft told the crowd?"

"Yes, ma. I was there."

"And it's the truth? He *did* ask you to marry him?"

Molly nodded mournfully. Presently she would be treated to a terrible harangue, and she had already stood enough for one day.

"It's all over town. Crowds on the corners talking. I was told by ten or a dozen people. But I couldn't believe it. You're sure it's no trick? I ran everywhere, hunting you."

"Mother, it's the bitter truth," said Molly, steadily.

"Bitter! Are you crazy, girl? . . . It tastes pretty sweet to me. . . . Did you say 'No' to young Traft?"

"Of course I did."

"But you're in love with him. That's what has ailed you ever since you went to Flag. Anybody could see you were lovesick. Aren't you?"

"Ma, I'm shore sick aboot somethin'," replied Molly.

"For Heaven's sake, then, why didn't you accept him?"

"Because I'm Molly Dunn of the Cibeque."

Then indeed the storm broke over Molly, though it was

so vastly different from what she had anticipated that instead of casting her down it began to do the opposite. In fact her mother presented a most interesting and amusing study, after the first tirade about Molly's lack of family pride. Molly learned that she was a granddaughter of Rose Hillyard of Virginia, and had bluer blood than any Traft who ever lived.

"Didn't I always try to keep these West Fork louts away from you?" demanded Mrs. Dunn, in protest at the outrageous way she had been foiled. "Didn't I bring you up different? You always were somebody, Molly Dunn. And that's where your father and me split. Now, it's proved. You're courted by a fine young chap. He must be *mad* about you—to tell it in the street. They said his being a tenderfoot didn't make him any the less a fighter from way back. . . . Molly, this young fellow will go far out here in the West. He's got stuff in him. He's nephew to old Jim Traft, they tell me, who owns ranches all over, and eighty thousand head of stock. . . . You can't refuse to marry him. Why, it'll be our salvation!"

Molly had to listen and she dared not voice her protest. Moreover she was as much amazed as her mother was indignant. She could not understand this sudden right about face in regard to her admirers. Temporary relief, however, came with an interruption in shape of the arrival of several young men, bringing Slinger home.

For once her mother's tongue stopped its wagging. Arch Dunn was a spectacle to behold. He could walk, but that was about all, and he rewarded the kindly offices of those who had escorted him by driving them off. Both Mrs. Dunn and Molly stood back, afraid to approach or speak, and almost afraid to look. Slinger dragged himself around to the back porch, where he sagged to his bed.

"Arch—can I do anythin'?" faltered Molly.

"Wal, I reckon since I cain't do for myself," was the surprising answer.

Molly hastened to get a pan of water, soap and bandages and salve, and hurried to his side. She divined that by this incident she would either gain or lose a brother. She unbuckled the long spurs, shuddering at the bloodstains on one of them. Arch had got what he deserved. The imprint of hobnails on his face appeared to be a brand. He had been treated to a dose of his own medicine. But the fatal issue might be now that he would kill Jim Traft. Molly prayed and hoped. Could not the same thing, almost, that had happened to her, happen to Arch? She pulled off his boots, and then his wet and torn shirt. The mixture of blood, sweat, and dirt actually made it heavy.

It was not pleasant to look into her brother's visage. Yet pity and tenderness came to her aid.

"Much obliged, Molly," he said, when she had finished what little she could do. "Was you in town when the cyclone hit?"

"Yes, Arch. I—I saw it," she replied, thrilled that he would talk to her in such wise. She prayed for something to make the moment helpful for this wayward brother.

"Did you see him lick me?"

She murmured an affirmative.

"My Gawd! who'd ever thunk it? A Missourie tenderfoot!—But, Molly, he had it on me. I never was so hurted in all my fights. He must have binged my nose a thousand times. I could have bellared out."

"Arch, you must 'have—have hurt him very much, too," said Molly. "He was all bloody."

"Shore. I reckon so. I'd have cut him to pieces—I was thet mad. . . . Molly, I got too mad. An' at thet he hurt me wuss with his sharp tongue."

"It'd not have been so—so bad if you hadn't tried to 'rooster' him."

"Wal, all's fair in thet kind of a fight. I don't care aboot thet any more'n I care aboot his lickin' me. He's simply a better man. I told them so. . . . But I reckon there's another way."

"Arch, you—you'll meet Jim—force him to draw?"

"Thet'd be natural-like, wouldn't it?"

"From the stand of the Cibque, yes. But there's a bigger way to meet it, If you forced him to draw, you'd kill him!"

197

"Huh! I'm not so damn shore of thet. Mister Jim Traft is a surprisin' hombre."

"Arch, I shan't beg you again," went on Molly, eloquently, "but I'll *pray*."

"Pray? What fer?"

"For you to see clear."

"How'n hell can I see anyway with both eyes shet?"

"Brother, I mean see with your spirit."

"Aw, you talk like thet parson who was shot heah onct. . . . Molly, did Traft want to marry you?"

Solemnly Molly nodded.

"I cain't see very well. Talk. Honest now—did he?"

"Yes, Arch—an' that justified my faith in him."

"Reckon a fellar could do no more. . . . An' you wouldn't take him up 'cause you was Slinger Dunn's sister?"

"That was one reason," admitted Molly.

"What you mean?"

"Well, you've a reputation that to civilized folks would look terrible."

"Molly, I'll gamble there's wuss men than me. It ain't nuthin' to pack a gun an' use it when you're crowded. . . . Now the day up the canyon. I shore gave young Traft a long time to shoot. An' he had a rifle in his hands."

"That's what's wrong aboot it, Arch. He wouldn't want to kill you in the first place—an' second, when you met him he'd forget he had a gun. Or be scared."

"Scared! Thet hombre? He was orful scared of me today! Nope, it's jest gun-slingin' wasn't brought up with him."

"It'd be plain murder."

"Wal, I'll let him off—providin' you agree to marry him."

"*Arch!*" whispered Molly, at once rapt and stricken.

"Only deal you can make with me, an you bet it's a hard one to swaller."

Molly knew Slinger Dunn and that she must grasp at straws. "I—I'll—take-you-up, Arch," she said, in a strangled voice. "If he—asks me—any more."

"Don't worry none, sister. Thet hombre will be heah to-day. An' you can make him ask you again. Reckon, though, he'll wait till dark—not wantin' you to see his mug. I shore bunged him up."

Molly trembled on the brink of the precipice to which she had been driven. She dared not look over. She must leap with closed eyes.

"Did you—rooster him bad?" she asked.

"Nope. Only scratched him. But I was shore leggin' it fer him when he ducked an' grabbed me. . . . Fetch me a drink. I'm shore parchin'.'"

Presently Molly stole away to her nest under the roof, thankful to let well enough alone, so far as Slinger was concerned. To secure his promise not to kill Jim was more than she had hoped for, at any cost. And that cost! What a terrible thing to take upon herself! If Jim did not ask her again and soon, he would not live very long. Slinger kept his promises. Molly felt that she would die for Jim and it was not so very much worse to have to marry him. The prospect dazzled and terrified her. If Jim would live in a log cabin and let her work for him! that would be heaven. But he would want to take her away from the Cibeque—from the woods! from Maple Spring! and wear stockings and live in the mansion of a ranch-house at Flagerstown, and meet his rich old uncle —his other relatives—and his mother. Molly was overcome at the thought. She could not do it. But to save his life she would do anything. She sank on her bed with a sensation as if her breast was caved in. And there she lay, like a wounded deer, for hours, and never could have accounted for them.

She crawled down to help get supper and she took some to Arch, who could not eat, and she sat at table more to avoid clash with her mother than to satisfy hunger.

In the dusk she wandered along outside the lane, irresistibly drawn. Her mother and brother were fools. Jim would not come. She longed for him, yet prayed he would stay away.

The bats were whirling in the clear cool air overhead.

The Diamond stood up black and bold, somehow strengthening her. All her life she had looked up to that mighty bulk. The smell of burning pine floated from the dark forest. A nighthawk flitted by with sharp note.

Then a whistle electrified Molly. She had been whistled for many times in this gloaming hour. It was one of the courting tricks of the Cibeque. But never before had a whistle sent a blade into her heart or lent her wings. Her moccasined feet pattered on the hard-packed ground.

She saw a dark form at the gate, leaning on the bars. She ran on. Yes—Jim! . . . Then somehow she was sitting on the top bar—one hand at her bursting breast and the other, which was her left, in Jim's grasp. He spoke, but she did not distinguish what he said, and she could not reply. She felt his rough strong hands. He was slipping something on her finger. A ring!

Then from the gloom behind rasped a low hard voice: *"Hands up, Traft!"*

Dark forms appeared out of the brush, almost without rustle. One man shoved a gun against Jim's back. Seth Haverly! Up went Jim's hands. Molly recognized Sam Haverly. The third man came close—laid a powerful hand on her.

"If you yap we'll kill him!"

Molly would have fallen but for his hold. It was Hackamore Jocelyn.

"Turn round, Traft, an' march," ordered Seth Haverly.

"What's this? A hold-up?" queried Jim, hoarsely.

"Keep still—or it'll be wuss!" hissed Haverly.

"Fellars, I'm takin' the gurl along," announced Jocelyn.

Haverly made a fierce gesture, which included his gun. "You air like hell! I'm tellin' you ag'in, Jocelyn, thet I'm runnin' this outfit. Stay heah an' keep her quiet till we git away with the hosses."

"But, Seth, I want the gurl," replied Jocelyn, low and doggedly. "I'll divvy my share of Traft's ransom with you."

—you Jocelyn!" cursed Haverly. "We'll have hell enough without that. Do you want Slinger Dunn on your

200

trail? . . . Stay heah an' hug the gurl who hasn't no use fer you, if you're that much of a sucker. But foller us pronto."

The Haverlys then forced Jim ahead of them, vanishing in the gloom of the lane. Molly heard the whinny of a horse at a distance. She seemed paralyzed. Hack Jocelyn loomed over her.

"Molly, I'm takin' you willin' or by force," he whispered, bending down to peer at her. "An' don't fergit—if you make even a peep they'll shoot Traft."

"Where they goin'?" gasped Molly.

"Up back on the Diamond. Thet wasn't my idee. They don't know Curly Prentiss. But they're goin' to hide Traft an' hold him fer ransom. But when they git the money they'll kill him. Hang him on the drift fence!—Thet's the plan. An' the only chanct of savin' his life is fer you to go with me."

"How'll that—save Jim?"

"I'll do it. I'll stick out fer lettin' him go. An' if it comes to a pinch I'll force them."

"You swear to Gawd!" demanded Molly in fierce passion.

"Shore. I swear to Gawd."

"Slinger will kill you. I cain't answer fer him. It won't be long till he's on my trail. I'm warnin' you, Hack Jocelyn."

"I heah you," he replied, grimly. "Reckon Slinger is— or would be—a stumper. But he's crippled, an' before he's out ag'in, it'll all be over. . . . I'll hev my stake an' we'll ride out of the country."

"You an' me?" she queried, marveling at the man's egotism and stupidity.

"You an' me, Molly Dunn. Shore it's been long in my mind. . . . Now, will I hev to hawg-tie you?"

"I'll go willin'. But keep your hands off me."

He led her down the darkening lane, out of the clearing into the forest.

19

WHEN JIM Traft heard that rasping command to throw up his hands, and felt the hard prod of a gun against his back, he came down to earth with a sickening thud.

Behind Molly he saw a dark form rise and loom. He recognized it. Hack Jocelyn! With a muttered curse at his heedless disregard of Andy Stoneham's warning he lifted his hands above his head. Then another dark form clinked into sight. He was ordered to face round. A swift glance was the last he had of Molly. Jocelyn's looming over her further added to his dismay.

The men had their short and disgruntled argument, then Jim was faced down the lane. Jocelyn's staying behind to "hug" Molly, as Haverly so vulgarly put it, made the heat dance back into Jim's veins. He turned once to call out to Molly, but a hiss and a move from Haverly dissuaded him. He could scarcely help her, and after a moment's reflection he saw the fallacy of Jocelyn's kidnapping her, too, and he had faith in Molly's wit and nerve. It galled him horribly to leave her there, to be subjected to rudeness, perhaps insult. And the uncertainty of the situation would grow on him until Jocelyn joined them again.

At the point where the lane entered the road to town three men waited with horses. Jim was amazed to make out his own horse, saddled and bridled. These kidnappers evidently were thorough and bold.

"What's your game, Haverly?" queried Jim, breaking into a whispered colloquy.

"We're holdin' you fer ransom," came the gruff reply. "We'll take you to a hidin'-place an' send a rider in to Flag."

"Well, I'll recommend my uncle's paying it, provided you agree to two things."

"An' what's them?"

"That the ransom isn't made out of all reason—and that Hack Jocelyn doesn't share in it."

Haverly let out a grunt which might have meant anything. Jim conceived an idea, which he proceeded to put into execution at once.

"This man Jocelyn is no good," went on Jim. "He had friends on the Diamond and he double-crossed them. He's not a straight shooter. He plays both ends against the middle. You fellows are a lot of suckers."

"Sam—you heah thet?" sharply ejaculated Haverly.

"Hell! I ain't deaf," replied one of the uneasy listeners.

"Jocelyn is using you Cibeque fellows to his own end and you can bet on it," concluded Jim, thinking this entering wedge enough for the moment.

"Seth, I'm gettin' leary myself," replied Sam Haverly. "An' I'm sorry I plugged Jocelyn's game. When he killed Andy Stoneham tonight, right in the road, I shore throwed a fit. Nobody but Boyd an' Hart an' me seen it done. But you can gamble West Fork will lay thet on to us."

"Killed Andy Stoneham!" ejaculated Seth, leaning forward. "When?"

"Jest now, almost. You ought to have heahed the shot."

"Wal, I'll be—! What on earth fer?"

"Jocelyn swore Stoneham was spyin' on him an' givin' us away to Molly Dunn."

"Ahuh. Jealous of poor Andy!—Gawd! but thet fellar is crazy aboot Molly Dunn. . . . We better not wait fer him. Tie his hoss, Boyd, an' we'll hit the trail."

Jim was told to climb into his saddle.

"Hart, you head his hoss. An' I'll foller behind him."

They started off at a trot and soon turned off the road into a trail. It was dark and overgrown with branches of trees that had to be dodged or brushed aside. Jim knew that he had not ridden down to West Fork by that trail. He settled himself for what he anticipated a long night ride and his thoughts were gloomy. He had been shocked to hear that Andy Stoneham had been shot by Jocelyn. Not an hour after Andy had warned Jim to keep indoors! But Jim had disregarded this advice, to his bitter regret. If only Jocelyn would catch up with them! His distrust of this cowboy had been more than justified. Jim realized now that Molly would be in peril. Jocelyn had insisted on kidnapping her, too. The chances were he would do it. Then, when he brought her along with him, there would be precipitated a complex situation. It might well be that Jocelyn in his passion had bitten off more than he could chew.

Jim grew darkly active in thought. He contended with the problem that presupposed Jocelyn was following with Molly. And while he cudgeled his brains he rode on into the denser forest. His captors were silent, and kept to a trot on level ground, and a walk over rough places and upgrades. The moon arose and sent a shadowed blanching into the forest. They rode down into a gully, where water ran over rocks, and the unshod horses slipped and splashed. It was weird and wonderful under the great pines, that moaned fitfully above. They climbed out of the gully to zigzag up a steep trail, soft and full of rocks. And after one of the halts to let the horses rest Jim made certain they were climbing the Diamond. The nerve of these Cibeque riders! Jim knew the Diamond was a big country, exceedingly wild and rough on the high west slope, but he would have staked a good deal on Curly Prentiss trailing them to their lair. Curly's reputation as a tracker would have to be sustained. How the outfit would drive him! As to that, they would each and every one ride out on the man-hunt. This aspect of the situation was thrilling, but Jim felt qualms at the possible outcome. He had come to know his men now.

The moon went down; the sky grew dark blue and

"Whar's our new boss?" he inquired, after greeting Seth, and his tone did not lack sarcasm.

"Matty, you can cut thet talk," replied Haverly. "Or I'm gonna get sore. . . . Jocelyn stayed behind." And in succinct words he gave his questioner a few details of what had detained him. And these elicited a short terse comment, mostly profane.

"If you're hungry come an' git it before I throw it out," called the other fellow, from the cabin.

"Make yourself to home," said Haverly to Jim, leading him in.

Whereupon these backwoods riders, precisely after the manner of cowboys, ate their breakfast standing or sitting or squatting, and one of them knelt with his. Jim very soon could have recommended the cook, and he made a hearty meal.

"What am I supposed to do now?" he asked, genially.

"Wal, you shore wouldn't expect me to sing fer your amoosement," replied Seth, dryly.

"No. I'm feeling pretty good now, considering, and I don't want to take risks," returned Jim, just as dryly.

This retort went home, for remarks were forthcoming anent Seth's opinion of his vocal powers. The men looked frankly at Jim.

"Wal, Traft, do I hawg-tie you or not?" queried Haverly.

"I'm sure I can't read your mind. As a matter of fact, Haverly, I don't think you've got much gray matter. Or you'd never have let Jocelyn persuade you into this deal."

Haverly took that retort gravely, as well as corroborative ones from Matty and the cook.

"If you'll give your word not to make a break I won't tie you up," went on Haverly to Jim.

"Man, I can't promise that. Would you?" protested Jim.

"Wal, I've done it, an' lied like hell. . . . Mister Jim, you pear to be a straight-talkin' fellar. Reckon we'll jest cut this idee of you bein' a tenderfoot. . . . You can set around heah in comfort. But if you run we'll wing you. Thet's my order. Do you savvy?"

"Sure. And much obliged. Molly was right when she said you were a pretty decent fellow. It was only bad company that was making an outlaw of you. She was glad Slinger quit your outfit," replied Jim, departing somewhat from literal veracity. But he had a deep game to play and he knew he could work hard in this simple, primitive mind.

"Wal, so Molly said thet!" he ejaculated, with a queer look on his face. And he fell into a profound reverie.

"Hyar we air," announced Matty, spreading his hands. "An' thet Jocelyn not in the outfit, Air we goin' to wait around, riskin' our necks, while he sparks a gurl?"

"Sparks nuthin'. He'll have to hawg-tie Molly Dunn, if he wants her near him," replied Seth, snorting.

Jim imagined he saw an opening. "Say, didn't you see Jocelyn grab Molly last night? If he hadn't she'd have run."

"I seen him. An' I'll bet you-all a hundred thet he packs her up heah," replied Haverly.

"Why, the man'd be out of his haid," said Matty. "It's bad enough to kidnap this heah Traft boy fer money. But to haul a Cibeque gurl up heah—for doubtful reasons!— Seth, this Jocelyn ain't no Cibeque fellar no how."

"Matty, you'd needn't rag me," rejoined Seth, sullenly. "I cussed him fierce last night. An' I said 'No!' If he fetches her — —; it'll be the wuss fer him!"

"An' it'd be wuss fer us, don't you fergit thet."

Sam Haverly spoke up, "Matty, you ain't heerd aboot Jocelyn shootin' Andy Stoneham last night?"

"Andy! Fer Heaven's sake, thet good-natured clerk of Enoch's!" exclaimed Matty, aghast.

"Hack swore Andy was informin' ag'in' us."

They all looked puzzled, and Seth Haverly shook his blond head broodingly. The expression of thoughts, opinions, criticisms, animosities, by these woodsmen seemed equivalent to the amassing of evidence.

"Fellows," broke in Jim, "Hack Jocelyn is too deep for you. He had the Diamond standing on its head. Even after I saw through him I had a job convincing some of them."

208

"S'pose you give us a hunch aboot this deal," suggested Seth Haverly.

"I will," declared Jim, "provided you agree to what I asked."

Seth turned to Matty, who evidently was an important member of the outfit. "Traft says he'll advise his uncle to pay a ransom, providin' it's not out of all reason, an' thet Jocelyn don't git no share."

"Strikes me hard," said Matty.

"Jocelyn will raise hell. He wanted to name the amount of ransom an' write the letter to old Traft. But he's not heah an' we've shore no time to lose."

Jim had a wild idea. "Haverly, would you trust *me* to get the ransom for you?"

That rendered the eager group speechless. Before Haverly regained his voice the cook, who had gone outside to empty a pan, whistled low and sharp. They all jumped, and it certainly startled Jim. Then Seth strode out, to be followed by the others.

"Jocelyn comin' down out of the woods—ridin' double," said the cook, pointing.

"Fletch, if you ain't correct!" ejaculated Matty. To this Seth Haverly added a volley of curses.

Jim's eyes roved and strained, at last to espy a horse coming under the pines carrying double. He stood stock-still, suddenly galvanized. How slowly the tired horse descended the slope! It was some moments before Jim made out Molly clearly. She was riding astride, behind Jocelyn's saddle, and appeared to sit there easily. Her dark head grew distinct—then her face—then her eyes. Jim wondered how he would ever have the courage to look into them. A long night ride through the wild forest with that vicious cowboy!

Jocelyn had a gray corded face—eyes like gimlets. He threw the bridle and, hands on hips, regarded the silent group.

"Missed the trail an' was lost till daylight," he explained.

Seth Haverly took a step out in front of his comrades. He was slow, guarded, but not afraid.

"So, Jocelyn, you kidnapped Molly?" he queried, harshly.

"Nope. She come willin'."

"What!"

"She come willin'. Ask her yourself," returned Jocelyn, coolly.

"Molly, is he tellin' me straight? Did you come up heah of your own accord?" demanded Haverly.

"Yes, I did, Seth," replied Molly, calmly.

Haverly stepped closer and peered up into Molly's face, as if to read not only confirmation of Molly's admission but of suspicions of his own. Again he made that striking gesture with his hand, and turning to Jim, baffled, eyes afire, he said, "Traft, will you take a look at Molly an' tell me if she's drunk, crazy or—or—"

He did not finish. There seemed to be eloquent manifestations about him that he had loved Molly Dunn.

Jim dragged himself forward to obey, and there might have been a chain with iron balls attached to his legs. Yet something sustained him despite the icy clutch at his heart.

Molly's face was wan. The big dark eyes gazed straight down into Jim's. He read in them love, hope, meaning.

"Mawnin', Jim!" she said.

"Good morning, Molly! How—are you?" he managed to get out.

"I'm all right, Jim."

"All—right?" he echoed. But he took little stock of her words. Jocelyn had acquired some control over her, probably lying to her about his authority in this kidnapping deal. Jim's whole inner being seemed to collapse with his sudden relief. Her eyes told him all he wanted to know.

"Shore. Only awful sleepy, hungry, an' sore," she answered.

"Did you come with Jocelyn willingly?"

"Reckon so, Jim. But I didn't have a lot of choice," drawled Molly, and from behind Jocelyn's shoulder she gave him a deep warning look that certainly could not have been lost by the others.

Jocelyn laughed sardonically. "My word goes a hell of a long way in this heah outfit."

"You fetched her ag'in' my order," declared Seth Haverly.

"Yes, I did. But I tell you she *would* come," snarled Jocelyn.

"Tell that to the chipmunks," retorted Seth, contemptuously, and turning to Molly: "Get down, gurl. You shore look fagged. Fletch will fix you somethin' to eat. An' I'll make a bed for you."

He picked up an ax and strode off toward a clump of spruce. Molly slid down, and limping to a seat under the extension she asked for a drink of water. Matty hastened to get a dipperful from a bucket and proffered it, not without kindliness. Here was a girl of the Cibeque—their own kind—placed in a queer predicament by a comparative stranger.

Jim's gaze had followed Molly devouringly. Happening then to shift it to Jocelyn, he was struck by that worthy's deep-set eyes, smoldering fire. Jim read intuitively that his very life was in peril, right at the moment. There did not appear to be any reason why Jocelyn could not and would not shoot him, as he had Andy Stoneham. It stilled Jim's emotion. Sitting down, back to a log, he studied the ground and tried to catch at whirling thoughts. And the first one he got hold of was that Molly's strength and composure were due to sacrifice. She was in possession of facts unknown to him or Haverly's outfit. Jim believed he could unravel the plot presently.

Seth returned carrying a huge bundle of spruce boughs, which he carried into the back of the cabin, where a stall-like partition hid a corner. Evidently behind this he made a bed, for he came out to get a blanket. After which task he reappeared, to approach Molly.

"You can sleep back there an' be out of the way," he said.

Finally Jocelyn dismounted, and uncinching the wet horse he threw saddle and blankets, unbuckled the bridle, and let him go.

"I'll eat somethin'," he said, "an' then we'll talk."

He went in to the fireplace and sat on a box, where he could not see Molly. And when he bent ravenously to his meal Jim ventured to look at her. Deliberately she held up her left hand, and slipping the ring round to the back of her finger, where the big diamond caught the sunlight, she gave Jim a smile that seemed reward for all his agony. Yet, on second thought, there seemed, beside love and loyalty, a sadness that might be renunciation.

Seth Haverly saw Molly's look, also the ring, and if he did not put two and two together Jim missed his guess. Moreover, Seth did not react sullenly to this revelation.

Presently Molly had satisfied her hunger and thirst and she repaired out of sight behind or in the stall at the back of the cabin. Jocelyn, about finished with his meal, watched her go, and there seemed that of a lean wolf in his gaze. A moment later he got up, and giving his belt a hitch he stalked out under the overhang of the roof, a strong figure, sure of himself and his resourcefulness. Among these men, anyway, he had no superior, and knew it.

"What's on your mind, Seth?" he queried.

"Shore there's aplenty, Jocelyn, an' you're part of it," replied Haverly, gruffly.

"Ahuh. Mister Traft's been talkin' to you. The man who gets your ear last has you on his side."

"Wal, if I'm not loco you stuffed both my ears prutty full."

"Come away from these crawfish of yours, an' we'll settle this deal pronto."

"Nope, not no more. Sam an' the rest of my outfit air goin' to heah every word I say."

Jocelyn rolled and lighted a cigarette. It struck Jim that he was prepared for most anything, and had little respect for the minds and abilities of these Cibeque riders. He leaned against the log post of the cabin and smoked, his hard eyes studying every one of them, and not missing Jim. Something Ring Locke had said to Jim seemed to be justified here. Jocelyn was one of the breed of far-riding cowboys, outlawed from many ranges, perhaps, and a dangerous man. He looked it now.

212

Seth Haverly, after a pause, went on speaking: "I'm sore aboot your shootin' Andy Stoneham."

"Thet's none of your bizness," snapped Jocelyn.

"But it is. You're in my outfit now. We'll all be held part responsible for thet. I reckon it don't make a hell of a lot of difference—if we get away with this ransom deal. But your stealin' Molly Dunn from her home—thet'll let us out."

"Haverly, I didn't steal her. You've got ears, man. You heered her say she came willin'."

"Bah!"

That nettled Jocelyn. He had lost grip here. "Haverly, you've no call to worry on account of Molly. She's goin' away with me to marry me."

"She is!—an' you're leavin' us heah?"

"Thet's your affair. I told you it'd be a good idea to light out fer another range or hole up till the thing blowed over."

Haverly got up, red in the face.

"It's none of my mix, if Molly means to marry you. But it looks damn queer to me. I *know* thet gurl. She wouldn't double-cross a Cibeque dog. . . . You're playin' a prutty high hand, Jocelyn, an' I'm admittin' you're too smart fer this outfit."

"Thanks. But it ain't so much of a compliment. . . . You've no kick comin', if you get your stake out of it."

"I wouldn't of had. But your murderin' Stoneham an' runnin' off with Molly—thet puts a bad complexion on the whole deal. I've a mind to back out of it."

"You will like hell!" asserted Jocelyn. "You'll go through on this deal or you'll have me to square up with."

The scarcely veiled threat had its solid effect upon Haverly. A break was imminent between them—a fact Jocelyn probably saw, but it would not come at once or openly.

"Wal, we ain't got a lot of time to palaver," said Seth. "Curly Prentiss is on Traft's trail, you can bet. The West Forkers air goin' to give him a hunch. An' wurst, Slinger Dunn has got to be considered."

"Dunn was beat so bad thet he'll be layin' up fer a week. Mister Traft played into our hands there."

"Jocelyn, you cain't figger Slinger, an' thet's why I've my doubts aboot you. Shore as Gawd made little apples Slinger Dunn is on your trail right this minnit."

Jocelyn looked up at the threatening clouds rolling from the southwest.

"It'll rain tonight an' then we can't be trailed," he said, confidently.

"Wal, thet'll only delay Slinger. He knows every hole in these hills, an' he's shore a hound on a scent."

Suddenly Jocelyn took hold of Haverly and dragged him out of earshot of the listeners. There in plain sight under a pine they argued, with Haverly growing less and less protesting. Finally they reached some kind of an agreement and returned to the cabin.

"Sam, we've made the best of a bad bargain," announced Seth. "The hitch was Molly. I jest don't care to be around if Slinger happens along. Wal, Jocelyn has agreed to take the gurl an' go to the haid of the draw up heah, an' stay hid in thet trapper's cabin at Turkey Spring. A rifle-shot will warn him to rustle. . . . As fer the deal—we'll send Boyd to Flag pronto with the letter to old Traft. Boyd's got the fastest hoss, an' allowin' half a day to get the money he can make it in lessen two days. What you say?"

"Suits me," said Sam, laconically.

"Wal, it ain't so slick," added Matty. "Tomorrer is Sunday an' no bank is open. Suppose Boyd don't find old Traft at home?"

Jocelyn waved this aside as if unworthy of consideration. "It's the letter thet'll fetch results. Blodgett or any of Traft's friends would dig up ten thousand."

"Oh, will they?" queried Matty, dubiously. "I'll write the letter. It'll be short an' sweet. It'll say if thet money isn't heah with Boyd in twenty-four hours we'll kill Jim Traft an' hang his body over his drift fence!"

20

JOCELYN OPENED a saddlebag, to take out a small packet, which he lay on the ground. Then, as if it was an
afterthought, he lifted out a large flask which he shook
with satisfaction. Placing it back, he next removed a
bottle half full of dark-red liquor. He drank from it. And
then he slipped that in his hip pocket.

Jim shared Seth Haverly's surprise at this act.

"Reckon it ain't no time for drinkin', onless your
nerve's pore," he said caustically.

The other wiped his mouth with the back of his hand.
"You're a bright fellar, Seth," rejoined Jocelyn, rising
with the packet. "But you ain't as bright as I am. My idee
is make Traft write this letter to his uncle."

"Shucks! I thought of thet long ago. An' fer thet
matter, he offered to do it."

"Who offered?"

"Traft heah. But he made it providin' I didn't ask fer
too much ransom, an' thet you wasn't to hev no share."

"Oh! The hell you say!" returned Jocelyn, with a dark
glance at Jim. Then he opened the packet and laid writing
paper, pen, and ink on the woodpile. "Fetch a box."

One of the party procured a box from inside. "Now,
Mister Jim Traft, I reckon you'll put one of your accomplishments to good use," declared Jocelyn.

As Jim rose from his seat Seth Haverly made that
singular gesture.

"Wait," he said, in lower tone. "Jocelyn, I'll agree aboot sendin' fer the money. But I'm daid set ag'in' your double-crossin' old Traft."

"Talk low, you— — —!" rejoined Jocelyn, swiftly. "She might be awake an' heah you. . . . Git it off your chest quick."

Haverly had paled so that his thin amber beard stood out in contrast. He knelt on one knee and whispered, huskily, "I weaken on two points of your deal."

"An' what's them?"

"Layin' the blame on Slinger Dunn, fer one—"

"Too late. I've already fixed thet in West Fork. Never mind your other point."

Jim had heard enough to divine Jocelyn's diabolical plot. Whether that ransom was paid or not, he realized Jocelyn meant to decorate the drift fence with his dead body, like a scarecrow hung up in a cornfield. There was one instant when it seemed Jim's whole internal machinery would fail. Then he rallied in desperate spirit. Right then and there he would have snatched a gun from one of these men, had he been close enough. He nursed the inspiration. If he could kill Jocelyn, that at least would save Molly. Slowly his muscles set to the terrible determination.

"You already fixed the blame—on Slinger!" ejaculated Haverly.

"Shore did. An' nobody but you fellars can prove *he* didn't shoot the store clerk."

"Jocelyn, you're orful smart, but you cain't work miracles," said Haverly.

"Let's don't argue. I've no time to tell you how I put the job up on Dunn. But it's *done*. If he has started on our trail, he'll never be able to clear himself. Thet's all."

"Gawd-Almighty!" gasped Haverly.

At this juncture Jim, whose eyes kept continually traveling back to the corner of the cabin, made the startling discovery that Molly was peeping round the corner of the stall. This added to Jim's uneasy sense of premonition and made him more restless than ever. He tried to move round where he could warn Molly to be careful.

216

"Somebody tie up this fellar," ordered Jocelyn, who apparently could see in all directions at once. "He's snookin' around. Reckon he'd like to get back there with my lady love."

But nobody lifted hand or foot to comply with his order. Snatching up a lasso he made at Jim, and swung the loose loops viciously, cracking on Jim's hip. It was just possible for Jim to resist leaping at Jocelyn, who he knew would shoot him upon the slightest excuse.

"Turn round an' lean ag'in' the post," he commanded. "An' put your hands behind you." With that he proceeded to bind Jim's hands and feet, and tied the last in intricate knots. "It ain't my rope, an' it'll have to be cut." Then he kicked Jim's feet from under him, letting him down. It so happened that Jim slid round in falling, and there he sat, back to the post, helpless and so devoured by wrath that he felt he was sweating blood.

Whereupon Jocelyn drew his bottle from his hip pocket and took a drink.

"To celebrate the day, Mister Traft," he said. "An' when I drink the rest of this I'll set the bottle on your head an' treat you to some real shootin'."

Repairing to the box, he sat down again before the writing-materials. "Hell! I was goin' to make him write the letter, an' now I've tied him up.... Wal, I'll write it myself."

And he did, laboring over the task like a schoolboy. Then he read it over with evident satisfaction.

Seth Haverly held out a lean hand. "I'm askin' to see what you writ."

Imperturbably Jocelyn sealed the letter. "Reckon you couldn't read it, if I let you," said Jocelyn.

"You're demandin' more'n we agreed on," shouted Haverly, beside himself with rage.

"I shore am. Ten thousand wouldn't begin to do me. You're a fool, Haverly. Old Traft will *pay* to save his nevvy's precious life."

"Yes, an' he'll pay all in vain," snarled Haverly, white to the lips.

Jocelyn gave little heed to him, and turning to Flick he

presented the letter. "Ride like hell, now. An' get this in Traft's hands today, or Blodgett's. An' if they ain't handy go to Tobin at the bank. Anyone of them will pile out the greenbacks. An' you ride back, pronto."

"I ain't stuck on the job," declared Flick, brusquely, rising to his feet.

"It's safer than waitin' here, you can gamble. . . . An' I reckon I needn't tell you what I'll do to you—if you don't come back."

Flick threw the letter in Jocelyn's face. "Go to hell! You cain't make me do your dirty job an' insult me to boot."

But Seth and Matty quickly intervened, one to rescue the letter and the other to lead Flick aside. Between them they persuaded him.

"All right, I'll go an' do my damnedest," said Flick. "But I'm tellin' you straight, Jocelyn has busted the Cibeque."

With that he picked up his saddle, blanket, and bridle, and disappeared round the corner of the cabin. Jocelyn stood up, to tilt his bottle and drain the contents. He was about to fling the empty bottle aside when he remembered something. Stalking over to Jim, he pulled him up to an erect sitting posture, rapped his head hard against the post and set the bottle upon it.

"There!" he exclaimed, with elation, and drawing his gun he flipped it in the air, catching it by the handle with great dexterity. "Anybody want to bet me?"

No one answered. Seth Haverly looked a protest he knew it would be useless to voice. Jocelyn had dominated the group. He had alienated them, but had them under his thumb. Jocelyn stepped off ten long paces and turned, his face singularly bright, to level the gun.

Jim saw that the hammer of the Colt was up. Next instant he looked into the small black tube-like barrel of the quivering weapon. All faculties but sight seemed to be in abeyance. And that deadly little hole suddenly belched fire. He felt a slight jar, just before the gun boomed. Particles of shattered glass fell on his head and shoulders.

"Ha! How's thet, Seth? Shot the neck off first crack!" cried the grinning devil.

"Wal, it's damn bad, if you ask me," growled Haverly. "Thet gun of yourn can be heerd fer miles."

When Jocelyn leveled it again Jim's consciousness seemed unclamped. Jocelyn was aiming a little lower this time. Back of the gun gleamed the eyes of a cat playing with a mouse.

Then came a rush and patter of moccasined feet. Molly flashed out. She struck up the gun so violently that it went off harmlessly in the air.

"Hey, gurl! You might get hurt," protested Jocelyn, as if he had been interrupted at a favorite sport.

"Hack Jocelyn, put away that gun," demanded Molly, furiously.

"Say, little lady, you cut quite a figger in my eyes, but you ain't givin' orders yet," drawled Jocelyn. But a keen person could have observed that here he was on uncertain ground.

"Put it away—or I'll—"

"What'll *you* do?" interposed Jocelyn, darkly. All the same he lowered the gun.

Seth Haverly, his brother, and their three comrades showed undisguised satisfaction at the turn of affairs. Seth, in fact, exhibited more. Molly Dunn, whatever her relation to this man or his villainy, was certainly not afraid of him.

"I'm liable to do anythin', Hack Jocelyn," she said, and she looked it.

Seth stepped out unsteadily. "Molly, you better stay back. Honest, gurl, Hack was only foolin'. He ain't really goin' to hurt Traft."

"You're a liar, Seth," snapped Molly. "You know better. An' you're a lot more than a liar. Flick was right, only the Cibeque *is* busted. You let Jocelyn drive Slinger out an' now you're—"

"Shet up," ordered Jocelyn, sheathing his gun. "Molly, you're damn pretty when you're riled, but you're goin' too far. Shet your mouth now, or I'll slap it good an' hard."

219

"You *dare* touch me!" she blazed, with such passion that it affected even Jocelyn.

Jim, loving Molly so deeply, and feeling her emotion so tremendously, had an intuition of a change in her that was not wholly explained by her fears for him. She had heard intimations not intended for her. She had realized Jocelyn's perfidy—that if murder was to be averted she would have to do it. This, of course, could have roused Molly's wild spirit to any extreme. Still, there seemed to be something else. Was Molly talking to gain time? Her suppressed air of suspense, her furtive glances, were slight indeed, compared with stronger expressions, yet they did not escape Jim.

"Wal, I'll touch you aplenty an' pronto," replied Jocelyn.

And that fetched Jim's gaze back to the leader in this woodland drama. He was in time to note Jocelyn, as he espied the ring on Molly's left hand.

"Where'd you get thet ring?" demanded Jocelyn, suddenly hot. "On your third finger! An' a big sparkler!"

"None of your mix, Hack Jocelyn," retorted Molly, and she put her hands behind her back. It was then that Jim imagined he saw her look over Jocelyn or behind him.

Jim peered across the grassy open to the wooded slope. On that side the pines were scattered, as by an expert landscape gardener who wanted a beautiful open forest. And on the instant Jim sighted the flash of a dark form vanishing behind a tree trunk. It resembled what he imagined an Indian would look like, and all his being responded in a concerted shock. Had Molly seen it?

"You two-faced hussy!" ejaculated Jocelyn, dark with jealous wrath. "Stick out your hand. . . . Lemme see."

Molly coolly brought her hand round and extended it, fingers spread, upper side exposed, and she preened it before the exasperated cowboy. She might have been actuated by many motives, but one of them assuredly was a woman's desire to inflict pain.

"Reckoned you was hidin' thet from me," declared Jocelyn, tragically.

"You just had that idea. Why should I hide it from you —or anybody else? . . . It's my engagement ring."

"Engagement!" echoed Jocelyn.

"Shore. . . . An' I may as well announce it."

"Wimmen shore air hell," muttered Jocelyn, more to himself, as if the puzzle of Molly Dunn's dual nature was beyond him. He seemed to be studying her as a species new to him, as fascinating as mysterious. And his doubt grew.

Jim took advantage of the moment to glance across the open to the slope, up and down, and to each side. He was about to believe he had been deceived, when far down to the left, at the edge of the forest, he saw something move —a shadow of a branch or the tail of a horse or—

"Molly, who gave you thet ring?" went on Jocelyn, coming to himself.

"Mister James Traft," replied Molly, blushing deeply. Even though she was playing a woman's wit against this jealous lover, she could not conceal her maidenly confusion, her pride and joy

Jocelyn bellowed like a bull.

"Since when? How long you bin engaged to this— tenderfoot?"

"I reckon—since the night of the *rodeo* dance in Flag."

Perhaps nothing else could have shaken Jocelyn as this mortal blow to his vanity. Perhaps Molly was working on that very weakness. If so, she was taking desperate chances and she knew it. A transformation took place in Jocelyn, not a swift one, but a gradual breaking up of illusive force, of the one vital, vulnerable link in his personality, and it left him a cold, hard fiend.

As he whipped up his gun Molly stepped in front of him, to shield Jim.

"You'll have to kill me first," she declared, resolutely. Certain it was, however, that she knew he would not shoot her.

Jocelyn was in no hurry now. He had a gun in his hand. He would torture as well as slay.

Seth Haverly, however, took him as seriously menacing Molly. "My Gawd, Jocelyn—put thet down!"

"Nope. I feel too much at home with my gun stickin' out in front."

Molly seemed to Jim to be at the end of her rope. Slowly Jocelyn backed her toward where Jim sat, his head against the post, still holding the broken whisky bottle.

"Oh, Seth Haverly, but you're a rotten coward!" cried Molly. "You leave it for a girl to face this devil."

"But, Molly, devil or not, I'm in a deal with him," expostulated Seth, as if stung. "An' it ain't no call fer me to risk my hide."

"Deal, yes—a dirtier deal than you know. He's—"

"Molly Dunn," cut in Jocelyn, "shet your jaw—or it'll be too late?"

"Too late! Why you poison-tongued snake—do you think I'd believe you again? . . . You can kill me an' Jim —an' this yellow bunch for all I care. But by God! I am givin' you away."

Jocelyn made a fierce reach for her. But he did not quite lose himself in the passion of the moment. He had to stand clear, to be free, to watch the Haverlys. So he dared not close in with her.

"I'm warnin' you onct more."

Molly must have kept her burning eyes on him, at bay, while she denounced him to the Cibeque.

"Seth, *he* cut the drift fence, even while he was workin' on the Diamond. An' after. He aimed to get you an' Slinger blamed for that. He's double crossed you as he did Jim. He means to take *all* the ransom money . . . to murder Jim an' lay that on to you. . . . Oh, I *know*. I see through him—now. He got me up heah—by swearin' he'd save Jim's life—if I'd give in to him. I agreed. An' then he kept at me—all night long—an' once I had—to fight him. But I—I wouldn't give in—"

"You pop-eyed cat," yelled Jocelyn stridently. Who wants you to give in?—I'll rope you like I would a mean hawse!"

Suddenly the gun banged. Jim felt the bottle blown off his head. Molly screamed.

"Right under your arm, Molly," said Jocelyn. "How's

thet fer shootin'?" And he began to step from one side to the other, the gun extended about even with his hip.

Molly did not back away from his formidable advance. She blocked his every move, interposing her body between the gun and Jim. Then like a cat she pounced upon Jocelyn's hand, shoving it out of line. Bang! The bullet scattered dust and gravel over Jim. Both her hands and then her teeth were locked on Jocelyn's wrist.

"Leggo!" he yelled, lustily, wrestling to get free. But he could not free simself. With his left hand he lifted Molly by her hair. He swung her clear of the ground, her weight nothing to his powerful arms. But he could not shake her grip. Blood began to drip from his wrist.

"Bite, —!" he cursed. And lifting her he tried to get the gun on Jim. But as he pulled the trigger she swung desperately, spoiling his aim. The gun roared and a bullet tore splinters out of the post beside Jim's ear, and whirred away into the forest. The recoil of the heavy Colt loosened Molly's teeth, but not her hands. She screeched like a wild creature. "Before Jocelyn could take advantage of this, she again buried her teeth in his wrist. He swung her aside, but she alighted on her feet. He fought her to and fro, until they entered the cabin. Haverly and his men were caught in a trap. Like rats they ran to dodge behind the stall, yet to peep out at this extraordinary encounter.

Jocelyn took another snap shot at Jim, narrowly missing him. The shock of this explosion, right at her ear, appeared to weaken Molly, for she let go with her teeth, and her weight sagged on Jocelyn's arm. He shifted his left hand from her hair to her neck, where his long fingers shut like a vice. Yet on the instant he could not get loose. His malignant cry, however, hoarse and exultant, attested to the victory he saw. Molly could no longer move. He was lifting her, and the gun.

Jim's distended sight caught a shadow of something passing him. He could not move, even his eyes, but out of the tail of his right he saw a buckskin-clad figure that had appeared as if by magic.

223

"Hey, cowpuncher!" rang out the voice of Slinger Dunn.

Jocelyn jerked up his head and a fleeting consternation showed on his convulsed face. He let go of Molly's neck. And as his hands slipped loose she slid down.

Like a whipcord Jocelyn's gun leaped. But as it leaped Dunn's crashed. Jocelyn appeared to be arrested. Then shot through the heart, he staggered forward, with an awful look that set blankly, and plunged step by halting step, to fall clear outside of the cabin.

21

A HEAVY breath escaped Slinger Dunn as he removed his gaze from the twitching Jocelyn to Molly and then to the bound Traft. His battered face was scarcely recognizable, but his eyes were wide open.

" 'Pears like I didn't get heah none too soon," he drawled.

"Slinger! Just—in time!" gasped Jim.

Molly sat up dazedly, her hair disordered, blood on her chin and nerveless hands. "Oh!—Oh!—Oh!" she moaned.

"Air you hurted, Molly?" asked Dunn.

She stared wildly. *"Arch!"* she cried, in recognition. "Is —he daid?"

"Wal, I reckon, onless he wears a big watch in his breast pocket."

Molly got shakily to her feet and ran unevenly to Jim, where she fell, still game, still proof against the collapse that had taken her strength.

"Cut—this—rope," she whispered, huskily, plucking at Jim's bonds.

Dunn, with a wary glance at the back of the cabin, dropped a knife in front of Molly.

"Jim—did he—hit you?" she asked, fearfully, as she freed his hands.

"No. But I sure know what a bullet sounds like. . . . Let me have the knife. . . . Molly!"

"I cain't heah you," she said. "His gun deafened me."

Jim severed the knotted rope and got up, lifting Molly with him, which action assured her that he was uninjured.

"Oh—thank heaven!" she cried, sinking against him. "Jim! Jim! I thought—he'd hit you."

Jim held her tight, and probably no other moment of his life could ever equal that one. Following it he became aware of Dunn sheathing his gun.

"Come out heah!" he called, and his voice was piercing enough to penetrate more than a board stall.

Seth Haverly came out first, livid of face, and Matty followed, visibly shaken, but unafraid.

"Slinger, he had us buffaloed," explained Seth.

"Who else back there?"

Sam slouched out, then Hart Merriwell, and lastly Fletch.

"Where's Boyd?"

"Jocelyn sent him with a letter to old Jim Traft."

"Ahuh." Then Dunn turned to his sister.

"Molly, you was shore fightin' thet skunk, an' I needn't ask if he got the best of you. But Seth, heah, an' Sam—did they stand around an' let thet hombre bulldog you?"

The moment was critical and Molly reacted to it as might have been expected from Slinger Dunn's sister. If Jim had had the impulse to check her he suppressed it.

"They shore did," she cried, lifting her pale face from Jim's arm. "An' what is wuss, Arch, they *believed* him . . . believed I'd got thick with him an' come up heah, a willin' hussy. . . . I agreed to give in to Jocelyn—if he saved Jim's life. No use lyin'—I'd have done it. . . . But I never trusted him. I lay back there in the stall—listenin' an' watchin'. An' pretty soon I knew his game. . . . Arch, I was 'most crazy. I prayed—an' I peeped out through a chink between the logs. An' I saw you comin' under the pines! ... *Oh!* then I had to brace an' keep Jocelyn off his guard—till you—could get heah."

"Wal, I reckon it's aboot good fer Jim Traft thet you *air* Slinger Dunn's sister," drawled Dunn.

"Good and fine and wonderful," declared Jim, fervently. "I'm thanking God she *is* Molly Dunn of the Cibeque!"

"Thet squares you with me, Jim Traft," replied Slinger, gruffly. "Take her away from the cabin. ... An' wash the blood offen her."

Jim was not loath to lead Molly away, half supporting her in his arm. He lifted her across the brook, surprised and pleased to find she was a pretty heavy little chunk. He led her on, across the open grassy flat and up the first gentle slope to a pine tree, where a fragrant brown mat, and shade, invited a stop.

"This is far enough," he said, letting her down. "I'll run back—"

"Don't leave me. There'll be a fight," she cried, clinging to him.

"But only to the brook to wet my scarf. ... You're all bloody."

"Then hurry."

Jim made short work of the trip down to the brook, and while soaking his silken scarf he heard a loud angry protest of Haverly in the cabin, and the cold ring of Slinger's voice. He ran back to Molly. She was spitting like an angry cat.

"I bit him, Jim, I bit him! I'd have chewed him to pieces. ... But now it's over I'm sick—sick with the taste an' smell an' sight of his blood."

And as she spat out she did look sick.

"Never mind, darling. Your biting saved my life. ... My God! how wonderful you were—how I love you!" And he kissed her passionately, stained lips and chin and hands.

Evidently this treatment effectually checked her nausea.

"Oh—Jim—somebody'll see," she whispered.

"Who cares?—But let me scrub you good," laughed Jim, and he did scrub her mouth inside and outside, and nearly washed the skin off her chin, and likewise the little strong brown hands.

"There goes one. Slinger's let him off. Look!" said Molly.

"That's Matty," replied Jim, recognizing the tall member of Seth's outfit. He was in a hurry, and snatching up a saddle and bridle he strode off up to the park, looking back over his shoulder. "He didn't seem a bad sort of fellow."

"I'm glad. Slinger is hell when he's—like you saw him. . . . Oh, but wasn't Hack Jocelyn the dastardliest—"

"Sweetheart, don't think of him," entreated Jim.

"But he's daid! An' Slinger killed him—all on my account."

"No, not at all. Some on mine, and some on his own. . . . Honey, did you really mean you'd accepted me —when you threw it up to Jocelyn—that we were engaged?"

"Yes, Jim—but, man alive, you cain't make love to me now! I tell you Slinger will *kill* Seth Haverly, an' like as not Sam, too."

"I'm afraid, but I hope not," declared Jim. "All the same, Molly Dunn, while they're palavering I *can* make love to you."

"Funny tenderfoot from Missourie you are—I guess not," she declared. "You're almost another Curly Prentiss."

"Thanks. You couldn't pay me a compliment that'd please me more."

"Jim, I'd have liked Curly if he hadn't the cowboys' weakness," said Molly, thoughtfully.

"And what's that?"

"Bein' too gay with a girl—the very first thing—all same like an Easterner I met once."

"Ha! Ha!—Where'd you meet *him*, Molly?"

"I reckon it was in Flag. . . . Oh—Jim—" She was surrendering to his arm, when suddenly she started up. "Look! Another leavin'."

"That's the cook. Fletch, they called him," said Jim, watching the man, who lost no time in imitating Matty's example in making tracks from the cabin, burdened by his saddle.

"Hart Merriwell left, besides Seth an' Sam. Slinger will let Hart go. Now you watch."

Presently Jim espied Merriwell come out, in no great hurry, and instead of striding away he slipped round to the back of the cabin and peered through a chink.

"Well, there must be something up," declared Jim, anxiously.

"Listen! That's Slinger shoutin'." rejoined Molly.

Jim did distinguish Slinger's voice, with its high ranging note, but only the sound carried so far. What meaning he could attach to the harangue he had to supply himself. But as Slinger kept on it was no great task to imagine the storm of violent backwoods profanity with which he was berating the brothers who had betrayed him.

"Just like I heahed once at a dance," said Molly, with a sigh. "There!" She jerked spasmodically at the crack of a gun, and clapping her hands over her ears she sagged against Jim.

"Gosh!—That didn't sound like Slinger's gun!" ejaculated Jim, and all his being seemed suspended upon his hearing. Bang! "That *was* Slinger's," he went on, huskily, tightening an arm around Molly. Shots followed, three or four, so swiftly as to be hardly separated. Then again came the heavy boom and a volley of lighter reports. There was a pause that might have been a suspension of hostilities. Jim dared believe it was over. Then followed loud reports, a heavy one—more of the sharp rifle shots —another heavy, and quickly the boom. Silence! Smoke drifted out of the cabin, showing blue against the green pines. Hart Merriwell, who had evidently run off appeared coming slowly back, halting, waiting, then approaching again. But there were no more shots.

"All—daid!" whispered Molly, lifting her head. She must have been able to hear the shots even with her ears covered.

"I—I'm afraid so," replied Jim, huskily. "I see Merriwell coming back. . . . There. He's going in. . . . Molly, I'll go, too."

"That's the end—of the Cibeque," she murmured. "Poor Arch! . . . He wasn't all bad."

"Stay here, Molly," admonished Jim. "I'll come back— if—if—" He squeezed her hand, and getting up he ran down the slope, leaped the brook, and soon reached the cabin. As he peeped round the post, against which he had sat not many minutes past, his hand came in contact with the place splintered by Jocelyn's bullet.

The interior of the cabin was still smoky. Jim saw one of the men huddled in a heap. Then on the other side he espied Merriwell kneeling beside Slinger, whom he had propped up.

"Is he—alive yet?" called Jim, breathlessly, and he ran in.

"Hullo! Shore, Slinger's alive, but shot all up," replied Merriwell. "Help me carry him out of this smoke."

They lifted the bleeding, broken body and carried it out to the shady side, where they laid it on a blanket. While Jim lifted Slinger's head Merriwell placed a saddle under it.

"Reckon you'll—cash in, Slinger, ole pard," he said, gulping. "Anythin' I can do?"

"Where's Molly?" asked Dunn faintly.

"She's across the brook. I'll call her," replied Jim, and he got up to go round the cabin. Molly was coming. She had seen them carry her brother out. Jim went out to meet her.

"Molly, he's alive. He asked for you." He had to run to keep up to her.

"Oh, Arch!" burst out Molly, dropping on her knees. "Are you—bad hurt?"

"Wal, Molly, I ain't hurt atall—but I reckon—I'm done fer," he said, feebly.

"Where there's life there's hope," interposed Jim, as he too knelt.

"Oh, cain't we do anythin'?" cried Molly.

"You don't happen—to have some—whisky?" replied Slinger.

"There's some here," said Jim, leaping up. "Where did I see it? . . . Jocelyn had it." Jim ran to the saddlebags, and procuring the flask he rushed back. Dunn took a stiff drink.

"Wal, Jim Traft, you're lucky—thet you're not layin' around heah full of bullet holes," he said, in stronger voice, not devoid of humor.

"I guess yes," said Jim, fervently.

"I was fer killin' you myself—till Molly made me—a promise."

"What promise?"

"Molly, air you goin' to keep it?"

"Yes, Arch," replied Molly, as she bent over him, her bright tears falling.

"Good! Reckon thet'll be aboot all," said Slinger, with satisfaction.

"Molly, dear, tell me the promise," rejoined Jim, earnestly.

"Jim, he was shore set on killin' you. I begged him not to. An' he said he'd let you off—if I—I would make you ask me again—to marry you—an' take you up. . . . So I promised."

Jim took Dunn's limp hand. "Slinger, she'd never had to make me. I'd kept asking till doomsday."

"Ahuh. Then you're powerful fond of my kid sister. . . . Wal, I cain't thank Gawd fer much—but I do fer thet."

"Oh, let's *do* somethin'," burst out Molly, in desperation. "Hart, where's he shot bad?"

"Lord! He's shot bad all over," declared Merriwell.

"Jim, I tell you bullet holes are nothin' to Slinger Dunn. He's not bleedin' at the lungs, because he'd be spittin' blood. This cut on his haid isn't bad. His left arm is broke. There's a hole in his right shoulder. . . . Heah, low down is the bad one. . . . Oh, my Heavens!—But let's tie it tight."

The practical Molly prompted the stricken men to get busy and do what was possible for the wounded one. Jim believed the gunshot in the abdomen would have killed any ordinary man. It had gone clear through. They padded that and bound it up. He had another dangerous wound in the hip, which, according to Merriwell, like the hole in his abdomen, had been made with a rifle.

While they washed and dressed his wounds, as best they could do it with limited means, Slinger talked.

"Sam throwed fust on me, when I was keepin' two eyes on Seth. An' he got me thet crack in the belly. It keeled me over, or the fight'd been short an' sweet. . . . I nailed Sam. Then Seth showed his true color at last. He dove fer the stall an' began shootin' from behind. He had a Colt an' a forty-four Winchester. An' he shore pumped lead into me. . . . I sent a couple through the stall. Hit him, fer he cussed hard. But he come back at me. Then I flopped over along the wall, where he couldn't see me onless he come out. He'd used up all his shells fer the Colt. Anyway, he didn't take risk to load, an' stuck to the rifle. Reckon thet beat him. I got to the corner by the stall— leaned over quick—an' bored him—when he was tryin' to shift the rifle round."

Beyond a slight huskiness Dunn's voice did not depart radically from a tone of ordinary conversation. There was no trace of emotion, unless the mere fact of lengthy recital of the fray was one. He had a remarkable vitality. Jim knew that in case of injury, especially from gunshots, the next perilous thing to the wound itself was the shock to the consciousness. This probably had not occurred in Dunn at all.

"Now, Merriwell, what more is to be done?" queried Jim.

"I reckon nuthin', onless he wants us to pray. How about it, Slinger?"

"Nope," was the laconic reply. He lay still, with closed eyes, a limp and ghastly sight. Molly sat beside him, supporting his head.

"I heah hosses," suddenly spoke up Dunn, opening his eyes.

They all listened, and Jim shook his head.

"You ain't close enough to the ground. I shore heah hosses," added Dunn.

Merriwell got up to walk out away from the cabin.

"Bunch of cowboys comin'," he said, excitedly. "Reckon I'd better make myself scarce."

Jim joined him. "No need to run, Merriwell. That's Curly Prentiss and some of my outfit."

"By gum! An' they've ketched Matty an' Fletch," ejaculated the other.

So it appeared to be, and presently Jim made certain of it. Curly rode down the slope, followed by Bud and Lonestar and Jackson Way, who had in tow the late fleeing members of the Cibeque.

Curly threw his bridle and made one sweep of his long leg and slid to the ground. A blue flash of keen eyes took in the situation.

"Howdy, boss! Mawnin', Miss Molly!" he said, and lifted his sombrero from his bright hair. Then he bent his gaze upon the prostrate Dunn.

"Prentiss, you're a little late in the day," said Dunn. "But I'm recommendin' you let Matty an' Fletch go. I did. . . . It was Jocelyn an' Seth an' Sam. Take a look in the cabin."

Curly did as he was bidden, returning promptly, a queer cold look in his eyes.

"Wal, Slinger, it shore was a good job. But I'm sorry they got you."

"Wal, I ain't cashed yet, an' if I do it shore won't be owin' to Seth or Jocelyn. Sam's the one who bored me. I wasn't lookin' fer it from him."

Bud Chalfack and the cowboys came riding down, to halt before the group.

"Dog-gone, Jim, if it ain't fine to see you on yore feet," said Bud, heartily. "How do, Molly! . . . Somebody tell me what's come off."

Whereupon Jim briefly related the circumstances leading up to the stop at this cabin, the wrangle over the conditions of the ransom, the blackguard conduct of Jocelyn, and the several fights that succeeded. If Jim emphasized anything it was the wit and courage and ferocity of Molly.

"Dog-gone me!" burst out Bud, with worshipful eyes on the girl. "Molly, I always knowed you was the sweet-

232

est an' wonderfulest little devil in Arizonie, but now I jest haf to take off my hat to you."

And he did it, quite gallantly.

Curly's encomium was directed at Jim. "You lucky son-of-a-gun! To come out heah an' steal her from us!"

Slinger had missed nothing of all this. He seemed not only incredibly tenacious of life, but singularly possessed of receptive faculties.

"Wal, fellars, she's Molly Dunn of the Cibeque," he drawled.

Molly took exception to compliments on the moment. "You heartless cowpunchers! Heah's daid men all aboot an' Slinger dyin'—yet you talk an' make eyes at me. Jim, you're just as bad. Curly, haven't you got some sense?"

"Molly, I'm shore beggin' your pardon," replied Curly, contritely, as he threw off his gloves and knelt by Slinger. "Tell me jest where he's shot."

Molly and Merriwell together gave him the desired information. Curly got up, decisive though grave. "Mebbe he's a chance. You cain't kill some fellars. . . . Jack, ride to Flag an' fetch back the doctor. He can drive a buckboard clear to Cottonwood. You lead an extra saddle-hoss, an' then come rustlin' across country. . . . Holliday, you an' Bud go back to camp an' pack some of our outfit over heah. Fetch the boss's pack an' don't forget everythin' to make Miss Molly comfortable. . . . Boss, do you want to hold these Cibeque men heah? I reckon if we let them go they'll haid Flick off with thet ransom money. An' we shore don't want to lose thet."

"Hold them, then, till Flick comes back," replied Jim. "You and I can take turns on guard."

"Wal, Traft," spoke up Matty, "if you'd like to know, we're so darn glad the way things hev come off thet we won't need watchin'."

22

SLINGER DUNN sank into a pallid insensible state that Jim believed was the coma preceding death. Molly, too, succumbed to a fear that every moment would be his last. But the hours passed; the three prisoners played cards and made no trouble whatever; Curly and Jim erected a tarpaulin shelter over Dunn, and a spruce-bough bed for Molly beside him; they got supper from the coarse stores they found in Haverly's packs; the setting sun filled the forest with a mellow glory; the heavy buffeting wings of wild turkeys going to roost in the pines broke the silence. And Slinger Dunn still lived.

Night fell, and the wind moaned the threatening storm. Coyotes ranged the park and yelped a staccato whining protest at the camp fire. Weird flickering shadows played on the cabin and the improvised tent. Molly sat close to her brother, leaning against the wall, silent and watchful. The only way she could ascertain that Dunn still lived was by touch, and when his pulse grew imperceptible and his hands cold she laid her head on his breast to listen to his heart.

Jim stayed up with her, and seldom left her, except to replenish the fire and take a look at the inside of the cabin, where the prisoners slept. Curly lay across the opening, and every time Jim stepped near, though ever so noiselessly, he would awaken. The dead men had been moved to a corner of the cabin and covered with canvas.

Sometimes Jim paced up and down, finding action helpful to the surcharged condition of his mind. He never closed an eye, and seldom indeed was there an interval of any length when he was not watching Molly. In the dead of night there in that lonely forest he came to full appreciation of her sterling worth and a deep respect for the primitive life that had developed her. Many things considered by civilized people as necessary were merely superficial. Molly had the great qualities, virtue, courage, and love.

When he would approach her, as he did often, and sink down on one knee to peer at the pale Slinger, Molly would take hold of him. By the firelight he could see the big eyes, black as night, rest upon him with a glance that made him wonder how life had come to reward him so beautifully.

Towards dawn the wind ceased and despite the overhanging clouds the air chilled until it grew bitter cold. Jim wrapped his coat round Molly and laid his saddle blanket over Slinger. He kept the fire going, and stood close to it, burning his palms, turning from front to back.

It grew very black and still, the formidable hour before dawn when even the life of the forest seemed at lowest ebb. Slinger would go soon, Jim thought.

Molly called him. "He whispered somethin' just now," she said. "I think he called for Seth's sister. He was sweet on her. . . . She'll hate even his memory now."

Jim sat with her then, silently awaiting the end, holding her against him. It seemed the most melancholy and poignant of all the long night hours. How welcome the first gray streaks! Something ghastly and ghostly stole away into the forest. A fine misty rain began to fall. Daylight at last with Slinger Dunn still not dead!

Curly appeared around the corner of the cabin, yawning, and stretching his lithe length.

"Mawnin', you babes in the woods," he said, and dropped beside them, to lean over Dunn. "Wal, Slinger, old man, I reckoned you'd be long where the blue flags an' the cornflowers blow."

235

"Curly, not yet," replied Jim. "All night we've been expecting him to die. And every moment the last hour."

"It takes so long," said Molly, sadly.

Curly placed his ear over Dunn's heart and listened.

"Wal, you both got the willies," he declared, as he rose with a glad smile. "He ain't goin' to croak."

"What!" ejaculated Jim.

"Oh, Curly!" cried Molly, in an agony of hope.

"Shore he'll live. I ain't no doctor, but I've seen a heap of fellars pass out. An' Slinger don't show no earmarks of thet this mawnin'."

Molly's little remaining strength eked out here and she collapsed in Jim's arms. He let her gently down on the bed of spruce and covered her over. "Go to sleep, honey," he said.

"Boss, it's goin' to rain," announced Curly, when indeed it was raining already. "Let's rig up another tarp heah fer Slinger. . . . Look! Molly asleep all in a jiffy. Poor kid! . . . Jim, I don't see how I kin give her up to you."

"Don't you? Well, please be reasonable about it," replied Jim, dryly.

They stretched a tarpaulin over the makeshift canvas shelter. "Thet'll do fer a spell. Mebbe we kin move him into the cabin after Doc Shields looks him over. . . . But say, boss, how aboot them stiffs in there?"

"They'll have to be buried, of course."

"Wal, the Haverlys ought to have decent burial, I s'pose, but thet Hack Jocelyn, —, he ought to be throwed to the coyotes."

Jim followed Curly inside. He stripped the scant covering off the bodies. It was not a pretty spectacle. Jim recoiled. But Curly viewed it differently.

"Daid center on thet left vest pocket," he muttered, bending over Jocelyn. "Slinger's fancy shot, I've heahed say. Wal, I'm durned if I want the jasper slingin' one at me."

Jim went back to rouse the three prisoners.

"Roll out, you buckaroos, and help get breakfast."

Matty lumbered up cheerfully, and the others followed

with an alacrity that presupposed a desire to please. Probably they did not hold themselves guilty of the deal hatched by the Haverlys and Jocelyn.

"Say, you Cibeque duffers," said Curly, facetiously, "I fell asleep purpose last night so you could sneak off."

"Prentiss, I'd hate to of tried it. But all we own in the world is this pack outfit," explained Matty.

"Wal, thet ain't a hell uv a lot."

While they ate breakfast the rain ceased and blue sky showed overhead, soon to be obscured, however, by fast scudding clouds out of the southwest.

Molly slept on, and even the bells on the Diamond packhorses ringing down the slope did not wake her. Jim did not recall ever being so glad to see cowboys as then.

"The whole night long!" sang out Bud. "The whole night long!"

"Say, Bud, if it was long for you, what do you suppose it was for Molly and me?" retorted Jim.

"I see you haven't covered Slinger's face, so he mustn't hev croaked yet," replied Bud, practically.

"Howdy, boys! Sure glad to see you," said Jim, running his eye over the group. "Where's Hump and Uphill?"

"Don't know. Cherry will tell you what he thinks, an' it ain't no cheerful news," announced Bud. "We left some uv the hosses an' packs. Jeff is comin' somewhere back. He shore hates a saddle."

"What's up, Cherry?" queried Jim, approaching Winters, who was dismounting.

"Boss, I reckon Stevens an' Frost hev struck somethin' out at the head of Derrick. We left a note fer them to hit our trail. An' I reckon they'll be along, mebbe tonight."

Jim did not see in Cherry's words much to be worried about. But still less did he like Cherry's expression than the hint in Bud's remark.

"Well, unpack and make camp," he ordered. "If Dunn pulls through we'll have to stay here for days. Put up the little tent for Molly, if you fetched it. But first thing after you unpack bury these dead men."

One by one, Bud leading, the cowboys went up to have a look at Slinger and Molly. Strange to say, no remarks were forthcoming, which was probably owing to solicitude for the girl. Then, after the fashion of cowboys, they set to work. Jeff Davis rode down into camp, and added his efficient hands to the task.

The rain held off till early in the afternoon, when it began to fall in earnest. Molly slept on through it all, dry and snug under shelter and blanket. Slinger showed no change. The three Cibeque men had been unceremoniously moved out of the cabin, which the cowboys had thoroughly cleaned. Jim, after a short stay beside Molly and her brother, watchful to see any change in the latter, went inside the cabin to wait. There was nothing much to do now, but wait.

Bud appeared to be industriously working over something. It was a section of aspen tree, split in half, on the white surface of which he had carved some words. Jim bent over Curly, who was intent on the artist.

Hackamore Jocelyn, N. G.
Drift Fence Cutter
Died with his boots on, Sept., 1889.

"I clean forgit the date," said Bud, viewing his work with satisfaction.

"Reckon it's aboot the twenty-third. Towards the end of September, anyhow. An' what's the date amount to? Jocelyn should never hev bin borned. All we aim to celebrate with this heah tombstone is thet he's damn good an' daid," replied Curly.

The other cowboys noted Bud's work with quite different points of view."

"Bud, anyone could see you once worked in a graveyard," said Cherry.

"What's the idee—cuttin' out a haidpiece fer thet greaser?" inquired Lonestar, scornfully. "There'd be sum sense in it if we'd buried Slinger."

"Shore. But it's good practice in case Slinger croaks," observed Bud.

"Hev I gotta tell you fellars any more thet Slinger will

live?" queried Curly, annoyed that his judgment was questioned.

"He might, Curly. Life is darn oncertain. I'll bet you Slinger croaks," returned Bud, much animated at the prospect of a wager.

"Aw, hell!"

"Wal, then, I'll bet you he croaks before Doc Shields gits hyar," went on Bud.

"You'd gamble on your grandma's coffin," asserted Curly, in supreme disgust. "Funniest thing, too. You always lose."

"Like hob I do! Right this minnit your spurs an' chaps belong to me. You'd be naked 'most but fer my magnanimity."

"But, it shore ain't no wonder no gurl will stick to you," replied Curly.

"Wot's a gurl got to do with games uv chance? I'm a born better, as you know to your cost."

"But you'll bet on anythin' in Gawd's world," protested Curly.

"Thet's the secret. How much did I clean up when the boss licked you—an' Cherry an' Up an' Lonestar? Huh! I got it all down, an if we live to reach Flag ag'in, I'll be rich."

"Shore. An' you'll be drunk, too."

"Curly, you make me so orful tired. If I wasn't so all-fired fond uv you—fer no reason thet any human bein' could see—I'd be riled at your insults. . . . Now listen. Money talks. Put up or shet up. Hyar's my roll."

Bud exhibited a roll of greenbacks that made Curly's eyes stick out and likewise excited Lonestar and Cherry.

"Where'n hell'd you git thet?"

"I bin holdin' out. Now produce your roll. It'll look like a peapod thet a hoss stepped on. . . . Wal mebbe not so flat," added Bud, as Curly retaliated by surprising him. "Now, hyar's a bet thet'll show how game I am. My roll ag'in' yours thet Slinger *won't* croak!"

Curly's face was saved, and the risk of his money, too, by the arrival of Jack Way and Dr. Shields. The latter was a little man, lost in a heavy slicker. From the exchange of greetings he was well acquainted with several of the Diamond. He got off, and out of the slicker, then removed a small medicine-satchel and a parcel from the saddle-bag.

"Where's your man?" he queried, after being introduced to Jim. "Fetch clean hot water."

Jim did not think it necessary to awaken Molly. The job would be gruesome and she would insist on helping. Dr. Shields felt of Dunn's pulse and heart, and said, "Hum!" which meant little to Jim. Then he cut open Dunn's blood-caked garments, and first removed the bandages from the wound in the abdomen. At sight of this he shook his head. When he saw that the bullet had gone clear through he nodded his head. So Jim inferred it was both bad and good.

Cherry fetched a pan of hot water. Whereupon the doctor went to work, and with Jim's assistance, in an hour had all six wounds dressed.

To Jim's amaze Slinger opened his eyes. No doubt all the while he had been conscious.

"You ought to be a hoss-doctor," he said. "Hurtin' me wuss'n the bullets. . . . Am I goin' to cash?"

"Dunn, that shot in your belly ought to have killed you long ago," replied the doctor. "The one on your hip is bad, but not critical. The others just gun-shots."

"Did you fetch any whisky?"

Shields made haste to supply this evident pressing need.

"Jim," said Slinger," I knowed you gave me some whisky of Jocelyn's. But I shore didn't want to live on thet."

Suddenly Molly sat up, wide-eyed and bewildered.

"Hullo, wood-mouse! You've shore slept a lot," said Dunn.

"Oh, Arch!—Jim!"

"Molly, this is Dr. Shields from Flag. He has just attended to your brother's wounds, and—"

But Jim could not reply to Molly's mutely questioning eyes. And Dr. Shields, blunt as he was, shrank from their wonderful eager look.

"Molly, I'm further from bein' daid than last night," spoke up Slinger for himself.

"Don't talk. Don't move," admonished the doctor, and he led Jim and Molly away. "Very likely he told the truth," continued Shields, presently. "I can't make predictions. He ought to have passed out long ago. Some of these cowboys are like Indians, to whom bullet holes and knife-cuts are nothing. Your Curly Prentiss is one. . . . Miracles happen. This man *might* live. If he lasts till tomorrow I'd say there was hope. I'll stay."

The rain dripped through the roof of the old cabin, in some places in little streams, one of which happened to go down Bud Chalfack's neck. It had the effect of a lighted match dropped in gunpowder.

"Bud, why don't you git used to water?" complained Curly, when the explosion had subsided.

Molly had dinner in the cabin and she was the object of much solicitude. She went back to her shelter, claiming it dry, at least. The three Cibeque men became restless as the afternoon grew late. Boyd Flick did not return. All the cowboys save Bud passed the time playing cards. Bud had evidently become enamoured of his carving ability, for he spent hours over the other half of the aspen log. When he exhibited his latest bit of sculptural genius the cowboys were spellbound. Bud had hewn out a masterpiece of a wooden headpiece for a grave. And he had engraved upon it: "Curly Prentiss. Died——. Unmarried." This he presented to Curly, before the bursting cowboys.

"You bow-legged, kangaroo-rat!" declared Curly, who could not see the joke. "I could of married a hundred gurls."

And so the day passed, every minute of it with less strain for Jim. He was attentive to Molly, who began another vigil over her brother. The rain roared on the canvas, but Molly was comfortable.

"Traft, you look fagged out," said Dr. Shields, when night fell. "Go to bed. I'll keep tabs on Dunn and wake you if there's any turn for the worse. He simply amazes me."

Jim slipped under Molly's shelter to encourage her and

241

say good night. In the dark he was feeling round for her when she tugged at him.

"Sssh! He's asleep," she whispered.

"Molly, you'll not sit up all night again? Dr. Shields said he'd watch."

"I'll lay down when I get sleepy," she said. "Jim, I'm beginnin' to hope."

"So am I," replied Jim, and put his arms around her. Molly gave a start and then slowly relaxed. Jim waited to see what she would do. After a long moment she stirred, and in the dim light of the smoldering camp fire he saw her head come up. Then shyly and sweetly, but surely, she returned his embrace, and just brushed his cheek with her lips. Thrilled and utterly grateful and content, he bade her good night.

He sought his own bed in the stall behind which Seth Haverly met death. Once stretched out, Jim discovered how weary he actually was, and that was the extent of his conscious mental activity for this trying day. He slept till the ring of ax and stirring of men roused him. It was a dark, wet, gray dawn, but evidently the rain had ceased. While pulling on his boots, he heard Curly speak:

"Wal, Doc, how's your patient this mawnin'?"

"I give up, Prentiss. You cowboys are not made of flesh and blood. Dunn just asked for a cigarette," replied the doctor.

Jim went to the fire in a hurry.

"Then he must be—be—" he faltered, just overcome with hope for Molly.

"Traft, I reckon he'll pull through. I'll look him over after breakfast. Then you can send a man with me. I left my horses tied in a corral over here where the road ends. Guess they'll be all right, but I'd like to hurry."

"Boss, it shore is good," said Curly. "My hunch was all right. But I was scared stiff fer the little gurl."

Jim felt too grateful for expression and had to restrain himself from rushing in to Molly. At the breakfast call she appeared, pale, yet somehow glowing, and to Jim's delight she chose a seat beside him.

The morning showed a prospect of clearing weather. A

242

bit of sunlight tipped the spear-pointed spruces on the ridge. Jays and squirrels were noisily in attendance upon the cabin.

Dr. Shields seemed vastly relieved, and not a little glad.

"Miss Molly, you can rest easy," he said. "Your brother will live. . . . Traft, I'm leaving only a few instructions. Give Dunn a little whisky and water now and then, for a couple of days. If fever sets in send for me. But there's no sign of that or other complications. His wounds have closed clean in this forest air. Then begin to feed him nourishing soups, beef tea, and presently light food. But don't overdo. In about ten days make a canvas litter and have four men pack him to the road, where you can safely haul him in a wagon to Flag."

When the genial doctor had said good-by to all and ridden away with his guide, Bud ejaculated plaintively: "Nourishin' soup! Beef tea! I need somethin' like thet myself."

"My Gawd!" added Curly, his loyal champion, at times. "So do I. This heah fence-buildin' has run me down to skin an' bones."

"I'll bet a two-dollar bill thet if I got shot up our deaf-an'-dumb cook would feed me salt mackerel," ended Bud, in disgust.

Long since Jim had learned this apparent discontent and garrulousness were just their perennial spirit of fun, but he still found occasion to pretend he did not understand them.

"Curly, you and Bud are so darn full of energy— suppose you split some shingles and repair the cabin roof," he suggested, dryly.

"Boss, it ain't a-goin' to rain no more," replied Bud.

"I think it might. It's clouding up just like Curly's face now."

"Boss, I'm as weak as a sick cat," protested Curly.

"You'll feel better at work. That's what you boys need. Good hard work."

"Wal, fer cripe's sake!" exploded Bud.

"Come on, Bud," said Curly, with resignation. "No turkey-huntin' this heah mawnin'. We gotta work while our Mizzourie boss looks at his gurl like a dyin' duck in a thunderstorm."

They hailed Cherry on the way out, "You're helpin' us split shingles."

"Who said so?" demanded that worthy, affronted.

"We said so. Orders from the boss."

It was well that Jim had advised this job, for no sooner had it been completed than the swift-moving clouds rolled up black and the rain poured down in a gray deluge. It rained all day. The cooped-up cowboys talked and played and joked and quarreled. Once Jim heard a thought-provoking speech from Curly, evidently made in deep argument: "Wal, *I* tell you gazaboos there's only one man in Arizonie who could fill Jocelyn's boots on the Diamond."

Jim saw Molly at meal-times. She had grown shyer as the strain of anxiety lessened. And the cowboys, now that her cause for distress had been removed, began to pay pretty compliments and make sly little speeches and eye her with flirtatious longing. She seemed even shyer with Jim. But he was happy, and when night fell, with the rain teeming down, he could not resist a moment alone with her under the canvas. Slinger, however, was awake, evidently suffering, and cursing Dr. Shields about the limited nips of whisky. Jim could only squeeze Molly's hand and say good-night.

It stormed that night, a regular equinoctial gale. The old cabin groaned and threatened to fly away on the wings of the wind. Jim thought there really was risk, for the rafters were heavy. Nevertheless, like the cowboys, he took the risk. It was wonderful to lie snug and warm, however, and listen to the crash and roar of the gale through the forest, and the intermittent and varying spells of rain on the roof. Now and then a faint flash of lightning showed the lashing pines, and dull thunder reverberated across the heavens. Toward morning the fury of the storm abated and it turned cold. When daylight came the sky was fast clearing, the air had a keen cold edge, and the color of the forest had perceptibly changed. There were hints of red in the maples, brown in the oaks, and the aspens showed a splash of gold. The willow leaves were gone. Autumn had come to this low part of the Diamond, and he ventured a guess that winter had laid a white mantle on the high promontories. This caused Jim concern, for he had hoped to get the drift fence finished before the snow fell.

He went outside to wash. The morning was beautiful, with rose and gold clouds skimming the tree tops, and the sky a deep blue. The brook was a rushing torrent of amber water, full of floating aspen leaves, and it was cold enough to make his fingers ache.

He was wiping his face with his scarf when Curly and Bud appeared, each with a rifle and a fine turkey gobbler.

"Mawnin' boss, did you hev enough sleep?" drawled Curly.

"Boss, you ain't risin' with the larks no more," added Bud, with pretended solicitude. "I hope you've no wuss ailment than—"

Jim swore mildly at them. "You went wild-turkey-hunting without taking me! It's a low-down trick. When I've been waiting and longing to go. . . . I'll get even with you."

"Boss, I'm downright sorry," replied Curly, with profound regret. "But it was dark an' cold, an' Bud says—"

"Aw, don't lie it on to me," interrupted Bud, scornfully. "You know you said, 'It'll jest aboot make the boss weep if we waddle in with a couple of turks'."

"It just has done that," said Jim.

"Wal, wait till Jeff roasts these young birds!" added Curly. "Boy, yore mouth'll water so you'll swear you've got dropsy."

"Ahuh. Do I get to go along next time? Of course there's a lot of odd jobs around camp—"

Vociferously and in unison Curly and Bud gave remarkable evidence of their regret and how they would make amends that very day.

It turned out that Jim would not leave Molly. Her brother was in agony most of the time, with fever threatening, and not until late did he grow easier. They were all concerned about Slinger, except Curly, who said: "Wal, the third day is the wust. From now on he'll mend fast."

Next morning, however, Jim routed Curly and Bud out so early that they could not see even a tree for half an hour.

"Boss, wild turkeys is wild, shore, but they ain't owls," complained Bud.

And Curly, loyal as always, vowed that Jim was not going to be permitted to shoot a turkey while still on the roost.

"Thet's pot-huntin', boss, an' not sporty atall."

"After eating that turkey drumstick last night, I'd perpetrate any kind of a dark deed to get another," averred Jim.

"Didn't I tell you? Wal, now don't talk so much, an' mebbe, if it ever gits daytime, we'll see a flock," rejoined Curly.

Jim, therefore, kept his exuberant spirits under restraint. He noticed, however, that Bud and Curly talked right on as usual, and after a few moments he dryly mentioned the fact.

"Wal, you see, these heah turkeys air used to us cowboys ridin' around in the woods," explained Curly. "They know our voices."

Daylight came, with rosy color and nipping air, with frost like diamonds on the gramma grass, and so quiet that a falling aspen leaf rustled loudly. Evidently they had come up to the head of the park, for they crossed a brook and passed a tumble-down log cabin, where Hack Jocelyn had elected to hide with Molly and wait for the ransom. Curly remarked about how the plans of crooked men went wrong more often than right.

"Flick ought to ride in today," he added. "He might be cute enough to savvy the way the deal has turned out an' skedaddle with the money."

"I don't believe—" began Jim, when he got a prod from Bud.

"Hist!" he whispered. "Shet up, you elocuteners! Turkey!"

Jim heard the well-known gobble of a turkey, and it certainly resembled that of a tame turkey at home. Bud led the way over a rise of ground, under green and gold aspens into an open glade, wildly closed at its upper end by a confusion of maples, oak, and pines. There were logs on the ground, and one huge pine across them. Something crashed ahead through the brush, snapping twigs. Then came a rap of bone on wood.

"Elk. Never mind him," whispered Bud. "*There!* A big gobbler—lookin' at us." He forced his rifle into Jim's eager hands.

"Where? . . . That thing? It's a stump."

"Take a chanct, boss," said Curly, with a chuckle. "If it's a stump it ain't a-goin' to run. An' if it's a turkey, keep on shootin'."

"Aim low an' be quick," added Bud.

"But I tell you that thing is a black stump," remonstrated Jim, always and forever looking for tricks from these boys.

"Honest to Gawd, boss, it's a turk," appealed Bud.

"Well, to please you. But I know it's a stump. I can see," replied Jim, and he leveled the rifle and fired. To his utter consternation the motionless stump turned into the most magnificent bird he had ever seen. It ran swift as a deer. It thumped the ground. It was black and bronze, with a wonderful speckled tail, like an immense fan.

"Stump, huh? Why didn't you peg him while he was runnin'?" queried Bud.

"Gosh! I forgot I had a gun. What a sight! Say, that wasn't a turkey, but an ostrich!"

"Wal, it was shore a rotten shot," said Curly. "But he didn't scare the flock. . . . See them scratchin' over heah —under the jackpines?"

Jim did see them and grew wildly excited. It was an enormous flock, some of which exhibited signs of nervousness.

"Duck now, an' crawl after me," whispered Bud, getting down on his knees. "They've seen or heerd us, but we'll get a shot if we're smart. . . . Now boss, don't crawl like a elephant with a broken laig."

Jim did not see anything but grass and leaves, the ground, logs, and tree trunks for several strenuous moments. But he heard turkeys gobble, and then, close at hand: put-put, put-put-put.

"Damn!" swore Bud. "It's always the hens thet bust up everythin'. . . . O Lord! hyar they come. . . . Now stand up an' shoot."

Jim got to his feet and certain was it that he shook. The great black and bronze gobblers, the sleek, smaller, less conspicuous hens, were coming under the scrub pines, out into the open. They no longer resembled tame turkeys. The huge-breasted gobblers, with their long beards, their stately nodding walk, suddenly halted. Jim picked out one that looked as high as a church and pulled the trigger.

Then ensued a terrible crashing, buffeting, roaring *mêlée*. The turkeys burst into united action. A dozen or more launched themselves marvelously into the air, and flew as swiftly as quail, only with tremendous flapping of wings, right at Jim. But most of the flock ran. Jim shot at this one and that one. He could not get the bead on them. How they ran! Curly was yelling and shooting. Bud was shooting and yelling. Turkeys darted right between them, here, there, everywhere. Jim kept working the lever of the rifle, aiming and firing. Then the uproar ceased. Jim stood holding a hot rifle, looking bewildered, while his two companions held their sides.

"Dog-gone!" gasped Curly, as soon as he could speak. "They shore stampeded us. Boss, about how many did you knock?"

"Gosh! I never touched a feather, that I could see. Oh, it was wonderful! . . . But why in the dickens didn't you prepare me for such a charge?"

"Boss, I know turkeys orful well, but I didn't hev this bunch figgered," said Bud. "Didn't you plug one?"

Jim shook his head sorrowfully. "I'm as bum a hunter —as—as everything else."

"How many times did you shoot?"

"I don't know. . . . The gun's empty."

"Gee whiz! So 'tis. It had ten shells in the magazine, one in the barrel. Countin' thet stump thet wus a turkey, you've shot eleven times."

"Good Lord! I must have. But didn't you boys shoot a lot, too?"

"I picked out a buster an' lambasted him," replied Bud, laconically.

"Boss, I shore hated to break in on you," added Curly. "But I seen you was shootin' over their haids an' between their laigs, so I jest had to pulverize one fer supper. You ought to hev heahed him hit the ground. Sounded like a bull."

Bud walked across logs and grass and picked up a beautiful hen turkey. Curly went somewhat farther in the opposite direction and picked up a gobbler that dragged head and wings on the ground. Both cowboys returned with much pride and sang-froid, to lay their quarry at Jim's feet.

"Plumb center, mine," said Bud.

"Boss, I always hit turkeys in the neck," said Curly. "You see thet shot doesn't spoil any meat. I always pick out a turkey either runnin' towards me or away from me, straight. You cain't hit one of them runnin' crossways or even quarterin'."

"It was a great shot, Curly," replied Jim, admiringly. The big gobbler was a rare specimen of the finest game bird, glistening, purple and black, bronze-flecked and white, with plenty of red-brown. And heavy—Jim could hardly lift him.

"Boss, your shootin' can be improved on a little," said Curly, seriously. "If we'd get holed up by the Cibeque bunch, as might have happened, or by thet Hash Knife outfit, which is shore goin' to come off an' be wuss, wal, I'd hate to have my life dependin' on you."

"So would I, Curly," replied Jim, very sober and self-accusing.

"Wal, let's mozey back to camp. You practice all day, shootin', an' we'll try again tomorrow."

Upon returning to camp the excitement of the hunt was dispelled by an astonishing fact. Boyd Flick had ridden into camp with the ransom money, which he was glad indeed to get rid of, and he and the other three members of the Cibeque were packing to leave.

"Traft, it wasn't no deal of mine," said Flick, frankly. "But I don't need to tell you thet. Jocelyn had us all buffaloed. I'm glad Slinger croaked him an' thet the Cibeque is done fer."

They had breakfast with Jim's party, bade them and Slinger good-by, and rode away into the forest, manifestly glad to get off so easily with whole skins.

Some time after they had gone and camp life had resumed normality, Molly called Jim, "You come heah." She led him around the cabin, out of sight of the others. Jim's instant perturbation subsided when he saw that she was smiling, though her gold-black eyes were full of fire.

"The sons-of-guns! Devils!" she exclaimed.

"Who?"

"Curly an' Bud. All of the bunch. Listen heah. I happened to be near when Bud an' Curly got Lonestar an' Cherry behind the corner of the cabin there. I could tell they were up to some mischief, so I listened. Heah's what Bud said: 'Fellars, it's so darn good I near bust waitin' a chance to tell you. Me an' Curly took Jim huntin'' (they always call you Jim behind your back, an' I shore like thet), 'an' soon's it got daylight we seen a gobbler as big as a hill. Jim swore it was a stump. But we made him shoot. Laws! he was funny when thet stump ran off like a wild steer. We located the flock an' sneaked up on them. Say, it couldn't hev worked out any better if we'd had a deal with them gobblers. They got skeered an' come at us. I said to Jim, stand up an' shoot. He did an' then hell busted loose. Me an' Curly turned loose our artillery an' let go all we had. I even took a peg with my six-gun. Neither of us so much as winged one of them turks. But Jim killed two—them we fetched in. Thet gobbler will weigh thirty-five pounds. Only we seen pronto thet Jim reckoned he'd missed. Never touched a feather, he said, an' was shore down in the mouth. Curly gives me the wink an' so we hands Jim a deal. Curly an' me only shot one each, an' as a matter of course downed a turk. Curly enlarged on how he always picked one out comin' or goin' straight, an' shot him in the neck. Kin you beat thet, boys? My Gawd! . . . Wal, Jim swallered the whole deal. He was shore nice aboot it, an' grateful to me an' Curly, an' as humble as pie. . . . My land! nuthin' we ever did tickled us so much!' "

Molly paused a moment breathlessly, her eyes alight. "An' Jim, the devils doubled up like poisoned coyotes, an' howled an' yowled, an' rolled over on the ground."

Jim surely wanted to howl and yowl himself, but he limited himself to jumping up and down in mingled rage and mirth. Then he vented it in all the language he dared use before Molly.

"Aren't they maddenin'?" she asked. "But, Jim, they're strong for you, an' I cain't help lovin' them."

"Neither can I, only, Molly, I've got to have revenge for that—or die," he declared.

"You bet. An' I'll help you. Heah's an idea, Jim. These two boys cain't hunt wild turkeys. They don't know the least bit aboot it. Now I do. Slinger taught me. I could call turkeys before I was ten."

"Call? What do you mean by that?"

"I can call them right up to you, so you can knock them over with a stick, almost. I've done it a thousand times."

"But *how* do you call them?"

"With a turkey-caller. We make that out of a wing bone. But I can call with a hollow weed, too. I'll show you an' teach you. Heah's my plan. You tell Curly an' Bud you think they're not so good, after all, an' you're goin' with me to kill a few turkeys. Then we'll go, several mawnin's an' evenin's, too. I like sundown best. We'll fetch turkeys in. An' after we get a dozen or so you can say to Curly an' Bud: 'Boys, I quit huntin' with you, 'cause when I killed turkeys you lied an' swore you did it. That mawnin' when you claimed the big gobbler an' hen —all the time I knew. *All* the time I was shore of your low-down trick!' "

"Great! Wonderful!" exclaimed Jim, beside himself with the joy of such a double prospect. "Molly, darling, run or I'll hug you right here."

She ran, laughing over her shoulder.

23

◈

WHEN JIM dryly remarked to the cowboys that he guessed he would not hunt with them any more, they looked nonplused and then blank. And he realized that if Molly could live up to her part of the program, he would crush the tricksters forever.

That morning, too, Dunn showed a decided turn for the better, and Jim, losing all his misgivings, was happy for Molly. She loved this backwoods brother and had faith in him. Jim generously waived the ambush on the trail and the rooster trick to which Slinger had treated him, and vowed he would share Molly's faith. Long before that he had decided to reward Slinger for saving his life.

The atmosphere of the camp grew merry, with only one drawback now, and that was the failure of Hump Stevens and Uphill Frost to arrive. Jim grasped that the cowboys were concealing anxiety from him, if not more. To his queries, Curly made evasive answers. But there was a cloud in the cowboy's flashing blue eyes, and Jim read its portent. He decided to send Jackson Way and Cherry Winters to Tobe's Well to ascertain if the missing cowboys were there. If they would only come in, or if news arrived that they were safe, Jim felt that he would be happy, and could even face that grim old Westerner who had entrusted him with such responsibility.

252

There were only two rifles in camp and they belonged to Curly and Bud.

"You boys don't need to go hunting, anyway," said Jim, as he appropriated the rifles and all the shells in sight. "Considering how many thousand turkeys you've killed, Bud, and how many you, Curly, have shot through the neck, running at you, there certainly shouldn't be any excitement left in it for you. So just think of *me*, going out with Molly, after wild turkeys!"

That last thrust was almost revenge enough, Jim thought. Still, after a moment's recall of past suffering, he steeled his heart. Supper was had at four o'clock, after which he started off with Molly, scarcely able to contain himself. And after he got out of sight of camp he no longer did.

"Jim, are we goin' huntin' or makin' love?" queried Molly.

"Can't we do both?"

"No. If you keep on huggin' me an' kissin' my ear— how am I to heah turkeys, let alone call them? . . . If you *must* make love, let's set right down under this spruce an' do it."

"Oh, Molly Dunn!" cried Jim, in the throes of temptation he knew he must resist. How bewildering she was! Her simplicity sometimes stunned him. He divined that his reward would be infinitely greater if he let her take her own time to respond to him.

They climbed a slope, scaring squirrels, rabbits, and deer on the way, and came out on top of a ridge where the forest made Jim ache with its wildness and beauty. Towering yellow pines and stately silver spruces lorded it over the green-gold aspens and the scarlet maples. The ground was soft with pine needles and moss and decaying wood. Everywhere lay logs and windfalls, which had to be climbed over or avoided. The setting sun lent a glamour to the dry, sweet wilderness. Here were thickets of young pine, impossible to penetrate, and there was a long shade-barred aisle down the forest. They came to an open oak glade, and here Molly pointed to turkey scratches on the ground.

"Fresh tracks. They're after acorns. Now, Jim, when we see turkeys, you shoot pronto," she said.

Jim's four months in the West had been productive of numberless experiences, of late merging upon breath-arresting agitation, but he counted high among them this slipping through the forest, close at the stealthy heels of little Molly Dunn. She was a wood-mouse, as Slinger called her. Not the slightest sound did she make. When Jim cracked a twig or brushed against a bush she admonished him with finger to her red lips and a dark disapproving glance. Then when Jim nearly fell over a log, she whispered, "You big clodhopper!"

Nevertheless, despite his awkwardness, she led him within sixty yards of a flock of turkeys that appeared to Jim to cover a half-acre in extent. They were of all sizes, from that of a large chicken to gobblers as large round as a barrel.

Molly cocked her rifle. "Get ready, Mizzourie. When I count three—shoot. But only once. . . . Ready. One—two —*three*!"

Both rifles cracked in unison. Jim seemed deafened by the crash of wings. The gobbler he had fired at bounced straight up, ten feet, and went lumbering through the woods, hard put to it to get into flight—then he flew as fast as the bullet that had missed him. When he disappeared Jim sought the others. Gone! And also the uproar had ceased. Far off he heard heavy wings crash through foliage. In the middle of the glade lay a dead turkey, feathers ruffled. Jim hurried to fetch it.

"Two-year-old," said Molly, as she surveyed the fine young gobbler. "Jim, that flock's made up of old birds, hens, a lot of two year olds an' yearlin's. We're shore lucky. Now come heah."

She led him to a log just on the edge of the glade. "We'll set down heah, an' I'll call."

A few thin bushes partially screened them from the glade. Molly sat down beside Jim, and slipping a hand under his arm leaned her head on his shoulder. "Oh, but this's goin' to be fun. I'm just tickled. We'll shore make Bud an' Curly crawl. Now, Jim, the way to do it is to wait a little. Listen! . . . There. That's a hen squawkin'. An' there's a yearlin' yelpin'.''

Jim not only heard these clear sounds out in the forest, but a deep gobble-gobble, farther away. He agreed with Molly about the fun of it; and whatever else it might be to her it was absolute bliss for him to have her so close, to feel her hand squeeze his arm, her head against his shoulder, her hair touching his cheek. And only a half year back he had been at odds with life!

Molly produced a short thing that looked like a quill to Jim, but which, upon examination, proved to be the small wing bone of a turkey, with a hole through its length.

"Listen, now, you boss of the Diamond," she whispered, gayly. "First I'll call the yearlin'."

Sitting up, she put the bone in her mouth, keeping the other end partly covered in the hollow of her hand. Then she sucked air through it, and the result was a perfect imitation of the yelp of the young turkey. It was answered immediately, not once but several times, and each reply sounded nearer.

"He's shore comin'. Now I'll call that fussy hen out there." And she produced a high-pitched, prolonged squawk, likewise a perfect counterfeit. Answers came from all sides, one of which was a deep gobble.

"Get your gun ready, Jim. Shoot restin' on your knee. Take lots of time. It's murder, shore, but we have to eat. . . . Look! There's the yearlin'. But don't shoot him. . . . Look! Over heah! A whole bunch—mixed."

Cluck-cluck, put-put, all around him! Then he saw turkeys coming on a run, from this side and that.

"Heah's the gobbler. Knock him, Jim," whispered Molly, as she leaned back away from him. "Wait till he stops. An' after you shoot look sharp, you may get a crack at another."

The gobbler entered the glade, stalked out majestically, and suddenly stood motionless, head up, not forty feet from where Jim sat. He scarcely had to move the rifle. Even as he aimed carefully, quivering as he put pressure on the trigger, he could not help seeing the glossy beauty and superb wildness of that giant bird. He shot, and the turkey appeared to pile up with a great feathery roar.

"Quick," whispered Molly, pointing. "Knock this young gobbler. Heah. He's crazy, standin' still there."

Jim located this one and killed it. The others had vanished.

"Drag in the game, Mizzourie," directed Molly.

Hurrying to comply, Jim lifted the smaller turkey, and then lay hold of the giant gobbler. It was huge, and so heavy that indeed he did have to drag.

"You didn't do so bad, then," said Molly, when he returned. "That big gobbler is an old bird. We don't often fool one like him. Set down now, an' I'll call again."

"But, Molly, surely you can't call them up again?" queried Jim, in amaze.

"Cain't I? The show's just begun. Arch an' I used to call half a day on a big mixed flock like this. But I reckon no more old gobblers will come."

In excitement just as tingling as before Jim listened, and heard, and watched, under precisely the same thrilling circumstances. Molly called to the turkeys and whispered to him. No doubt his delight was infectious. Presently a string of yearling turkeys came cluck-clucking into the grove, and Jim, out of three shots, got two.

Then again Molly began to call, and confining herself to the yelp of the yearling, she gave it a wailing note. Answers came from near and far, closer and closer. But it was long before Molly lifted a hand to indicate she had espied one.

"I've been callin' too fast an' often," she explained to Jim. "But I was shore so anxious to have you heah an' see them. We'll wait a little."

It turned out she did not need to call again, for a fine hen turkey followed on the heels of a yearling into the glade. Yet they did not come close. Put-put. Put-put-put. Jim made a capital shot on the suspicious hen, but missed the yearling.

"That'll be aboot all we can pack to camp," said Molly. "Heah's a string. We'll tie their feet together an' run a stout pole through."

"What a load! Gee! but won't Bud an' Curly be sick? . . . Molly, this has been just glorious. I always loved to hunt. But there was never any game except rabbits and squirrels, and sometimes a partridge. And to think—all this grand sport with *you* Molly!"

"I'm glad, Jim. Shore I never felt so good aboot huntin' before."

"Would you mind kissing me?" he asked.

"Jim, you put such store on my kisses," she replied, wistfully. "I reckon they're not—not so precious as you imagine."

"Yes, they are, Molly."

"I told you once—I—I'd been kissed a lot," she went on, shamefaced, yet brave. "Not that I was willin'. . . . An' now I know what love is I—I wish my lips had been for you alone, Jim."

"No, Molly. You were a child. That you can feel as you do now is enough for me, regarding the past. You are a dear, good girl, and I couldn't begin to tell you how I love and respect you."

She kissed him, then, absorbed with the seriousness of it, rather than the sweetness of surrender.

"I reckon I'll let myself go, pronto, an' eat you up," she said.

Resting often, they packed the string of turkeys down through the forest, across the park, into camp. Somebody whooped, and there stood Bud and Curly, transfixed and staring. Neither came out of his trance until Jim and Molly halted under the cabin shed, breathing fast, and glad to lay down their burden.

"For the land's sake!" ejaculated Bud, which speech, considering his proclivity for profanity, merely attested to his mental aberration.

"Didn't I heah you boys talkin' aboot how Jim couldn't hit the side of a barn?" inquired Molly.

"Wal, I reckon you might of—sumthin' like," replied Curly.

"He's a daid-center shot."

"Ahuh. So it 'pears. But what you mean? At gurls' hearts or turkeys?"

257

"I reckon both," replied Molly, and she fled.

Much was made of the turkey-hunt at supper-time. It appeared apropos inasmuch as the meal consisted of roast turkey, gravy, and mashed potatoes. Jim was really concerned over the gastronomic feats of the cowboys, especially of Bud and Curly. And the result of talk and supper was to inspire the two cowboys to get up before daylight to hunt for more wild turkeys. Molly and Jim left an hour after that, and returned with three fine birds before Curly and Bud got back. At length when they arrived, tired from much climbing on foot—which certainly was not their forte—empty-handed, with all kinds of excuses that implicated each other, they were allowed to talk some before being shown what Jim had bagged. Presently Jim directed their attention to the three fine gobblers hanging in bronze and purple splendor on the cabin wall.

"Dog-gone!" said Bud, sagging.

"Huh! Turkeys walked right in camp, so you could knock them over with a club?" queried Curly, snorting fire.

"Nope. I went out for half an hour."

"This heah mawnin'?"

"Yes, after you left. You'll observe they are all shot high up in the neck. I got them coming and going. Straight, you know."

Curly let out a feeble groan. Bud had submitted abjectly.

"Boys, I hope this will be a lesson to you," went on Jim, eloquently, impressive before all the listeners. "Don't go out with an old hunter, and when he kills birds claim *you* did it. And brag about your prowess!"

"Jim, was you onto us—aboot them two turks, the other mawnin'?" asked Curly, in misery.

"Yes, I've long known of your perfidy."

"Aw! Aw!" yelled Curly, in pain. "Bud, this heah is too much. Jim has dun fer us."

"Yes," ripped out his partner in shame, "but we can lay it to the root of all sorrow fer cowboys—a gurl!"

On the following day Slinger Dunn had improved so materially that Jim began to hope it would be safe to move him at the end of another week, perhaps sooner. That forced him to consider the coming situation. Mrs. Dunn had been sent word by Boyd Flick that Molly was safe, and her brother mending favorably. Jim began to incline to a plan to take Molly also into town. The very good excuse of a wounded brother would suffice. How about the Flagerstown feminine contingent when they scented this romance? Jim indulged in a gleeful laugh. Uncle Jim might be destined to have his heartfelt desire fulfilled long before he anticipated any hope of it. But Molly was so young—only sixteen!

Another more perturbing question, for the moment, was the continued failure of Hump and Uphill to appear. Probably they would show up soon with Jack and Cherry. Jim dismissed that, too, as something to be combated another and perhaps more favorable day.

Early in the afternoon he slipped off alone with one of the requisitioned rifles, but not to hunt. He wished to have a long, lonely walk in the forest. It turned out, however, that he did not go far, hardly out of range of Jeff's ringing ax on a dead aspen log.

He took a peep into the old log cabin where Hack Jocelyn had planned to hide Molly. It was full of debris, leaves, pine cones, woodmice, and insects. The place showed evidence of having once been lived in by human creatures. What had happened there? Perhaps once the very thing Jocelyn had wanted! Jim felt a haunting story in that lonely cabin.

Then he followed the draw, up under the spreading silver branches, to a spot where he simply had to stop. Frost had turned the aspens gold. The wondrous hue blazed against sky and forest. All the tranquil little glade appeared to have absorbed light from the aspen leaves, that quivered so delicately and silently, each separate one fluttering like a golden moth.

Jim sat down and gloated over these quaking aspens, and the towering pines and spruces. A hawk sailed across the blue opening above. A dreamy hum pervaded the forest. He did not wonder at a backwoodsman. Here was strange, full, strength-giving life. Molly Dunn seemed a composite of all that he saw and felt there.

Deep in his soul, now that he had time and place to face it, he thanked the God of chance, and the higher divinity to whom all events were subservient, for her love and her promise.The West had dealt harshly with him, yet made greater amends. He had served his apprenticeship under these fire-spirited cowboys; and he sensed more and yet more hardships, problems, pangs, of that elemental range life.

He had had his eye teeth cut. In the future he might hide his stern acceptance of labor and duty under a guise such as that of Curly Prentiss, if he could aspire to this prince of cowboys' mask. But recklessness and boyish desire for adventure for adventure's sake, carelessness and loss of temper, deliberate seeking of trouble—all these must not only be suppressed, but done away with. His responsibility had quadrupled.

Jim wrought over his many failings like a blacksmith hammering malleable iron. If he must build drift fences, he would do well to add something of Slinger Dunn to his conception of Curly Prentiss, in his intelligent acceptance of that which made a Westerner.

That was the clearest of his many hours of self-teaching.

Late afternoon found Jim descending the slope toward camp. He espied a curling column of blue smoke after he had smelled a camp fire. Saddle-horses in camp, grazing with dragging bridles! He quickened his pace. Probably the cowboys had returned. He made sure of this when he saw Cherry's pinto horse hobbling up the park.

Approaching from behind the cabin, he could not see anyone until he turned the corner. But he had heard a merry voice and a deep laugh. There outside the cabin on a bench sat his uncle, holding Molly's hand. Jim was thunderstruck.

"Uncle! . . . Where'd you come from?" he exploded.

"Howdy, son! I rode in with Locke a while ago," replied Traft, his keen eyes sweeping Jim from head to toe. "I haven't been lonesome, as you see."

"I do see," replied Jim, and he could have shouted to

the skies the good of what he saw. Molly did not look as if she wanted to run from Uncle Jim. A blush slowly rose under tearstained cheeks.

Traft exposed the back of Molly's little supple brown hand, on a finger of which the diamond sparkled, as if in gay and treacherous betrayal.

"Son, I see you've been goin' in debt for diamonds," drawled Traft.

"One. Has Molly—told you?" replied Jim, and it was his turn to blush.

"Wal, she only said *you* gave it to her."

Molly gently disengaged her hand. "If you'll excuse me I—I'll run back to Arch," she said, shyly, and fled.

Traft looked up at Jim. "You pie-eatin', soft-spoken, hard-fisted Mizzourie son-of-a-gun!" he ejaculated.

"Yes?" returned Jim, hopefully.

"Doc Shields told me first of these doin's," went on the rancher. "So Locke an' I hooked up the buckboard an' dragged a couple of saddle-horses along. We left the team at Keech's where . . . but that'll wait. Curly told me the whole business. So did Bud. I had a little talk with Slinger. An' then I got hold of Molly. . . . Jim, you've done it. Winnin' the Diamond was a real job, but nothin' to that girl. It took me a minute to fall in love with her myself, an' a whole hour to get the story out of her. Son, she's real Western stuff."

"I—I'm awful glad you like her—Uncle Jim," said Jim, and weak in the knees, he sat down.

"So much for that. We can come back to it later. . . . I've got tough news for you."

"Uncle, I can stand anything now," replied Jim, and indeed felt that he could.

"Hump Stevens is at Keech's, all shot up, but I reckon not so bad as Slinger," went on Traft. "I had him hauled to Flag. Up Frost got to town night before last, an' he's crippled. The darn fool reported to me before he went to a doctor."

"Oh! I'm more relieved than surprised. I was worried. Who shot them, Uncle?"

"Up told me he an' Hump run plumb into some of the

Hash Knife outfit, cuttin' your drift fence, an' there was a bit of a fight. Hump thinks he killed one of the gang. There was five of them, an' they rode off with one hangin' across a saddle. Then Up packed Hump across to Keech's an' come on in to town."

"Hash Knife outfit!" ejaculated Jim, thoughtfully. "The boys used to argue. Curly always said: 'Wait till the Cibeque falls down on the job. Then see!' . . . Uncle, who and what is this Hash Knife outfit?"

"Humph! They're a heap, son. The Hash Knife used to be the king-pin cow outfit of central Arizona. That was twenty years ago. Now, it's got the Cibeque beat to a frazzle for hard-nut hombres, exceptin' Slinger. Old-timer named Jed Stone runnin' the Hash Knife. He used to ride for me, years ago. Killed one of the best foremen I ever had. An' I'd hate to say how many men he's shot since. . . . Wal, Jed an' his bunch haven't any boss or ranch, or even a homestead. They ride from camp to camp, like Injuns, an' believe me they eat more beef than this Cibeque outfit stole."

"Their own beef or somebody else's?" asked Jim, gruffly.

"Haw! Haw! I'll tell that one on you, if I get hard up. . . . Jim, listen to the worst! The last nine miles of your drift fence is down. An' some of the aspen trees are fresh decorated with Jed's trade-mark, a plain old hash-knife cut in deep."

"Well, the nerve of him!"

"Jim, that outfit drinks six cups of coffee a meal, to keep their nerve quiet, Jed bragged to me once. . . . Now you're up against a far worse crowd than the Cibeque. Old cowboys, gunmen, rustlers!—Wal, you've still got up sixty miles or more of fence. An' that'll have to do for this year. Fact is, I'm more than satisfied. I'm darn proud of you, Jim."

"Thank you, Uncle. But soon as I see what's to be done about Slinger and—and Molly, we'll go right back to fence-building."

"No more till next spring, Jim. You don't savvy. That

262

end of the Diamond is high, an' this storm spelled winter. The cattle had drifted off before this snow came."

"Snow!"

"Shore. Two feet at Tobe's Well now, an' deeper as you climb south. Tough luck, son, but don't ask too much. Mebbe Jed Stone will get his deserts this winter, though *that's* plumb too much to hope for."

"Aw! I put such store on finishing our drift fence before the snow flies," exclaimed Jim, poignantly.

"That was a dream, son. An' Locke an' I let you dream it. . . . Listen! I've got an idee that may suit you, since Molly Dunn talked so hopefully about her brother. It seems *she* thinks you had good influence on Slinger. Wal, follow it up. If you can get Slinger Dunn into the Diamond—why, you'll have it all over the Hash Knife.— Son, it's turnin' tricks like this that is genuine Western."

"I had that idea myself, Uncle! If I can only get him! Why, Molly would sing for joy."

"All right, then. Let's put our heads together. We've got to take Slinger to town, an' so we'll take Molly along. Then we'll send for her folks an' keep them at the ranch. I wouldn't rush that kid into marryin', not before a year. She's backward, an' it'd be good for her to meet people, an'—"

"Great! Uncle, you're just the finest ever!" cried Jim, wildly fired with enthusiasm. "Molly could go to school, or at least have private lessons, and what could not that bright girl learn in six months?"

"You'll have some trouble talkin' Slinger into it, mebbe," went on Traft. "I sat talkin' to him a little while. He's got one weakness shore, an' that's Molly. An' I'll gamble he has another—a ranch. Play these cards strong."

"Ranch?" queried Jim, eagerly.

"Shore. I happen to own the Yellow Jacket. It's a big, wild range, run down, with only a few thousand head of stock. I took it over on notes of Blodgett's not long ago. Some rustlin' down there. It's a fine winter range. Just the place for the Diamond this next six months. You talk up the Yellow Jacket to Dunn. Tell him you'll take him in with you as partner, or half shares, providin' he'll throw in with the Diamond. That'll fetch him, unless you an' Molly have him figured wrong."

Jim got up trembling, and put a hand on Traft's shoulder.

"Uncle Jim! . . . So this is one of the things that makes you a great Westerner? Oh, I've heard a lot! . . . I couldn't ask more in this world—than—"

But he choked over that utterance and rushed round the cabin to drop in upon Molly and Slinger. He was half sitting up and looked better, especially as one of the boys had shaved him, and his face had regained some of its clean tan. Jim swallowed hard and strove for calmness. He did not dare look at Molly, whose eyes he felt.

"Howdy, Slinger! You seem to be doing fine. I'm sure glad. How about a little talk?"

"Suits me, if you do the talkin'," he replied. "Molly is aboot talked out, an' I never had nuthin' to say."

Whereupon Jim sat down next to Molly, and took time to settle himself comfortably.

"We'll be riding you into Flag, pronto," began Jim.

"Say, I don't hanker aboot thet. I'd only meet up with Bray. An' fact is, I'll be sorta sick fer a while."

"Bray won't get near you," went on Jim, warming to his subject. "But Doc Shields will. We'll take Molly along an' go right to Uncle Jim's ranch.—And send for your father and mother to come up. . . . You see, Slinger, it's this way. Molly and I will be getting married in a—a year or so"—here a half-stifled gasp at his elbow disrupted him—"and you know she's pretty much of a kid. We won't let her go back to the Cibeque—ever—except, of course, on visits—and you just ought to be where you can see her often."

"I reckon I ought," agreed Dunn.

"Fine. I thought you'd agree. Now, here's another angle. Do you happen to know the Yellow Jacket ranch?"

"I shore do."

"What kind of a place is it?"

"Wal, no ranch to brag aboot—only a cabin an' corrals. But, Lord! what a range! Water an' grass an' timber!"

Jim really needed no more than the light of Slinger's eyes.

"Uncle has turned it over to me, lock, stock, and barrel," laughed Jim. "Only three thousand head of cattle. But great possibilities for development. . . . Now, Slinger, I want you to go in with me—be my partner in making a big ranch out of the Yellow Jacket."

Dunn grew quite red in the face for him.

"Molly, is this heah fellar of yours drunk or crazy?" he asked, turning to her.

"I—I don't quite know—Arch," she faltered. "But I reckon you can trust him."

Jim had further impetus to his enthusiasm. A small trembling hand slipped into his and clung.

"Sure there's a string to the offer, Slinger. There always is in business deals. Sure it's a big chance for you—not to say how wonderful for Molly. But I'm quite selfish in the matter. You're more than worth the deal to me, provided, of course, you agree to my terms."

Jim felt another pressing little hand stealing up around him, over his shoulder.

"Ahuh. An' what's them terms, Jim Traft?" queried Dunn.

"Do you happen to know Jed Stone?" counter-queried Jim.

"I shore ought to. Jed an' me drawed on each other aboot a year ago. Reckon we was so durn scared we missed. But we hevn't met since."

"Do you know his Hash Knife outfit?"

"Better'n anyone who rides the Diamond."

"Well, it was Jed Stone and his outfit who cut the last nine miles of our fence. And he has cut his brand on the aspens. Next spring we'll go back on the job. Slinger, to complete that fence and keep it *up,* I need you. Savvy? Will you throw in with me and the Diamond?"

"Gawd! Jest gimme the chanct!" replied Dunn, hoarsely.

"Here's my hand. And with it is an end of the bad blood between us."

When Jim extended that hand he naturally released the little one that had clung tighter and tighter to his. Suddenly, while he came to grips with Slinger, and their eyes met in the understanding of men, this little hand flashed up before him to lock with the other one behind him. As he had reason to remember, these little members were strong, and now he had more proof of that. Moreover, Molly's arms were inseparable from them, and they twined and twined. *"Mizzourie Jim!"* she whispered. And between Jim and Slinger, while yet their hands gripped, intervened a pale little face, with wet eyes, dark in passionate gratitude, with red parted lips that came up and up and up—

"Wal, Jim, I reckon thet'll be aboot all," said Slinger Dunn.